"I SHOULD GO."

His eyes darkened, and his gaze traveled down her body and back up to her face. His look was so hot it was almost like a caress. " 'Tis late and I've disturbed your sleep."

Megan's heart thumped violently in her chest. She wanted him to take her, to fold her up inside of him, so she could forget who he was for this moment.

Bryan held her gaze for what seemed an eternity, until she was certain he was preparing to leave her with a lonely ache for him. Then his hand rose, pushing the neck of her shift off her shoulder. She swallowed and let her eyes drift closed. His hand moved under her hair, along her back, to cup her neck. Her trembling was stopped by his mouth on hers, hard and demanding. He pulled her into the circle of his arms, his hands running over her, his tongue parting her lips.

She curled her arms around his neck as he pushed her backward on the bed. She could sense his impatience, and it excited her. He gathered the material of her shift in his hand and pulled it over her head. SUPER ROMANCE

"I should stop," he murmured in a thick voice. "I should leave." Then he was trailing kisses down her throat to the swell of her breast.

She whimpered in response. "No . . . " she managed to gasp between ragged breaths. "Stay."

Other Books by
Jen Holling

A TIME FOR DREAMS

JEN HOLLING

Forever, My Lady

HarperTorch
An Imprint of HarperCollins*Publishers*

This is a work of fiction. Names, characters, places, and incidents are products of the author's imagination or are used fictitiously and are not to be construed as real. Any resemblance to actual events, locales, organizations, or persons, living or dead, is entirely coincidental.

HARPERTORCH
An Imprint of HarperCollins*Publishers*
10 East 53rd Street
New York, New York 10022-5299

Copyright © 2001 by Jen Holling
ISBN: 0-06-101437-0

First HarperTorch paperback printing: January 2001

HarperCollins®, HarperTorch™, and ◈ ™ are trademarks of Harper-Collins Publishers Inc.

Printed in the United States of America

Visit HarperTorch on the World Wide Web at www.harpercollins.com

10 9 8 7 6 5 4 3 2 1

My thanks to Shauna Grimme, for her honest feedback during the writing of this story; to Brenda Brandon, for her insight through the revisions; and to Robin Stamm, whose guidance has been invaluable to me.

The Lament of the Border Widow

But think na ye my heart was sair
When I laid the mould on his yellow hair?
Oh, think na ye my heart was wae
When I turned about, away to gae?

No living man I'll love again,
Since my lovely knight is slain,
With ae lock of his yellow hair
I'll chain my heart forever mair.

Unknown Author
Collected by Sir Walter Scott
Minstrelsy of the Scottish Border, 1869

Prologue

East March, Scotland,
1581

The pain hit Megan again full force. It was like a metal band circling her abdomen, crushing her.

"Oh God! Help me!" she screamed. Her knees buckled and she wrapped her arms around her belly, sinking to the floor. A strong arm circled her, under her arms, and lifted her back to her feet. "I can't, Innes! I can't!"

His voice was low near her ear. "Of course you can, love. Come on, up the stairs."

She turned her face into the rough wool of her husband's tunic. He lifted her, his arm beneath her knees.

" 'Tis naught, Meg. You shall see. Why, lasses are birthing weans every day. Once the babe is out, everything will be fine."

His voice was low and soothing, and she curled her fingers into his sleeve. The pain began to subside, but did not leave her body. She could breathe now. She could hear the women behind her, climbing the stairs, murmuring about towels and water.

He laid her on the bed and turned to leave.

"No! Don't leave me!" she cried, still clutching at his sleeve. Another pain hit, and her face contorted as she moaned.

Innes's skin was pale and sweat dewed his brow, but he sat beside her on the bed. "I won't leave you." He took her hand between his and held it tightly.

She looked up into his light blue eyes, hoping they would give her strength. His short copper hair was standing up in the front where he had pushed it away from his forehead, and freckles stood out darkly across his ashen face. He was trying to be strong for her.

The pain drained out of her and her muscles loosened. One of the women, her mother-in-law perhaps, though Megan wasn't certain, handed Innes a wet towel. He wiped Megan's face gently with it. Megan was unaware of anyone else in the room except her husband. She allowed herself to focus solely on him. His sky blue eyes, his soothing voice, his long reddish-blond lashes.

The pain gripped her again. "Oh God, Innes! It hurts!" He gathered her close and rocked her. The pain was like those that often accompanied her courses, only magnified to an unbearable level.

The door burst open and her brother-in-law entered. He stood over them, his eyes wild. "Innes! Cedric Forster and his men are here! They've set the village alight and are on their way!"

"Has the beacon been lit?" Innes asked.

"Aye, it has, but they'll never make it in time!"

Not the Forsters! Not tonight! She was giving birth! Another pain ripped through her and she let out a scream.

Innes stood. "I must go."

Megan wouldn't release his hand. She writhed with pain. "No! Stay with me! Please! I don't care if you're the warden. Send your damn deputies. What else are they good for?"

But his eyes had already taken on the familiar cold stare. His mind had left her and the babe, moving on to other, "more important" matters such as murderers and criminals. She turned her face away and released his hand, not having the strength to argue with him. It always ended the same way.

When he was gone, fear filled Megan, making her clench tighter against the pain. What if her child lost his father tonight?

Her mother-in-law, Cora, took Innes's place on the bed. "Shhh. He'll be back. Don't you fash now, you've a babe to birth." She caressed the swell of Megan's belly. Cora's red hair, liberally streaked with white, was pulled into a tight knot at the nape of her neck. Her pale blue eyes were the same as Innes's.

It seemed as if hours passed, but Megan knew it was only minutes. The pains came faster and harder, and the women of Innes's family gathered around her. Sweat rolled off her, the sheets were soaked beneath her. She felt something strange and gasped. Fluid rushed between her thighs.

"What's happening?" she cried.

" 'Tis only your water. It broke. Everything is fine." Cora was still beside Megan, trying to ease her discomfort. She rolled Megan on her side and kneaded the cramped muscles of her lower back. It was some relief, and Megan let her eyelids drift shut.

Her eyes sprang open when she heard shouting outside. One of the women ran to the window and threw the shutters open. The woman's hand flew to her mouth.

"What is it?" Megan asked.

"They're here!" The sharp crack of splintering wood reached their ears as the door downstairs was forced open.

"Hurry! Secure the bolt!" Cora yelled.

Loud voices and the clomp of boots resounded up the stairwell, followed by hammering on the door. "Open up or we break it down!"

Cora hurried to the door but didn't open it. "I pray you, leave us in peace! Lady Dixon is giving birth!"

From the other side of the door came Innes's voice. "Damn it, Cedric, do you not have enough? Let my family be!"

His plea was met by Cedric's laughter. "Good e'en to you, Warden. Just the man I was looking for."

Megan met her mother-in-law's fearful gaze.

"Not my wife, Cedric. If you lay a hand on my family, I won't discuss a thing with you ."

Another laugh from Cedric. "I 'ave not noticed you to be overly talkative in the past. Nay, I'm not 'ere for 'er, but for you, my friend. Your bonny wife is an added pleasure I shall 'elp myself to."

Cora moved her face away moments before an ax slammed through the door. A roar of pain and rage was followed by the sounds of a struggle. Megan was still wrapped in a blanket of agony, but she sat up, straining to hear the outcome of the fight.

"String 'im up in the doorway!" Cedric yelled and the ax bit into the wood again.

"No!" Megan screamed and stood. Her legs almost gave way beneath her, but she ran to the door. Cora tried to hold her back, but Megan raised the latch and threw the door wide. Cedric stopped in midswing, almost burying the ax in her forehead.

"Christ, lass! I could 'ave killed you!" he exclaimed as if he cared.

"Let my husband go!" She clutched at his sleeve. Another pain stabbed her and her knees gave out. "Please," she gasped through a moan. "Take me prisoner instead. He'll pay the ransom. You have my word!"

He grinned. " 'Tis too late for that, lass. Your 'usband will be an ache in me bum no longer. 'Tis 'is own fault, for being so disagreeable."

"No!" She pulled herself to the railing. Cedric didn't stop her. Cora was beside her, helping her down the stairs. She stumbled and almost fell at the bottom. But it was too late. Her husband's limp body hung in doorway, swinging gently in the breeze.

 # One

East March, Scotland,
1585

Sir Bryan could ignore the ache in his bladder no longer. The afternoon was late and the light was fading. He decided to relieve himself while he still had daylight. He glanced over his shoulder at the party of disreputable looking men farther down the road. They had been hanging around an alehouse where he had stopped for dinner. He had ignored how they stared at him during his meal, but when they followed him out of the alehouse, he began to get suspicious. They had been behind him for several miles now, and he feared the worst.

He veered off into the woods that lined the road. He left Arthur nibbling the grass, his reins trailing the ground. His dog, Pellinore, trotted at his heels.

He was traveling to the East March garrison where he was to be the new warden. It had been an impromptu decision. His cousin, Francis Hepburn Stewart, the fifth Earl of Bothwell, had met him in Lieth when his ship had landed a month earlier. Francis told him that a position had recently opened, and he had petitioned the king in advance about Bryan filling the job. Bryan had accepted reluctantly. Francis was his only real family left, so he felt somewhat obligated. Bryan was just returning from fighting in the Low Countries and hadn't put much thought into what he was going to do next, other than stop fighting and find a good woman to wed who wasn't a liar and a harlot. But he was glad to be in Scotland again, after having been away for many years.

Bryan tensed. Had he heard something in the trees nearby? Unease washed over him. Could this be the very wood where his predecessor, the previous warden, Leod Hume, was rumored to be scattered about in pieces?

He rushed through his business and made his way back into the sunshine. The men were gone. Bryan scanned the horizon, but they were nowhere in sight. Surely he would have heard them pass. Arthur's head dipped to nudge his hand. Bryan was leaning over to gather the horse's reins when he noticed Arthur's ears twitch and swivel, his eyes rolling to look at something behind them. Bryan swung around.

Three men emerged from the wood behind him—the same men who had been following him from the alehouse. The one closest to Bryan jerked his hand behind his back, but he couldn't hide the thick tree branch clutched in it. He gave Bryan a jagged smile. "Gude day, sir! Hiv ye a few bits ta spare?"

"No." He didn't want to give them anything, but there were three of them and one of him. "I have some bread."

"My thanks, kind sir!" said the one with the branch. He came to stand beside Bryan, using the branch as a walking stick, the rotting hole of his mouth still curved into the semblance of a smile. An oily smell accompanied him. Bryan didn't want to turn his back on them to rummage through his saddlebags. He was about to tell the man to back away when Pellinore gave a short bark and fled into the trees. Pellinore always ran when there was danger.

Bryan's sword was strapped to his saddle. He grasped the hilt and was pulling it from the scabbard when something crashed against the side of his head. He staggered, but caught himself before he fell. There were five of them now. Two were trying to control Arthur, who neighed and reared in alarm, hooves pawing the air. The other three advanced on Bryan with a variety of weapons. One held a lance and an ax, another had taken Bryan's sword and pistol, and the rotten-mouthed man still held the tree branch.

"Laddie, gi' it up. Ye canna win," said Rot-mouth. "Just gi' us yer clothes and those fine dirks . . . and yer dog and horse . . . and all yer money, and we'll leave ye ta yer business."

Rot-mouth appeared to be the leader. Bryan had dealt with this kind of rabble before. Only the others had been clad in Spanish uniforms. They preyed on the weak. They were scavengers. They made Bryan sick.

When Bryan didn't respond to his request, Rot-mouth signaled the men to attack. Bryan blocked a clumsy lance thrust with his forearm and captured the weapon, ducking an ax swing and yanking the lance from his attacker's hands. He kicked the man in the stomach and slapped another with the butt end of the lance.

The man with the gun was trying to determine how to operate it. Bryan crashed his fist into the man's face. Rot-mouth called for help and swung the tree branch, hitting Bryan in the shoulder. Bryan stumbled, fire coursing through his biceps. All five men fell on him.

Something wet was on Bryan's face. It was Pellinore's tongue. He pushed the whining dog away and shook his head to clear it. He was lying on his back. His shoulder throbbed dully. The setting sun stabbed his eyes. He groaned. Rot-mouth had beaten him over the head with his tree branch while the other men held him down. He stood and staggered to the rutted dirt road, Pellinore at his heels.

This was not a good first day for the new warden of Scotland's East March. His horse, his weapons, his food, his doublet, his boots, and all of his money were gone. He was sure they would have taken Pellinore, too, if the dog had an ounce of courage.

The sun was dipping below the horizon when Bryan crested the hill and the garrison that was his to command came into sight. As he stopped to gaze at the ruined fortress, an unfamiliar lethargy seeped into his limbs. *Fortress* wasn't quite the right word. It looked as though Leod Hume had done little in the way of upkeep during his tenure. The grayish-green

stone tower rose above a crumbling curtain wall surrounding it. Large holes pocked the wall. The stones
were green with mold, and vines of ivy had claimed
the wall at the back of the castle. The castle boasted a
portcullis and a decaying gatehouse, which were useless since invaders need only crawl through the holes
in the wall to take the tower.

From his cousin's account, invaders from both
sides of the border ransacking the garrison had
become a problem. And the past warden either
couldn't or wouldn't enforce justice. With such a
weak central government as Scotland had, it was easy
for the post to become corrupt. The borderlands were
separated into six marches, three on the Scottish side
and three on the English side. Each march had a warden who governed his area with the help of his various
deputies, captains, and sergeants. The borders had
been in a steady decline for years, and, as his cousin
warned him, were extremely resistant to the enforce-
ment of justice, particularly from an outsider.

And this was Bryan's new home. It had been a very
long time since he felt as though he had a home; when
he had imagined one, however, the ruin before him
had not been the picture his mind drew. His heart sank
as he started down the road to meet his new charges.
He had spent the past ten years following the Prince
of Orange around the Low Countries, trying to drive
the Catholic Spaniards out. He was ready to stop
fighting. He desperately wanted a home, a wife, children. After the last woman he loved betrayed him, he
trained himself to not think about such things, to get
along without the comforts of women and home. But
of late, it had become difficult.

He was still questioning the wisdom of accepting the post of warden. The borders didn't appear much different from a battlefield. He hoped the missing warden would turn up so his commission would be brief.

He heard hoofbeats behind him and moved aside so the galloping rider wouldn't run him down. The rider passed, but reined in his mount, jogging back to ride beside Bryan.

"Have you been robbed?" the man asked.

"Aye, I'm afraid someone beat you to it."

The man looked offended. He removed his metal helmet, resting it on his thigh. He was older than Bryan's thirty years, forty-five, mayhap. His hair was graying at the temples and his skin was lined and leathery. "I am no thief. I'm Willie Hume, the deputy warden of the East March."

"Ah, Willie, 'tis you who wrote me. I'm Sir Bryan Hepburn, your new warden."

"Sir Bryan!" Willie instantly became flustered, and dismounted. The deputy was a head shorter than Bryan and twice as thick about the waist. "Well met, sir, well met! Who has done you this grave injustice?"

"I know not, Willie. I was hoping you might be of some help answering that question."

"Prithee, take my horse. I will walk to the fort."

"I don't want your horse."

Willie grabbed the reins and walked beside Bryan. "Where were you attacked?"

Bryan nodded behind him. "Just over yon hill."

"Hmm, could be it was one of the Cranstons; that Jock is always into mischief. Or mayhap it was a Dixon. They've never been much into the foraying, but I have reason to believe the widow Dixon is giving some payback these days."

"So the reiving isn't only confined to the men? The ladies partake in it, too?"

Willie grinned. "Not most of them, but the widow Dixon isn't most women, and she has it out for the Forsters. She believes the only good Forster is a dead Forster."

"You seem to find this blood feud amusing."

Willie gave him a shrewd look. "Reiving is a common practice, sir. The stealing of cattle is most difficult to control. By allowing the clans to feud amongst themselves, a balance is usually struck."

Bryan looked down at Willie, masking the contempt he felt at such a suggestion. If Bryan wasn't so completely friendless, he'd replace the deputy immediately for such an attitude. "Is this not Hume land? Mayhap it was your kin who robbed me and left me for dead."

Willie didn't respond. He rubbed his chin, his thick fingers rasping loudly against the gray whiskers. "That's a fine hound you have, Warden. A bit long in the tooth, though."

Bryan raised an eyebrow at the quick change of subject. "Aye, he is a fine dog." He bent to run his hand over Pellinore's shining gray fur. "He's reached his twelfth year and still not too old for a good hunt."

"Sleuth dog, aye?"

"He's the best tracking dog there is, but a bit of a coward."

"We don't have much use for gutless hounds on the march. I'd say 'tis time to lay him to rest."

Bryan tried not to become indignant at the idea of

killing his dog. True, bravery was not one of Pellinore's strengths, but he made up for it in loyalty, a
quality Bryan prized above all. He whistled and
slapped his thigh. Pellinore hurried to trot beside him.
His tongue lolled out of his mouth, and he looked as
if he was smiling. "He's got more years in him yet."

They continued in silence until Willie asked, "Will
the wife be joining you?"

"I am unmarried."

Willie looked him over curiously. "And plan to stay
that way?"

"Nay, Scotland is too cold to be sleeping alone."

Willie nodded his approval. "I was a bit surprised
when Lord Bothwell informed us we were to have
another landless warden. The warden usually operates
out of his own estates." Willie's voice was censorious.

Bryan tried not to take offense at the reference to
his low station. "This isn't a permanent appointment.
Lord Bothwell brought me in to investigate Leod
Hume's disappearance. I'm sure you will soon have a
landed gentleman as your employer."

They entered the gate of the fort. The disrepair was
even worse than it had appeared from far away. The
distance had flattered it. Bryan stopped inside the gate
to view his charges. He couldn't remember the last
time he saw so many raggedy-assed men in one place.
The men's breeks and tunics were worn and thread-
bare. The guards wore leather jacks and metal bonnets, and leaned casually on their lances as though
protecting the keep were not among their duties.

"This way, Warden. I'll show you to your chambers
and locate something for you to wear until your things
arrive."

The keep was in little better shape, and it looked as though the rushes hadn't been changed in years. Bryan wrinkled his nose at the thick odor of decay. His quarters were on the bottom floor. A small sleeping chamber adjoined an audience chamber with a desk and a bookcase filled with volumes concerning border laws and cases on file. The only other furniture was a table and a few chairs.

"Are there no women to clean?" Bryan asked.

"Aye, some Hume women come down twice a week to clean. My wife lives here and will see to any of your needs—water, food, whatnot."

A quick scan of the quarters assured Bryan a bath was not in his immediate future. Perhaps a tub for bathing was located elsewhere? But Willie's rather scruffy appearance seemed to indicate there was none to be had, either.

"Well, I'd like to speak to whoever is in charge of the cleaning. The place is a sty. It can't be good for the men's constitutions to live in such squalor. What is the state of the finances? The wall is in sore need of repairs, and the men need proper equipment."

Willie smiled patiently. He pointed to the ledgers on the desk. "Here are the most recent entries on our accounts. But don't pay it any mind. We don't really have the money it says we do. We were raided just last week by the Forsters, and they took everything." He patted Bryan on the back. "Rest tonight. I'll have my Lauren bring you some dinner, and we'll talk on all this in the morn, aye?"

Pellinore, already sprawled on the narrow bed, raised his head tiredly.

"Aye, I think I might like to just sleep."

Willie left him. Bryan stood in the middle of the bedchamber and stared at the bleak cell. The sheets were dingy, but looked clean enough. He sat on the low straw bed beside Pellinore.

"I suppose you don't care where you call home so long as I'm in it."

Pellinore rolled his eyes to look at Bryan, but didn't move his head.

"I don't even have a pair of boots thanks to your coward arse."

Once again Pellinore must not have felt this warranted a response, and he lay motionless.

What had he gotten himself into? Bryan rubbed his face wearily. Francis had convinced him it was an honor to be given the wardenship and had knighted him for his service in the Low Countries fighting for the Protestant faith. His cousin had even intimated there was a gift of land to be had in the bargain. Now Bryan was beginning to fear the appointment was punishment for fighting battles that had no victors. Had he not been punished enough when the Dons killed his woman? She had been a heartless wench, but she never deserved death. Her murder had left him aching for a revenge so great it had been unachievable. Her own people had killed her. The people for whom she had betrayed him. No matter how many Spaniards he killed, it was never enough. He pressed his fingertips against his eyelids. *Will not think of that now*.

He lifted his foot to look at the bottom of his stocking. There was a hole in the toe. He stood and began unlacing his breeks. He was interrupted by a knock on the door.

"Aye?"

A tiny lass with a mass of sable curls entered, carrying a ewer of hot water.

"Are you Lauren Hume?" he asked, trying to hide his amazement. She couldn't have been more than fourteen.

"Aye, Warden. I'll be bringing your meal shortly." She set the water on the table and scurried out.

He forced the picture of Willie and the wee lass as man and wife out of his head. He washed up and was feeling fresher when Lauren returned with his dinner. Her face was small and filthy. She had enormous dark eyes but completely avoided making eye contact with him.

The tray she left on the table held a flagon of beer and a pewter tankard, a wooden bowl full of thin porridge, a hunk of overcooked beef, and two greasy oatcakes. When she was gone, he inspected the inside of the tankard, then washed it in the ewer before partaking of the weak beer.

Pellinore padded over to him with sleep-stiff legs and whined softly. Bryan started to drop the hunk of meat on the floor when the saw the filthy rushes. He scanned the room for something to set the meat on and decided on a piece of paper. He knew Pellinore didn't care if rushes and lice clung to his dinner, but Bryan did. Bryan liked order and discipline in his life, and though he was used to the dirty life of a soldier, he had left it behind, with the intention of never returning.

He thumbed through the account ledger while he ate. It did nothing for his appetite. He was appalled at the paltry subsidy the king allotted for the running of the garrison. No wonder the fortress was in its present state. He would write the king tomorrow and detail the situation. Surely, if King James knew the complete disrepair the fort was in, he would increase the amount.

Later, he lay on the bed with Pellinore curled warmly against his side. He stared into the dark. He was drifting to sleep when something bit his neck. He slapped it. Suddenly he felt as if he was crawling with insects. He jumped off the mattress and lit the candle, holding it over the bed. He didn't see anything. *Fleas, probably.*

Pellinore looked annoyed; finally, Bryan blew out the candle and went to sleep.

Bryan cracked his eye open. It was morning, and someone was in his chamber. He grabbed for the dirk he never removed from his belt. It was gone. He slapped at his waist a few times, but it didn't materialize. His shoulder hurt. The events of the previous day came rushing back. His weapons, including his dirk, had been stolen. He was at the East March garrison.

He sat up. Pellinore was standing in the center of the room watching Willie lay clothes over a chair.

"What ho!" Bryan exclaimed. "My doublet. And my boots. And there's my dirk. Where did you get them?"

Willie scratched the gray stubble on his chin. "I had a suspicion as to who had taken your things, so last night I went out to Jock Cranston's place, and sure enough, he was wearing these dandy clothes and fine boots. I told him he had robbed our new warden."

Willie shrugged. "He didn't know you were the warden or he wouldn't have attacked you. He asked me to give you his sincerest apologies, and he returned your clothes and weapons."

Bryan began dressing. "You didn't arrest him?"

Willie frowned, his fuzzy brows pulling together. "Now why would I do that when he gave your clothes back?"

"He assaulted me! He could have killed me."

Willie waved that away. "Nay. He knew he didn't kill you. He says he had to knock your senses from you. Why, laddie, you're a bull compared to him and his men, and he could tell you were ready to fight it out with the five of them. He did it for your own good, so he didn't have to kill you."

Bryan had been warned about this border law, that it wasn't really law of any civilized sort. He had also been told there was little he could do about it. But this offended Bryan's sensibilities. There was nothing fair or honorable about the whole situation. He had been robbed and beaten. And where was his horse, anyway?

"Did he return my horse?"

Willie looked uncomfortable. "Well, no . . . I tried to make him see reason, but he felt he was returning a goodly bit of his livelihood to secure your good graces. He didn't think he needed to lose the horse as well."

Bryan stared at Willie blankly. " 'Tis my horse."

"Aye, but Jock has a litter of bairns and bonny fat wife to feed."

"I will speak to Jock myself."

"Uh . . . Sir?"

"Aye?"

"He already sold it."

Bryan's irritation was growing. "To whom?"

"To the widow Dixon for two crowns."

"Then we shall pay a visit to the widow Dixon," Bryan said, shrugging into his doublet. He might as well begin immediately showing these border people how he planned to execute his office. This "border justice" would not do for Bryan.

Lauren darted in and out of the room, leaving ale behind. When Willie turned to follow her, Bryan caught his arm. "How old is your wife?"

"She's fourteen. Why?"

"No reason." Bryan shook his head stiffly and focused on buckling his belt.

"There's some bonny young ones in the march if that's what you'd like. Why, I know of a fine lassie— she's about thirteen, I think—and her mum is looking to marry her off. I'm sure she'd think you were a fine husband."

"I'm sure she's lovely—"

"Oh, aye, and when you get them so young they learn their place quick."

"Really, I didn't mean—"

Willie's eyes lit up. "Aye, that's what you need, laddie, an extra set of hands about to keep the place clean and a warm body for your bed. I'll speak to Cora straight away."

"But—"

"Don't you worry about it," Willie said as he walked out the door. "You have other matters to concern yourself with. I'll find you a horse, too."

"But—"

He was gone. Bryan stared after him in frustration.

He did not want Willie to find him a wife. Certainly not one who was not yet a woman. He sighed and went after Willie. He'd have to set the old deputy straight, but not now. He wasn't in the mood. He just wanted his horse back.

Willie was able to round up a mount for Bryan, and they rode into the rich green of the Merse, Willie explaining a bit of the history of the East March. It was some of the best farmland in all of Scotland. Since the East March was north of Berwick, and the Tweed in that area was easily fordable, the march usually sustained heavy devastation when the English invaded. But the Merse always seemed to spring back, the shoots of oats and barley finding what they needed in the soil.

Lairds abounded on the borders. Their dwellings ranged from fortresses to cramped stone towers. The widow Dixon had such a small, square tower for defense, but, for comfort's sake, the Dixons lived in a brick house a quarter of a mile from the tower. It was enclosed by a stone barmkin wall about fifteen feet high. The house and tower were in the center of acres of green fields. Bryan and Willie followed the narrow dirt path to the gates, where they were allowed in unmolested.

Inside the walls were several pens and stables. One pen was so full of woolly sheep they could hardly move; another held a large hog and several piglets. Small cottages lined the barmkin where men and women were busy working and talking. The place exuded warmth and comfort.

An older woman with white hair stepped out of the house and waved.

"Is that the widow Dixon?" Bryan asked Willie as they dismounted. She didn't look very threatening, nor so sprite. He had a hard time visualizing her raiding and killing.

"Aye, one of them. But we just call her Cora."

"How many widows Dixon are there?"

"Too many, thanks to Cedric Forster." They climbed the steps where Cora stood watching them. Willie waved his hand in Bryan's direction. "Cora, this is the new warden, Sir Bryan Hepburn."

Cora looked him over critically.

"Well met, Cora."

"The warden's looking for a wife," Willie continued. "Fiona just turned thirteen, didn't she? Has she been troth-plighted yet?"

"What?" Bryan burst out and looked at Willie incredulously.

"No," Cora began cautiously as another woman came out of the house. She was younger, in her early to mid-twenties. Tall and slim, she crossed her arms over her chest and regarded Bryan with large eyes the color of spring leaves. Golden hair hung in a thick plait down her back.

Willie's brow furrowed in confusion. "I thought as long as we were here, and you were searching for a bride, you could have a look at Fiona, see if she meets your standards."

The blond woman raised a well-shaped eyebrow. "I hope you can abandon your search for a bride long enough to attend your duties."

"Of course I can." He shook his head. "I mean, I'm not looking for a wife."

The blond woman raised both brows in surprise.

"We borderers don't look kindly on men who ravish wee lassies. You should at least propose marriage first."

Bryan closed his eyes and took a calming breath. "I don't want any young lassies, or to wed." They all looked at him blankly. "Where's my horse?"

"Did you lose it?" she asked.

"It was stolen." He paused and when he received no reaction from his statement he said, "I'm Bryan Hepburn, your new warden."

"Megan Dixon. Most call me the widow Dixon."

"So you do have my horse."

"The only horses here are mine." Her bland stare never wavered.

Bryan couldn't decide if he was annoyed or amused by her studied indifference. A little boy with coppery hair and freckles poked his head out the door and examined Bryan curiously. Megan slid her hand around the boy's shoulders and drew him against her skirts. Her waist was small and her breasts ample. She had fair skin, but with a warm glow that reminded him of a peach. It was becoming clear to Bryan that he found her to be something quite apart from amusing or irritating. His palms started to sweat. He wiped them on his breeks, feeling foolish and awkward.

Willie was saying, "Jock said he sold it to you, Megan. 'Tis the warden's horse. I think you should give it back."

She went past them, brushing Bryan's arm and turning at the bottom of the steps to give him a hard look. "And will the warden be arresting Jock for selling stolen goods? What about my five crowns? Will I ever see it again?"

"You can file against him at the next Truce Day. But for now, I'm taking my horse back." Bryan frowned at her. "I thought you only paid two crowns."

"Did you?" She turned on her heel and walked into the stable.

Bryan and Willie followed. Bryan's black stallion, Arthur, was eating oats. He rubbed the horse's neck. Arthur whickered a greeting and nudged his shoulder.

"He sold me the saddle, too." She indicated the high-back leather saddle lying over the side of the stall.

"I thank you . . . Lady Dixon?"

"Aye, my husband was Laird Dixon, so you may call me lady if you wish. But Megan will do." She moved close to stroke the horse's nose. " 'Tis a fine horse. A bit spirited, but well behaved. I was going to keep him for myself."

Bryan didn't comment. He had a sudden, ludicrous urge to let her keep the horse. He stamped it out. "Do you have a beacon to alert me if the English should trouble you?" He lifted the saddle and settled it on Arthur's back.

"Aye. At the top of the tower. If I light it, will you come to my rescue?" She was gazing at him openly. Her eyes captivated him, wide and clear, and *so green*.

"That's why I'm here," he said, pulling the strap snug around Arthur's belly.

"That's a comfort. The last warden thought he was here to get into my kirtle. I didn't like him much."

Her remark brought Bryan up short. What exactly was she implying? Surely she didn't have anything to do with Leod Hume's disappearance.

"Let me give you some advice, Warden," she said

softly. "Give up trying to be our friend and start sleeping while the sun's up, aye?" She smiled at him, showing a row of pretty white teeth. She swept by him, stopping in front of Willie. "Come inside for some ale, Uncle Willie." She patted his arm and walked out of the stable.

Bryan gaped at his deputy. "Uncle Willie?"

Willie shrugged sheepishly. "Aye, she's my niece." He inclined his head for Bryan to follow. "Come on. Megan brews a good ale and doesn't water it down for company."

Bryan, scratching his head, trailed after his deputy.

Megan was pouring ale into three tankards when she felt a tug on her skirt. "What is it, love?" she asked, kneeling so she was eye level with her son.

"Who is that man with Uncle Willie?"

"He's our new warden. He's here to protect us and stop the raiders from stealing our kine and sheep."

Innes nodded solemnly. "That's good. He's very big. He could just clout them, aye? Or scare them away?"

"Aye, that he could." She straightened his hair. "You go with your grandmum until I'm done speaking with Uncle Willie and the warden."

Innes ran up the stairs. Megan looked around to see if anyone was watching. She turned an empty tankard over and looked at her distorted reflection in the shiny bottom. She looked hideous, she saw with dismay. She smoothed back her hair with both hands and removed her apron. She was wearing an old blue woolen kirtle and bodice. It would be obvious if she

ran upstairs and changed. Not only had she not
expected the warden to show up on her doorstep his
first day on the march, but she had never expected him
to be so comely. She clenched her jaw, annoyed at
herself. Why did she care? Why was she getting herself all in a lather about the new warden? He was
likely to be gone in a few weeks anyway. Outsider
wardens never lasted long.

She filled the three tankards and carried them into
the next room. Uncle Willie and the warden were
seated at the table. The warden's long legs were
stretched casually in front of him. He didn't wear a
hat or helmet like other men, and his short chestnut
hair curled around his ears. He straightened when she
entered and smiled.

Her heart skipped a beat. Deep dimples grooved his
cheeks when he smiled. His eyes were warm and
brown with thick, dark lashes. She sat at the head of
the table between him and Uncle Willie. The warden
thanked her and took a drink. He was so polite and
mannerly. His clothes and horse and saddle spoke of
something better than the border life she lived. She
had known that the horse Jock sold her was stolen
when she bought it. She hoped the act of returning his
horse convinced him of her goodwill. It would be nice
to have the law in her favor for once.

"You have a nice place here, Megan." Sir Bryan
regarded her steadily. "It seems you've been immune
to the raiding."

"Not necessarily. We're under Douglas Hume of
Leadwater's protection, plus the Dixon men can run a
fine hot trod when they're put to it. The raiders don't
get far . . . unless they're Forsters. Cedric Forster has

burned my crops to the ground on more than one occasion. I hope to make it to harvest this year."

Willie nodded ruefully. "Aye, most don't even bother to plant, but Megan keeps at it, every year."

Sir Bryan nodded courteously then asked, "How much does Douglas Hume charge for his protection?"

Megan glanced at Willie. He stared back at her, his face completely expressionless. *So that's the way it was.* Bryan Hepburn was one of those honorable types who saw the law as black and white.

"Why, the protection's free. The laird of Leadwater is kin."

To her dismay, he appeared disappointed. He didn't believe her, she could tell. It was a major crime to pay ransom or protection money. It was actually a bigger crime to pay it than to extort it. She pushed her unease aside. It wasn't as though the warden could do anything about it. He couldn't arrest everyone in the East March.

Sir Bryan sighed and tapped his fingers on the table. His hands were large and strong. Dark hair dusted the backs of them, and the fingers were long. "Is that your boy?" he asked, looking toward the stairs.

She turned and saw Innes peeking at them through the railings. He giggled and ran up the steps.

"Aye. His name is Innes; he's four."

A smile curved the warden's firm mouth. "Does he look like his father?"

"Aye." She looked into the tankard of ale, feeling the usual stab of anger that her son was fatherless.

Willie cleared his throat. "Megan's husband, Innes, was killed four years ago. He was one of Cedric Forster's first victims."

"My condolences," Sir Bryan said.

She shrugged, forcing the memories away. It was better to never dwell on it. There was nothing she could do about it but defend her family against further injustice.

"Cedric Forster is still about, after committing this murder? Is he an outlaw?"

Megan met the warden's eyes. "No, he's not. He lives just across the border, protected by the warden of the English Middle March, Sir John Forster."

Sir Bryan's look of horror was almost comical. Megan sighed, thinking he had a lot to learn before he would be able to deal with the borderers effectively. The silence drew out.

She smiled suddenly. "So, Warden, you're looking for a wife?" He started shaking his head, and she pressed on. "My sister-in-law is thirteen and needs a good husband. I could call her down now for you to meet." She started to rise.

He grabbed her arm. "No! No, please!" His eyes darted to Willie, who was watching curiously. "I'm sure she's bonny, but I prefer . . . older women."

"I know!" she exclaimed. "The Bromfield widow!"

Willie nodded his approval of her selection.

But the poor warden was having none of it, shaking his head again, a look of desperation in his eyes. "Really, Megan, Willie. This isn't necessary. I have no intention of getting married any time soon." He stood abruptly. "I think we should go."

"I didn't mean to scare you off. I won't send the lassies after you if you don't want me to," she said, a note of teasing in her voice.

He was full of excuses and apologies, but his neck

was red. She followed him and Willie to the door, admiring how broad his shoulders were. His hair almost brushed the top of the door frame—which had been made unusually high to accommodate her late husband's great height. They disappeared into the stable. She wondered why she had driven him off. She had done it purposely, knowing that what she said would embarrass him.

She had surrounded herself with a cool wall of words ever since Innes was murdered, not wanting to give her trust to someone again, only to have it torn violently from her grasp. After a few minutes with Sir Bryan Hepburn she had felt herself thawing, wanting to know him. That was why she had run him off. She had no business feeling such intense interest in another lawman.

The warden emerged from the stable and rode over to her. He looked like some mythical warrior atop the enormous black steed. Larger and more powerful than mortal men . . .

"I thank you for the return of my horse," he said, interrupting her thoughts.

She nodded stiffly, mortified by her fanciful musings. "I'm pleased I was able to help."

He flipped two coins at her, and she caught one. The other fell in the dirt at her feet. They were crowns.

"Only two?"

He grinned. "You don't lie well."

Francis Hepburn Stewart gained entrance to the garrison with no trouble; everyone knew who he and his men were. It was the wee hours of the morning, the sun not yet trying to cast her glow on the world. He entered the keep and went straight to Bryan's chambers. No men were guarding the room. Francis shook his head. Soon every reiver on the march would be plotting to assassinate Bryan. He should hire personal guards. Such was the life of a warden.

Francis lit a candle, appalled at the squalor his cousin was living in. He went to the bedchamber. Bryan's mongrel raised its mangy head. It whined in fear, then seeing it was only Francis, laid its head back down. Francis sat on the bed beside his cousin and pushed at his shoulder. Bryan was so tall his stocking feet hung off the end of the bed. He definitely didn't get his length from the Hepburns. Francis wasn't a short man, but neither was he a giant like his cousin.

Bryan grunted, and a second later the blade of his dirk was pressed against Francis's throat.

Francis pushed his cousin's hand away. "You'll have to be quicker than that, Cousin. I could have stoned you to death ere you knew I was here."

Bryan dropped his hand. "What do you want?" He rolled over, putting his back to Francis.

"I want to know if Leod still lives."

"How should I know? I was robbed on the way to the garrison. I've been trying to recover my belongings the past two days."

"And you questioned no one while doing this?"

Bryan sighed, but didn't answer.

"If he is alive, I must have him. If he is dead, I must have proof. If you find the killer, I must speak to him, face-to-face, to determine if he is lying."

"This smells foul to me."

Francis stood, grinning. "Naught smells foul but that ferocious beast you keep company with. Why, he nearly bit my head off when I entered. What a dog!"

Bryan turned violently toward him. "Why me? Why can you not find another of your lapdogs to do this task?"

"Because I trust none but you. You are the only man I know, since your father died, who holds honor and justice dear. I know you will do as I ask. You will make a fine warden."

Bryan's face grew dark at the reference to his father. James Hepburn, despite a strong sense of honor, had died in a foreign prison, a traitor in exile. It was a sore spot with Bryan. Francis turned to leave.

Bryan's voice stopped him. "What business have you at the witching hour, riding about the march like the warlock they all accuse you of being?"

"The devil's business, Cousin, what else?" He walked out the door, cackling.

Two

Megan chewed the inside of her lip as she viewed the bags of grain stacked against the wall. If the Forsters raided her before harvest, this would be all the grain they had. She shuffled some bags aside, looking for moisture. It wouldn't do if the grain were to rot.

She was making one of her frequent checks of the weapons and provisions stored in the tower. After murdering her husband four years ago, Cedric Forster had taken all of the Dixons' kine and burned their crops. They had nearly starved to death. Megan would not allow such a thing to occur again. Worry gnawed at her insides, as it always did. *It's not enough food.*

She went to the window, trying to put the nagging thoughts out of her mind, and spied the warden riding for her house. Her heart leapt, and her hands flew to her hair in distress. She curled them into fists, willing this strange excitement at the sight of Sir Bryan to go away. She continued watching his approach. His size was compelling. He wore no covering for his head and rode alone. Few wardens would dare venture out so exposed. He was so different. His name was Hepburn. The Hepburns had held the earldom of Bothwell for many generations. The current earl was a Stewart, but his mother was a Hepburn. She wondered if the warden had that noble blood running through his veins. Most people wouldn't consider Hepburn blood entirely noble, even though the current earl's predecessor had styled himself the king of Scotland for a time. Most folks believed witchcraft ran strong in that family.

The surge of excitement transformed to irritation. Why had the warden returned today? She had tired of the former warden, Leod Hume, paying so many unexpected visits. Cora met Sir Bryan outside, then led him into the house. Megan sighed. She would have to go down and see what he wanted.

She found him in her parlor, his back to her. Cora had offered him refreshment; he held a tankard in one hand and was examining a tapestry. His head was turned to the side to study it. Chestnut hair curled around his thickly muscled neck. The sheer breadth of his shoulders was stunning. She had seen many powerful, rugged men; border life bred them that way. But none had the height to match the brawn as Sir Bryan did.

A shield, an ax, and a sword were mounted on the wall next to the tapestry, and Bryan moved to them. He was inspecting the sword hilt when she finally made her presence known. "They belonged to my late husband's grandsire. He cut down a few English at Flodden with those."

"Obviously not enough, or things might be a wee bit different, aye?"

"Not here on the borders."

"I'm beginning to see that things are quite different here." He tore himself away from the weapons and finally looked at her.

"Different from what? I've known little but this all my life."

He stared at her, not responding, then turned abruptly and went back to scrutinizing the weapons. "What did you ask me?" He was intent on the sword hilt again.

"Nothing. So what brings you here again so soon?"

He turned back to her. "You asked me something. Forgive me, I was . . . distracted. We were talking about things being different on the border."

"I was asking about you. What is it different from?"

"Antwerp, Brussels, Luxembourg, Anjou . . ."

She understood now what he meant by *different*. Backward, uncivilized, uncultured. She had been right that there was an air of aristocracy about him. Pretentiousness. She decided she didn't like him. He was all pretty manners and fine clothes, too good for the poor borderers he was sworn to protect. She felt coarse and common suddenly, embarrassed by her plain dress and work-roughed hands. She wanted him out of her house. His presence only seemed to make its lack of refinement more prominent.

"Aye, well, whatever you might think, we're not a bunch of dullards. Why are you here?"

"I have yet to meet a dullard since I've arrived."

"I pray you, Warden, state your purpose."

His brows drew together in confusion at her abrupt

manner. He pulled a letter from his belt. "This was waiting for me when I returned to the garrison yesterday. Would you like me to read it to you?"

"I can read," she snapped, her embarrassment increasing at his assumption that she was unlettered.

He unfolded the letter and handed it to her. She scanned the contents. It was from Lord Hundson, the warden of the English East March, opposite them. It seemed the Selbys were complaining that she was grazing her kine on their land. They not only wanted her to stop, but expected some kind of restitution for the grass her cattle had eaten. She handed the letter back to him.

"Is this true?" he asked, watching her carefully.

"No. They must be mistaken. I graze my kine to the east."

He opened the letter again. "So the big *D* on the kine's bums doesn't stand for Dixon?"

"Mayhap it's Dodds' kine, or Davisons'. And I'm not the only Dixon living on the Merse."

He folded his arms across his chest. "They recognized your shepherd."

"So they say." Was she really so transparent? Could he tell she was lying right now? Those damn Selbys. Who cared if her cows ate English grass? Perhaps now all her cows would become pompous windbags. She was not paying any sort of restitution for their bloody grass.

He scratched his temple, then sighed. "Just stop doing it, aye? And that'll be the end of it. I'll bother you no more."

"Do you not have more important things to attend to, Warden? Murders and the like? Do you really care whose belly English grass goes into? Perhaps you should be trying to determine where the Forsters are going to raid next."

He smiled sarcastically. "That should be simple. Everyone I've met is so honest and cooperative. Maybe if I ask them prettily they won't plunder at all anymore."

She could sense his frustration. He was strung tight, hands on hips, scowling at her. She knew some things, from being a borderer, being a laird, and having been married to a warden. Things that could aid an outsider. Things that no one else would offer to show him and that he was too proud to ask. She could help him. She was tired of being raided, and he was useless to her as a warden if he didn't know what he was doing. But did she want to help him? Did she want to spend more time in his unsettling company?

Before she answered her own questions, she heard herself asking, "Tell me, Warden, have you ever been on a hot trod?"

"No."

She walked to the window and looked at the morning sky. "What have you planned for the day, Warden?"

"I was going to write some letters; I have a half sister I haven't seen in years . . . investigate some stolen kine, then there's the warden of the Middle March I need to speak with."

"I'll show you something far more interesting than some letters or the crooked warden, Thomas Kerr. I can show you how a warden really dispenses justice."

"Very well. All that can wait. What are you going to show me?"

*   *   *

Instead of taking the road back to the garrison, Megan
led Bryan out the gates of her home and around the
barmkin wall. He had no idea what she wanted to
show him, but he was open to any help or advice.

She rode down the hill, and he stayed close behind.
Her braid bounced against her back, reflecting the
sunlight like a thick chain of gold. She had changed
into breeks, tall boots, and a soft leather doublet
before leaving. It was a major effort not to stare; her
legs seemed to go on forever. She was a rather uncon-
ventional woman, and he had been shocked at first by
her attire. But he had seen women do far stranger
things in war than don a pair of breeks.

She was a hard woman, too. He had been surprised
by her invitation. And somewhat suspicious. He
didn't want to be, but he was powerfully attracted to
her. After his last experience with love, he didn't trust
easily. Most people didn't give without expecting
something in return. She would be no exception.

He urged Arthur faster so he was riding beside her.
"Where are we going?"

"Stop worrying about where we're going and start
watching how."

He hung back again and paid attention to his sur-
roundings. The countryside had been mostly flat with
gentle swells; now it became bleaker with hills and
valleys. There was no road, nor even a faint trail. It all
looked the same to him, and he wondered what he was
supposed to be watching for. If she wanted him to be
able to find an exact spot in this repetitious countryside, he was afraid he would disappoint her.

After riding in a northeasterly direction for a long

while, they entered a low valley surrounded on all sides by steep hills. There was one way in and an exit to the south. Otherwise you would have to climb the hills to get out. She stopped in the center of the valley.

"Is this what you want to show me?" he asked, looking around.

"Warden, if you can understand the significance of this, I might be able to teach you something." Her green eyes were full of challenge.

He raised an eyebrow and jogged his horse around the valley. She dismounted and sat on the ground, watching him. Her gray horse munched on the thick grass. It was as if they were in a bowl, or tub. An enclosure. He scanned the floor of the valley. The grass wasn't so thick everywhere. Something else had been grazing here.

"Is this where the reivers hide the kine they've stolen?"

She gave him an appreciative look. "It's one of the places, though they're not dumb enough to use the same place every time."

He left Arthur to graze with Megan's horse and joined her on the ground. "Why are you showing me this?"

She shrugged and looked away from him, watching the horses. "I know not. I feel sorry for you."

He didn't want her pity. "I appreciate your aid, whatever your motives."

"This by itself isn't going to catch you any reivers. Nay, Warden, we've just begun." She stretched her long, slim legs out in front of her and turned partway toward him. "Imagine it's late at night." She waved her hand across the valley, as though transforming it to darkness. "A party of Forsters have attacked Edington and are riding away, laden with plunder, herding kine, and they even have prisoners across their saddles. If the raid went well, they've a good head start on the wardens, and if they destroyed the village properly, none of the villagers will be hot on their tail."

Her eyes were the color of the grass around them, he noticed with a slight quickening of his pulse. He nodded for her to go on.

"You saw the ride out here. Imagine it in the dark. And the reivers know all the tricks, all the good hiding places, all the shortcuts." She poked her finger at his shoulder. "You are the one at a disadvantage if you're bumbling around the hills, lost yourself. What kind of hot trod is that? No one will take you seriously if you can't keep up or haven't a clue what's going on."

She had a point. "And you'll show me around these parts?"

"I'll show you some, but I suggest you start sleeping till noon."

"Why?"

"The hills look a good deal different at night; it would be best if you learn your way around then. Most of the reivers, the Forsters in particular, don't strike unless the sun is down. They prefer a full moon."

"You seem to know a lot about the Forsters. Are you training me to catch your husband's murderer?"

Her lips thinned. "You'd be the first. But if you catch him, you better guard him well. If I get near his prison I'll cut his head off and stick it on a pole."

He stared at her until she looked away. He had discovered what she wanted from him. She wanted him on her side against the Forsters. Her anger went deep. He wondered if she ever grieved the loss of her husband, or if she just turned it all into hate. He had almost convinced himself she had no ulterior motive for inviting him on this little training session. His disappointment was sharp, but he still wanted her help.

"Don't do that," he said. "Then I'd have to arrest you for murder."

"How could I be guilty of murder? I'd say I'm serving justice by killing him."

"You should leave executions to the proper authorities."

"Why, when the authorities are incompetent? Or care only for themselves?"

She tried to stand, but he grabbed her arm. "I think you judge me too quickly. I'm neither pathetic nor incompetent, and I do care about the families on my march. But I can't do this if no one wants me to." She was staring at his hand on her arm and he released her. "Would that you were my deputy, then I could get something accomplished."

She stood and looked down at him. The sun was at her back, shadowing her features, but her hair shone like a golden halo in the sun. She reached her hand out to help him up. He took it and noticed she still wore her wedding ring. He stood over her. She was tall for a lass, but she still had to tip her head back to look at him. Her mouth was wide but well formed and turned up slightly at the corners. Her eyes were searching his face, her look expectant. He realized he was still holding her hand and she was trying to remove it from his grasp. He released her and stepped away.

"I do want you to succeed," she said, "or I wouldn't be here with you now. But competence alone won't get you far. You must be wily and think like a thief. Go to the garrison and take a nap. Come back to my house at sundown." They climbed on their horses. She started to leave without him, and he caught up with her.

"I don't know my way back," he said, feeling foolish. He had been so busy admiring the female attributes visible in her masculine attire that he hadn't been paying much attention.

They rode in silence for a long time. She finally reined in her horse. She pointed to his left, and he saw the garrison in the distance. The idea of leaving her company and going back to the rotting tower was depressing. She was watching him, waiting for him to give her leave to go. The quiet was becoming awkward.

"I'll see you tonight, then," he said, but made no move to leave.

Indecision warred on her face. She sighed. "If you come a little earlier I can give you something better than old meat and pottage for dinner."

"I'd like that."

She gave him a hesitant smile and galloped away. He watched her until she disappeared over the horizon.

His good humor dissolved at the garrison when he found a crowd of angry borderers in the hall. As soon as they saw him they began shouting.

"Hold!" he yelled. "One at a time!" They quieted. "Who was here first?"

"I was!" one man shouted.

"Ye bloody liar! 'Twas me who was here first!"

Bryan groaned. He pointed to a young man waiting quietly. "You, lad, come with me." He raised his voice. "Everyone else, stay here and wait your turn." He gave them all a hard look. "And no fighting!"

Bryan sat at the desk and offered the lad a chair. He was a big, muscular young man with a neck like a tree trunk.

"I've come to offer you my services as a personal guard, Warden. My name's Rory Trotter." His large frame filled the chair. His hands rested easily on his thick thighs. There was a calmness about him, an air of self-possession unusual in one so young.

"Why would I need a guard? I'm surrounded by soldiers and I've got Willie."

"Willie couldn't save the last warden from being murdered."

"Does someone want to murder me?"

"Well, not yet."

He supposed Rory had a point: once the borderers realized he meant to clean up the East March, there would probably be threats to his life. "Who do you think killed the last warden?"

"Some say it was the widow Dixon, others believe it to be the witches that finally got him."

Bryan was having a hard time finding his voice. "Lady Dixon?"

"Och, aye. Can't say I blame her . . . if she was the one who did it. I only said that's what people think. I don't know myself, and I'm not troubling myself on it. His death was no loss to the march."

"Why would she kill the warden?"

"For one, he was over-fond of her and I don't think

she liked him. And he was protecting the Forsters. Everyone knows she would kill Cedric with her bare hands if she could."

Bryan contemplated Rory's words, wanting to dismiss them. It was too obvious. It was no more than talk, gossip, he told himself. His stomach clenched sickeningly, remembering the last time he had such thoughts. Tried to make excuses for a woman. A worthless whore. He could not allow himself to become weak and misjudge Megan.

He studied the large young man before him. He had an open, honest face, and there was no doubt he was strong as a bull.

"What are your recommendations?"

"I've been running raids and counter-raids with the best since I was fifteen, four years now. The Trotters and the Grays have been feuding for decades; I know the way a reiver thinks."

"Why would I want a reiver as a guard?"

Rory grinned. "You will find, sir, the borderers see naught dishonorable about thieving kine. Why, even the nobles have a hand in it. There are no greater reivers than the wardens of both the Scottish and English Middle Marches! But I will refrain from any acts that might compromise my position with you."

Bryan was thoughtful. He could use a man at his back with such knowledge and experience, and a personal guard was one of the few things for which the king provided a special allotment. "How are you with a sword? Or a gun?"

"I can wield a sword fine, but I've never used a gun. I'm good with an arrow and a dirk."

Pellinore trotted in from the other room and began

sniffing the lad. He nosed Rory's hand and was rewarded with a vigorous ear scratching. Pellinore apparently approved.

"You're hired. You will live in the garrison and accompany me on business," Bryan said. Rory smiled, but Bryan didn't return it. "I expect your loyalty. I will pay you well, but I don't want you to be loyal to my purse."

Rory became serious. "Aye, sir. I carry your safety foremost."

Bryan considered bringing Rory with him when he went to Megan's that evening but decided against it. "I'll have Lauren ready the room next to mine."

Rory left, and Pellinore nudged at Bryan. He stroked the dog's back idly. So Megan was thought to be a murderess. It appeared his visit with her would have a dual purpose.

 Three

"Tell me everything you remember about Leod Hume," Bryan said as they sat down to eat.

The light from outside was beginning to soften with evening, though they still had several hours of daylight left, and the candelabras were lit. The smelly rush lights had been put away for the occasion. Everyone who lived with Megan was at the table, and they all stared blankly at Bryan. Megan wondered why he was asking about the dead warden. Had he heard the rumors circulating that she had killed him?

"He tried to kiss my mum," Innes said, craning his neck to look up at the warden. Megan had situated Bryan between herself and Innes.

Bryan's eyes narrowed on her, but when he looked back at Innes, his smile was genuine. "Did he? Well, I hope your mum set him straight."

"Aye, she did." Innes said nothing else and left that hanging in the air.

Megan smiled stiffly and tried to explain, "The East March doesn't see as much trouble as the Middle and West Marches. But the last four years things have been very bad because of the Forsters across the border. The Humes had always been a strong clan and able to repel offenders, but they've been failing of late. Every time I build the land back up and I'm operating at a profit, I'm raided."

"What has this to do with Leod Hume?" Bryan asked.

The others had not touched their food, and Megan glared down the table. Spoons and knives were suddenly raised, and low feminine talking commenced. She was surrounded by in-laws, mostly females, but they were her family as if they were blood kin. They had pulled together after her husband was murdered. They had struggled and suffered together. Loved and worked until their fingers bled. She loved them completely. "I have reason to believe our missing warden kept Cedric Forster apprised of my circumstances."

Bryan nodded and looked down at his plate.

"That doesn't mean I killed him," she said.

"I didn't say you did. I have not accused you of such a thing."

She was becoming irritated. Of course he wasn't accusing her of anything. He had no evidence, merely hearsay. But that didn't mean he didn't suspect her, or even more appalling, think her capable. Her comment about putting Cedric Forster's head on a spike echoed back to her.

"Why don't you ask Tavish Marshall about Leod? He's certain to know more than anyone else. And what about the witches? Mean you to check out that story as well? 'Tis as plausible as the one that I killed him."

Bryan frowned. "Who is Tavish Marshall?"

"He's your deputy."

He raised an eyebrow. "Indeed? The only deputy I am aware of is Willie. So I have another? I wonder where he is."

"I suggest you take stock of your situation, Warden. Last I heard he was visiting his brother in the north."

From the coolness of his unwavering stare, Megan was quite certain he did not appreciate her patronizing comment. She forced herself not to look away. His indifference this evening was at such odds with his earlier warmth that she was becoming uneasy.

"From whence do you hail, Warden?" Cora asked, abruptly changing the subject with a cross look at Megan. She was sitting across from Bryan to Megan's right.

He hesitated, but smiled at the older woman. "I was born here in . . . in Lothian, actually. My mother sent me to my uncle in the Low Countries, where I stayed and eventually fought for William of Orange against the Spanish. I have only just returned since his assassination."

"Who are your parents?" Cora asked. "I have kin in Lothian; mayhap our families are acquainted."

"I don't think so," he said in a tight voice, not answering Cora's question.

Cora looked at Megan with raised eyebrows but didn't pursue the topic.

"How is it that a man raised in the Low Countries

finds himself a post as warden of the East March in Scotland?" Megan asked. He seemed extremely uncomfortable, which continued to pique her interest.

"My . . . cousin, the Earl of Bothwell, had me appointed to the position."

The others began asking him questions about the Prince of Orange and the war in the Low Countries, and he visibly relaxed, warming to the subject. Megan watched him silently, not contributing to the conversation. He had been in countless battles over the past decade and in the personal service of William of Orange for the last seven years. He told of Calvinist towns he defended and Catholic towns he attacked.

His table manners were exemplary; even as he told his stories not a crumb of food went anywhere but on his plate. Her family, who generally had food falling out of their mouths, were making an effort to imitate him. Innes was watching, mesmerized, as Bryan used his knife to cut a piece of meat without touching it with his fingers. When Bryan noticed Innes watching him and not eating, he leaned over and cut the boy's meat into little pieces for him.

"Did the prince choose you because you're so great?" Innes asked in awe.

Bryan laughed. "Aye. I was serving in the Scottish regiment seven years ago. The king of Spain had put an enormous price on the Prince of Orange's head, along with a promise of complete pardon and a title of nobility to anyone who assassinated the prince. There were many attempts on his life after that. My commander thought I fought well, and I was larger than the other men in the regiment, so he offered me to the prince. I was with him until he died, though it was not

I who was on duty when he was murdered or things might have been different."

"But then you wouldn't be our warden," Innes said, giving him a shy smile.

Bryan grinned back, his cheeks dimpling. He turned to Megan and caught her staring. She looked away quickly. Blood rushed to her face all at once. She spent the remainder of the meal with her eyes riveted to her plate, mentally chastising herself for mooning over him in awe as if she were the common rustic he thought she was.

Afterward, Cora dragged Sir Bryan to the solar, where she was making an enormous tapestry of the Merse as viewed from their tower. Almost against her will Megan was drawn to follow and found him sitting in front of the large frame that held the tapestry. "Did you make the bonny one in the hall? Next to the shield and swords?" he asked Cora.

"Aye," Cora said, and Megan saw her blush.

He peered closer at the stitching on the tapestry. "That's a fine job, Cora. You've captured all the colors. Do you dye them yourself?"

"Aye, I do." And with shining eyes and flushed cheeks, she launched into a description of how she dyed the thread.

Megan scowled and decided to put Innes to bed. It was dark, and she was anxious to begin her lesson with the warden so she could be through with it. She resolved that this would be a singular occurrence. She didn't want him hanging around her home and becoming friendly with her family.

Innes was peeking into the solar. Megan took his hand and led him to his room.

"You didn't let me bid good evening to the warden."

"You'll see him again soon enough." She sat on his narrow bed while he stripped to his shirt and hose. He started to crawl into bed. "Did you use the pisspot?"

"I'm not going to do it in front of you."

"Oh? You're a big lad now, I suppose, and need your mum to go away?" She sighed dramatically and stepped out of the room. It was time to put up a screen. Her eyes burned. He wasn't a baby any longer. Soon he wouldn't need her at all. He needed to be in the company of men. He needed a father.

"I'm done!" he called.

He was under the covers. She sat beside him.

"Did you clean your face and your teeth?"

"Aye."

She smiled down at him. He looked just like his father, with light blue eyes and freckles covering his face. He was already big for his age. He would be tall like Innes. "I can't tell you a story tonight, love. I have to show the warden something, but tomorrow I promise to tell you a long one."

"Is the warden coming back tomorrow?"

"I don't know. I doubt it."

He looked sad. She pressed her cheek against his. Innes's immediate fondness for Bryan only reinforced her feeling that the boy needed a father. There were men around, his uncles, but they only visited. There was old Hob, but he was nearly eighty years old. Her throat tightened, and she knew it was time to think of remarrying. She hadn't even considered it since Innes's death. She would speak to Douglas Hume soon. He had a son about her age, Charles, who had taken a fancy to her. He was a distant cousin and would bring wealth and security to her home, as well as able-bodied men. It really would be the best thing for Innes.

She kissed her son and blew the candle out. She went to her room to dress for the nighttime ride. She had worn one of her few good fustian gowns for dinner. It was emerald green, and the neckline was low and square. Her stays were pulled tight and pushed her breasts upward. She gazed at her reflection in the looking glass, trailing her fingers down her neck to the swell of her breast. She would have another man touching her as her husband had. She tried to imagine Charles Hume's lips pressed against hers. Instead, she envisioned the warden looming over her, and she quickly shoved the image away.

She had noticed how he looked at her. It made her restless with a strange yearning she couldn't fathom. She felt disloyal to Innes's memory. She never had such strong, heart-pounding thoughts about her late husband. She had never wondered how it would feel to kiss him.

She shook herself. She did not intend to involve herself with another warden. That road only led to heartbreak. Besides, Sir Bryan was too good to be interested in someone like her for anything more than pleasure. She was too low and coarse. He would want a real lady who smelled sweet and wore silks and velvets, not wool and homespun. He probably had a lass waiting for him at King James's court.

She had even put her hair up. She yanked it down in disgust and it fell around her shoulders. Was she as obvious as everyone else? She was acting the fool, too, trying to look pretty. After changing her clothes and braiding her hair, she went downstairs. He was waiting for her, and he followed her out of the house.

A big gray dog ran at them on their way to the barn, startling Megan. Bryan knelt to scratch its ears.

"Is it your dog?" she asked.

"Aye. His name's Pellinore."

She ran her hand over the dog's back. "Pellinore? Is he so fearsome that even King Arthur must have Merlin's help to defeat him?"

Bryan took the dog's face between his hands and grinned. " 'Tis what I hoped when I named him, but the only manner in which he resembles the ferocious King Pellinore is his long naps in the woods with his tail between his legs."

Megan laughed. Pellinore leaned against her legs and moaned when she scratched him. "If you had told me you brought company I would have fed him, too."

"Cora gave him dinner while you were putting Innes to bed." He followed her into the stable. She started to saddle her horse, but he took the saddle from her. "You didn't have to stay, you know."

His hands brushed hers, and she recoiled as though she had been burned. "What are you talking about?" she asked, flustered by her reaction to his touch.

"After your husband was murdered. Most lasses would have run home to their family. And you've a big family. I know you're a Hume. They would have taken you back in easily enough."

"You've been asking questions about me."

"I've been looking into the circumstances of your husband's death and what the last warden did to bring Cedric Forster to justice."

She held her breath, waiting for his next words.

"The Dixons had naught after Cedric's raid four years ago," Bryan said. "He killed many of the menfolk, excepting old Hob, thank the Lord. Instead of letting Innes's family fall apart, you held them together. They look to you with respect as they would any male laird."

His admiration warmed her. "I do it for my son, so he has something of his father's. And I wouldn't call myself a laird. We're a small clan, mostly women, old men, and bairns. I hire most of my labor from neighboring clans since I have few tenants to call on."

He walked around the horse, tugging the saddle to make sure it was secure. "Would such a strong and determined woman let anything stand in her way? Even brutal men trying to take her home?" He leaned casually against the stall beside her.

His nearness did strange things to her, made her unable to think straight. He smelled like leather and something else, warm and unique. She raised her eyes to his. His face was cool and expressionless. She forced herself to match his demeanor. "Just because I would murder, doesn't mean I did."

"Did you kill the warden?"

"No."

"Do you know who killed him?"

"No. It could be anyone. Everyone hated him."

He held her gaze for a long time. "I want to believe you, Megan, really I do."

"But you do not?"

He pushed away from the stall. "I feel that I can't trust anyone."

"Well . . . you are the warden."

He gave her a narrow look. "Is that what you're afraid of?"

The urge to be honest with him was strong. She knew she should reject it, but something deep inside told her he was different. "This is difficult for an outsider, I know. That's why I'm trying to help.

"Did you offer any help to the last warden?" His voice was cold.

"No," she answered, confused. "He didn't need my help."

"What was your relationship with Leod Hume?"

She shrugged. "He was a distant cousin. I didn't even know him until he was warden."

"And then?"

Did he really want to know? She didn't want to keep lying to him, but wondered how he'd take the truth. For some reason she longed to trust him, longed to lean on his strength and let him take away the guilt and worry. She blurted out, "I paid him to kill Cedric Forster."

He took a step back and stared at her in shock. He turned his back to her, running his hand through his hair. His change in attitude made her nervous. She shouldn't have told him. She reminded herself that Cedric was still alive and thriving, so she had done nothing wrong. Anyway, she would deny it if he dared bring charges against her.

He didn't say anything for a long time. He let out a breath. "Well, since he didn't kill Cedric, I think I shall just forget you said that."

"I thank you, Warden. Shall we go?"

He gave her an odd look, but took Arthur's reins and followed her out of the barn, ordering his dog to stay. Pellinore didn't look pleased, but he disappeared into the shadows beside the house.

They rode through the countryside for several hours while Megan pointed out trails and landmarks Bryan should be familiar with, thieves' roads and river fords. She showed him hidden ways to get in and out of the larger homesteads. He was impressed with her knowledge of such things and was again grateful she was sharing it with him.

But he was even more uncertain about her than before. He wanted to believe her when she said she knew nothing about Leod Hume's death, but her revelation that she hired him to kill another man was a shock. He found himself rationalizing for her. Cedric Forster *had* killed her husband and raided her property repeatedly.

Irritation at himself simmered just below the surface. He had only heard Megan's side of the tale. There was always another side. He'd been through this before! The last woman he cared about had done nothing but lie to him and use him. He had made excuses for her, too. He had sensed the same half-truths in her as he did in Megan.

They stopped half a mile from a small stone cottage. Smoke rose in a thin stream from a hole in the roof, white against the dark sky. Bryan and Megan were hidden in one of the little copses of trees that littered the area. He recognized the house. After retrieving Arthur from Megan, Willie had given Bryan a brief tour of the march, introducing him to some of the inhabitants. A widow named Cathy Armstrong

lived here with her two children, a cow, and a pig.
Cathy had a little garden behind the house, and she
managed to scrape out a living. She made baskets and
pretty embroidered handkerchiefs. Bryan had bought
several handkerchiefs and baskets on his visit. They
sat back at the garrison serving no purpose.

He gave Megan a sideways look. She watched the
cottage intently. She looked different. There was a
large leather bag on the back of her saddle. After they
left the walls of her home she had pulled a short
leather jack and a metal bonnet from it. She had dag-
gers concealed in several places on her body. She
made him nervous.

The jack had plates of metal sewn into it so it was
like a coat of armor but not so heavy. It completely
hid her well-shaped upper body. He had been quite
entranced by her at dinner. It amazed him that she
could transform herself from soft and feminine to
something so hard.

"Are we waiting for something?" he whispered.

She glared at him and brought her finger to her lips.
He scanned the area where she was looking but didn't
see anything out of the ordinary. The cow was tied to
a post. It was too dark to see the pig, and a dog was
walking around by the cow. He peered intently at the
dark forms. That wasn't a dog. Bryan's body tensed. It
was a man, and he was on his hands and knees, unty-
ing the cow.

Bryan quickly looked at Megan. They'd been sitting here close to fifteen minutes. Had she seen him
the whole time? Megan's lips were compressed in a
grim line. She leaned close to him. "He's not going to
herd the cow back on foot," she whispered. "I suspect

he's not alone. There's probably another one holding the horses just over that rise." She indicated a low hill to their right. "That's the direction he came from. I'm going back through the trees to confront the other one from behind. As soon as you can't see me anymore, apprehend that man. We need to be quick. *Look,* the cow is untied, and he's going for the pig."

Bryan strained his eyes. She was right. The man was crawling toward the pig's pen. Bryan turned to say something to her, but she was gone. He twisted in the saddle and saw the swish of her horse's tail disappearing into the trees. He spurred Arthur and galloped toward the man skulking around the cottage. The man saw him and, instead of running as Bryan had expected, he yelled wildly and brandished a small ax. He hit the cow on the backside. It ran for the hill where Megan said his accomplice would be hiding. Bryan drew his sword.

The man grabbed the struggling piglet under his arm and raced after the cow. When Bryan was close enough, he kicked the man in the back, sending him sprawling to the ground. The piglet squealed and scampered away. Bryan jumped down from his horse and approached the thief, who was lying face-down.

"Get up!"

The thief didn't move. Bryan hadn't kicked him that hard. He nudged the thief with the toe of his boot. The thief's hand shot out, latching onto Bryan's ankle. The man rolled over, raising his ax as he tried to pull Bryan down. Bryan brought the heel of his other foot down in the middle of the man's chest. The ax grazed his thigh, cutting through the material of his breeks. The thief released his foot, and Bryan knocked the ax out of his hand. He dropped a knee onto the thief's throat. The man squirmed convulsively for air.

Bryan felt over the man's body and pulled a knife from the thief's boot and another from his waist. He tossed them out of reach and hauled the man to his feet. He was suddenly fearful for Megan's safety and ran toward the hill, dragging the man with him. When he crested the rise, he saw two figures on the ground. Megan was on top of the man. Her bonnet was gone and blond hair streamed over her shoulders. At first, he thought they were still fighting and almost released his prisoner to go to her aid until he heard what she was saying.

"I should slit your stinking throat right here!" She held a dirk to his throat and a wad of the man's hair in the other hand, and beat his head against the ground to emphasize her words. "You piece of dung! If I killed your sorry arse, no one would miss you."

"Megan!" Bryan yelled sharply. "Leave off!"

She didn't move at first. Then she rose slowly, slamming the man's head against the ground one last time and spitting in his face. The man crawled away from her, toward Bryan. Blood ran down his face from various cuts and scratches. Bryan was so astounded at Megan's behavior, he didn't know what to do at first. She went to her horse and retrieved a length of rope.

Bryan took the rope from her. Her cheeks were flushed and her eyes glinted like emeralds in the moonlight. A thin stream of blood ran from her nose, staining her lips red.

"Round up the cow and pig and take them back to the cottage," he ordered.

She nodded and did his bidding. He tied the men's hands and tethered them to the horses. As they rode silently back to the garrison, Bryan struggled to pull his thoughts together on the evening's events. Megan had been ready to commit murder. It shocked him that a woman could be a vessel of such violence. Yet he couldn't deny a certain grudging respect—admiration even—for the way she had ambushed and fought the reiver.

Willie ran out to meet them, rubbing the sleep out of his eyes. "What's this, Warden?"

"We caught these men trying to steal Cathy Armstrong's beasts. They say they're Kerrs, so we'll send them back to their warden in the morning."

Willie motioned to some men to take care of the thieves. Megan was sitting dejectedly on her horse, all the fight drained out of her.

"Come on," Bryan said. She followed. In his chambers, with the door shut, he turned on her. "What the hell was that all about?"

She removed the leather jack and threw it on a chair. "If you haven't figured it out, Warden, you're not fit to hold that title."

Her hair was still streaming down her shoulders wild and thick. She had tried to wipe the blood away, but had only managed to smear it across her cheek. The sight of it sent new fear coursing through him that quickly transformed to rage.

"You know damn well what I speak of! You were a few seconds from killing that man."

"He showed little conscience when it was my gullet he was trying to slit!"

He rubbed his hands across his face, trying to make some sense of what happened. "Did you know they were going to be there?"

"No."

"Then why this?" He grabbed the jack and held it in her face. "Why the dirks concealed all over your body?" He reached around her and grabbed one she had strapped to her lower back.

"You must open your eyes if you're going to protect your people. We're yours now. And they are out there every night, during the daylight even. 'Tis common sense in the borders." She snatched her dirk out of his hand. "You'd be surprised. Raiding parties oft run into each other in the night, and then you've got yourself a bloody battle to clean up, because they'll decide they want to plunder what the other's got."

"You could have been hurt."

"No!" she yelled. "I could have been killed. Do you not understand?"

"Why do you stay?"

She laughed incredulously. "Where shall I go, pray tell? I don't have the soft life you're accustomed to. Great lords don't shuffle me around at their whim. This is my home, and God damn the man who tries to take what's mine!"

Her passion left him speechless, which was aggravating because he wanted to comfort her. He wished he had the words to say that he was sorry for what she had lived through. Even if he tried, she was too proud and would take it as an insult. She shook her head and took her jack, starting for the door.

He grabbed her arm. "Where are you going?"

"Home."

"Nay. You're not riding out by yourself at night."

She rolled her eyes and tried to yank her arm away but he held tight.

"Let me go!" Her voice was rising and taking on a hysterical edge. He pulled her against him and held her tightly. She struggled, trying to push away. Just holding her, the smell of her hair, like wildflowers, and the feel of her body, both firm and soft, were arousing him. God help him, but he wanted her.

"I'm sorry," he said soothingly. "You're right, I don't understand." She stopped struggling. "Teach me."

She raised her eyes to his. One of his hands was buried in the soft hair hanging between her shoulders and the other was on her lower back. He could feel the swell of her bottom beneath his fingers. Her eyes were so green, and she seemed to have stopped breathing . . . or maybe it was he who had stopped breathing; he wasn't sure. He wanted to kiss her, but when he looked at her lips, he saw the blood. He stepped away from her, disturbed that he had almost acted on the impulse.

He grabbed one of Cathy Armstrong's handkerchiefs and wet it at the ewer. He handed it to her. Her hands were shaking when she took it. He wondered if he had frightened her.

"You have blood on your face." He gestured to her mouth without touching her.

She scrubbed at her face until it was clean again. She looked down at the handkerchief. "This is one of Cathy's. She does fine work."

"Aye." He grabbed the rest of them and held them out to her. "Do you need some?"

"Everyone in my house has at least two," she said.

He laughed softly and shrugged. "Mayhap a basket? To put your sewing in?" He handed her a basket.

"My thanks, Warden."

He smiled at her, but her face was drawn and tense, and she averted her eyes. He regretted touching her the way he had. He had made his feelings clear, and she was uncomfortable now.

"Let me ride back with you." He took her jack and the basket from her. Her cheeks turned pink when he opened the door and waited for her to walk through.

"Well, you did leave your dog there, so I guess it's fine," she mumbled.

The sun was rising when they reached her house. Pellinore was standing at the gate, wagging his tail. "I didn't forget you, old man." He handed her the basket and jack. "Well . . ." he said, stupidly not wanting to leave. He had things to do, and he was tired.

She hesitated, biting her bottom lip, then blurted out, "Would you like to see something before you leave?"

"Aye," he answered too quickly.

They left the horses at the stable, and he followed her to the tower. It wasn't a big tower like some of the chieftains of the larger clans lived in, but it was solid. Inside there were several rooms, their wooden doors shut. On the bottom floor, bows and arrows and a pile of rocks to throw down at the enemy were stacked in a corner. He followed her up the curving stone steps.

In the room at the top, bags of grain and barrels full of provisions were stacked against the wall. There was a ladder leading to the roof where they could light a beacon to alert him if they were under attack.

She stood at one of the narrow slit windows. He joined her, and she pointed. His breath caught at the beauty. From the tower the land looked deceptively flat, and the entire horizon was a deep pinkish-orange. There was a cottage in the distance, and smoke drifted lazily from the crude chimney.

He looked at her profile, lovelier to him than the view before them. Her skin seemed to glow in the soft light. Her nose was straight and her chin firm. They stood very close in order to see out the narrow window. Her shoulder brushed against him. She turned her face, raising her eyes to his.

Before he could stop himself, or even think about it, he lowered his head and kissed her. Her lips were warm and yielding, and a fire stirred in his body. He pulled back after the light kiss. Her eyes were closed, the long blond lashes lying against her cheeks. She opened her eyes and returned his gaze.

She wasn't pushing him away or telling him to stop, and he wanted to kiss her again. He lowered his head. She turned her face away. Her hand went to her mouth, covering it as she stared across the landscape. She backed away from him.

"You better leave before Uncle Willie thinks he lost another warden."

"Megan . . ." he started, but she hurried out the door and down the steps. He followed her, but he was greeted in the bailey by a slamming door. He cursed himself and kicked the dirt. He was more confused about her than ever. What the hell was the matter with him? How could he be so foolish? He whistled for Pellinore. As he rode back to the garrison he doubted he would get any peace that day.

 Four

Bryan and Rory followed the narrow path through the dense wood until they saw the gray tower of Ferniehurst rising high above the curtain walls. The Middle March warden's garrison was in far better shape than Bryan's. The two prisoners, on foot and tethered to Bryan's and Rory's saddles, were feeling the previous night's beatings, stumbling and falling.

Some rough-looking men-at-arms questioned Bryan and Rory at the gates, and grudgingly allowed them entrance.

A rugged man with a head of wavy gray hair greeted them in the bailey.

"Sir Thomas Kerr?" Bryan queried.

Kerr's eyes darted to the prisoners and back to Bryan. "Aye."

"Sir Bryan Hepburn, warden of the East March. I captured these men trying to thieve a lone cow and pig from a widow who had naught else. They say they're kin to you."

Thomas Kerr scratched his head and sighed. He slapped one of the prisoners on the head. "Christ Jesus, Buggerback! What the hell is wrong with you?"

The man Sir Thomas called Buggerback gave Bryan a sideways glance then looked down at the ground in feigned embarrassment. "I dinna know they belonged to a widow, sir."

"You didn't know they belonged to a widow?" Sir Thomas mocked incredulously. "I don't care if they belong to the king himself! Stop stealing the kine!" He emphasized his words by kicking Buggerback and the other man in the backside.

Sir Thomas cut the rope on the men's wrists. "Now git out of here, both of you! Your wives are at home worrying!" The men ran for the castle gate. Sir Thomas turned back to Bryan's frowning face.

"I think you've missed your calling, Sir Thomas. You and your puppets should take that act to the road."

Sir Thomas ran his tongue over his teeth.

Bryan could already see his decision to visit with his neighboring warden had been a useless one.

Sir Thomas looked at Rory and raised a gray brow. "I'd get more than one thug, Sir Bryan, if I were you. I can see you're going to need some protection." When Bryan didn't respond, Sir Thomas motioned for him to follow. "You didn't come all the way to Ferniehurst just to deliver Buggerback and his brother. You can tell me your troubles over a draught."

Bryan followed him into the keep. He was finding it

annoying to have Rory shadowing his every move. The Prince of Orange used to have fits of irritation in which he would order Bryan and the other guards to stay away from him. It had been frustrating to those sworn to protect the prince's life, but Bryan was beginning to understand. Sir Thomas had three personal guards. They all looked like hardened criminals, but Rory was bigger. Bryan knew from experience that a show of force was often deterrent enough. Rory served that purpose.

They sat at a long table in the hall, and Sir Thomas called for some ale. He stared hard at Rory, who stood behind Bryan's chair. "Laddie. Go away. See those men?" He gestured toward his guards, who had entered the hall but were now loitering across the room. "Do what they do. Mayhap then you can be a real guard."

"Go on," Bryan said to Rory.

"Where did you get that whelp?" Sir Thomas asked when Rory had moved away to lean against the wall.

"He'll learn."

"Let's just hope you live through the lessons, aye?" He laughed.

Bryan just stared at him.

Sir Thomas frowned and started licking his teeth again, close-mouthed. His tongue looked like a big worm moving beneath his skin. "So tell me, Sir Bryan, what do you think I should have done with Buggerback and his brother?"

"Imprison them for a period of time. Six months perhaps. Or fine them."

Sir Thomas nodded sagely. "I don't have room in my gaol for such fancies. I had a mass drowning just last week to make room for some more of them Forster scuts that can't keep their sticky fingers off Scottish soil."

"Did you say you had to *drown* men to make room in your prison?"

"Ah, son, am I scaring you? I don't want to give you and your sweet guard there nightmares."

Bryan's temper was simmering. "Next time I catch Buggerback or his brother thieving in my march I'll cut their hands off, just as the Turks do."

Sir Thomas exploded with laughter, spraying ale across the table. He scrubbed his forearm across his mouth and belched. "Laddie, they'll be butchering you up in no time." He slammed his tankard on the table, sloshing ale on his hand, and leaned close to Bryan, his face gravely serious. "They are the enemy!"

"Who is the enemy?"

Sir Thomas leaned back in his chair, becoming calm again. "The Forsters, the Scotts, the Selbys, the Turnbulls . . ." He stabbed the air with his finger in Bryan's direction. "You'll understand afore long."

Bryan raised his eyebrows. He could see neither sanity nor impartiality were prerequisites for being a warden. " 'Tis actually the Forsters I was wanting to ask you about."

"Nary a loch in Scotland breeds such scum as they."

"So I've heard. I would like your counsel on a matter of concern to me."

"Oh, aye?" Sir Thomas suddenly became interested and attentive.

"Are you familiar with Cedric Forster?"

"Aye, verra familiar. In fact, he resides in the bowels of my keep at this moment."

Bryan leaned forward. "Indeed? On what charges?"

Sir Thomas shrugged. "None. I was asking a ransom for his life. Sir John Forster captured my deputy in a raid and I'm trading Cedric for him. I'm releasing him today. What's your concern with him?"

"He murdered Innes Dixon four years ago and has never stood trial."

Sir Thomas rolled his eyes and dismissed Bryan's words with a wave of his hand. "I care not about that hoyden Megan Dixon. She's been crowing about that injustice for years." He gave Bryan a knowing grin. "Has she used her wiles to enlist you to her cause?"

"No."

Sir Thomas raised a sardonic eyebrow. "Cedric has caused more deaths than Laird Dixon's in the last four years. Why is it his you've come to investigate?"

" 'Tis the only one I know about."

"Well, if I were you, I would be worrying about who killed Leod Hume and why."

"Do you think Lady Dixon had anything to do with the warden's murder?"

Sir Thomas inhaled deeply and took a long drink from his tankard. "Now that's a fine question, laddie. Seeing as how she and Leod were lovers, and had a falling out afore he disappeared, that would put her at the top of the list, aye?"

Lovers? Bryan's gut clenched. "H-how do you know they were lovers?"

"Leod told me. Sitting just as we are now, over a draught."

Bryan was stunned. "But did you see them together? Or did you just take him at his word?"

"You didn't know Leod. He was popular with the ladies. Why would he lie?"

Bryan shook his head. He had believed her . . . he still wanted to. Maybe it was a mistake, or maybe Leod had lied.

Sir Thomas was watching him ponder this revelation and chuckled. "Worry not. I don't think she killed him. If you ask me, you should be talking with Douglas Hume of Leadwater."

"Douglas Hume?"

"Aye, he and Leod were at each other's throats last year. Douglas made a fine living protecting most of the folks of the East March, doing Leod's job for him so he could carry on with his women and raiding. But last year Leod started trying to tell Douglas whom he was to protect and when, regardless of whether they paid faithfully." Sir Thomas gave him a wicked grin. "Methinks Douglas had enough."

Bryan drained his tankard and stood to leave. "I thank you for the draught and your time, Sir Thomas."

"Tell that damn Dixon widow if I catch her reiving my sheep again, I'll put a hole through that bonny head."

Bryan sat back down. "What?"

"If you ask her, she'll no doubt give you some rubbish about me stealing her sheep first. But don't listen to her, ye hear? She's a thief, that one."

"I see . . . I'll certainly speak to her about it." He hesitated, then asked, "Do you think I could see Cedric before I leave?"

"You want to speak with him?" Sir Thomas asked in surprise.

"Nay, I just want to get a look at him since he's such a plague to my march."

Sir Thomas pushed away from the table, and Bryan followed him through the keep. Rory and the other guards were close behind.

"He's evaded the law for such a long time," Bryan said, "how did you manage to get your hands on him?"

" 'Twas a surprise to me as well." They descended the curved stone stairs. Torches were lit at intervals along the wall. The deeper they went, the stronger the smell of decay became. "The Forsters and the Fenwicks have been hitting the Middle and West Marches hard the past year. I authorized my deputy to take a raiding party into their lands and get back a wee bit of what we've lost. That old bag of bones Sir John Forster captured my deputy. But some of my other men managed to seize Cedric."

He stopped in front of a thick wooden door and looked at Bryan quizzically. "It was most unusual, too, for he's a slippery one most of the time. It seems he was more concerned with helping someone escape from the raid than with his own safety. When my men were gaining on them, he actually stopped and engaged four men in battle single-handedly, simply to buy time for his fugitives." He motioned for a guard to open the door.

"Were your men able to catch who he was protecting?"

"Nay, haven't a clue who it was. So his ruse worked. 'Twas probably some outlaws, now living comfortably in the Debatable Land."

"They're out of reach, then," Bryan muttered. The Debatable Land was home to a nest of reivers and thieves. It was nothing more than a narrow strip of disputed territory that neither Scotland nor England would lay claim to, neither wanting the responsibility of enforcing justice there. So, it remained a haven for criminals of all sorts.

The door swung open. It was dark inside, but two guards walked in and stationed themselves on either side of the door, holding torches. The prisoners sat on the floor. There was no need for restraints; it seemed hunger and fatigue did the job of subduing them rather well. The men were filthy and hollow-cheeked. Their eyes were dull and their lips cracked. The cell smelled like a cesspit.

"That's him, Cedric Forster," Sir Thomas said, pointing to a man hunched in the corner. The man straightened upon hearing his name. Sir Thomas said louder, "You ready to go home, Cedric? Or would you like to stay wi' me a bit longer?"

"Who's 'ere for me?" a deep voice asked. Cedric stepped forward into the light. He was a big man and didn't appear to be ravaged by hunger as the others were. His hair was black and curly, and his skin very dark. "Aye, I'd like out of this hole." He turned his dark eyes on Bryan. "I do not know you."

"He's the new warden of the East March. He wanted to have a look at you."

Cedric smirked. "Well, get an eyeful, Warden." He turned away from Bryan as if bored and stared at Sir Thomas expectantly. "I thought you said I could leave."

"Sir Bryan would like to stretch your neck for killing Innes Dixon," Sir Thomas taunted, smiling.

"Innes Dixon? Ah, I remember 'im. The warden

with the bonny wife. He had a problem minding 'is own business."

Bryan's eyes narrowed. "What mean you?"

Cedric gave him an obscure look. "I'll be seeing you around, Warden."

Faster than Bryan would have ever thought he could move, Sir Thomas plowed his fist into Cedric's stomach. "The warden asked you a question!"

Cedric doubled over. He straightened and lunged at Sir Thomas. Sir Thomas's thugs surrounded the warden immediately, one blocking Cedric's attack and tossing him to the ground.

Sir Thomas laughed. "Throw him outside." Two of the guards dragged Cedric from the cell. Sir Thomas gave Bryan a shrug and ushered him out.

Once they were in the clean, open air of the bailey, Bryan asked, "What do you think he meant by that? About Innes Dixon not minding his own business?" Bryan watched as Cedric was led to the castle gates and shoved out. Cedric turned to glare at Sir Thomas and his men, but one of the guards made a threatening move with his lance and Cedric ran, kicking up dirt behind him.

Sir Thomas rolled his eyes. "Who can know? Naught probably, just blathering, trying to get your hackles up."

Bryan and Rory's horses were brought around. "You mentioned Lady Dixon and Leod Hume had a falling out. Did he say what it was about?"

"Nay, but knowing her, she was probably in a chuff because he was rutting with a Forster lass."

Bryan nodded grimly. "I'll be seeing you at the

next Truce Day. Let's hope I don't have to bring any of your kin back before then."

Sir Thomas just licked his teeth.

On the way back to the garrison the conversation with Sir Thomas Kerr dominated Bryan's thoughts. What did it all mean? At least he had another lead. He would have to speak with Douglas Hume soon. He was disturbed by Kerr's reference to Megan having an affair with Leod. When he kissed her, he didn't get the impression it was something she did very often. Even though she was a widow with a small child, there had been an innocence to her kiss.

He was making excuses again. It was pride rearing its head. He had vowed he wouldn't fall for another faithless woman, and now, here he was, dangerously close to being completely smitten. Whether or not she had been Leod's lover was beside the point. She had obviously withheld some important information from him. She hadn't mentioned a falling out right before Leod's disappearance. She was already proving herself unworthy of his trust.

He turned to Rory, remembering what the lad had said during his interview. "You told me Leod Hume was over-fond of Lady Dixon, but she didn't like him."

"Aye."

"Sir Thomas seems to think Megan and Leod were lovers. Could such a thing be?"

Rory scratched his auburn hair. "I don't see how. I've known Lady Dixon all my life . . . before she was Lady Dixon and was just Meg Hume. We both grew up in Edington where my father is a blacksmith. I think I would know if there was something more to their relationship. I saw them only a month past at the fair. They were going at it like two cats. I thought she was going to scratch his eyes out."

That must be the falling out Sir Thomas spoke of. Bryan reined in his horse. "Could it have been a lover's quarrel? She was angry because he was untrue?"

Rory frowned. "If they were lovers, and I don't think they were, she would have known he wasn't true to her. The man probably had the pox he spread himself around so much. He was known to rape the unwilling as well. Once he set his eye on a woman, he meant to have her. I suppose their fight at the fair could have been viewed that way." Rory shook his head firmly. "But I don't believe it of her. If she did kill him, it had naught to with such trifles."

Bryan hoped what Rory said was true. But he also knew how Megan felt about the Forsters. Didn't Willie say she thought the only good Forster was a dead Forster? She might not care about Leod's other lovers, but what if it was a Forster lass? Since she had paid him to kill Cedric and he hadn't succeeded, the situation could have become volatile.

Bryan's mood became even darker when they arrived at the garrison and found Megan there. She stood at the gatehouse talking animatedly with one of the guards. Bryan felt a wave of unease, seeing them together. A felt hat with a floppy brim shaded her eyes from him, but the sight of the smooth curve of her jaw, the graceful line of her neck, sent his pulse racing. The guard touched her familiarly, his hand on her shoulder. He stepped away from her when Bryan approached.

"Lady Dixon," Bryan said. "Is there anything I can do for you today?"

She gave him a chilly smile. "I thought you might need me as a witness to last night's events. But Johnny tells me you've already returned the reivers to their home." Her eyes were accusing and Bryan grew uncomfortable. Johnny tried to excuse himself, but her hand closed around the shaft of his lance, holding him there.

"Aye, I returned them to their warden."

"And I'm sure he punished them harshly," she said sarcastically.

"If you want to speak to me, we can go to my chambers."

"Oh no, I don't think so, Warden."

Johnny was purposely looking in another direction. Bryan grabbed her wrist, prying her fingers off the lance, and dragged her into the keep.

"Let go of me!" she cried indignantly. He pushed her down the corridor. She whirled on him outside his door, hands on hips, cheeks flushed and green eyes snapping with temper. "You touch me again and you'll be sorry!"

"Will you hire someone to kill me?"

She released a slow angry breath. "I knew I'd be sorry about last night! What possessed me to offer my assistance to you?"

He regretted the remark instantly. "Forgive me; I didn't mean that. I value the counsel you have given me and hope you will continue to take an interest in enforcing peace on the borders. However, it appears you aren't doing everything in your power to help me meet that end."

"What mean you?"

"Sir Thomas claims you've been picking off his sheep."

"He's a liar," she said with a wave of dismissal. "There is no bigger reiver in all Scotland than Sir Thomas Kerr."

"Did you take his sheep?"

"No! He took mine! I merely took them back."

Bryan sighed tiredly, rubbing his forehead.

"You don't believe me!"

"Megan, this has to stop. I don't wish to take you into custody to curb your activities, but I will if you force me."

"Are you quite through?" She was nearly trembling with rage.

Bryan decided it wasn't a good time to bring up her alleged affair with Leod. But he still felt they had other matters to discuss. "No, I'm not. I want to speak with you privately." He tried to maneuver her into his chambers, but she wouldn't budge. "I promise not to kiss you."

Her face flushed crimson and she averted her eyes. "We have nothing to discuss!" She stalked past him.

He sighed, wanting to go after her, but not relishing an argument. He needed to be away from her anyway to put his thoughts in order. He entered his chambers and viewed the room with dismay. His things had arrived while he was gone and had been dumped in the middle of the audience chamber. A piglet was rooting through a stack of papers piled in the corner. Pellinore stood a few feet from the pig, watching it with a puzzled expression.

Willie came in behind him. "Good, you're back. A messenger from the king is here to see you."

"Why is there a pig in my room?"

" 'Tis a gift from Cathy Armstrong. She was so pleased with your heroics on her behalf, she sent you a gift." Willie shoved a basket full of handkerchiefs into his arms.

"I can't accept her pig."

" 'Twould be an insult not to."

He couldn't send it back. He would have to return it to her in person so she didn't feel slighted. "What are the papers?" Bryan inclined his head to the papers the pig was pillaging. One was stuck to the pig's snout, and it was trying to scrape it off with its little hoof.

"Shoo, pig!" Willie pushed the pig away. He removed the paper from the pig's snout and set the stack on the table. "These are some of Leod's correspondence. I thought you might like to read them, to see what he was doing the last few years."

Bryan set the basket on the table next to the papers. "How long was Leod warden?"

"Four years. Ever since Innes Dixon was murdered."

The pig threw itself on the ground near Pellinore and began wriggling on its back in the filthy rushes. Pellinore jumped back in alarm and became still again, staring at the odd creature. It was male, Bryan observed.

"I thought I told you to have the women come in every day to clean. These rushes still haven't been changed."

"They aren't going to clean for free. We don't have any money to pay them."

"I don't care. I'll pay them myself until the king sends funds. I want this place cleaned up."

Willie cleared his throat. "Sir, Leod never made the men train or the women clean . . . so much, that is. I just don't know how they'll-"

"I am warden now," Bryan said louder than he had intended.

"Aye, sir." Willie turned to go.

"Feed the messenger, then send him in." Bryan had written to the king a few days ago, and he hoped the messenger was bearing his grace's response. He grabbed a coarse woolen blanket off the bed and folded it on the ground.

"Pig, lay down," he ordered, pointing toward the blanket. The pig didn't even look at him, but Pellinore walked to the blanket and stretched out on it. "No one listens to me," Bryan muttered.

Who was this Johnny fellow? He couldn't stop thinking about Megan's familiarity with the young man. He mentally flogged himself for wasting so much time thinking about her. They had no relationship! He had kissed her, and she had responded with hostility. He had no right to these possessive thoughts. But he couldn't stop them. His gaze swept the hovel he lived in, looking for some way to distract himself. He leaned his head out the door. "Rory!"

Rory wasn't far and came running. "Aye?"

"Go find Lauren and tell her to bring a broom."

By the time the messenger showed up at his door, Lauren and Rory were removing books from his trunk and stacking them in the bookcase, and Bryan was sweeping rushes into a pile outside the door.

"Warden?" the man asked, looking around as

though surely he couldn't be the warden, so there must be another man hiding in the room.

Bryan leaned on the broom. "Aye? You've a message for me from his grace?"

"From his grace's treasurer." He wasn't jingling with coin, so apparently the money wasn't immediately forthcoming. Perhaps it was arriving separately?

Bryan opened the letter. His heart sank. Not only would there be no money, but the letter was practically a reprimand for daring to ask. The treasurer wrote that the subsidy the march currently received was more than adequate, and if the march wardens could control the pillaging and thieving they might not find themselves so short of funds.

Bryan threw the letter at the pig. The pig immediately began snuffling at it, making little grunting noises. The messenger stared at him incredulously.

"You may leave now."

The messenger backed out of the room.

"What the hell am I going to do now?" Bryan asked the pig. Without an increase in the subsidy he couldn't pay soldiers, servants, *and* make improvements to the garrison.

"Uhm . . . Warden, sir?"

Bryan turned to see Lauren standing by the books, looking at him hesitantly. "Aye?" Even Rory appeared surprised to hear her speak. Bryan thought it was a shame she was wed to a man three times her age. He had noticed how she seemed to change when Rory was around; she drew more into herself, if that was possible.

She stared at the floor, her cheeks impossibly red. "My da was a deputy warden and he worked the land around the keep and he grew barley and vegetables and it was more than enough to feed the garrison and so my mum and I would take it into Berwick on market days and sell it." She was speaking so fast Bryan had a hard time keeping up with her. She twisted her hands in a dirty cloth she had been using to wipe down the shelves. "And he also kept kine to sell and butcher and he had sheep and we made wool cloth and sold it, too."

Bryan sat in a chair beside her so he wasn't towering over her tiny frame. She moved a few steps away from him. He suspected Rory's presence did nothing to calm her, and with a look, he sent Rory from the room. "Where did your da get the money to do all this, Lauren?"

"Well, some of it was my mum's, but he sold some things and sometimes after one of the other clans attacked us, he would attack them and take back more than they took from us and then he would have extra to do more . . . but he and my mother were killed in a raid and everything they did was destroyed." She swallowed visibly. "And forgotten."

Bryan had some money. If he made a profit it wouldn't be too painful to use. Their subsidy was due in a week's time; after he bought provisions, he might be able to buy some beasts.

"Thank you for your counsel, Lauren. You have given me something to think on." She was still twisting the filthy rag, but gave him a small smile. He reached into the basket and handed her a handkerchief. "Here's a clean one, lass."

"Thank you, sir," she said and looked at the handkerchief. "Cathy Armstrong does fine work."

Bryan grabbed another handkerchief from the basket. "Aye, she does," he mumbled, inspecting the finely embroidered edges. "What else does Cathy make?"

"Och, she makes lots of things." Lauren was beginning to warm to him and her talking slowed, becoming more articulate. She took a few steps closer, pushing wisps of tangled brown curls behind her ear. "She makes bed sheets and bonnets." She pointed to the basket. "She can make finer baskets than this. She used to have a little stone oven behind her cottage where she made clay dishes and bowls and cups, but the Forsters destroyed it when they killed her husband."

" 'Tis dangerous for a woman living out there on her own."

"Aye," she nodded sadly.

"Is she attached to that wee cottage, do you know?"

"Sir?"

He leaned closer, an idea forming. "What do you think she would say to moving to the garrison under my protection? In return for lodging and food—and my protection—she could provide me with her services. I would build her a big oven right here in the castle walls. She could bring some of the other widows with her, and we'd have a wee sewing ring."

Lauren grinned. "I don't know, sir. But I can't see why not. They don't know where their next meal is coming from most of the time, and they're always in fear of the raiders leaving them destitute." She averted her eyes. "I am fortunate to have a good husband like Willie."

Bryan hesitated, uncertain how to respond to her

practiced reply. "And he is blessed to have such a good wife." Bryan squeezed her shoulder, pleased with the plan that was growing in his mind. "You have just made my life easier, lass."

It was dark when Anna Beaton finally found the cottage. She was tired, hungry, and annoyed the directions in the letter hadn't been better. After living on the borders all her life, she still couldn't find her way around if she didn't stick to the main roads or rivers. She could see the glow of a candle in the open window. She was relieved the man from the letter had waited.

She dismounted and led the horse to the small loch to drink. She walked in the open door. A fire blazed, and the air smelled of meat and oatcakes. Her stomach rumbled. A man sat in a large chair by the fire. He was very attractive in a rugged fashion. Black curly hair, broad and muscular. She moved closer. He was scrutinizing her with hard, blue-gray eyes.

"Anna Beaton?" he inquired.

"Aye. I almost didn't make it. Are you Cedric? The author of that letter?"

"Aye." His mouth was sensual, with a full bottom lip. He was smiling slightly.

"Well, the directions were awful. I've been riding around for hours. I think I came upon this place by accident."

"Hmm." He continued looking at her. "My uncle says you are clever. So far I am unimpressed."

Her face grew hot. "What does Warden Forster have to do with this?"

He stood and approached her. He was looking at her through half-lidded eyes, and her blood rushed through her veins. "You are Sir Bryan Hepburn's sister?"

"Aye, half sister; we share the same mother." She was almost as tall as Cedric and met his eyes boldly when he was standing before her.

"In spite of this, I 'ave 'eard there is no love betwixt you and your brother. Is this so?"

"This is about my brother? I spent the day searching for this place to be questioned about Bryan?" She waved her hand in disgust and started for the door. He caught her wrist and pulled her close. His eyes burned into hers.

"Answer my question."

His authoritative manner was making her hot and restless. She lowered her lashes in mock submissiveness, liking this man. She ran her tongue over her lips.

" 'Tis true we disliked each other growing up. His father is James Hepburn, he who killed Queen Mary's husband and tried to seize the kingship for himself. He was a wizard and treated my mother like a whore. Nay, I bear no love for his spawn."

Cedric smiled broadly and released her. "You 'ave told me much now, and I am pleased with you. What think you of the current earl? Francis Stewart?"

"He is evil. A wicked man. I like him not."

His hand slid behind her, around her waist. He drew her close. "You are a very beautiful woman, Anna. I 'ave revised my opinion of you."

She smiled at him and eagerly met his mouth when he kissed her.

Five

Over the next few days Megan heard a great deal about Bryan's doings, usually from one of her besotted female relatives as they swooned over the new warden and laid out plans to snare him. Bryan had moved Cathy Armstrong and several other widows, along with their children and animals, into the stronghold. He had his men filling wagons with stones to repair the holes in the curtain wall, and he was building Cathy an oven with his own two hands to bake pottery to her specifications. Megan was jealous. She hated the stupid, petty thoughts, but that didn't stop her from having them. He had kissed her. Regardless of the fact she deeply regretted the incident and had since violently rebuffed him, she couldn't take such a thing lightly. Yet that was exactly what he was doing. Had he thought of her at all since then? Her pride stung.

She found herself having ridiculous thoughts such as, *I'm a widow, why does he not ask me to live with him*? She knew very well the reason was that she didn't need his financial help, nor would she leave her home.

"Madame! Have your vegetables angered you?" Marie, Johnny's very pregnant French wife, knelt beside her. Since Megan was their nearest neighbor, still miles away, the couple was staying with her until the child was born.

Megan was on her hands and knees, brutally ripping the weeds from her vegetable garden. She told herself, as she grabbed a green weed threatening to choke her turnips, that it didn't matter. She was probably going to marry Charles Hume anyway. She shouldn't be thinking about another man. Certainly not one who was a warden. Of course, with Charles being a Hume he could one day be warden, too. She sighed at the turn of her thoughts. She always seemed to find a way to keep potential suitors a bay.

"Aye, Marie, the weeds are trying to take over!"

She sat back on her heels and viewed her garden. Neat rows of leeks, cauliflower, turnips, onions, and spinach grew strong and hardy. There was another garden on the other side of the house devoted to hop buds for making ale and beer. She wiped her dirty hands on her gray wool kirtle and stood. Marie stood, too, sighing and running her hands over her belly. She was a stunning woman, even as heavily pregnant as she was. Her dark brown hair was in a knot atop her head, and wisps fell down to frame her heart-shaped face.

Marie's dark eyes lit up and she let out a little

exclamation of surprise. "Monsieur Warden! Look, Madame! It is the warden."

Bryan was walking toward them from the stables. Megan looked down at her hands. They were coated with dirt; it was even crammed under her fingernails. She was always forgetting to wear gloves when she worked in the garden. Marie had remembered hers and pulled them off in a very ladylike manner. Megan hid her hands behind her back. Marie waddled over to Bryan, and his face beamed with pleasure.

"Warden," Megan said as he drew nearer.

"Good day, ladies," he answered.

Megan turned back to her garden and knelt on the ground again, searching frantically for another weed to pull. Unfortunately, it seemed she had conquered them all.

"Forget about the silly weeds! You have company!" Marie pulled her to her feet, a gleam in her eye. Megan knew what Marie was thinking and scowled at her. Marie had nothing nice to say about Megan considering marriage to Charles Hume. She thought it was unromantic and pathetic to marry a man one didn't love. She had merely snorted delicately at Megan's lofty retort that love was for those with no responsibilities.

"What brings you here today, Warden?" Megan asked, pulling her arm away from Marie.

"You don't have to address me so formally; Bryan will do." When she didn't answer, he sighed. "I come on business."

"Of course." Her tone was nasty. What was wrong with her? She didn't need to make an enemy of a warden who already suspected her of murder. She smiled tightly. "What can I do for you?"

"Business!" Marie cried dramatically and trudged to the house. She turned and called over her shoulder, "I will get the basket ready. Monsieur Hume will be here soon."

Bryan raised a speculative eyebrow at Marie's comment, but Megan offered no explanation.

"I'd like a price on some kine. It seems we've been buying our meat from Douglas Hume for over a decade, and, if you ask me, his price is criminal."

Megan appraised the man before her. Bryan looked more like a borderer now. He wore leather breeks and a wool doublet. His boots were tall and black with silver spurs at the ankle. The wind tousled his golden brown hair, the burnished locks catching the sunlight. His skin was dark from hours spent outdoors. *Before long he'll be one of us,* she thought. But his brown eyes were still warm and friendly. They hadn't taken on that hardened glint so familiar among borderers.

She forced herself to focus on what he was saying to her rather than on his overwhelming presence. This business he brought to her was quite pleasing. Since the Humes usually held the wardenship there had never been a question of who they bought provisions from.

"Laird Hume won't be pleased to hear he's losing business to a Dixon."

He shrugged. "I care not."

"The laird's eldest son, Charles Hume, has proposed marriage to me. If I accept, I am certain this shall sweeten the deal for Douglas." She rubbed her hands together; forgetting about the dirt caked on them. Something passed across Bryan's face, but he quickly masked it. It seemed he hadn't heard about Charles's proposal. Was it disappointment she had seen?

She noticed Rory Trotter hanging back at a distance. "I'm relieved you've hired a guard, though I think you should have more than one."

"Were you concerned for my safety?" He made the comment lightly, but his face was grim.

"Any warden who does his job should fear for his life."

"I've put together a watch to ride the march at night. That duty has been neglected for the past four years."

"You should use care with your words. When you talk about going *riding* to a borderer, they will assume you mean you're going raiding. I'd be certain the men you're assigning know the difference."

He was so completely taken aback by her statement, that she knew he hadn't clarified his meaning to the men. She had to laugh.

" 'Tis no laughing matter," he said gravely. "How would that be if the men I send out to protect the march are the ones causing the damage?"

She shrugged. "We'd simply think we had another Leod Hume on our hands."

"What would I do without your counsel?"

She walked past him to the house. "You'd do fine, I imagine. Certainly any one of your widows would be eager to direct you."

He followed her inside. She went to the ewer and washed her hands. She was glad they were so filthy now, so she could keep her back to him while she industriously cleaned the dirt from beneath her fingernails.

"I was wondering if there was anything else I should know about a hot trod that you haven't shown me."

"I could show you every secret on the march, but until you're able to apply them, it means naught. Come back after your first hot trod and mayhap I'll show you more."

He was quiet for a long time. "Are you dismissing me?"

She turned to him, her hands dripping. "No. 'Tis I who have been dismissed." *There*. She said it. She was hurt that he dared kiss her and neither followed it up with an apology nor called on her again to make his intentions known. Never mind how she flayed him back at the garrison. She was no loose woman and didn't appreciate being treated as one. She feared he had heard the rumors of her and Leod and was acting on them, thinking she would be willing. It was more upsetting that the kiss had affected her so deeply. She started to dry her hands on her gown, but it was already covered with soil. Before she could search out a towel, Bryan pulled a handkerchief from his waist with a flourish and handed it to her.

"You must never be at a loss for a clean cloth these days," she said dryly, accepting his offering.

"Cathy keeps me well supplied." He grew serious. "I didn't dismiss you. I have thought of little else."

"You keep your thoughts well hidden."

He regarded her for a long time, then shrugged. "What matter? You are betrothed, are you not?"

She pursed her lips at such logic. She almost denied it, since she had accepted no proposals. But to what end? "Aye."

His voice was distant when he asked, "Will you consider supplying provisions to the garrison?"

"Aye."

Marie bustled in with an enormous basket over her arm. She started to walk between them, then changed her mind and walked behind Megan, her round belly shoving Megan forward, closer to Bryan. Megan side-stepped quickly so she wouldn't come in contact with him.

"Good day, ladies," he said shortly and turned to leave.

"Monsieur Warden!" Marie caught his arm. "Don't leave. We're off to the coast for an outing, I pray you to join us. It will be so much more amusing with you and your big guard."

Megan glared at Marie, and Bryan began to protest.

"*S'il vous plaît!* It would mean much to me if you would bring Johnny back some dinner." Marie fluttered her eyelashes at Bryan, who appeared more confused than charmed by her wiles. A clatter of hooves sounded outside. Innes darted into the room and hid beneath the table.

Megan leaned down to look at Innes's red head. His blue eyes were round as an owl's.

"What are you doing?"

" 'Tis Charles Hume. Don't make me talk to him, Mum! Or play with him again!"

Marie giggled, and Megan gritted her teeth together. "Please, Innes. I will be there and so will Marie."

Marie grabbed Bryan's arm and pulled him to the table. "Innes, *mon petite chou*, perhaps you can convince Monsieur Warden to join us?"

Innes emerged from under the table. "Are you coming with us, Warden?"

Bryan smiled and shrugged. "How can I refuse?"

Megan narrowed her eyes at him, but he didn't even glance in her direction. He took the basket from Marie and carried it outside to meet Charles Hume.

A short time later the six of them were riding southeast. Charles had not been pleased to discover that Bryan and Rory would be joining them. Megan had whispered to him that it was Marie's doing, and he gave her a warm look of understanding. With hair so blond it was almost white and eyes a pale greenish-blue, his looks were not as pleasing as the warden's, but that wasn't important. The protection his father's wealth offered was what made him a good choice.

The outing wasn't all Charles had hoped for, Megan knew, but she was relieved. She hadn't spent much time with Charles, and none alone with him. There would be plenty of time for that later, though, when they were wed.

If they wed. When she considered the union of land and wealth, it seemed like the best possible choice. But when she tried to imagine coming to him as a woman, his bride, the idea left her cold.

Her son needed a father. But she wasn't sure Charles was the man for that job, either. Innes was ecstatic to be spending the afternoon with Bryan, and he insisted on riding with him rather than with

Megan. Perched in front of Bryan, Innes chattered nonstop about the piglets their sow had birthed. Rory and Marie rode on either side of the pair. Megan was behind them, next to Charles.

She was having a difficult time paying attention to what Charles was saying, since the conversation going on in front of her was so much more lively and interesting.

"I have a pig," Bryan said when Innes stopped talking long enough to take a breath.

"Oh?" Marie asked.

"Aye, 'twas a gift from Cathy Armstrong and she wouldn't take it back. It sleeps on the floor in my room."

Innes giggled, and Marie asked, amused, "It sleeps in your room?"

"He slept in my room the first two nights, then when I tried to pen him up with the rest of the pigs, he cried. The guards thought they might go mad. So I ended their misery and he sleeps with me."

Megan edged her horse up closer to the others. Charles kept pace with her, babbling on and on about the game of dice he had played the night before. "What does Pellinore think of this pig?" Megan asked, interrupting Charles's stream of words.

Bryan looked at her over his shoulder. "Och, he doesn't mind him, so long as he stays off the bed."

Megan shook her head at this strange, accommodating man.

"I must name him, Innes. Perhaps you could help me."

Innes became so excited he bounced on the saddle. By the time they reached the coast, Bryan and Innes

had decided on Curly. Megan had protested the name
was too obvious and Bryan should stick with his
Arthurian names. Rory had come up with some silly
ones like Swinetail and Hogsbreath. Marie's names
were all French and Innes could hardly pronounce
them.

They spread a blanket away from the rocky shore of
the North Sea. The wind that blew off the water was
cold, but fresh. Megan closed her eyes and inhaled
deeply. The air smelled clean and invigorating. She
sighed and opened her eyes again.

Her mood fell when she caught sight of Charles. He
was being very quiet. She went to him and took his
arm, drawing him near the plaid blanket. He resisted.
His usually ruddy lips were drawn into a thin white
line. Suddenly she felt awful. She had interrupted him
and then ignored him for the remainder of the ride,
never asking him to finish his story.

"Mayhap I should eat with the horses. I don't
think anyone would notice my absence," he said
petulantly.

"Oh, Charles, come sit with me."

He relented with a grudging smile and followed her
to where the others were sitting.

Megan brought out the oatcakes, cheese, and pears
from her orchard, and everyone was hungry. It had
been a long time since Megan had spent any time with
Rory. When she and Rory were children they had
played together in the woods and fished in the many
steams. Her parents had never liked their friendship
since her family was of high standing in the commu-
nity, her father being an important burgess, and
Rory's father was a mere blacksmith. But Megan

never cared and openly defied her father, despite the repeated whippings she received.

"Aye, you must be very careful, Warden," Rory was saying. As they ate, he had been entertaining them with stories about raids gone awry.

Bryan grinned. "That's why I have you, so I can be as reckless and foolish as I please."

"Well," Rory became serious, "some things can happen that I won't be able to aid you with. You should take care."

Bryan didn't look overly concerned. Megan wished he would heed Rory's words.

Charles raised his eyebrows at Bryan's casual attitude and asked Rory, "Was there not a warden, on the West March I believe, who rounded up some men and set out on a hot trod only to become the victim himself?"

"Aye." Rory nodded. "He and the men were riding through the forest and the next thing he knew, the very men who were helping him pointed their guns at him and stole everything. His horse, his weapons—even the poor man's clothes. But I suppose he was fortunate his life was spared."

"Your concern is misplaced," Bryan said. "I have much experience in these matters. And I can't afford any more guards. As it is, my keep is falling down around my ears and I can barely keep my men in ale."

He reclined on his side and looked at the water. Apparently, he was finished with the subject. Innes was by the shore with Marie, building a house made out of stones and sand. Rory joined them, and Megan heard Marie's tinkling laughter against the roar of the surf. She watched them for a while before turning back to Bryan. He was staring at her intently, his expression guarded. A flush immediately crept up her neck.

"So, Warden," Charles said loudly, "have you learned anything about Leod Hume?"

"I don't know what to think. I've heard plenty of rumors and opinions, but I have yet to come across any facts. And no body has been found." He shook his head in confusion. "Who started this story that he's chopped up and buried in the woods? Everyone I ask says they heard it from someone else. What if no one killed him? What if he just fell in the river and drowned?"

Megan frowned. "I doubt that. He had too many enemies."

"Aye," he said, watching her closely. "I heard you had a disagreement with him the day he disappeared. Is that true?"

A chill crept into her limbs at his words, though she struggled to maintain her composure.

Charles's pale face turned crimson with anger. "Just what are you implying, Warden? Out with it!"

Bryan's expression immediately became cool. "I merely asked the lady a question, one she is under no obligation to answer."

Her fingers curled into fists as she was overcome with unease. His questions had made her angry before, when she felt he couldn't prove anything. But many people had seen her with Leod at the fair. The possibility that she could actually be convicted of murder terrified her. She didn't want to answer the question, and she searched her mind to come up with a lie. Refusing to answer would sound like an admission of guilt, and yet the truth was so incriminating she couldn't bear to reveal it. She could just let Charles keep blustering to cover her silence, but Bryan wasn't a stupid man and would heed her actions.

"I was angry with him," she said lightly, looking away. "He was supposed to be protecting the people of the march. I was raided. We lit the beacon and he never showed up . . . neither did the Humes." She glanced at Charles, who quickly averted his eyes. "I had a few more able men then, plus I had hired some from neighboring clans. We were able to defend ourselves as it was only a small party of Forsters." She shrugged. "I think he didn't show up on purpose, that he knew about the raid and allowed it to happen."

That was partly the truth, so she felt somewhat better. It had been one of the topics of her argument with Leod.

"Do you think he ordered Douglas Hume not to come to your aid?" He darted a quick look at Charles before returning his attention to her. "I know you're paying him for protection, so don't lie to me about it. I won't charge you with anything. But I do hope it soon becomes unnecessary for the march people to pay for protection."

"You dare to speak of my father thusly? He will not be pleased to hear of this slander!" Charles's face was red again, but his pale eyes were frightened.

Megan laid her hand on his arm. "That's enough, Charles."

Charles turned his angry look on her. "He is a fool!" He glared at Bryan. "Look you to the witches if you want answers." He stood dramatically and marched farther down the shore, away from the others. He plopped on a rock with his back to them.

She was embarrassed that she was actually thinking of marrying him. He was so childish. She found herself mentally comparing him with Bryan. Charles was lean and colorless. The man leaning on the blanket beside her was so alive and male. Dark and muscular, every fluid movement from him captivated her attention. The rise and fall of his chest when he breathed, the way his dimples lined his cheeks the slightest bit when he wasn't smiling, the sensuous curve of his lips, the powerful hands she could imagine touching her . . .

She could not allow such thoughts to continue! Her clothing was becoming constricting, and she felt the dew of sweat forming on her upper lip. "I'm positive Leod ordered someone not to protect us. I think he used his position as the law of the march to threaten someone, though I'm not certain it was Douglas. Regardless of what you might think of Douglas, when he was warden over ten years ago, he did a fine job of it."

Bryan's brows were raised in disbelief. "I plan to speak with the laird myself, but I'd like more information before I do. What is this rubbish I keep hearing about witches?"

Megan shook her head; she was mortified Charles had even brought it up. "It is said there is a coven of witches on the borders." She raised an eyebrow. "And that your cousin, Lord Bothwell, is their master. Many murmur that the murders on the march are actually sacrifices to Satan."

"Hmm." His brows were high, but he looked at the ground, a small smile on his lips.

"I didn't say I listen to such tales. Leod probably started the rumor to cover up some dirty doings of his own."

Bryan nodded at that, obviously finding it more plausible than a coven of witches led by a prominent border lord.

She smiled thinly. "The borderers are a superstitious lot. Even my late husband believed your cousin to be a warlock. He was rather vocal about it, too. At one point Lord Bothwell challenged him to meet secretly and make the accusation face-to-face."

Bryan shook his head ruefully. "Francis is very . . . exuberant. But he is young. How did your husband manage this challenge?"

"He fully intended to meet with the earl, even though I pleaded with him not to. I was with child at the time. He, of course, didn't listen to me. But the encounter never took place. Innes was murdered by Cedric Forster the night before they were to meet."

Bryan frowned deeply, but made no comment. They were silent for a few moments, and when he spoke again, his voice was diffident, "You aren't really going to wed that man, are you?"

The thought of sharing her bed with Charles was nauseating. "I don't know." She didn't want to speak on personal topics. "What about the kine? We haven't spoken of a price."

"I trust you. I'll send one of my men down tomorrow to fetch some. Just name your price, I know you'll be fair."

"I thought you didn't trust me."

He held her gaze a long moment, his eyes probing her thoughts. She felt exposed, and her pulse sped up with anxiety. She longed for him to deny it, to claim he did trust her. His eyes dropped, the thick, dark lashes hiding his expression. He was looking at her mouth. Her breath was coming short. Her gown felt hot and confining. She moved away suddenly, closer to the edge of the blanket.

He turned his head away, looking at the sea. "You're right, I don't trust you. But I want to. You cannot imagine how I want to."

She could not speak, could think of nothing to say. His words hurt. They shouldn't, she argued to herself. What did it matter if he trusted her or not?

He looked back to her. "But I do believe you won't cheat me."

She took a deep breath. Normally, his trusting nature would have been an open invitation for her to overcharge him, but he was right; she would give him the best price she could afford. And she would do it for him. The others were returning, except Charles, who was still sulking, and Megan knew the outing was over.

Bryan and Rory said their good-byes and left first. Her eyes were trained on Bryan's broad back as they rode away. Her interest in the outing left with him. Everything was dull and flat. Charles had returned from his pout and was talking to her. She nodded in the appropriate places while folding the blanket, still watching the figures growing smaller in the distance. Bryan turned suddenly, looking back at her. He raised his hand to her. Her heart skipped a beat, his gesture flooding her with intense pleasure. But she turned her back on him, not waving in return.

Six

Bryan was feeling frustrated as he and Rory rode away from the sea, heading west, toward Leadwater, to speak with Charles Hume's father. He had some questions to ask Douglas about Leod. He didn't relish this meeting. No body had been found, a fact that certainly wouldn't escape the laird.

A large, square tower, surrounded by a high curtain wall, was in sight. A herd of kine was being ushered south for grazing. When Bryan and Rory entered the bailey, a barrel-chested man approached from an outbuilding. The years had stolen his vigor, and he looked sunken and gaunt in spite of his large torso. He scowled when he saw Bryan. Hands on hips, he waited for Bryan to close the distance.

"Douglas Hume, laird of Leadwater?" Bryan asked.

"Aye."

"I have some questions for you."

The laird's eyes were the same pale bluish-green as his son's, except one eye protruded more than the other, lending him a froggish look. "I didn't kill Leod Hume, though I wouldn't have minded the honor. You can leave now." His bulging eye trembled.

"I'm afraid I still have some questions."

Douglas's scowl deepened, and he didn't move. Apparently the interview was to be conducted in the center of the bailey.

"Willie said Leod's things were sent to you. May I see them?"

"You can have them." Douglas stopped a man hurrying by. "Tell Joan to send out Leod's things." He turned back to Bryan expectantly. When Bryan didn't speak, Douglas smiled unpleasantly. "I ken who you are, Sir Bryan Hepburn."

Bryan returned the laird's gaze without emotion. "I ken who I am as well."

"Your mother was a Beaton, aye? Your father a Hepburn?"

"Aye."

"It makes a bit more sense to me now why Bothwell made you warden. Your father was a fine lieutenant; too bad he wasn't a very good king."

"He wasn't given the opportunity."

Douglas's nasty smile grew. "What would the king say if he knew one of James Hepburn's spawn still lived? And with the witch Janet for a mum!"

Francis had told Bryan that Douglas Hume had petitioned the king to be appointed the next warden, but Francis wanted an outsider. He felt the Humes had dominated the post for too long, and he suspected many unethical doings on their part. And Francis had the king's ear. Bryan assumed that was the cause for the laird's spleen. That and the black memory of Bryan's father, James Hepburn.

Bryan said, "The Earl of Bothwell has no personal feelings of disdain against you, but I was chosen as your warden and I suggest you get used to it. You help naught by giving me your choler."

"The Earl of Bothwell is a wizard," Douglas said vehemently.

"I'm not here to dispute charges of sorcery against the earl."

"Because you share in the black arts? You are the issue of two witches, after all."

"Enough of this," Bryan said, overcome with annoyance. He turned back to Arthur, but the laird's voice stopped him.

"Hold!" Douglas laughed suddenly. "Don't go getting in a chuff, lad. Your secret is safe with me . . . so long as you stay out of my business, that is."

"I have no interest in any business you conduct unless it causes harm to my march."

Douglas smiled humorlessly. "The marches aren't a safe place for an outsider, Warden. The Humes usually hold the wardenship, but the Earl of Bothwell is apparently not pleased with our recent service to him. I can't say I blame him. Leod was trash, and I am ashamed to claim him as kin. However, you should beware. My grandsire cut the head off the last outsider warden and rode through the East March with it tied to his saddle. A trophy, if you will."

Bryan's jaw clenched in anger. "Are you threatening me?" He felt Rory's presence move closer behind him.

The laird's eyes darted to Rory and back to Bryan.

He shrugged. "Nay. I'm merely recounting history. 'Tis probably somewhere in your ledgers if you'd care to check on it."

"Did your grandsire get away with the murder?"

"Aye, he did."

The old man was made of iron, that was for certain. Bryan could see it in the blue of his eyes. He held Bryan's gaze without blinking, even his large eye had stopped its twitching. Bryan didn't know what to make of his little story. Was it a threat that outsiders could find trouble in the march? Or was it a veiled confession that he murdered the last warden and would never be caught?

A woman approached carrying a parcel wrapped in a plaid blanket. She handed it to Rory.

"That's Leod's things," Douglas said, nodding to the bundle.

Bryan didn't see any point in staying. He turned to leave, then hesitated. "Oh, I almost forgot," he said with a polite smile. "Don't send any more kine to the garrison, nor provisions. We are concluding our business with you. We'll be dealing with the Dixons from this time forward."

Douglas's eye bulged and his face reddened. "You can't do that."

"I did it." Bryan mounted and looked down at the furious laird. "I find your prices to be larceny. Lady Dixon was more accommodating."

"Aye, I've heard how accommodating you've found the fair widow."

Bryan narrowed his eyes, waiting for Douglas to further slur Megan. But he took one look at Bryan's face and his mouth clamped shut.

"Thank you for your help," Bryan said as they left.

"You're welcome, Warden *Hepburn*," Douglas called after him.

On the way back to the garrison, Rory looked a bit pale.

"What is it? You're not looking well."

"I think you ought to consider hiring more guards, sir. You have angered Douglas Hume."

"Think you he'll try to have me killed?"

Rory nodded. "I'm certain of it."

"Good."

Rory didn't appear so pleased. Bryan thought it was a perfect opportunity to get Douglas where he wanted him. Unfortunately, this meant Rory's life was also in danger. "You may resign, Rory, if you'd rather."

Rory looked as though he'd been struck. "Sir! As if I would! Nay, I have sworn to protect you and I shall with my life, if it comes to that."

"Let us hope it doesn't. I think, though, when we return, we'll see how you do with a pistol."

When they reached the garrison, Bryan sent Willie to fetch pistols from the armory.

Willie returned with four guns and two powder horns. The guns were rusty and in need of cleaning. "Why are these pistols in such disrepair?"

Willie shrugged. "I know not. 'Tis not my responsibility to care for the weapons."

Bryan did not like that answer. "Pray tell, whose responsibility it is?"

"Tavish's, sir."

Ah, Tavish Marshall, Bryan's absentee deputy. Tavish hadn't been attending his duties properly.

Bryan would have to speak to him about it when he returned. "When Tavish isn't present, Willie, his duties fall to you. If they are too much for you, then I expect you to delegate."

Willie was abashed. "Aye, sir. I will take care of it immediately."

After gathering some of the misshapen clay cups Cathy deemed unworthy for sale to use for targets Bryan and Rory rode away from the garrison to the stand of woods where Bryan was attacked his first day. He sent Rory into the trees to make certain no one was nearby before they fired in that direction.

Bryan was upending a large rock so the flat side was up and they could set the cups on it, when Rory called to him. Pellinore was barking excitedly.

"Warden! Hurry!"

Bryan ran into the trees, but didn't see Rory or the dog. "Where are you?"

"Over here! I found something!"

Bryan followed the barking. Rory stood near some boulders with his hand over his nose and mouth, waving away swarming flies. Pellinore sniffed at something on the ground. As Bryan got nearer, the stench became unbearable and he was forced to use one of Cathy's handkerchiefs to cover his face.

He joined Rory, looking down at the body on the ground. Flies covered it thickly, and it was severely bloated. Insects were crawling in the hair, and the eyes had already been scavenged. Bryan urged Pellinore to back away from it.

"Is anyone else missing from the march?" Bryan asked.

"Well, aye—but none recently. Only Leod Hume."

"We'll have to try to determine how he died."

"He?" Rory asked. "How can you tell?"

It was impossible to identify the body. It was naked, for one thing, and parts of the genitals were missing. But Bryan was certain the corpse was male. Rory was looking rather green, so Bryan handed him a handkerchief. Rory took it gratefully and covered his face, so only his hazel eyes, peering at the body, were visible.

"Well, I don't know many lasses with so much body hair, and it has no breasts."

"It has no eyes, either," Rory muttered.

"Go back and fetch men, horses, and a litter, as well as heavy blankets."

Rory nodded and turned to leave. He hesitated. "Mayhap I shouldn't leave you alone?"

"He's already dead, lad. I've naught to fear from him."

After Rory left, Bryan went to Arthur and retrieved a pair of leather gloves from the saddlebag. He slipped them on and knelt beside the body. The murderer had stripped everything from the victim. Scavengers had been at the corpse, so Bryan doubted that any of the warden's identifying marks would be distinguishable. No eye color. But the hair was still present, and it was brown. He rolled the body on its side and almost retched. The back side was in far worse condition. He had to step away from the body for several minutes to calm his stomach.

The victim had been stabbed in the back several times. Bryan was suddenly irritated at the incompetence of his deputies and officers. Why hadn't the woods been searched after Leod Hume's disappearance? The body would have been found while it was still identifiable.

The corpse was probably riddled with disease. They should bury it immediately. He left the woods to wait for Rory. When Rory returned with the men and litter, he also had Willie.

"So you've found Leod?" Willie asked as they walked into the woods.

"I think so, but you'll have to identify him."

Willie stood over the body, not even covering his nose from the stench. He walked around it and returned it to its back with the toe of his boot. "I'd have to say, aye, it's Leod."

"How do you know?"

"Leod is the only one missing recently, the height's right, and his hair was brown. Other than that, I can't tell. But who else could it be?"

Four soldiers arrived, carrying between them the litter, piled with blankets. After the body was loaded onto the litter, Bryan slowly circled the area, kicking the underbrush out of the way, looking for anything left behind. Pellinore snuffed about the clearing, his nose to the ground. Signs of a struggle would be long gone, but maybe . . .

Pellinore's sharp bark interrupted his thoughts. The hound's tail poked out of some shrubs. By the time Bryan joined him, Pellinore had backed out with a boot dangling from his mouth. It was stiffened from rain, but it was a boot. Pellinore retrieved the mate and dropped it at Bryan's feet, tail wagging proudly.

"Good work!" Bryan scratched Pellinore's head and called his deputy over. "Do you recognize these boots as Leod's?"

Willie looked the boots over and grinned. "Aye! Good work, Warden! These are definitely Leod's boots."

Bryan frowned. "How can you tell?"

"Leod had an uncommon small foot." He indicated the smallness of the boot. It was true; it looked more like a boot a woman would wear. "Aye, it appears whoever killed him stole his clothing as well, but when the murderer found he couldn't wear the boots, he left them behind."

Bryan couldn't argue with that theory. It seemed he finally had a body.

Megan escaped into the kitchen with the excuse of checking on dinner. Cora stirred a large pot over the fire, and Marie made decorative flowers out of radishes. She held one up with a big smile when Megan walked in.

"It's a tulip."

"How can I eat it when you make it so pretty?" Megan asked.

Marie just kept smiling and humming as she worked. Megan stood at the large wooden table in the middle of the room. The women stopped their work.

"Is he still here?" Cora asked in disbelief.

"Aye. I've given him plenty of hints, but he won't leave."

"How can you marry a man that you cannot endure two meals with?" Marie asked.

"My son needs a father."

"What about Monsieur Warden? He's so tall and

handsome. Innes likes him better than Monsieur Hume."

Megan glared at her.

Marie lifted her shoulders and sighed. "You are right, of course. I keep forgetting marriage is a business transaction. I married my Johnny for love and look at where it has gotten me." She rubbed her large belly and waggled her eyebrows lasciviously.

Megan laughed, but shook her head. "I don't love the warden, Marie."

"I see him look at you, Madame; his blood runs hot for you."

"Marie, stop!" Megan felt herself turning red. She was especially embarrassed to be having this conversation in front of her mother-in-law.

They heard a rider in the yard. "That must be Johnny," Megan said. "Maybe when Charles realizes how late it is, he will leave."

Megan had no such luck. When she came out of the kitchen, she found Charles leaning back in the large chair that her late husband once sat in every evening to clean his weapons. Except Charles held a goblet in his limp grasp and was swirling wine around in it. He had already drunk too much and would probably pass out in Innes's chair.

"I think it's time for you to be heading home," Megan said.

Charles stopped swirling the wine and raised his bloodshot eyes to hers. "What about dinner?"

"I'm told there's food served about this time at Leadwater."

He tried to rise out of the chair quickly and indignantly, but he stumbled and almost fell. "Are you throwing me out?"

"No, Charles. I'm merely saying, it's late and it isn't proper for you to be staying here any longer."

A door opened and closed at the front of the house.

"Not proper?" Charles slurred and walked toward her. "But we are to be wed, you and I. 'Tis common for a man to sample his bride afore the nuptials."

"I haven't accepted your proposal."

He flung his arms out. "Then what was all this? The outing, aye?" He came closer and gripped her arms. "I love you, Megan. I will do anything to make you my wife. What is it you want?"

She swallowed. His breath stank. "Let's not discuss this now."

He tried to kiss her, but stopped, his face inches from hers and contorted with pain. He let go of her and began moving backward. Johnny had him by the side of his neck and was pinching the muscles so hard, Charles was completely helpless.

"Hold . . . hold . . ." Charles kept repeating pathetically.

"Get out until the lady summons you to her presence again," Johnny said and released him with a shove. Charles hurried out of the room. Johnny and Megan looked at each other for a moment then they both burst out laughing.

"Tell me you aren't going to marry that man. You do a sorry injustice to Innes's memory by even considering it."

She scowled at him for making such a comment. She had been fond of Innes, but he had been far from the perfect husband. They had fought endlessly about his reckless nature. Once she was pregnant, she had lived in constant fear that her son would grow up without a father. And that was exactly what had happened. She knew now to trust her instincts. And her instincts about Charles were screaming at her to run. It was time to listen.

Johnny removed his leather jack and sat in the chair across from Innes's. "Leod's body was found today."

Megan's eyes widened.

"The warden and Rory Trotter came upon it in the woods."

Marie brought Johnny a tankard of ale and perched on his knee. His arm slipped round her enormous belly. Despite the fact that she was huge with child, Johnny still dwarfed her with his muscular frame.

Megan sat in Innes's chair, gripping the arms. "He thinks I did it."

Marie asked, "Who thinks you did what?"

"The warden thinks I killed Leod."

Johnny shook his head. "Don't be a lackwit. How could he think such a thing?"

Megan chewed her lip anxiously. Johnny was wrong. She sensed it. Bryan somehow believed she was capable of killing a man. Maybe she *was* capable of it, but she didn't kill Leod. It was odd, since most men didn't think women capable of such violence. Innes had known it, though. He had once executed a woman accused of murdering her husband. Megan hadn't believed that the woman did it, but Innes couldn't be swayed. She had gone to witness the execution, as a protest against Innes's pigheadedness. His eyes had been cold as blue ice when the woman twitched at the end of the rope, her tongue protruding from her mouth.

Later Megan had told him how upsetting the whole ordeal had been for her. He had smiled, as though she were complaining about something as simple as a torn kirtle. He told her not to watch anymore if it bothered her so much. His attitude had chilled her, but now she realized he must have needed to detach himself from it, to look at the facts, not the person's gender. He couldn't become emotional about everyone he had to execute. Tragically, not long after, it was discovered that the woman had been innocent. *Too late.*

Megan shivered. The world was full of innocent corpses.

 Seven

Megan looked around furtively before entering the wood. No one was in sight. She tried to walk quietly, but the soft crunch of leaves underfoot echoed in her ears. The smell of the trees and earth filled her senses, injecting her with an excitement she shouldn't be feeling.

From the trampled ground, she knew she was at the spot where Leod's body had been found, but she saw nothing unusual. She poked through the bushes and shrubs, inspecting everything thoroughly. Finding nothing of interest, she sat on a fallen tree to think. She wasn't sure what she was looking for—something that would convince the warden she was innocent of murder. There were so many people who had a motive to kill Leod. Douglas Hume of Leadwater. Any one of the women whose husbands he had a hand in killing. Or one of the lasses he had raped. Since she was lacking clues, maybe what she needed was to give Bryan another suspect. But then it would look as though she were trying to remove suspicion from herself. And that would be the truth. She buried her face in her hands. She could do nothing but sit and wait.

The worst part was, she didn't want Bryan to see her that way, as a murderer. She almost laughed. She actually cared more what he thought of her than for the charge of murder! How could he think such a thing about her? *Easily*. She felt ill, remembering all the evidence she had given him that she could be violent.

She was submerged in her thoughts when an acorn flew out of a nearby tree, landing at her feet. She stared at it dumbly, then stood, looking up at the treetops around her. She shaded her eyes against the morning sunlight streaming through leaves and branches. Seeing nothing, she began turning in a circle. Another acorn hit the leaves nearby, sending up a spray of needles and dirt.

"Who is there?" she called. "Show yourself!" Her hand went to the dirk at her waist.

Bryan landed with a thud a few yards away. He had been up in a tree the entire time, watching her. A bevy of emotions coursed through her, ranging from horror to delight. He closed the distance between them, another acorn in his hand.

"Looking for something?" he asked, his face bland.

"I thought I'd have a look around."

"Really?" A dark brow arched. "Why?"

"Why do you think?" she said in a tight voice.

His eyes raked over her, taking in her male attire and lingering on her canvas-covered thighs. She raised her chin a notch.

"I don't know what to think." He walked around her to the log she had vacated and sat. "I came here today, thinking, when the murderer heard we had found Leod's body, he or she would return to the scene."

She took a deep breath and turned. "That would be foolish."

"What makes you say that?"

"That would certainly incriminate that person if he was caught."

"My thoughts exactly." He gave her a little grin, his dimples indenting in his cheeks. "Imagine my surprise to find the widow Dixon poking around this clearing."

"Hmm." She crossed her arms beneath her breasts and tried to look thoughtful and innocent.

"What are you doing here, Megan?"

"The same thing you are. I'm trying to discover who killed Leod Hume."

He tossed the acorn. It skipped across the ground, landing at the toe of her boot. "Are you certain you weren't making sure you didn't leave anything to indicate your identity behind?"

"If you believe me to be the murderer then you should be fearing your life right now, Warden. I killed one man here, aye?"

"Oh, I have no intention of putting my back to you, lass."

His response infuriated her. He was serious, too. His eyes were guarded; his posture on the log one of relaxed readiness.

"I did not murder Leod Hume!"

"Where were you after the fair?"

"I went home."

"Can someone vouch for that?"

Her stomach dipped. "No . . . everyone else stayed at the fair."

He watched her pensively, not speaking. He stood. "What did you find out, poking around here in the wood?"

He was beside her, looking down at her from his great height, so much taller and broader than most other men. She could smell him, leather and horse. She took a step back, her neck growing warm.

"Nothing."

"Hmmm." He was thoughtful, his hands on his hips.

She began to feel a prick of annoyance. He was trying to scare her, to make her squirm. She stared back at him, unwavering. "Where is Rory? I'm surprised he let you out of his sight, especially to come here."

He shrugged. "He doesn't know I'm gone."

"You took quite a chance, coming here, unprotected, looking for a killer."

"You underestimate me if you think me unprotected."

He was right; she had underestimated him from the very beginning. Had she been wise, she would have been careful to show the new warden in everything she did that she was not capable of murder. But wise had never been a word applied to her. Reckless and headstrong, but never wise.

"Shall we go?" he asked, gesturing for her to lead him out of the wood.

"Where? Are you going to charge me?"

"Should I?"

His answers were making her angrier. "No! I am innocent! But you suspect me. I need to know, am I free to leave?"

"Aye."

She tried to brush past him, but he stopped her, his hand circling her arm. She swung around angrily. "What is it you want from me?"

His eyes searched her face before moving down to the arm he held in a firm grip. "The question that most perplexes me is this: Could a woman kill? Is it within her nature, as it is in a man's?"

She hesitated, caught off guard by his question. "Is it not in everyone's nature to protect themselves and those they love from harm?"

He nodded. "Aye, but women are the givers of life and are of a much gentler disposition. It is not instinct for them to kill. Defend, aye." He moved closer to her, still in possession of her arm. "I have seen women defend their children, their homes, even their wounded husbands. After the initial blow that incapacitates their attacker, she does not stay to bludgeon or stab him half a dozen more times. *That* is an act of hate."

He looked into her eyes again. A shudder trembled through her. How inopportune for her to desire this man. Her cheeks were burning, she could feel them glowing. He had to see it, but his expression didn't change. She forced herself to speak, though her voice cracked as if she hadn't used it in a long while. "What if this . . . *villain* who attacked her were a scourge? Would she not stay to be certain he was obliterated, never able to cause harm again?" What was she doing? Confessing to a crime she didn't commit? But the words were out there, and she couldn't take them back.

His hand tightened on her arm, then became caressing, stroking and kneading the tight muscle. "That is conceivable. What about strength? Women are lighter, more delicate. They do not possess the power to overcome a man." His hand strayed to her shoulder, then to her neck, where his thumb traced circles in the sensitive flesh.

She could hardly breathe, or think. She knew she should step away from him, but could not. "What of stealth? Surprise?"

His touch paused and he nodded. "Aye. Surprise. An ambush?"

"She could sneak up behind him and stab him in the back. He'd never know what hit him."

His grip on her throat tightened, and he used it to pull her closer. When she met his eyes her breath lodged in her throat with fear at the fire blazing in them. "I never told you Leod was stabbed in the *back*."

Her breath came in gasps as she struggled to understand what he was saying. Her mouth was open but nothing came out.

"I instructed my men to tell no one, including you, the details of the murder."

"I didn't know," she gasped, shaking her head, straining backward against the painful hold he had on her neck. Her hands went to his, trying to pry them off her. Emotions flooded her, memories of another such situation, of another hand at her throat. "Let go of me!" She shoved at him with all her strength.

He released her, stumbling backward. He eyed her

with surprise. "You're quite strong. For a woman."

"What were you doing? Trying to suffocate me?" She was angry now. He had twisted her words into some kind of confession and made her prove she was strong enough to spar with a man. "That was some kind of test, wasn't it? I guess I failed. What now?"

He shook his head, his brow troubled. "Nothing."

She snorted derisively and turned, stalking through the trees. Her horse grazed just outside the wood. She looked furtively over her shoulder. Bryan appeared at the edge of the trees. He leaned against a tree and stared at her. She gritted her teeth, conscious that everything she did, every move she made, somehow incriminated her more, that her smallest actions proved her guilt or innocence. It had been such a foolish notion to come here today. She suddenly wanted to cry. She was certain his interpretation of tears would not be good. She mounted and rode over to him, determined not to appear suspicious.

He grasped her horse's bridle and looked up at her. "I want you to be innocent, Megan."

Tears welled in her eyes unbidden. She desperately wanted him to believe her. "I am."

"I wish it were that simple."

She swallowed and averted her eyes before the tears fell. "It is."

He shook his head in resignation, releasing her horse. She rode away, trying to ignore the pain in her chest.

Eight

Another week passed, and Megan heard nothing from the warden. She thought constantly about their encounter in the woods, trying to make sense of it. Why had he let her go free? She had been certain he believed she was a murderess. Why didn't he pursue her as a suspect with more diligence?

The anxiety from waiting for something to happen was driving her mad. She decided to pay him a visit. She had an excuse. She needed to collect money from him. He had sent men twice now for provisions, and she had provided them on credit. She knew he was waiting for the subsidy from the king and he would pay her when it came, but it was still pretense enough for a visit. She would determine his feelings by how he acted toward her. She was tired of worrying about it.

She dressed with care, being certain not to look too nice but neither too coarse. The gown she chose was a deep forest green. She knew it made her eyes appear even greener. It was soft, brushed wool and very flattering, if a bit plain.

She braided her hair and donned a hat with a wide brim. Looking in the glass, she was satisfied with the result. "Why am I doing this?" she asked her reflection. She could see the flush in her cheeks, the excitement in her eyes that the mere thought of Bryan Hepburn could create. She hesitated. Perhaps this was a bad idea, asking for more trouble. She did seem to have a problem guarding her tongue when he was near.

She wandered to the window, her stomach churning with indecision. Why couldn't he be someone else, she thought angrily. Her decision was abruptly made when she spied Charles Hume riding into the courtyard. She grabbed her things and hurried out of the house.

"Megan," he said, bowing gallantly as she approached him. His white-blond hair was too long, and it fell in his eyes. He took her hand and pressed a wet kiss against her knuckles. She yanked her hand away at the earliest possible moment, her skin crawling.

"I'm so sorry, Charles, I was just leaving. Cora will see to your refreshment. Good day." She started toward the stable. He caught her arm. "This is how you entertain your suitors?"

Her teeth clenched, and she pulled her arm from his grasp. She loathed offending him. She paid his father to protect her in the event of a raid. The Humes were known to be very vengeful. "I am not entertaining suitors at this time."

He hurried after her into the stable. "Don't play your feminine games with me! I won't have it!"

"Fine. My answer is no. I will not marry you."

He looked as though he'd been slapped. "You're saying no to me?"

"Aye, I am." She was nervous suddenly. They were alone in the stable. She hurried to her horse and began saddling it. He didn't move, but stood rooted to the spot.

"It's the warden, isn't it? He is nothing! He has nothing! He wouldn't even have employment if it weren't for his wizard cousin! And he's a bastard."

She whirled around. "He has more than you could ever wish to have! He is a good warden and good man!" She was trembling with rage, her hands balled into fists.

"You're smitten!" he cried, his face crimson with anger.

She went back to saddling her horse, but her fingers were shaking so badly it was proving a difficult task.

"You will be sorry for insulting me!" He stormed out of the stable.

She released the breath she had been holding. She had just made yet another enemy she couldn't afford.

By the time the garrison was in sight Megan was feeling better about her decision not to wed Charles. Bryan had made more improvements to the castle walls. Even from a distance she could see the change. The wall was finished and looked spotted from the repairs. It had become a defensive structure again.

She raised her hand to Johnny at the gates. He

helped her down and sent the boy who had accompanied her to the stable with her mount.

"What brings you out here, Meg? Is it Marie? Is she ready to have the wean?" He looked alarmed suddenly then fought to control himself.

"No, no," she assured him. "I'm here to see the warden."

"Aye?"

"On business," she said quickly, to hide her embarrassment.

His eyebrow twitched, obviously not fooled, but he held his tongue.

She walked slowly to the keep and found herself mesmerized by the flurry of activity going on around her. She was even more surprised when she entered the hall. She had been to the garrison when Leod was in command, and it had been filthy and run down. The men had been lethargic, playing at dice and cards, half of them drunkards.

Now clean, scented rushes covered the floor. The smell of marjoram mixed with the aroma of roasting meat filled the air. Children were everywhere. The widows were gathered around the fire, all engaged in some industrious activity. The smaller children were playing on the floor while the older ones were at a long table with, of all people, Lauren Hume giving them lessons! They were bent over their hornbooks and chalkboards, scratching out lessons.

Cathy spotted Megan standing slack-jawed in the entryway and called to her. Megan moved around the children to where Cathy was seated by the hearth.

"Lady Dixon! Greetings!" Cathy stood, placing her sewing neatly in one of her exquisite baskets.

"To what do we owe this visit?" She was acting the perfect lady of the manor, and Megan felt a stab of annoyance, since the only lord of the manor could be Bryan.

"I've come to speak with the warden—but if he's too busy, I can call another time."

"Nonsense! He will be delighted! Follow me."

Megan followed her outside and around the back of the keep. Men were assembled, shooting arrows at straw targets. There were more men along the back wall, stripped to their shirts, swords clashing. Bryan was not among them. But Cathy was still hurrying along, her ample hips swaying gently. They came to the corner where several men were cutting away the ivy that had claimed the wall.

Bryan was there, but not directing the labor. He and Rory were shirtless and soaked with sweat. They were both quite a sight, Rory laden down with bulging muscles and Bryan, his long bones covered with thick ropes of sinew. With scythe in hand, he hacked at the ivy, ripping it off the wall and throwing it in a pile. A small crowd of lasses had gathered, pretending to be stretching laundry out on the ground to dry, but in fact gaping at the muscular torsos.

"Warden! You have a visitor!" Cathy called.

Bryan set the scythe aside and wiped the sweat from his forehead, pushing wet brown curls off his brow. He surveyed the wall a moment before turning. The broad smile that lit his face when he saw her left her knees weak. She was unable to stop the answering curve of her lips any more than the flush creeping up her neck.

He slipped his shirt back on. "Thank you, Cathy."

"Shall I send some cool ale to your chambers?" Cathy asked solicitously.

"Aye, that sounds fine."

Cathy smiled affectionately and hurried back inside. Megan didn't know what to say and could only stand there mutely staring at him. His white linen shirt was hanging open, becoming damp with his sweat. In clothing he looked lean and rangy, but it was merely a deception because of his height. His chest was brawny with muscle, matted now with wet, brown hair. Broad shoulders tapered down to a narrow waist. His biceps were bunched-up hard and round from the work. There wasn't a bit of fat to spare on him.

He placed his hand on the small of her back and propelled her into the keep. His large hand seemed to burn through the material of her bodice to her skin. She moved away from his touch immediately. She was beginning to perspire and fought for a calm nonchalance on the way to his chambers. His attitude toward her was nothing but warm and pleasant. That was a good sign. Surely if he thought her a murderess he wouldn't be so friendly.

They were greeted at the door by Curly the pig, who refused to step over the threshold, but stood at the open door. Bryan patted the pig's back and murmured a greeting.

"A moment," he said, indicating his wet shirt and disappearing into the connecting room. The pig followed. Pellinore was lying on a blanket and stretched. He came to her and wagged his tail, waiting patiently for his greeting. She scratched the dog's head and looked around the room. Papers and ledgers were in neat piles on the desk, the workspace clear. Two book-shelves overflowed with books.

A young lass knocked discreetly on the door and placed a pitcher of ale and two mugs made from glazed clay on the table. Megan removed her hat and inspected the mugs. Cathy Armstrong creations. She wondered if the plump widow was fishing for husband number two.

"I'm glad you're here."

She whirled at his voice, almost dropping the mug. He was fully dressed in clean clothes. He had washed, and his hair was combed.

She set the mug down. "I came about our business arrangement," she blurted out. She regretted it when his smile faded.

He brushed past her and poured the ale, offering the mug to her. She met his gaze, but could read nothing. She took the mug eagerly, glad for something to do with her hands. He went to the cupboard and unlocked a cabinet, removing a wooden box from it. Sitting at the desk, he took coins from it, stacking them on the table.

She searched furiously for something to say. She hadn't come here just to collect her money! If she didn't think of something soon she would have to leave and not know for certain if he still suspected her.

"I also wanted to inquire how you are fairing. As warden, that is."

He looked up. "Aye?"

She nodded. "It seems you're better suited to the post than anyone thought."

The clink of coins started up again. He had resumed counting and stacking the coins in neat little piles. A small frown pulled at his brows. Her face flushed with embarrassment. She hadn't meant to say it that way. It sounded more like an insult than a compliment.

He removed a little bag from the box, put the coins in it, and tied it closed. After methodically locking the box and replacing it in the cabinet, he offered her the bag.

"It's all there if you'd like to count it."

She wanted to throw it in his face, but it was her money. She snatched it out of his hand. "I trust you. If I have your leave?"

He didn't say anything, only continued to frown at her. His silence increased her unease. She started to turn when his voice stopped her. "Is it merely a rumor that you have agreed to wed Charles Hume?"

" 'Tis rumor indeed. I have refused his suit."

He raised an eyebrow. "Walk with me," he said suddenly, startling her and setting her heart racing. He smiled slightly, the dimples only shadows. "If you still want to hear of my doings, it will take some time, as I have been very busy since we last spoke. Would you walk with me?"

Her stomach coiled into a knot of tension, but, almost against her will, she gave him a small nod. Her hands became clammy as she watched him tidy up his already neat office. Why was she doing this? *Tell him you just remembered something. You have to return home. You apologize, but the matter is pressing.* But nothing came out of her mouth. Instead, she stood by the door twisting the brim of her felt hat in her hands. It was ridiculous really. Why did she get so excited at the thought of spending time with Bryan? Why didn't

Charles have this effect on her? But she knew. Bryan was everything Charles wasn't. He exuded confidence and command. He made her imagine things a proper widow had no business imagining.

He opened the door for her, and she went out, trying to calm herself and wondering if perhaps she should send for the boy who accompanied her. Rory was leaning against the opposite wall and straightened. He had cleaned himself up nicely, too, his auburn hair combed and curling around his thick neck. She let out a sigh of relief. They wouldn't be alone. Rory attended the warden constantly.

She ignored the little grin Johnny gave her as they left the gates. It was a beautiful day, but she was too wary of the motives behind the invitation to enjoy the walk. Would it be another veiled interrogation?

They followed the wall around to the back of the stronghold, neither of them speaking and Rory following at a distance, and started down the hill to the distant wood. It was the same area where Leod was killed, where Bryan had practically accused her of murder a week ago, though that spot was farther down the main road.

"Tell me about you and Innes . . . big Innes. Was the marriage arranged?"

His question gave her pause. She answered without looking at him, "No, but when he asked, my father thought it a good match and was well pleased." The day was warm and her tight wool sleeves itched. She fought the urge to tug at the high collar of her gown.

"So it was love . . ."

"Well . . . love is a strong word. I was very fond of him." His silence made her uncomfortable, so she tried to fill it. "I had little choice of who I was to marry. My father had a few merchants in mind, but he never expected a laird to ask for me. Innes was quite a bit older than I. Probably your age, yet I was only seventeen."

"I am thirty."

"Aye, he was thirty. He was more than I had expected, so I was pleased." She didn't want to talk of Innes. "What about you, Warden? The people of the Merse know little of your past. Are you a widower?"

"Nay . . . there was a lass once—but we never married and she's dead now." He was gazing off at the trees; his eyes squinted against the sun.

Did he mourn her still, Megan wondered. "How did it happen? Was she in the Low Countries?"

He didn't say anything for a long time, so long that she thought he wasn't going to answer. Then he said, "She was a Don."

A Spaniard! Megan's eyebrows shot up.

"She said she was Protestant and came to me for protection. I was the Prince of Orange's man, so it was a likely tale. She claimed to have been hurt. Raped and hunted because she had information on Don John's army. I, of course, fell for it . . . and for her."

Megan was quiet, but felt sick for him. She waited for him to continue.

"I told her things . . . I shouldn't have, when we were . . . alone. I wanted to reassure her that I would never allow the Dons to hurt her again." He wouldn't look at Megan. He seemed ashamed of his weakness, of leaking information.

"I was told one day that she was a spy. I thought I

might kill her for deceiving me. When I confronted her, she told me it was true, but that she loved me and would not leave me. She said," he spat the words out, "that our love had changed her. She could never betray me. I believed her—again—making her escape possible. She promptly reported everything to the Spaniards."

"Oh, Bryan . . ." Megan breathed. She reached out impulsively, laying her hand on his arm. He looked down at her, surprised. She started to withdraw her hand, but he covered it with his, holding her there.

He continued, "I'm not sure what happened after that. I think they wanted her to kill me but she refused. I only heard about it from our own spies. She was later found dead from poison. Her husband—" His gaze flicked to Megan when he heard her quick intake of horrified breath. "Aye, I didn't know she was married. He claimed it was suicide. I do not believe it."

He was silent for a long time. His face was hard. "The prince was a good man, and though I didn't deserve it, he kept me with him. His second wife was a treacherous woman who had caused him much grief, so he didn't blame me for being fooled. I . . . wanted to avenge her, despite what she had done to me; she didn't deserve to die. She had served them well, and they killed her for it. I thought of little but killing Dons . . . better ways to kill Dons . . . more painful ways to kill them, until the prince was assassinated. Then it all lost its meaning to me."

"How awful," she whispered, her words sounding empty. They had come to the woods, and the trees loomed green and dark over them. He didn't enter but turned her to walk along the edge, in the trees' shadows.

"I feel sick now when I think of all the men I killed. All the nameless, faceless men who had nothing to do with one woman's deception. Now, even the fight appears to have been in vain. Since the prince was murdered, the Spaniards have taken back much of what we won over the past decade. The heart went out of the Low Countries the day the Prince of Orange was assassinated.

"Queen Elizabeth finally sent English troops, after years of solemnly vowing to send aid and casually breaking her word. When the Earl of Leicester stepped off the ship in Flushing, I boarded one headed for Lieth."

Both their moods had become maudlin. She didn't want their walk ruined thinking about such horrors. She asked, "Why did you live in the Low Countries?"

He turned his dark brown eyes on her. She was startled that his look had become guarded, after such an outpouring. The hand that covered hers dropped, but she didn't release his arm.

"My mother felt it wasn't safe for me here."

"Why?"

"I was only twelve when she sent me to live with her brother, so I didn't understand it much myself. She said it was because of my father . . . everyone thought he was an evil man; if it was known that I was his son . . . I might meet with harm."

"Who was your father?" she asked, but her mind was already fitting the pieces together. Bryan's surname was Hepburn, he was related to the current Earl of Bothwell, and if he was twelve when his mother sent him away, the year would have been 1567.

Before he could answer, she blurted out, "James Hepburn, the fourth Earl of Bothwell."

"Aye," he said, looking at her warily.

"My God . . . I didn't know he had any children."

"None that are legitimate. My mother said I have two other brothers, though not of her issue. My father . . . was rather popular with the lassies."

"So I've heard. Did you know him?"

He shook his head. "Nay. He did come to see me on occasion and brought me gifts. I went to visit him while he was imprisoned at Malmö in Denmark. He was very upset with me. He told me never to visit him again. Like my mother, he feared I would be used against him if anyone knew I was his son."

She was astounded by his revelation and unable to even properly digest it. She had heard that the earl had died a horrible death seven years ago in prison.

"Are you sickened by this?" he asked. "My mother, Janet Beaton, was believed to be a witch, as was my father. Does it disgust you to think I am witch's spawn and the son of a murderer?"

"No!" she answered explosively, then more calmly, "Of course it doesn't sicken me. You have no control of such events. . . . Anyway, I don't believe in witches."

He smiled down at her. A rush of warmth filled her, affecting her breathing. This was not at all what she had expected, for him to bare his soul to her. It was even more dangerous than the interrogation she had anticipated. When he was questioning her, she could keep the cool wall between them, but in the space of an afternoon, he had torn the wall down and left her heart open and wanting. She turned her face away, certain all these feelings were evident in her expression. She dared not open her mouth for fear of what she might say, what she might confess.

"I'm glad to hear that," he said, taking her hand again, only this time threading his fingers with hers.

The intimacy that had sprung up between them frightened and excited Megan. Her stomach fluttered with anticipation, though she tried to tell herself it meant nothing. His hand holding hers was warm and strong, and she couldn't ignore the stirrings of desire. She found herself unable to speak and thankfully he filled her silence.

"I'm learning that witches are much feared here, almost as much as in Denmark."

Megan breathed a sigh of relief that the topic had turned impersonal and turned back to him with a smile.

The light was fading from the sky when Bryan and Megan walked back to the garrison. He had spent the past week arguing her innocence to himself, and when she had shown up at the garrison, as fresh and lovely as spring itself, he found he no longer cared. He sensed some change in her, also. A softening, her guard dropping. He was relieved. He didn't know what had possessed him to reveal that James Hepburn was his father. If she heeded all the vicious rumors, she could believe he was the son of a warlock, rapist, murderer, and power-hungry despot. Bryan didn't even know that any of those claims were untrue, though his mother had assured him that they were and that anything his father had done was done out of necessity.

But Megan hadn't recoiled; in fact, he had seen something in her eyes, something that made the blood pound in his veins. Being with her now, it was impossible for him to believe she had killed a man, impossible to believe any evil of her. He swore to himself he would find the real culprit and clear her name.

He wanted to know everything about her. "How long were you and Innes married?" he asked as they made their way back up the hill to the garrison.

"Two years."

He didn't want to feel jealous of a dead man and young Innes's father, but the sadness in her voice gave him a pain in his chest. "It must be hard for wee Innes, not having a father around."

"Aye, very hard. Once he was out of nappies and I was teaching him how to use the chamber pot and go outside without drenching his breeks, I realized just how difficult it was. That really is a manly thing, and I don't know much about it."

Bryan couldn't help but laugh. "So how did you manage?"

"Och, well, I enlisted the help of old Hob. He was the only man about I felt comfortable asking. He did the job, though it took him longer than I might have expected."

"Old Hob taught him how to make water like a man, aye?"

"The only problem is, he stoops over to do it." She illustrated by hunching her shoulders like an old man. "And I had a terrible time convincing him he doesn't need a cane to piss."

He burst out laughing, not knowing if she was jesting or not. Her green eyes were glinting with humor.

It was late, and he knew he should see her home. But he wasn't ready for their time together to end. "You should return before dark," he said as they walked into the keep.

"Aye."

She had left the money he paid her in his chambers, so he steered her in that direction. He gave Rory a look over his shoulder. Rory headed for the hall to get dinner. Bryan closed the door once they were inside. She jumped and glanced apprehensively at the door, then at him. He held her gaze, wanting to say things to her that he had no business even thinking. A snorting behind her broke the spell. She stepped back and looked down at his pig.

"So this is Curly?"

He knelt and the pig came to him. He stroked its hairy back. "Aye, and he's clever, too. Why, he listens better than Pellinore." The dog raised his head from where he lounged in the corner and looked at them haughtily.

"I've never really thought of pigs as any more than food. He's rather sweet." She leaned down to scratch him between the ears and Curly snorted. "It will be a shame to butcher him."

"Good God, woman! As if I would!"

She raised her eyebrows then burst out laughing.

"I don't jest!"

"I know. That's why I'm laughing."

He felt a little embarrassed and wondered what she thought of a man who took a pig as a pet and refused to butcher it.

"What are you going to do when he's great and fat?"

"He certainly won't sleep in my chambers any longer, but he will still be a good pig."

She was staring at him, a smile curving her full mouth. He returned the look and took a step closer. Their eyes were locked and her smile began to fade, but she didn't move away. Rational thought was rapidly leaving his head. He wanted to be alone with her, to have his hands on her, to taste her.

He slipped his arm around her waist. She trembled for a moment and seemed to pull back from him. Then her blond lashes dropped, the creamy skin of her cheeks deepening to rose.

When he kissed her she made no facade of shyness and met his mouth, matching his pent-up desire. Her hand went to the back of his neck, pressing him closer and immediately deepening the kiss. The sweet taste of her combined with her response was intoxicating. He had meant to steal no more than a kiss, but good intentions faded to nothing. He yanked at the ribbon holding her braid. When it was gone he pulled her hair free from its weaves with one hand, never taking his mouth from hers.

Her hands moved to the buttons on his doublet, working them free as he pushed her backward to his bedchamber. By the time they reached the inner room she was shoving his doublet off his shoulders. He shrugged out of it impatiently. Using the grip he had on her hair, he pulled her head back, kissing the smooth, tight skin of her jaw. He would have gone lower, but the damn gown she was wearing came almost up to her chin. Frustrated at being thwarted, he released her and set to work on the buttons.

Her breathing was rapid and her hands gripped his

biceps, but she kept her head tilted back and her eyes closed. His fingers were fumbling with the tiny buttons.

"Damn," he muttered, as he ripped one off and it fell to the ground. He dropped to his knees, impatient, searching the rushes for it, but couldn't see where it went.

He looked up at her. "I'm sorr . . ." he trailed off. She had finished taking the bodice off and stood before him in a thin linen chemise. Her breasts were full and straining against the material, the dark outline of her nipples clearly visible. He forgot the button and stood, gathering her in his arms and kissing her. He held her closer, loving the warm, soft curves pressed against him.

There was a pounding at his door. "Warden! Warden!" He jerked his head up. Not now! He wanted to ignore it, but her eyes were frantic. He grabbed her bodice from the bed and handed it to her. He was still dressed and went into the other room, closing the door to his bedchamber.

"Warden!" The pounding grew more insistent. He opened the door. Willie and Rory stood before him looking panicked.

"What is it?"

"The Dixons have lit their beacon, sir! They're being raided! We must hurry!"

Rory and Willie had pushed their way into his room, so there was very little to say when his bedchamber door flew open and Megan exited, buttoning her bodice, golden hair spilling down her shoulders.

He could see she was distressed and didn't care about Willie's and Rory's gaping jaws.

"We have to go! Now!" she yelled at them.

"Get the men together and let's head out!" Bryan ordered. Willie roused himself from staring at his niece and left.

Megan was tying her hair back. "Are you ready for your first hot trod, Warden?" she asked, but didn't wait for his answer. She was out the door behind Willie. Bryan grabbed his doublet and hurried after her. He caught her before she left the keep.

"I want you to stay here."

"Like I hell I will!" She tried to pull free.

"You're safer here. Stay with the other women."

She jerked away. "I don't have time for this! My family is there! My son." Her eyes suddenly widened in horror. "Marie . . . she's due to have that child any time now!"

His teeth were set on edge. He didn't want to go into this worrying about her safety, but he could see any attempt to dissuade her would be useless. Rory was bringing forth their horses in the bailey. The other men were readying their mounts to head out.

"Where's Johnny?" she called out.

"He went home over an hour ago," someone yelled back.

Bryan took a party of twenty men, Willie and Rory included. Megan was single-minded, trying to leave the garrison before Bryan's men were ready. She became angry with him when he made her wait. He didn't care, she could get mad, but he wasn't going to let her be hurt or kidnapped.

They rode furiously through the darkness. Megan and Bryan were leading. She bent over her horse's neck, digging her heels into its sides to make it go faster. The beacon still flared when they arrived. The women and children were leaving the tower. Cora held Innes, his head buried in her neck. Megan jumped off her horse and grabbed her son.

"Mum!" he cried and wrapped himself around her. Tears squeezed from her tightly shut eyes.

"Where are they? What happened?" Bryan asked Cora.

Cora was thoroughly shaken and stroked Innes's red hair. "Johnny sent everyone up to the tower. It was Kerrs."

"How many? Where is Johnny now?"

"It was a small party. Five, I think. They took the kine and raided the house." She turned to Megan, her face white with fear. "They took Johnny. Marie has started having pains. . . ."

They heard a low cry from the tower door, emphasizing Cora's words. A man and a woman were helping Marie to the house. When she saw Megan she began crying.

"Madame! They took my Johnny! Monsieur Warden, please do not let them kill him!" She cried out in pain and began chanting, "*C'est mal! C'est mal!*"

Megan kissed Innes and handed him back to Cora, then she was back on her horse, yelling for the men to follow her. Bryan swung back up into his saddle. He grabbed the reins of her horse.

"Marie needs you. Innes needs you. Stay here. Let me take care of this!"

"How many hot trods have you been on, Warden?" she asked, wiping her damp cheeks. When he just stared angrily at her, she answered for him, "None. I know better than you where to find them."

His lips thinned. He was wasting time arguing with her. "Then put on your jack at least and arm yourself."

She ran into the house and was down minutes later clad in breeks and a jack. The other men knew their way. Bryan stayed close to Megan. He was pleased to find he was not nearly as disoriented as he expected to be. He remembered some of the territory from his night ride with Megan. They sped over the hills, the thick grasses appearing gray in the dark, stopping every so often to be certain they were on the raiders' trail.

It wasn't long before they caught a glimpse of riders ahead in the moonlight. The raiders traveled far slower than Bryan's party since they were herding Megan's cattle. The Kerrs spotted them at the same time and an arrow whistled through the air next to Bryan's head.

He withdrew his pistol and rode straight into the fray. The Kerrs' horses were laden down with the valuables from Megan's house. One of them had a limp form draped over his saddle. Johnny Oliver. He had to be alive, otherwise they wouldn't be burdening themselves with the extra weight. He was worth a great deal to the raiders. If Bryan didn't pay the ransom to retrieve his guard, they knew Johnny's wife would.

Bryan discharged his pistol into the air. The cattle stampeded. Three of the five Kerrs were trapped in the melee of crazed beasts. One of their horses reared, and its rider fell into the kine. The two remaining Kerrs left the cattle behind and galloped away. Bryan

yelled orders for the others to stay with the kine and
capture the three Kerrs.

Bryan, Rory, and two other guards pursued the
escaping reivers. Megan ignored his order to stay with
Willie and followed. They reached the river and
splashed into it. Several of the horses balked at such a
violent fording but Arthur kept after the thieves. The
water reached the horses' bellies, seeping into Bryan's
boots. The raiders' booty was slowing them down, so
Johnny was shoved into the river.

Bryan caught up to one of the men as they cleared
the river. He reached for him, to pull him from his
horse, but the Kerr held a lance. He swung it at Bryan,
striking him in the chest. The blow was glancing.
Bryan grabbed the lance and yanked. The man fell
beneath Arthur's hooves. Arthur reared, almost sending Bryan to the ground.

As soon as his horse calmed, Bryan jumped down.
One of Arthur's hooves had struck the man's head,
and he was having trouble standing. Bryan hauled
him to his feet. He had no intention of returning these
men to Sir Thomas Kerr. He would punish them himself.

He didn't see Rory, Megan, or his other guard. The
Kerr Bryan had captured was thoroughly dazed and
not putting up a fight. Bryan tethered him to Arthur
and dragged him back across the Tweed.

Willie had everything under control. Two of the
Kerrs were dead. One had been trampled, and the
other had tried to fight it out and lost. Megan, Rory,
and one of the guards had not returned. The other had
stopped to pull Johnny from the river. He was con-

scious and held his head between his hands. "Marie . . ." he said hoarsely.

Bryan laid a hand on his shoulder. "Marie is fine. She's giving birth."

Johnny stood quickly and almost collapsed.

After giving orders to herd the kine to Megan's, Bryan returned to the river. He started to cross when he saw Megan and Rory approaching. The last Kerr wasn't with them. They forded the Tweed while Bryan waited patiently on the opposite bank. His heart stopped when he saw Megan's face. She definitely had an encounter with the raider. Blood was smeared under her nose and dripping from her eyebrow. Her lip was swelling.

"Bloody hell, Rory! How could you let this happen?" Bryan yelled. He touched her chin gently to inspect the damage. His hands were shaking, and he tried to control his anger.

"Don't yell at Rory. He wasn't even with me."

He glared at Rory. "And why not?"

"I'm sorry, sir. My horse stumbled in the river and when I finally forded it, she was gone."

He inspected her body and noticed she was rather laden down. She had recovered some of her stolen possessions. The shield from the wall, as well as the rolled-up tapestry, lay across her lap.

"Where is the Kerr?"

"He got away," she said shortly.

The blood seemed to crystallize in his veins. "Yet you recovered your things?"

"I fought with him. He hit me and escaped, but he dropped these."

Bryan found it hard to believe that a woman, no

matter how tough, had scared the Kerr reiver into leaving his plunder. He and Megan studied each other's expressions a full minute.

Her lips thinned. "He knew I wasn't following him alone, Warden."

If she killed him, why wouldn't she tell him? She would have done it in self-defense, and he certainly wouldn't hold her accountable. Unless she was afraid it would incriminate her in another murder. Anger infused him at the thought of her deceiving him. He said nothing else, but gestured for them to join the others. He took care to observe her feet without her noticing. For a woman, they were quite large. Too big to fit into Leod's boots.

Nine

"She still has a while yet," Cora said, drawing Megan out of the room where Marie was in labor. "Let's see to those cuts now."

Megan allowed Cora to fuss over her, shocked at the level of rage and indignation she felt. It was like a living thing inside her, growing with each memory of the accusatory look on Bryan's face, the disbelief in his voice. She sat in a chair, barely feeling the sting as Cora gently wiped the cloth across her brow, *tsk*ing the whole time. "I don't understand why you do this! One day those reivers are going to kill you. Where would that leave us? And you a mother!"

Megan didn't comment. She knew Cora's feelings on this subject, and Cora was well aware of Megan's. If she was going to care for her people she needed to do it in every aspect. She couldn't rely on anyone but herself. The unsettling sensation of another, stronger presence in the room made her look up. Bryan stood in the doorway, his arms folded across his chest. His hair brushed the top of the door frame, as usual, and his shoulders filled it horizontally. He kept his eyes on the floor, as though deep in thought.

"Leave us, Cora," Megan said stiffly.

"But your face—"

"I said leave us!"

Cora pursed her lips together and stalked from the room. Megan didn't stand. She was feeling the fight with the Kerr throughout her body. He had done a lot more than hit her in the face. He had kicked her and punched her, too. Her arm was wrapped around her ribs, trying to contain the pain that stabbed her side when she moved. But she had paid him back in kind . . . if not worse.

"What happened, Megan? And I want the truth."

Anger welled up in her chest, threatening to choke her. "I told you what happened. And it *is* the truth."

His eyes narrowed. "How is it you got the shield and tapestry back, and no Kerr? It just doesn't make sense."

She sprang up out of the chair and winced, her breath locking in her throat from the pain. He was beside her instantly, unfastening the hooks of her jack and gently pulling it off.

"Christ! Where else are you hurt?"

"I'm fine." She pushed his hands away.

He grabbed her shoulders tightly, forcing her to look at him. His eyes were filled with worry and anger. "For all you think you're a man, you're not one! Capable or not, lasses' bones break a hell of a lot easier than a man's. Now let me see."

"Cora will tend my wounds when you've left. If you're so eager for me to be mended, I suggest you get on with your accusations and leave me in peace."

His face darkened.

"That is, unless I'm to be charged with murder," she sneered.

"Warden?" Willie queried from the door as Bryan was opening his mouth to reply. His fingers tightened on her shoulders, then he released her.

"Aye?" He turned to Willie, but stayed close by, as though he thought she might try to escape.

"The rest of the men have returned. They met up with Duff just past the Tweed. He caught the last Kerr—said he chased him almost to Kerr lands." Willie grinned and winked at Megan. "If it weren't for this lass maiming him, Duff says he might not have caught him at all. Fine work, Megan!"

Willie left the room, but Bryan didn't turn to her immediately. She stared at the broad shoulders, hoping he felt like a fool. When he finally faced her, his expression was apologetic.

"It seems I have made a terrible mistake."

"Get out of my house," she hissed through her teeth.

"Megan . . ." He seemed to be at a loss for words. He reached for her but she shoved his hands away, jerking from the pain in her side. His hands went to his hips, and he said, "I never accused you of anything."

"Oh, you!" His comment left her seething. " 'Twas all in your eyes—no need to put words to it!" She wrapped her arm protectively about her ribs.

"You're hurt. Let me help you." His face reflected nothing but genuine concern and regret, but she didn't care. He had immediately assumed the worst of her, automatically believing she had brutally murdered the Kerr and tried to cover it up.

"If you don't leave right now, I shall scream and not stop until the whole house is awake!"

"Then scream! I will be certain you are not mortally wounded afore I leave."

She glared at him, yanking the shirt out of her breeks and pulling the ties, leaving the two at the top secured to cover her breasts. Pushing the linen aside, he gently probed at her ribs. She winced, but not from pain. He paused, leaving his large, callused palm pressed against her flesh.

"Does this hurt?" he asked, kneeling in front of her, his head lowered.

The room seemed to be closing in around her, and she was grateful he wasn't looking at her face. "A bit," she lied, needing an excuse for why her voice had suddenly become hoarse. She wanted this examination over. His hands were in motion again, one resting on her hip to steady her, the other moving warmly over her ribs. Something tightened unbearably in her chest so that when he asked her to breathe in and out, it was most difficult.

Finally, he straightened. "It looks nasty, but 'tis likely just bruised."

She turned away from him, clutching her shirt closed. "Now you can leave. Please don't come back, unless you're on warden business. And then I'd rather you send my uncle."

She climbed the stairs, leaving him staring after her. She stood at the top, listening. When she heard nothing for a long time, she almost went back down to force him to leave. His footsteps echoed across the floorboards, and the door opened and closed.

In her room, she eased a shutter open to peek outside. The men from the garrison were ready to leave with their prisoners and the bodies. Rory was waiting, holding Arthur's reins. She watched Bryan climb into the saddle. He looked back at the house once, then they were filing out of the gate.

She lay on her bed in the dark room. Her chest was tight and her throat thick. She tried not to cry, but the sobs came anyway. The salty tears stung the cuts on her face and jarred her ribs, but she couldn't stop. How was it she was feeling these things? And for the wrong man! He was wrong in every way. He was a warden. He thought her a liar and murderess. But everything else about him felt so warm and right. When she finally had herself under control, she changed into an old dress. She had made a fool of herself over him and now everyone would know it.

Had she really burst out of his room, half dressed, her mouth probably swollen from his kisses? She felt weak with shame and even more disgusting, lust. The memory of his kiss, his touch, was burned into her mind. Had she lost all her judgment? She had other things to think about now. She had to put the warden from her mind.

Where was Douglas Hume during the raid? She paid him to protect her! The memory of how she rebuffed Charles earlier that day came back to haunt her. Could it be revenge? She would worry about it later. Right now Marie needed her. She hurried down the hall to join the birthing.

* * *

"Shall I take the Kerrs back to the Middle March at daylight?" Willie asked.

Bryan slumped in the chair behind his desk. "Nay. Lock them up until I decide what to do with them."

Willie left, and Rory leaned in the doorway. Bryan stared at the wall, drumming his fingers on the desktop.

"I'm sorry I wasn't able to stay with her, sir. This wouldn't have happened if I was doing my duty."

Bryan frowned at him. "Your duty is to guard me, not Lady Dixon. Apologize no more. 'Twas not your fault." He looked back at the wall. Rory had, of course, overheard their whole argument since he was always hovering nearby.

His words didn't mollify Rory. He suspected what Rory wanted was to see the warden not glowering at the wall. Bryan couldn't help him. Rory finally backed out and closed the door.

He had really mucked things up. He was very angry and it was all directed inward. It suddenly seemed ridiculous. What did he think she did? Chopped the man up and buried him? As if she had enough time! How could he be so foolish? He was treating her as though she were a madwoman! She had every right to throw him out and insist he never return. Perhaps she was telling the truth about why she was in the wood that day. He had shown nothing but distrust for her. It was reasonable for her to believe that she would have to prove herself innocent.

Curly was snuffling at something in the corner. It was the bundle of Leod's things Douglas Hume had given him. Bryan scratched at the growth of whiskers on his jaw. The only way to persuade Megan to forgive him was to prove her innocence. And if she was guilty? He wanted to believe she wasn't capable of it, but he had seen her with the reivers before; he was certain she could kill if she felt it was necessary.

The same strength and passion that attracted him so powerfully were what made him suspect her. She was the first woman he had ever met whom he felt was capable of anything, and she probably had greater ability to do it than most men. His fists clenched in annoyance and impatience. She had been his until he had messed it up. He shouldn't have left. He should have stayed until he made her forgive him.

Sick of his own thoughts, Bryan opened the parcel of Leod Hume's things, given to him by Laird Hume, and was extremely disappointed with the contents. Letters. Lots of letters. Most of which Bryan could have done without reading. He was shocked. Even Cathy Armstrong had been rutting with Leod. He could think of no better place for the letters than the fireplace, but since they were all love letters—some fairly innocent and even sweet, others of a more lewd nature—he had to look for Megan in them. So, he ended up knowing far more than he wanted to about the women lodged at the keep.

He realized he would now have to talk to some of these women and reveal that he knew the nature of their relationships with Leod. He was not looking forward to it. It would be easiest to start with Cathy. He sent for her, and while he was waiting, tried to figure out how he would phrase his question.

"Cathy," he said in a strained voice when she entered. "Prithee, close the door behind you. This is a private matter."

She raised her eyebrows and obeyed. "A private matter, Warden?"

"Aye, have a seat." He gestured to the chair across from him.

She sat down and gave him an enormous smile. "What can I do for you?"

"I . . . uh . . . have some letters . . . written by you."

"Me?"

"To Leod Hume."

Her eyes widened.

"Now, I am not concerned about what went on between you and Leod," he said hastily. "What I am interested in is what he might have talked about while you were . . . visiting."

She yanked at the sides of the crisp white hood that covered her hair, her dark eyes averted. "We didn't talk verra much."

He waved his hand at the pile of letters on his desk. "Were you aware Leod had so many other . . . interests?"

"Aye, everyone was." She was no longer smiling, but sullen.

"I need your assistance, Cathy," he said, allowing a note of pleading to enter his voice.

Her expression softened, her smile returning.

"I don't mean to dredge up anything that is unpleasant or hurtful to you, but I need to find out who killed Leod. With so many lovers, could his killer be a jealous woman? Or husband?"

"I couldn't tell you if it was another woman who killed him, but it wasn't a husband."

"How can you be certain?"

She raised her eyebrows. "Leod was many things,

but he wasn't stupid. He steered clear of the married ones . . . until they were widowed, that is."

Bryan leafed back through the stack of letters on the desk. "All these are from widows?"

She shrugged. "I know not, but I'm sure many of the widows he laid with wouldn't be able to write. So likely there's more than you have there. And then there's the . . . others."

Bryan looked up from the stack of letters. "Others?"

She was twisting a kerchief in her hands. "Well . . . not all of them—or so I've heard—were willing."

Rory had mentioned this also. Bryan leaned forward across the desk. "What mean you by that? Did he rape them? Or force them to be his doxies through blackmail?"

"Both." She looked as if she might say more, then shook her head.

"Cathy, I pray you," he said gently. "Tell me."

She sighed and her voice shook slightly. She wouldn't meet his eyes anymore, but stared down at the kerchief she was wringing. "He and I, well, we had a falling out one night. He said to me that if I wasn't more . . . pleasing . . . in the future I would find my cottage raided."

Bryan's throat was tight. "Did he mention who might be doing the raiding?"

She shook her head. Bryan rested his chin on his hand. He would have to interview all of these widows now. What the hell had that man been up to? Other than running some kind of personal brothel on the East March. His killer could very well be some widow who did not like his tactics. One face immediately came to mind, and he shook his head to make it go away.

He folded his hands on the table. "How did your relationship with Leod begin?"

"My husband was killed by Cedric Forster during a raid. Leod began to stop by frequently to see to my welfare. Things just . . . happened." She was blushing furiously.

"Did Leod make any efforts to capture Cedric?"

"Aye. He said he was going to catch him and hang him."

Bryan hesitated over the next question, but thought it necessary. "How did your acquaintance with Leod end?"

"He began to frequent another woman and stopped coming around." Her voice was bitter and angry.

"Was this woman recently widowed?"

She nodded.

"A raid?"

"Aye."

He had humiliated her enough. "My thanks, Cathy, for your help. I have no more questions." She stood to leave, but he suddenly thought of another, more important one. "What was your opinion of Leod?"

She smiled. "He was verra sweet most of the time. Even after our affair ended, he continued to protect me. I wasn't raided again until you arrived, Warden."

After she left, Bryan read the letters more carefully. There was a pattern, though the majority of them were undated. Leod seemed to jump from one newly widowed woman to the next. After a frantic shuffle through the stack, Bryan satisfied himself that

none of the letters were from Megan. But Sir Thomas
Kerr seemed to believe Leod had no reason to lie
about his paramours. Bryan could understand why
Kerr thought that, since it appeared many women had
fallen to Leod willingly. Could Megan have been one
of the unwilling? She had brawled with men bigger
than herself on two occasions that Bryan knew of and
come out the victor. What would the outcome have
been if Leod had attempted to rape her?

The clouds were thick and dark overhead. Bryan
hoped the sky wouldn't open up on them before they
returned from the market. A pen had been built, and
he was taking Rory and Willie to Edington to purchase sheep. There was an old woolshed in the garrison that Bryan had the men fixing up so they could
make their own cloth.

It had been several days since his conversation with
Cathy. In that time, he had questioned all of the widows living in the keep. Each one of them had had
some sort of relationship with Leod. Some had tried
to lie until he set their letters before them. Most had
been willing participants. One revealed she had been
raped, and two others he suspected were unwilling
parties, but refused to speak of it. All of them had
been approached by Leod an unseemly amount of
time after their husband's deaths. And Cedric Forster
had killed most of their husbands.

Bryan, Rory, and Willie entered the village, making
their way past merchants selling meat and vegetables
on stalls, the mercer selling his cloth, and still others
displaying metalware. The beasts were at the far end

of the street. Bryan set Rory loose on the man selling sheep.

Willie and Bryan stood at the fence watching Rory haggle with the sheep vendor. They couldn't hear over the bleating, but Rory appeared to be angering the man.

"Willie," Bryan began. He spoke lightly, wanting to ensure this was a friendly conversation. "Were you aware of Leod Hume's dealings with the widows in the march?"

"Aye."

"And why did you allow it to continue? Did you not see anything wrong with his doings?"

Willie sighed, his hand rasping across his gray whiskers. "Since they didn't object, what was I to do? Leod didn't like people in his business."

"What happened to those who found themselves in his business?"

Willie met his gaze gravely. "They found themselves dead in a raid."

"Was Innes Dixon in his business?"

"Aye."

Bryan shook his head, frustrated. "Why haven't you come to me with this before? You're my deputy, but I don't feel as though I can trust you. I fear before long I will have to dismiss you."

Willie's face was grim. "Do what you must, sir. I was only trying to keep you out of Leod's business, as well. If I were you, I'd let dead men lie. He deserved whatever he got. He was a wicked man. I don't know what he was involved in, but it was more evil than he was, and I think it overpowered him. He killed more innocent men than I'd care to count, though he didn't strike the death blows himself. I'd say his murderer was a hero, and if caught I will not be party to their punishment."

Bryan was taken aback. "I'm finding I tend to agree with you, but just the same, a warden was killed. There are other channels to remove a corrupt official than murder, and 'tis not an example I want being set on my march. I am the warden now. I won't have folks thinking they can do away with me whenever they like."

"You're a fair man, Warden, and the march is better for having you. But you're too soft. These men don't think twice about killing if someone stands in their way. You must decide the appropriate battles to fight. Your successor may not be as good a man as you are."

Bryan mulled over Willie's words. Sometimes he also wondered if this was a battle better left unfought. If it weren't for Bothwell's direct order to find Leod's killer, he might be tempted to take the deputy's advice.

Willie cleared his throat. "I feel 'tis my duty to inform you, sir, Douglas Hume is a wee bit disgruntled with you. I'd have Rory sleeping in your chamber from now on and mayhap even hire another guard."

"What? Why?"

"The cotters are losing confidence in him. You've thwarted two raids and recovered all of the victim's possessions. That doesn't usually happen. And the watch you've sent out has been keeping the peace. You're taking the bread off his table. He can no longer collect protection money from the widows who moved into the keep."

"Good," Bryan said, allowing himself a moment of smug satisfaction.

"I heard," Willie continued, "when he went to see

Megan yesterday, she refused to pay him. She thinks mayhap the Kerr raid was Charles Hume's way of taking revenge on her. She told Douglas now that the people have a real warden to protect them, the Humes should find someone else to blackmail."

Bryan was both pleased and alarmed. He was proud of Megan for standing up to Douglas and refusing to pay the money, but he was worried that the laird might seek further retribution on her. "When we return to the garrison I want you to send some men to Lady Dixon's. They are to stay there until I give them further instructions."

Willie nodded. A ragged brown dog barked and ran into the flock of sheep. They began bleating and milling about, kicking up a cloud of dust. Bryan waved his hand in front of his face to clear the air. Through the cloud he saw the sheep merchant yank his hat off and throw it on the ground, yelling at Rory.

"When is Tavish due to return?" Bryan asked.

"I'd say the end of the week. He's been gone over a month. I didn't think he'd be away so long."

"How did Leod and Tavish fare?"

Willie was thoughtful. "They were close, I'd say. He took Tavish with him on most business. I was left to run the garrison."

"Did Tavish leave before or after Leod was murdered?" Bryan said, suspicious of the mystery deputy.

"Before. He goes to see his brother every year. Nay, Warden, it wasn't him that did it, of that I'm sure."

Then Tavish wasn't a likely suspect, though Bryan didn't discount him totally. He wanted to speak to him, especially if Leod took him on his business, whatever that was. It seemed Leod's business had little to do with protecting the march.

"When we return to the garrison I want you to send a messenger to his brother, requesting Tavish return immediately as I need his assistance in the murder investigation."

Rory returned, grinning broadly.

"Well?" Bryan asked.

"I got a very good price. In fact, I purchased the entire flock. He said he'd have them herded to us, but I told him we would do it ourselves. I had the feeling he might pluck a few out for himself."

Bryan glanced over Rory's shoulder and saw the merchant in animated conversation with his shepherd. He was making lewd gestures at Rory's back.

Rory said, "While Willie and I are readying the sheep, there's some business you might be wanting to attend." He nodded behind Bryan.

Bryan turned. Megan, Cora, and Innes were down the next lane talking to a fish peddler. Megan was even more beautiful than he remembered. Her hair was in a thick golden plait. She looked tall and slim in a blue wool gown. His eyes lingered on the smallness of her waist, the full curve of her breast, remembering how he had held her in his arms and touched her. His arms ached to hold her again.

The brim of the floppy hat she often wore shadowed part of her face, but he could see her brows draw together as she argued with the peddler. Innes said something, and when she looked down at him her whole face lit up as she laughed. But then she looked in Bryan's direction. When she saw him, her expression became bland, and she turned away.

*　*　*

He was here. Megan felt sick. So were Rory and Uncle Willie. She felt like a harlot after how they had seen her in the warden's chambers. She didn't want to see Bryan again, but there he was, standing by the sheep pens, staring at her. She quickly turned back to the peddler. She decided to take the fish for whatever price he quoted. She just wanted to get away.

"Lady Dixon?"

She closed her eyes, taking a moment to compose herself. She turned to him. "Warden," she said coldly.

"Warden!" Innes cried and ran to him. "Mum said you were not coming to see me anymore!"

He looked at Innes hesitantly. "Megan," he said, dropping the formality, "I must speak to you."

"I'm busy."

"A moment of your time. I won't take any more."

"Go on," Cora said. "I'll see what the mercer wants for his canvas."

Cora knew Megan didn't want to see Bryan. But Cora and Marie had both been at her, expounding unendingly on all the warden had to recommend him as a husband and trying to convince her to encourage his affections rather than repel them. Megan glared at her mother-in-law for her underhanded trick. Cora merely smiled and grabbed Innes's hand, dragging him away. Innes looked back at them in confusion.

Bryan moved closer. It was a warm day, even with the sky overcast, but it was her nervousness that was making her perspire. She wasn't ready for this confrontation. The hurt was still raw. "There isn't anything to talk about," she said, tucking damp strands of hair under her hat.

"There is." He took her elbow and steered her away

from the people milling in the street. He stopped at the sheep pen.

She looked up at him expectantly.

"How are you?" he asked, gesturing to her face and midsection.

She touched the scab near her brow self-consciously. "Fine. I told you it was nothing."

He glanced around, as though to be sure no one was eavesdropping, then said in a low voice, "I've learned a great deal about Leod over the last few days. I think he deserved whatever he got."

Dare I hope? She tried to hide the surge of happiness his words created. "Does that mean the investigation is closed?"

"Nay." He shook his head, his dark eyes regretful. "It means the decision about how I deal with the murderer depends on the reason they killed Leod."

Her bubble of hope burst, and was replaced with incredulity. "Are you still trying to induce me to confess? Because this little talk is completely transparent; the fact that you would even broach the subject with me is astounding. Don't speak of it to me again unless you plan to act on these accusations."

His shoulders slumped as she swung away, but he caught her elbow again. She was of a mind to make a scene, screaming and kicking him, but she turned back stiffly.

"He raped you." His voice was low and his gaze probing.

She was speechless. Did he know? Or was he seeing if her reaction gave her away? She worked to control her expression. "Who told you that?"

"I've been told many things, and one was that you

and he were lovers." He still held her elbow and tried to draw her nearer. She resisted.

"That is a lie!" she said loudly. "And if you believe that you're an even bigger fool than I thought you were."

"I don't believe it. I never did. Well, not entirely. But he wanted you. And he was known to force the unwilling. Did he force you?"

She couldn't speak, could think of nothing to say. His intense gaze bore into her, willing her to tell him all, but it was beyond her to admit it, for that would mean thinking of it. She felt hysteria rising and fought for calm.

Seeing she wasn't going to answer, he began to speak quietly, "If I were to find that a woman who had been raped by him was his killer . . . I would forget."

Indignant rage filled her and her fists clenched. He was not going to give up on it. No matter what she said or did, he would never believe her. "Death is too good for a rapist, Warden. Were I to exercise justice on a rapist, it would be through castration! So once again, *I did not kill him!*"

Thundered rumbled overhead, punctuating her words. He released her arm and she walked away. She felt his eyes on her back, and she held her spine straight and her head high.

The weather did nothing to improve Bryan's black mood. He was soaked to the bone and shivering by the time he and Rory reached the garrison. The rain fell in sheets, completely obscuring his vision. Willie had taken the sheep and holed up at one of the Hume farms. He would follow Bryan and Rory in the morning.

They went straight to Bryan's chambers, leaving a trail of water behind them. Two enormous men were stationed outside his door. He frowned at them, but they didn't try to hinder him. His room was illuminated when he entered. A fire blazed and candles were lit. A pair of shiny black boots with silver and gold spurs at the heels were propped on his desk.

"Ah, Bryan, you have finally arrived." His cousin, Francis Hepburn Stewart, the fifth Earl of Bothwell, lowered the letter he was reading to smile at Bryan. His long brown hair was pulled into a love-lock at his nape, and his mustache and short beard were immaculately barbered.

"Cousin . . . how unexpected." Bryan nodded to Rory, giving him leave to retire for the night. Rory left, closing the door behind him.

"What is this?" Francis waved his hand, indicating the pig snoring loudly in the corner. "I didn't realize the garrison was in such disrepair it was necessary to stall the livestock within the keep."

Bryan went to the bedchamber to change. "The pig was a gift."

He heard Francis's boots clomp as he stood and followed Bryan. When clad in warm, dry clothes, Bryan asked, "What is it, my lord?"

Francis gave a little laugh. "You flatter me with such pretensions. 'Milord!' " he mimicked. "I've only come to visit my cousin. Am I not allowed such pleasantries?"

Bryan raised an eyebrow, knowing this wasn't a

social visit, and not in the mood to ferret the true reason out of him.

Francis's gaze swept the bedchamber. "Is this the best accommodations you have?"

"Aye. You're welcome to my bed tonight, I will sleep elsewhere."

"Hmm. I think not. I shall continue on to Jedburgh and stay at the royal lodging."

"That's a long ride in the rain. Surely my garrison is not so base you can't bring yourself to stay with me."

Francis shook his head. "Nay, I have a matter to discuss with Sir Thomas Kerr. I am receiving many complaints about him harassing the English. Do you know anything of this?"

Bryan turned away, not willing to be the earl's snitch. "Nay. He seemed a fine warden when I met him."

"Oh, pah! You are so honorable. I know you, Bryan, and the man had to have set your teeth on edge. He's a beast."

Bryan opened the door. "Send one of the servants with refreshment," he ordered the earl's guards who were still standing outside the door. The men were borderers and didn't take kindly to being ordered about by anyone but their master. They both glared at him, then one of them nodded curtly and started down the hall.

When he turned back Francis was at his desk reading Leod Hume's love letters. He laughed and began reading aloud, " 'Oh, my love, if only to feel you inside me one last time.' Who is this lass?" He scanned to the bottom of the paper. "Cathy Armstrong, aye? I shall have to pay her a visit. She must be very lonely with Leod being food for the worms, aye?"

"I doubt it, since he discarded her long before he died."

Francis looked at the letter with new interest. "Oh? Did he hurt her, know you? Abuse her, perhaps?"

"Not that I'm aware of."

"Does she have reason to hate him?"

Bryan sat in the chair across from him, frowning. "What is this all about?"

Francis stroked his beard, smiling wickedly. "I have a way with women, mayhap she would speak to me."

"What way with women? You're a lech."

Francis set the letter down and sighed expansively. "You never change. Always so serious! Your father wasn't like that, you know."

"The last time I saw him he had little to jest about."

Francis smoothed his mustache thoughtfully. "That is because Uncle James was a warrior, not a statesman. He foolishly thought the sword mightier than the word. I know better."

Bryan couldn't help grinning. "Do you plan to ravish the king?"

Francis looked momentarily ill. "I fear our good *Queen* James might enjoy that too much." He eyed Bryan thoughtfully, lips pursed tightly together. "We have a problem."

"We?"

"You and I."

Bryan crossed his ankles and leaned back in the chair. "What is our problem?"

There was a knock on the door. "Enter," Francis called before Bryan had a chance to. He smiled apologetically. It was Lauren bearing a tray with cool ale and honey cakes. She set it down on the desk and bowed her head to Francis.

"Leave us," Bryan said.

"Thank you, sir," she said in a voice barely above a whisper and hurried out of the room, never raising her eyes.

Francis continued to look at the door after she left. "Who is she?"

"She's married, my lord."

"Married?" he cried, then sighed deeply and turned his attention to the plate of honey cakes. He picked through them until he came up with a large, odd-shaped one. He took a big bite of it. "Very good!" he exclaimed in surprise.

"Our problem?" Bryan asked impatiently.

"Your sister."

"What? Anna?" Bryan's older half sister was a Beaton and no relation to Francis. She and Bryan had never got along as children. They were both bastards, but Anna always felt she was better than Bryan and had christened him "Devil's Spawn." She called him nothing else for many years. It had been nearly a decade since he'd last seen her. He'd been meaning to send her word of his return, but couldn't bring himself to write the letter. He tried to recall something pleasant about their relationship, but simply couldn't.

"Has Anna not been in contact with you?" When Bryan shook his head Francis scowled. "Damnation! What is that woman up to?"

"What?" Bryan asked in exasperation.

"She came to me a sennight ago. She said I wasn't the rightful heir to the earldom." Francis paused to watch Bryan closely before continuing. "She claims your mother and father were handfast, and that makes you the legitimate heir. Did your mother ever mention such a thing to you?"

Bryan shook his head. "Nay. When did my mother tell her this?"

"On her deathbed. She wanted Anna to right your father's wrongs. She claims your father threatened to kill her if she came forward with this information."

Bryan frowned deeply. "I don't believe it. Why then have I never heard of it? Of what threat was there after he was outlawed and imprisoned? Anna is foolish. She means you harm. She was always malicious."

Francis relaxed. "I agree. So you have no intention of pressing your claim?"

"God's blood, Cousin! As if I would! I wouldn't live long after making such an announcement. Nay, I am no threat to you."

Francis smiled. "Very good." He raised an eyebrow. "Anna has become a beautiful woman, but she still reminds me of the nasty bairn she always was. Didn't she do something to that hound of yours? Jasper, was it?"

"Aye," Bryan said grimly, "a fine example of Anna's humor, digging up corpses as a jest." He pushed the ugly memory away. "When she came to you, what did you tell her?"

Francis gave him a level stare. "I told her if her handfasting tale were true, I would rid myself of you."

Bryan had a sudden, frantic urge to look over his shoulder.

Francis's serious countenance broke into an amused grin. " 'Tis what everyone expects me to say, so I hate to disappoint. Don't worry, Bryan. I wouldn't kill you. I still need you. Have you any idea who murdered Leod?"

Bryan waved his hand at the stack of letters. "One of them likely. He was a rapist, too, it seems."

Francis nodded. "That sounds like Leod."

"I don't suppose you could do me a wee favor?" Bryan asked.

Francis raised his brows in question.

"I need men and money. The king's treasurer has refused my request. Is there anything you can do? Persuade him to reconsider?"

Francis slammed his fist on the table. "This is extortion!" When Bryan began to protest, he laughed and stood. "You're still so damn gullible! Aye, I'll see what I can do. I'll even lend you some of my men."

Francis was pulling on his fine wool surcoat when Cathy entered, looking especially pretty in a new dress with her hair pulled on top of her head. "My lord." She did a clumsy curtsy before Francis, who had stopped putting his coat on to smile at her.

"The pleasure is mine. How might we help you?" he asked, moving closer.

Her cheeks were turning pink and she turned to Bryan. "I readied a room and a bath for his lordship to pass the night with us."

"My thanks, Cathy, but the earl isn't staying the night—"

"Nonsense!" Francis cut him off. "After the lass has gone to such a bother o'er me, how can I refuse?" He took his coat back off and draped it over his arm.

"Please, pretty Cathy, show me to my room."

He gave Bryan a lecherous smile on his way out and Bryan caught his arm. "How's the countess?"

Francis gave him a narrow look. "Very well, thank you."

Bryan could see reminding him of his wife wasn't going to stop him. "She's under my care, Francis, do you understand?"

"Perfectly," he said, but he wasn't really listening; his eyes were fixed on Cathy's swaying hips.

Bryan let his cousin leave, not in the mood to defend Cathy's honor. Perhaps Francis was right. It was true that he had a way with the lassies. Francis would probably get more information out of Cathy through seduction than Bryan had through interrogation.

He thought of what Francis had told him, and how he had been concerned enough to make a personal visit in the pouring rain. Bryan had no wish to be earl. He wondered what kind of mischief his sister was planning.

Ten

Megan and Johnny rode out together collecting rents. Marie and the wean were doing well, and Johnny didn't want Megan out alone after the Kerr raid. She did feel better with his presence near. Bryan had sent some men from his garrison to guard her house, and they resisted all her efforts to send them home. She supposed she was grateful, since Johnny was one of them. They did help her rest easier at night. Douglas Hume had paid her a personal visit and had been very angry when she accused him of shirking his duty to her and indulging his son's petty desire for revenge. She could trust no one. It was disheartening.

Ever since her encounter with Bryan in Edington, Megan had been unable to stop thinking about Leod—and all he had done to her. She tipped her face up, letting the breeze cool the heat of humiliation from her cheeks. It was a beautiful morning. After two days of heavy rain, the sun was shining and every-thing was green and blooming. Drops of water sparkled on the grass and leaves. Their horses sped across the Merse at a lope. The pace should have been invigorating, but Megan could derive no pleasure from the beauty.

She came out of her thoughts enough to realize Johnny was watching her worriedly. He was surely aware of the parallels between the recent Kerr raid and the raid in which Innes had been killed.

"What has happened to you, Meg?" he asked.

"What do you mean?"

"You've changed . . . since Innes died."

Shaking her head, she said hesitantly, "Leod Hume happened to me."

"Tell me."

Johnny had been Innes's best friend. Innes's confidant. If she couldn't tell him, who could she tell? "He . . . he came to me . . . after I gave birth to wee Innes. I didn't want to go on living after Cedric murdered Innes. But Leod convinced me that it was a betrayal to Innes's memory not to be strong and raise my son. Be the laird my people needed."

Johnny looked surprised, clearly not expecting to hear good things about Leod.

"I was grateful to him at first. He *was* the new war-den. He swore to protect my child and me. He made me feel safe."

She smiled thinly at Johnny's confused frown. She knew this went against everything he knew and heard about Leod. "Then he tried to extract payment for these kindnesses. When I was unwilling, he tried to force me."

Johnny paled. "Did . . . he . . . ?"

"Not at first. I cracked his ribs the first time, and he stayed away, but he kept coming back. Then one day he told me he could make Cedric leave me alone—that he could have Cedric killed—for a price."

Johnny's mouth dropped open in shock. Megan smiled slightly and shook her head. "Aye, that was the price he named, but fash not, I didn't pay it . . . willingly at least. I paid in coin instead. When I found out he took my money and never intended to kill Cedric, I confronted him. We argued and he . . . he raped me."

Johnny let out a slow breath. "I don't understand, Meg. I can't believe any man could get the best of you. I mean, you fought him off for years."

"This time was different. . . . He had a knife to my throat and threatened to kill my son."

Leod. How she had hated him. She could feel no remorse at his death. She only wished he had been alive when the scavengers had picked those lovely blue eyes out. He was always so sure of himself, confident he would never be punished for abusing his position. How had Bryan guessed that he had raped her?

"Meg . . . I'm so sorry. I never should have left you to him. I should have stayed."

She could hear the guilt in Johnny's voice, and she knew he felt as though he had failed her late husband. She shook her head vehemently, regretting telling him. "Nay! Then you wouldn't have met Marie and had a son. You had your life and I had mine. Innes never expected you to give yours up to protect me."

She gave him a tight smile and his frown deepened. They arrived at a stone cottage and she dismounted, glad for something to do before he asked any more questions. The occupants came out to greet her. She noticed immediately something was wrong. They looked frightened.

"Is something amiss, Elliot?" she asked.

Elliot's wife poked her head out the doorway. She was an English Selby and from what Megan had heard, she had actually been of some consequence before Elliot stole her heart. Now she lived in a tiny cottage. They always seemed happy, though. Now they looked anything but.

"Aye, m'lady," Elliot said. "We dinna hiv the rent. We've barely enough to feed ourselves."

Johnny was still on horseback, but drew closer to hear their exchange.

"What hardship has befallen you?" Megan asked. "The crops have been good. Have you sustained a raid I am unaware of?"

" 'Tis the Humes. Charles was here and he raised the price of protection."

Megan was speechless, and Johnny muttered an angry oath. Elliot became flustered, apparently thinking they were unsatisfied with his excuse. "Please dinna evict us. We hiv nowhere to go."

She shook her head. "Of course I'm not going to evict you, Elliot. But why did you pay it?"

"Ye know what happens when ye dinna pay."

Johnny spoke up. "We now have a warden who won't let such things occur."

Elliot became even more upset. "Charles said he thought we would be having a new warden ere long."

"Is that so?" Megan was incensed. She had a mind to go to Douglas Hume herself. Charles was taking this too far, and his bug-eyed father was turning a blind eye. But at the moment she was more concerned with the threat to Bryan's life. And she knew he hadn't hired any more guards. All he had was Rory. *The fool.* He didn't take this seriously. He found the rotting corpse of the last warden in the woods and still didn't think it could happen to him.

Johnny spurred his horse forward.

"Johnny! Wait!" She quickly mounted and rode after him. He slowed impatiently for her. "Where are you going?"

"The warden must be informed," Johnny said.

Megan chewed her lip thoughtfully, then came to a decision. "Go back to Marie. I will warn the warden."

Johnny looked as if he might protest, but Megan knew that was where he wanted to be, with Marie and his new son. Spurring her horse forward before he could stop her, she raced for the garrison.

Bryan received two messengers in his chambers. Rory was with him, sprawled in a chair. They were both young lads and appeared very hostile toward each other. At one point, before Bryan had the opportunity to address them, their shoulders touched and they began shoving each other and yelling obscenities.

Bryan pushed them apart. "What is the meaning of this?"

They glared at each other. They were both tight-lipped and not about to reveal the source of their dispute.

"What message have you for me?" Bryan asked the redhead.

"I am only to tell you in private. I certainly cannot say it in front of this scum."

The other boy was vaguely familiar with his curly black hair and blue eyes. Bryan asked him, "Can you reveal your message in this lad's presence?"

"Aye, sir." He proffered a letter.

Bryan broke the seal and read it, staying between the lads. It was from Sir John Forster, warden of the English Middle March, announcing the Day of Truce. It was a time when wardens of opposing marches came together to judge offenders and mete out justice. It was to be held in a sennight at Windygyle. Included was a list of offenders from Bryan's march who had allegedly committed offenses against the English Middle March.

Bryan gave the dark-haired boy a closer perusal. "Are you a Forster?"

"Aye."

"Any relation to Cedric?"

"Aye," he sneered.

"You are dismissed."

The boy took his time leaving, giving the redhead evil looks the entire time. Bryan was suddenly uncertain he should let the redhead leave at all with a Forster apparently after him. Rory closed the door.

Bryan stood in front of the redhead, arms folded across his chest. "What is this private matter?"

The boy looked at Rory uncertainly.

"You can say it in front of him. It will go no further."

"I've been sent by Lord Francis Russell. He requests a private meeting with you."

"Does he? I don't know a Lord Russell."

"He is son-in-law to the English Middle March warden, Sir John Forster."

Rory shook his head, indicating he didn't think it was a good idea. Bryan was inclined to agree. What would Sir John's son-in-law want with Bryan?

"Has he told you what this meeting pertains to?" Bryan asked.

"Aye. It is about the disappearance of Leod Hume. He said he owes the Earl of Bothwell a favor and that this makes them even."

Bryan was interested now. "When does he want to meet?"

"At the Day of Truce. I am to tell him what you look like, although all have heard you are a giant, and he will seek you out. He cannot be seen speaking to you. It could cost him his life and yours."

"Tell him I agree to this meeting."

The boy turned to leave and Bryan stopped him. "Stay here tonight. I don't like you going with that Forster lad out there. He has it out for you."

The boy grinned, showing a row of square, white teeth. He pulled an enormous knife from his boot. "Just let him come after me. I cut 'is 'eart out."

Bryan nodded approvingly and allowed the lad to leave. But as soon as the door closed Bryan turned to Rory. "Did you see that dirk? This place is an asylum! God help me!"

Rory laughed and Bryan shook his head, returning to his desk.

"What think you of that?" Bryan asked.

"I know not, but he didn't want the Forster lad to hear. That's interesting."

"Aye." He rubbed his chin contemplatively, wondering what kind of information Lord Russell had for him, when there was another knock on the door. Bryan rolled his eyes. "What now?" he asked under his breath, then, "Enter!"

He stood when Megan entered.

"Good day, Warden, Rory."

Bryan was so pleased he didn't know what to say. He could tell she had been riding hard by her flushed cheeks. Golden tendrils escaped her braid to curl around the slim column of her neck. Rory started to leave, but Megan held up her hand to stop him. "No, you should hear this, too."

Bryan sat back down, realizing she was there on business.

"Douglas Hume is putting such a squeeze on my tenants that they can't even pay their rents. He's also made some veiled threats to your life. I came to warn you to be on your guard."

"I will have a word with the laird of Leadwater about his black rents. I don't like it."

Megan gave a quick shake of her head. "I don't think that's a good idea. He wants to kill you."

"Surely he seeks to kill me secretly, not while I'm on an official visit."

She looked at Rory incredulously, then turned back to him. "Do you not understand, Bryan? *He wants to kill you.* You will disappear, just like Leod, and the next warden will find you rotting in the woods."

"You have little confidence in my abilities."

She threw her hands up in the air. " 'Tis not you! I have very great confidence in Douglas Hume's ability to murder!" She shook her head. "Take care of him," she said to Rory. Her hand was on the door to leave.

"Don't go!" Bryan stood. Her shoulders stiffened. Bryan nodded for Rory to leave. When Rory was gone she turned back to him, her face carefully expressionless.

"Why did you come to warn me?"

"Because I think you're a good warden and it would hurt the march to lose you."

It meant a great deal to him to hear those words from her. He walked around the desk. She didn't back away, but raised her chin a bit to meet his eyes. If anything, his feelings for her had grown stronger. Her courage touched him deeply, and he desperately wanted to make amends for how he had hurt her.

"Can you ever forget what a fool I've been?"

"I know not." Her face was still unyielding, then suddenly, her expression broke the smallest bit. "I . . ." Her lips hardened again as she tried to give words to what was bothering her. "Forgive me, for my brazen actions when I came here before. I am not a wanton, and I can't believe I acted in such a manner. If it isn't too late, I would ask that you and the others, my uncle and Rory, speak of it to no one."

He closed the distance between them, grabbing her arms. He could wrap his hands completely around her slim biceps. "It is I who should be on my knees begging your forgiveness."

She pushed against him. "Can we just forget it ever happened? I would like nothing more."

Her words cut him and he released her. She looked up at him, her clear green eyes watery. She was close to tears. He backed away from her, not trusting his own urges with her.

"Would you at least consider assigning another guard to your person?" she asked softly.

"I'll do better than that," he said, finding an outlet for his frustrated emotions, "I shall take Douglas Hume into custody."

"Are you insane?" Her voice was barely a whisper.

"Nay, it is punishable by death to collect black rents."

"So you're going to execute him?"

"I hope I don't have to. He will pay restitution to the cottars he took money or goods from. If he refuses, then I will hang him."

"Good Lord, Bryan! You must forget this foolishness."

"Why?"

"The Humes are a powerful clan. Douglas Hume isn't the only Hume lord on the march!"

"I know that, but the others aren't committing such flagrant crimes."

She was distressed and raised her hands to the sides of her head as though to help herself think straight. "You don't understand. They will avenge him. His wife is an English Graham. Do you want two such powerful clans vying for your death?"

"Do you hear yourself?" Bryan raked an angry hand through his hair. "This is why I must! I am the warden. Am I to live in fear of exerting the law? Then they shall get away with anything. They will wreak havoc on my march, and you suggest I huddle in the corner ignoring it?"

"Aye!" she yelled at him. "I don't want you to die!"

"That life is not worth living."

Her eyes were bright, her hands clenched in fists. "You are such a foolish man! All the wrongs in the world are not here for you to right! Do you not see? Innes wasn't looking to solve every problem and he died anyway. Look at you! You go out begging for it! *'Please, someone, assassinate me!'* "

She tried to open the door but he placed his palm against it, holding it shut. "You're wrong. Innes didn't lay down and take what was dealt to him, either. His death was no accident."

She whirled around. "What are you talking about?"

"It seems Innes was in Leod's business, although I don't know to what extent. But from what I've learned, even before Leod was warden, those who troubled Leod found themselves dead in a Forster raid."

He shouldn't have blurted it out, but he felt an overwhelming desire to justify himself to her. He couldn't bear her derision, nor being compared in any way with her saintly dead husband.

The color drained from her face and she began shaking. She pressed her palms over her eyes. "Oh God," she moaned.

He pulled her against him in alarm. "Megan, I'm sorry. I shouldn't have told you."

She pushed his arms away. "No! You should have told me as soon as you knew!" She glared up at him. "How could you even care who killed Leod, let alone try to punish them for it?"

"Megan—"

"No! It is justice that he is dead! I wish I had killed him! I wish he were alive right now so I could kill him again!"

He forced her into his embrace. He was not going to allow her to leave in such a state. She fought against him and finally began crying. Her fists were balled up against his chest, her face buried in his doublet. Her shoulders shook. He held her tightly and whispered soothing words to her.

She turned her face so her cheek lay against his shoulder. She wasn't crying anymore, but she sniffed a few times. "Don't kill Douglas Hume." When he didn't answer, she raised her head to look at him. Tears stained her cheeks and her long blond lashes were clumped together.

He pulled a kerchief from his waist and wiped her face. "I won't have to if he cooperates, and I hope he will if he knows the alternative is death."

She sighed and pulled away. "I have to get back."

"I will make him and his son leave you alone. I promise. They will bother you no more."

She said nothing.

He gathered his courage. "May I come see you? Afterward. To tell you how it went?"

She averted her eyes. "Bryan," she whispered in an obvious protest. He touched the satin skin of her cheek and she didn't stop him. "I don't want to feel this way." Her voice was almost inaudible, her lashes lowered.

"Mayhap it would be easier if we didn't have these feelings, but we do, and I can't just stop mine."

She met his eyes for a moment, then opened the door and left. He realized, with a small smile of satisfaction, that she hadn't told him he couldn't come.

 Eleven

Bryan had a score of men assembled in the bailey, ready to ride out to Leadwater to confront Douglas Hume. He had been told Douglas could command as many as three hundred men and that he could have them in the saddle in as little as half an hour. If things went well, Bryan hoped to come to an alliance of sorts and perhaps those men could be at his disposal, too. But he wasn't setting his heart on it. Not if Douglas wanted him dead.

A rider entered the gates just as Bryan was slipping his foot into Arthur's stirrup. It was the messenger sent to fetch Tavish Marshall.

"Warden!" the messenger shouted. He vaulted down from his horse, racing to Bryan's side.

"Aye?"

"Tavish Marshall never visited his brother."

"What?"

"Aye, sir. His brother said he received a letter from Tavish several months ago stating his intention to visit, but he never arrived."

"So we have another missing officer," Bryan mumbled. Except Leod wasn't missing anymore, he was dead. And Tavish was gone. "I think we might have located our murderer."

Rory nodded. "It doesn't sound good for Tavish."

Bryan wanted to act on this new information immediately, but he didn't have the time and Tavish could be anywhere. He could have left the country by now.

Bryan ruminated on this development as they headed for Leadwater. He wanted to be finished with this Douglas Hume business as quickly as possible. He had every intention of going to Megan tonight, even if he showed up after everyone had retired. She had come to him, to warn him. She had been worried about his safety. He was beginning to see the reason for her reluctance. She had lost one husband because he was warden. She didn't want to make the same mistake again. He would prove he was more careful than Innes.

He was roused from his thoughts by the sight of Hume keep in the distance. The brown stone tower rose against the dying light of the late afternoon, casting a dark shadow behind it. People were rushing inside the gates, the portcullis lowering unheedful of them. By the time Bryan and his men reached the walls, the wooden doors had been slammed shut. Bryan couldn't lay siege to the castle, even if he went back and rounded up all of his men. Diplomacy was in order.

"Laird Hume!" he called.

There was movement on the ramparts. Douglas Hume's head peeked tentatively from an embrasure in the battlement. "State your business, Warden."

"I come only to talk. I know you to be a man of intelligence who doesn't like to live amongst strife any more than I do."

"Then talk. I can listen from here."

Bryan exchanged a look with Rory. "Very well." Rory moved closer, his hand clutching the butt of his pistol. Bryan regretted not wearing a jack or chain mail. Perhaps he was being foolhardy. He was an easy target for an arrow. Rory's thoughts must have been running along the same line, because seconds later he ordered one of the larger men to remove his jack. It was handed to Bryan along with a metal bonnet.

"I request that you return the payment you have forced the people of the march to pay you. They are no longer in need of your protection." The jack was a bit snug through the shoulders and the sleeves came to just above his wrists. He struggled to hook it in the front.

"I beg to differ, Warden," Douglas called down. "That money is owed to me."

"The penalty for collecting black rents is death."

Douglas's laughter traveled down to Bryan. "Are you going to execute me, Warden?"

"If you force me to."

An arrow whistled through the air and landed in the ground next to Arthur. Arthur was a well-trained warhorse, accustomed to galloping headfirst into swords and pikes, and only snorted at the arrow.

"That wasn't very friendly," Bryan called. "I've been told you mean to take my life. I've written a letter to King James, informing him of your insolence. I have already spoken to the Earl of Bothwell, who was sore angry to hear of your lack of honor. I was hoping you might give me reason to retract my statements. But it seems I am mistaken." It was a lie, but if he left alive he intended to make it a reality.

There was quiet on the battlements. Douglas peeked his head out again. "Forgive, Warden. One of my men's hands slipped. It won't happen again."

"That's good to know. I am prepared to negotiate with you. Mayhap we can come to an agreement that will help compensate you for your lost income."

"I'm listening." Douglas was now hanging through the embrasure, unmindful of his safety.

"I've been told you can raise three hundred men on horseback in less than an hour."

"You heard right."

"Lord Bothwell has convinced the king to increase my subsidy. With this sum, I will appoint deputies and land sergeants to cover the march more effectively. Outsider or not, I'm not going anywhere. You can keep trying to kill me, or you can help me. You can't be warden, Laird, but you can be my deputy. You know how it works: I call on you and you raise your men to assist me in defending the march. What say you?"

There was a long silence, and Bryan wondered if he was conferring with someone. He waited patiently, his hands folded across the saddle horn. A slow metallic creaking began as the portcullis was lifted. The laird ducked his head and walked out the gates. He waved his hand, indicating for Bryan and his men to enter. He was grinning.

Relieved laughter and some admiring comments rippled through the ranks of Bryan's men. Bryan was feeling relieved, too, and pleased that his plan had worked, until Rory said, "Just don't turn your back on him, it could be a ruse."

"Well," Bryan said grimly, "we shall see."

Megan was in that shadowy place between wakefulness and sleep. She had been thinking of Bryan when she laid her head on the pillow, wondering if he would come to her as he had asked to. He hadn't, and she should have been relieved. But she wasn't. She was bitterly disappointed.

What she wanted and what she needed were in such direct conflict she didn't know what she was feeling any longer. Her judgment had become flawed. She wanted Bryan. But her family, and her heart, needed stability. Someone who wouldn't hurt them, however indirectly. Her family—Innes—was her priority. She must put all these fancies of loving a warden from her mind.

Her thoughts shifted and came back to him anyway, when she was too sleepy to care about anyone's needs but her own. She saw images of him, felt his kisses and embraces, but they were a ghostly, gossamer touch that made her ache for the real thing.

Then his palm was against her cheek and it felt real, firm. She turned her face into it. She opened her eyes in fright. It *was* Bryan. He was sitting on the edge of her bed. Her gaze darted around the room, searching for Cora, who usually slept with her, then remembered that her mother-in-law was sleeping with Marie's new baby. They were alone.

A candle was lit on the table nearby. He was looking at her with warm brown eyes. There was no mistaking what he was thinking. Her blood ran hot.

"How did you get in here?" she whispered. She was mortified at her immediate arousal, but as she came fully awake, her surprise at his presence quickly dissolved into anger.

"My men are guarding your home."

"Who gave you entrance?"

"Johnny."

"He certainly didn't invite you into my bedchamber!" She sat up and backed away from him. It was too hot for a quilt and she had only a thin sheet on her bed that she pulled up to her neck. "Do you mean to blacken my name more? So mayhap no one will ever have me?"

He sighed, but didn't move away. "Forgive me. I meant to be here earlier. But Douglas wanted me to stay for dinner, then he insisted I play a game of chess with him." He rolled his eyes. "I thought I'd never get out of there."

"What are you talking about? I though he wanted you dead?"

"Aye, he did. But we came to a compromise. He is my new deputy warden and has promised to return your tenants' payments."

Her mouth dropped open in astonishment, anger and indignation forgotten.

He grinned at her, his dimples deeply indenting his cheeks. "I'll be taking my men home when I leave, as you have no more need of them. He won't be seeking retribution."

"I can't believe you did this! And with no bloodshed!"

"I brought you something, too."

"For me?" she squeaked in surprise and pleasure. *A gift!*

He held up his finger and left the room. She stayed in bed, waiting. She wore only her thin night shift. It was sleeveless. The throat-tie was undone and gaping, exposing the tops of her breasts. She gathered the sheet higher, but her awareness of her scant clothing made her skin tingle. He was here, as if she had dreamed him up in her sinful mind. In her bedroom. In her bed, if she wanted him. She felt breathless and hot, and knew she wanted him. More than anything she wanted him to love her.

This wasn't good, she realized, but her body had its own ideas. She was conscious of the sensuous feel of the linen against her skin. Her breasts seemed fuller. She could even feel the softness of her own hair against her bare back. He returned, shutting the door quietly behind him. He was holding something behind his back. Her awareness of him was heightened, too. His broad shoulders, the sheer muscular length of his body, the thick, dark lashes.

"What is it?" she whispered, excited.

He sat on the bed again and brought the gift around from behind his back. It was a puppy! And so small it fit in his palm with its snout hanging off one side of his hand and its tail the other.

"Oh!" she cried, dropping the sheet and taking it from him. She cradled it against her breast. It made soft little whimpering sounds. It was covered with silky white fur.

He pet its head with one finger. " 'Tis a wee lassie. Douglas was going to kill her, her being a runt and all.

She couldn't get any milk from her mum because the other pups are so much bigger. So I took her. You don't mind? I noticed you and Innes have no dogs, and bairns love pups, so I thought—"

"I love her and so will Innes." She got out of bed and laid the puppy gently on her pillow. A basket was on the floor by the door. She lined it with a folded quilt. She lifted the sleeping pup, rubbing the incredibly soft fur against her cheek, and lay her in the basket.

Bryan watched her silently. She sat beside him on the bed.

"I should probably go," he said, but didn't get up.

He was right; he should go. But she didn't say it. Instead she said, "I'm glad you came to share your news."

His eyes darkened, and his gaze traveled down her body and back up to her face. His look was so hot it was almost a caress. " 'Tis late and I've disturbed your sleep. There will be talk if it's known I came to you so late. I've done enough damage to your good name." But still, he didn't go. Her heart thumped violently in her chest. Was he waiting for her to do or say something? Would he leave if she didn't? She wanted him to take her, to fold her up inside of him, so she could forget who he was for this moment. But she could not say these things.

He held her gaze for what seemed an eternity, until she was certain he was preparing to leave her with a lonely ache for him. Then his hand rose to her shoulder, pushing the neck of her shift off her shoulder. She swallowed and let her eyes drift closed. His hand moved under her hair, along her back to cup her neck.

Her trembling was stopped by his mouth on hers, hard and demanding. He pulled her into the circle of his arms, his hands running over her back and bottom, his tongue parting her lips, coaxing a deeper response.

She curled her arms around his neck as he pushed her backward on the bed. She could sense his impatience, and it excited her. He gathered the material of her shift in his hand and pulled it over her head, then he was trailing kisses down her throat to the swell of her breasts.

"I should stop. I should leave," he murmured in a thick voice, then flicked his tongue over her nipple.

She whimpered in response. She couldn't breathe, let alone speak, but she couldn't let him leave. "No . . . stay," she managed to gasp between ragged breaths.

He rose to his knees and swiftly shed his doublet and shirt. He was smiling. The muscles of his abdomen moved beneath his skin. His chest and belly were covered with curling brown hair. She reached her hands out to touch him. His body was hard as rock and his skin hot. Then he was leaning over her again, taking her nipple in his mouth. She gasped and her back arched. His hand slid beneath her, pressing her closer to his mouth.

The warmth in her lower body tightened to a sharp ache as his tongue traced a burning line through the valley of her breasts to tease her other nipple to hardness. Her hands were in his hair, combing the soft locks with her fingers as she moved her body urgently against his.

He stopped kissing her and was moving rather awkwardly. He was trying to kick his boots off, but it wasn't working. One of his spurs caught on her blanket and they both heard the rend of fabric ripping.

"Oh . . ." he said softly, looking down at the blanket. He sat up and pulled the offending boots off. They thumped on the floorboards. He turned back to her, looking down at her body in the soft candlelight. She shuddered, wanting to close her eyes, but compelled to watch his slow appraisal of her body. Breathing became an impossible task. The desire in his eyes was wild. She held her arms out to him and he came to her. She opened her thighs to him, her hands pulling him close. His mouth was warm as it moved over her belly and ribs. His weight pressed her into the mattress.

"God, they're so long," he breathed against her jaw as he caressed her legs. She was in a frenzy of need when he finally entered her. He pushed into her, harder and deeper with each thrust. She started to cry out when his hand clamped over her mouth.

"You've a houseful of people . . . guards outside . . . the window is open," he panted in her ear, then kissed her, pushing his tongue into her mouth. His whiskers scraped her skin. His hands slid beneath her bottom to bury himself deeper. When he finally spent himself she had to bite his shoulder to keep from crying out.

They lay exhausted, the sweat-soaked sheets tangled around their legs and the cool air from the open window drying the moisture on their skin. Her head lay on his chest.

She stretched languorously and lifted her head to look at him. His eyes were closed, the thick lashes lying against his cheeks. A small smile curved his lips, dimpling his cheeks. What did he think of this? She had been so absorbed in herself, her own wants and longings, she hadn't spared a moment for his feelings. Men were so casual about sex. Her heart twisted at the thought of this night holding no meaning for him. But she knew that wasn't how it was with him. If he was like that, he would have wanted her to cry out so all his men below knew what he was up to. It would save him the trouble of bragging about it later. But he was protecting her.

His eyes opened. "What are you looking at?" he asked, closing his eyes again, his smile growing. He was rather pleased with himself. His hand was tangled possessively in her hair, and he forced her head back down to his chest. She found herself smiling, too, and closed her eyes to sleep.

Bryan didn't rest much. It had been years since he had slept on a feather mattress and he tried to make the most of it, but he kept waking with her beside him, in his arms. He would only mean to gaze upon her or kiss her gently, but she was warm and yielding and he would take her again. The sky was beginning to lighten when he finally reined himself in. He had to return to the garrison. He didn't want to. He looked down at her. Her blond hair was tangled over the pillows; her eyes were open and guarded. He kissed her lingeringly and when he pulled back she smiled.

"I have to go." He slid out of bed and began dressing. "I have much to do today, but I will be back soon."

She sat up, a sheet covering her, to watch him. "Maybe we shouldn't be so obvious. . . ."

He grinned lasciviously. "Would you rather me stay away until we are wed?"

She flushed and lowered her eyes. "Of course not." She plucked at the blanket a few times before asking abruptly, "Did Tavish kill Leod?"

She must have heard this news from Johnny, since Bryan had refrained from mentioning it to her until he had more evidence.

He slipped a boot on. "It does look bad for him."

She was silent for a long time, then asked, "Am I clear?"

"What do you mean?"

"I mean, do you finally believe I am innocent?"

Something in her expression made him uneasy. He hesitated. Why did this conversation seem painfully familiar? Had not another woman taken him to her bed only to gain his trust? And had he not given it to her completely? Without so much as a question? Would he play the fool again? He didn't know for certain that Tavish killed Leod. Perhaps it would be better for them to avoid the subject until he knew something definite.

"What's the matter, Bryan? Can you not give me an answer?"

"Tavish is my primary suspect, aye."

"Meaning, there are still other suspects?" She was withdrawing from him, huddled against the wall, her golden hair like a veil covering her shoulders and breasts.

There was no way to go about this delicately. "Megan . . ."

"I can't believe this," her voice was choked with emotion, "how can you . . ." She bit her lip and continued staring at him. Her green eyes were enormous.

"Don't misunderstand—"

"No. I understand perfectly. I made a mistake. Nothing has changed at all." She had herself under control and her expression became unyielding. "I need your trust."

He gripped her bare shoulders. "Trust is something that must be earned. You have lied to me before and you know it. You ask for trust but you don't give it."

Her eyes blazed. "Let go of me and get out," she said through clenched teeth.

He released her shoulders and stood, shocked that she was ordering him to leave. What was happening dawned on him with painful clarity. Unless he told her he believed her, there could be nothing between them. She did not love him. He had kept his own declarations of love to himself, sensing she wasn't ready to hear them. Fool that he was, he had never suspected she would bed him merely to gain his trust, even though he had fallen into this trap before. The old feelings of betrayal flooded him. He was such a gullible fool! He had talked himself into this, whether he realized it or not. He had rationalized her behavior to death until he cared no more. This was the consequence.

He glanced down at the pup, not wanting Megan to see the desolation in his eyes. It was still sleeping soundly, curled into a little ball. "So that's what this was? Do you feel anything for me?"

Her gasp of indignation filled the room. "How dare you imply such a thing! I can't forget that you believed I killed Leod. I need your trust. Every time you look at me, I have to wonder what you see? A woman or a murderer?"

"Megan, it's not what you think—"

"Then tell me I'm innocent!"

"Megan—"

"Tell me!"

His teeth clenched, keeping in the words he wanted to say to make things right. "I can't. I hope you are. I hope Tavish did it. But Leod raped you—I would be a fool if I thought you'd allow him to live after such a violation." He stood and grabbed his doublet. "How could you make love to me with no intention of wedding me?"

"Do you think I wanted this to happen?" she asked.

"Oh, so I forced you now, did I?"

Her lips drew into a thin line. "Just what are you saying?"

She was making no sense and it only fueled his anger. "I'm not saying anything! I'm trying to understand you!"

"You think I would do such a thing? Love a man willingly in my bed, then cry rape when it was through? You think this of me as well as murder and blackmailing you with my body?"

He gaped at her, trying to collect his thoughts. How could they have gone from making love to having this absurd argument? He did not want to lose her. He loved her. Yet he seemed to have no control over this situation, and he was quickly losing ground. He was no longer certain of the assumptions he made only a few moments before, but still he felt wary of her.

"I see you can't answer my question," she said coldly. "Get out of my house and take your men with you."

"Megan, I don't think such things of you—"

"Bryan, leave! Don't make this difficult. Be gone!"

He left, closing the door quietly behind him. He felt anger, shame, heartbreak, confusion, and the emotions were so mixed up he wanted to hit something. How was it she made him feel like a blundering lad who hadn't a clue what he was doing? Rory waited for him in the stables. His very presence was annoying. Arthur was still saddled and he swung himself onto the horse. Rory quickly mounted his to follow, but Bryan turned to him, angry. "Leave off!"

"But, sir—"

"I said leave off!" He spurred Arthur and rode away, leaving Rory staring after him.

 Twelve

The sounds of the waking garrison drifted to Bryan's chambers where he slumped behind his desk. Rory had come trailing in earlier, and Bryan sent him to bed. Realizing he had been left to himself, he decided to make the most of it. Curly and Pellinore followed him out. He spied Lauren creeping into Rory's room, the lad's clean laundry piled up so high in her arms only her big eyes peeked out. Willie didn't make her serve anyone but Bryan; she saw to Rory's needs of her own will. And Rory hadn't a clue who did it all. He had commented to Bryan on more than one occasion that some lass working at the garrison had taken a fancy to him, but he never suspected it was Lauren. Which was probably for the best—Willie would not be pleased if he knew.

Bryan pretended he hadn't seen her and continued on his way. Few others were awake at this early hour,

but one or two were walking bleary-eyed through the
hall, readying the room for the morning meal. The
main gate was well guarded, so he went to the postern
door. Johnny Oliver stood sentry at the gate.

"Open the door," Bryan ordered.

Johnny stepped in front of the door. "Sir, I can't
permit you to leave." His face was grim with his duty.

"On whose orders?" Bryan asked, annoyed that he
couldn't even go for a walk alone unchallenged.

"Rory Trotter."

"I am the warden, Mr. Oliver, and I want to leave.
Open the door."

"Uh . . . I'll send someone to fetch Rory for you.
'Twill only take a moment."

"God's teeth! Let the lad sleep and let me alone."

"Sir," Johnny said, stepping in front of him again
when Bryan tried to walk around him.

Bryan glowered down at the guard in a way meant
to make him back down.

Though Johnny looked anxious, he held his
ground. "Meg-er, Lady Dixon asked me to watch your
back."

Johnny's words deflated Bryan's annoyance. "Very
well. You can join me."

They were both silent as they walked down the hill
the garrison sat on. Curly grunted softly with each
step and Pellinore ran far ahead of them.

"Do you see?" Bryan asked, turning to Johnny.
" 'Tis naught more dangerous than a mere walk."

"Just because Douglas Hume is no longer a threat
doesn't mean there aren't others who want you gone.
After four years of Leod's lawlessness, you can't help
but make enemies in droves. Leod had many friends.

Most will bide their time, waiting for the moment your guard is down."

"Did you serve Leod?"

"Nay. I served Innes Dixon when he was warden. After Innes was murdered, I stayed on a few months with Leod before hiring myself out for war."

"But you came back."

"Aye, I did. I love the march, beastly as it can be, and I was missing it. The Low Countries were no longer safe for Marie. I only came back to the garrison when I learned of Leod's death. I am honored to serve such a great warrior."

Bryan laughed. "Now I doubt the sincerity of your words. Where have you heard such rubbish?"

"I served under the Prince of Orange in the Scottish regiment. The stories of your valor were widely told by men who had served with you."

Bryan had seen little of the old regiment after moving into the prince's service. Johnny's gushing praise was almost embarrassing. Valor! The word used to describe him brought shame to his heart. He had been weak and divulged secrets to the enemy. There was no valor in that. He shook his head. "We were mercenaries. I killed men for money in wars that weren't my own. Valor. Nay, had I valor I wouldn't have been a paid killer."

"Just the same, all heard of your prowess in battle. And in the end, you know as well as I that we weren't mercenaries. I didn't see a penny in payment those last few years and I doubt you did either. I stayed for the prince."

Bryan grabbed a stick. "Pellinore!" The dog's head popped up from the grass. He tossed the stick, and

Pellinore bounded after it. He could not admit aloud that the opportunity to kill Dons had been payment enough for him. "There was enough senseless killing, I did naught worthy of such reverence. Look to those who solve their problems without bloodshed if need you a hero."

"I think you're wrong. There is only one solution as far as the Spanish King is concerned, and that is the complete extermination of Protestants. You can't tell me it isn't heroic to fight to live as you believe."

Bryan laughed again. What ideals! And after the lad had already been through the bloody, starving war. Perhaps he could learn a thing from this young man. Pellinore came jogging up to him with a stick and Bryan took it from the dog's mouth. It wasn't the same one he threw. He dropped it before Johnny noticed.

The sun was rising in the sky, dispelling the dark from the air. But the light around them still had a soft, rosy glow, and there was a bite to the breeze. It felt good to Bryan and helped clear his head.

"So you served Innes Dixon?"

"Aye." Johnny's mouth turned down at the corners. "And he was a good friend."

Bryan wanted to ask questions about the deceased warden, but was afraid it might be inappropriate. He knew Johnny and his wife, Marie, were staying with Megan. Perhaps he could tell Bryan something useful in his pursuit of the woman.

"I think Innes would be pleased with you." Johnny's light blue eyes were filled with amusement. He removed his helmet and tucked it under his arm, grinning. His long fair hair was pulled back into a love-lock.

"I know not of what you speak."

"Surely your intentions with Meg are honorable? I can't think of a better match."

"I'll wager she could."

"Sir?"

Bryan shook his head. "She won't have me. I suspected her of murdering Leod . . . she can't forgive me for that."

Only the rattle of Johnny's chain mail filled the ensuing quiet.

"Besides," Bryan added, a little bitterly, "I am not so saintly and perfect as Innes Dixon, so I probably am not good enough."

Johnny laughed shortly. "Innes was not a saint, but he did love her. She oft chided him to be more careful, but he rarely heeded her words. Innes, God rest his soul, wasn't a very good warden. Not for lack of trying, don't misunderstand; he did put great effort into it. But he was a borderer and felt he must resort to the border ways to maintain control. It was a bloodbath when he was warden."

That shocked Bryan. He had an image of Innes in his head that was beyond reproach. Perhaps that was because Megan saw Innes that way. "So he wasn't a fair man?"

"That's not what I said. His policy was an eye for an eye. But imagine the chaos it created when every damn clan in all of the marches felt duty-bound to avenge every slight. There were so many threats on Innes's life that if Cedric hadn't killed him he wouldn't have lasted long after. And Innes was always riding out alone, unprotected, something he and Meg were at odds about." Johnny shrugged. "At least you try to solve the disputes without bloodshed. Enemies you may have, but not like Innes. And you've already overcome the disadvantage of being an outsider. The men have confidence in you."

Bryan eyed Johnny consideringly. He could use an ally in Megan's camp, and she would be pleased to hear he was heeding her advice. "So," he said casually, "Lady Dixon asked you to watch my back, aye?"

A week passed before Bryan saw Megan again. He had been unable to contrive a meeting with her, until now. Thanks to warden business he was finally given the opportunity. When he rode into her courtyard, he spied two young men hitching a fine ox to a cart. He didn't remember that ox.

She was leaving the stable with something held close to her neck. A little white tail wagged between her hands. Her eyes passed over him, then lit up when she saw Johnny and Rory. She waved at them with a big grin. Annoyance knifed through Bryan.

"Is there something I can help you with, Warden?" Megan asked when he rode Arthur beside her and stared down at her upturned face. She squinted slightly against the sun behind him.

"Aye, I have a list of offenses you've been charged with against the English Middle March. You must needs be present at the Day of Truce."

She shaded her eyes, still holding the puppy against her neck. "You could have told me that in a letter."

He climbed off the horse to stand in front of her. "But I didn't. And I have more questions for you."

His shadow fell over her. She lowered her hand and

stared at him uncertainly. Her blond lashes swept down as she looked at the puppy.

"Mary's doing well. She drinks lots of milk, and I've gotten her to eat some egg."

He stroked the silky fur of the puppy with one finger. "Mary, eh?"

One corner of her mouth turned up in a smile. "Innes wanted to call her Bryan."

"May I?" He held out his palm. The pup began whimpering, but he quickly held her against his chest and she calmed.

Once in the house she brought him some ale, which he didn't really want, but took a drink anyway. Her slim, wool-covered arms were crossed beneath her breasts. She watched him warily. "Why did you come?"

"I told you, I have a list of charges filed against—"

"I asked you to send Willie."

"How unfortunate it slipped my mind," he ground out, angered at her aloof demeanor.

She stared at him for a long time. "I trust you aren't going to recite my crimes from memory."

He pulled the letter from his belt and handed it to her. She began reading and shaking her head. She laughed at one point, then exclaimed, "What rubbish!" She dropped it on the table. "This is going to cost me."

"Aye, and I can't help you with most of them, though I might be able to get them set aside." He opened the letter, cradling the now sleeping puppy on his forearm. "The Selbys can't prove your kine are eating their grass, so 'tis your word against theirs. And I think you're lying. How you plead is up to you, but I will stand behind you." He considered her a moment. She was still standing straight, her arms crossed and chin lifted defiantly. He pointed to the door with the letter. "That ox . . . 'tis the one in the letter, aye? I don't recall seeing that ox before."

She shrugged. "He's been in the fields."

He cleared his throat and with a quick flick of his hand, straightened the letter back out. "It says here, 'The widow Dixon is charged with the theft of one ox, stolen from Cedric Forster.' "

"He's mistaken."

"I'm not stupid. Don't speak to me of my life being in danger when you're reiving oxen from your husband's murderer."

She was stoic.

His temper flared. If anything, the cold wall between them had grown thicker! He was wasting his time. He tossed the letter on the table. "Well, just be ready to answer for the charges. Unless you stop lying to me I won't help you."

"And if I were honest, would you defend me and allow me to keep my ox?"

He stroked the silky white fur of the pup. "Am I to protect you as Warden Forster protects Cedric? Is this what you ask of me?"

"No. Because you are perfect. You are God of the March, handing down judgments on what you see as right and wrong. I ask naught of you!"

God of the March? Was that how she saw him? He put on no airs. He only tried to do what was right. Just because he loved her didn't mean he could allow her to steal beasts at her leisure.

"You're right if you think I don't understand your

definition of what is right and wrong. It is wrong to kill and steal, and it doesn't make it right simply because it's been done to you first." He handed her the sleeping pup and turned to leave.

"The ox isn't mine," she said quietly.

He turned back slowly. Her cheeks were pink, and she was looking down at the puppy. She laid it in a basket near the wall.

"But I happen to know Cedric's been picking off my kine. And I've lodged many complaints against him as well, but naught ever happens. Every so often, a few of us whom Cedric seems to harry the most ride out and take some back." Her face was completely red, all the way up to her hairline. She took a deep breath and raised her chin. "So now that I've told you the truth, has anything changed? Can you help me? Are you going to take my ox away?"

His relief was enormous. They were finally getting somewhere. "Nay," he said. "You've had that ox since I've been warden."

"I thank you," she said stiffly. "If that's all, I'll see you off."

He paused. "No, it's not all. I told you I have some questions for you."

She raised a brow expectantly.

"I've been asking around about Tavish, what kind of man he was, and what reason he might have for killing Leod."

She closed her eyes and sighed heavily. "I know not, Warden. I will be honest with you, it seems very unlikely to me that Tavish killed Leod. He was a rather harmless . . . useless deputy. More like Leod's pup, the way he followed him around. He was quiet." She swallowed hard, her face becoming tight. "He was a watcher, that one. He didn't participate in all Leod did, but he took pleasure in seeing it."

A wave of nausea went through Bryan as he realized what she was saying. *He was a watcher.* Tavish had stood by watching while Leod raped Megan. His hands curled into fists; the desire to get his hands on this deputy who stood by while Megan was violated was nearly overwhelming. When he found Tavish, murderer or not, the man would pay for not aiding Megan. But he couldn't say these things to her; the chasm she had created was too wide.

He cleared his throat, continuing with his questions, "And he was about the same size as Leod? He'd be able to wear his clothes?"

She nodded stiffly. "Aye, all but the boots."

This confirmed all Bryan had already heard about Tavish. Everyone was ready to lay Leod's murder on Tavish, yet no one could come up with one possible motive. Apparently, Tavish hadn't even been the violent sort.

Bryan scratched his head thoughtfully. "It just doesn't seem likely that Tavish killed Leod. Perhaps something happened to him on his way to visit with his brother?"

Her mouth flattened angrily. "So what now, Warden? Am I under suspicion again?"

He closed the distance between them. "No. I came to seek your counsel on the matter, not accuse you."

"Well, I gave it to you." She started for the door and he caught her arm.

"That's not the only reason I'm here."

Her jaw was set. She stood still, not looking at him, waiting for him to go on.

He was unaccustomed to this coldness—she had scalded him with her tongue on many occasions, but this freezing civility was unsettling. He released her arm. "I have been thinking about . . . the other night."

She turned her back on him and paced the length of the room. "I think we should both forget about that."

Bryan followed and hesitantly placed his hands on her shoulders. "Nothing has changed for me. I can't forget it . . . or change how I feel."

She turned slowly. He kept his hands on her shoulders, drawing her closer. He wanted to embrace her, to kiss the lips that had softened as she gazed up at him sadly.

"That's the problem, Bryan."

"What is?" he asked softly, his eyes on her mouth.

"That your feelings haven't changed. You don't have a murderer and you don't trust me."

She gently removed his hands from her shoulders.

He watched her walk away and knew she was right.

Anna Beaton looked down at Lord Russell's sleeping face. He had been so easy to seduce. She dressed quickly, anxious to get back to Cedric and tell him what she had learned. Her body was still flushed with lust. She felt sorry for Lord Russell's wife. He had no idea how to prepare a woman for lovemaking. No matter. It had been over quickly enough.

She had the horse at a gallop riding for the cottage where Cedric waited, her excitement growing. She met him there several times a week to report her progress. He had given her a special assignment, and she had done well. He would be very pleased.

When she arrived he was waiting for her, as he always was, by the fire. She removed the scarf from her head.

He turned. "Well?"

"You were right. He knew," she said. "He knows everything, but I couldn't determine how. . . . It seemed inappropriate to keep talking."

His dark eyes narrowed. "Then why are you here? Why did you not stay with him until it was appropriate?"

"Because he's married! I didn't want his wife to catch us."

He scratched his chin, looking straight through her. She was annoyed. He should be pleased. She brought him what he wanted.

"What about Bothwell?"

She nodded, moving closer to him and the warmth of the fire. "Aye, he is loyal to Bothwell for some reason, but he wouldn't tell me why. I spoke evil words against the earl and he became angry."

Cedric's brows raised. "Indeed?"

She smiled coyly and knelt in front of him, her hands on his knees. "Well, only for a little while." She pulled at the laces on his breeks. "Shall I go back to him? Find out more for you?"

"You'd like that, eh?" His eyes were cold. He grabbed her hair and kissed her, ravaging her lips. "You are a slut. You do not care who you get it from, so long as you get it."

"I want it from you now," she said, eyeing his mouth.

Desire smoldered in his eyes. She knew he hated such weakness in himself, and that made her feel powerful. He dragged her to the bed and took what he wanted.

 Thirteen

The English still hadn't arrived at Windygyle when Megan rode to the top of the hill. She searched the ranks of men in jacks and armor, most wearing metal bonnets. She saw many familiar faces and several raised their hands in greeting. There were so many! Megan usually absented herself from Truce Days, but it still seemed an uncommon amount of Scots to her.

She saw Bryan at the center front of all the men. Rory was beside him, and Johnny was behind him. Johnny had told her that Bryan appointed him a personal guard. This information had caused an argument between Johnny and his wife, but Megan was pleased Bryan was taking his situation more seriously.

The Humes were present in force, circling Bryan and his men. On his other side was Sir Thomas Kerr, replete in a metal breast and back plate, his helmet resting on his knee, and surrounded by his thugs. There were even more Kerrs than there were Humes.

She rode behind the crowd. She had debated with herself on whether or not she should come to the Truce Day. She would have to face Bryan sometime, and in the end, that was what made her decision, the desire to see him.

The crowd blocked her view of the enormous stone cairn that sat on the hilltop. When it was in sight she stopped to look at it, wondering who had built it and how long it had been standing there. Quelling the desire to go exploring, she pushed her way through the men until she was behind Bryan. Rory grinned and urged his horse to the side so she could be beside Bryan.

"Good morning, Wardens!"

Bryan turned to her in surprise, and Kerr leaned forward. He ran his tongue over his teeth as though trying to clean them.

"What brings the widow Dixon to the Day of Truce?" Kerr asked. "Is there a Forster to be hanged that I'm not aware of?"

She smiled sweetly. "Oh, I do hope so, or my travels will be for naught."

Kerr grunted, obviously annoyed his barb didn't find it's mark, and turned away.

Bryan's eyes raked over her possessively. His manner brought an immediate flush of pleasure to her cheeks. Images of the night they spent together crowded into her head, his mouth on hers, his arms around her.

"Did you come alone?" he asked her in a low voice.

"Aye, if I didn't come, you might think I was trying

to hide something. I want you to know I have nothing to hide."

"You shouldn't have come alone. Don't leave without telling me."

She rolled her eyes. "Please, Bryan—"

"I mean it!" His voice was still low, but there was a warning in it.

"Fine. I'll let you know my every move, sir. If I must relieve myself in the bushes, you can be certain you will be the first to hear of my intent."

"Good."

A smile tugged at the corners of her mouth, and she quickly looked away. The English topped the ridge in front of them. They stopped and aligned themselves. The Scots outnumbered them. That was good, since contrary to the name, Truce Days sometimes ended in battle.

Bryan was inspecting the English forces before him. Unlike most men, he was hatless. The morning breeze blew the hair away from his forehead. His face was lean and strong and darkly tanned. Although his dimples weren't visible when he wasn't smiling, their promise was always present in the faintest of lines beside his mouth. Even on horseback he was the tallest man in the entire cavalcade and probably the broadest. His eyes were squinted and all she could see were the thick eyelashes. His hands rested lightly on his well-muscled thighs, the reins wrapped loosely around his wrist.

The standoff continued for several minutes more before two Englishmen broke away and galloped toward the Scots. The riders stopped in front of Bryan and Kerr. "Do we have your word, Wardens, that peace will be maintained until sunrise on the morrow?"

"Aye," both Bryan and Kerr answered. The Englishmen turned and rode back. Once they had disappeared back into the ranks of English borderers, Kerr sent two Scottish riders across the valley to get the same assurance of peace from the English warden. Then the English and the Scots once again stared at each other. Finally, the snowy-bearded Sir John Forster raised his hand and Kerr gave him an answering signal. The English set out across the valley.

Megan had been to few of these, but this moment always set her heart beating. The Scots had suffered so much at the hands of the enemy across the border, seeing a company of them advancing was always a little frightening. When they were a few feet away, the wardens climbed off their horses and met in the middle. Bryan towered above the other two wardens. Kerr shook hands with the English warden and introduced Bryan, who nodded and smiled politely, shaking hands.

Once the wardens turned back to their men, the release of tension was like an enormous sigh of relief. English and Scots began to mix among each other until the field was a blur of activity. A table and chairs were removed from a wagon and set up on the field. The wardens, deputies, and men of respectability converged around the table to choose jurors.

Sir Thomas Kerr and Bryan stood in front of a group of Englishmen. Bryan had one of his arms folded across his chest and his other hand rubbed his chin thoughtfully. He stood before an Englishman and questioned him closely. Megan wanted to laugh. She knew what the holdup was: Bryan was going to interview each man before he appointed him to his jury. Kerr looked thoroughly annoyed, and periodically ran a beefy hand through his steel gray hair.

Megan shook her head, laughing to herself. Bryan was bound to puzzle the other wardens with his ideas of justice and fairness. The thought of his unflinching honor in the face of so much corruption made her heart swell. The powerful emotion left her confused. She had never felt this way about her late husband. Innes had never sent her heart racing with a look, inflamed her body with his touch, inspired such pride in her heart to watch him.

Musing on these feelings, she wandered through the groups of borderers waiting to be tried. Her own bills would not be called for some time, so she climbed back up the hill to the cairn. After so many years, the pale stones still held the huge slab of rock that served as the roof. She ran her hands over the stones and ducked inside. She couldn't stand up straight. She had heard that the cairns were where ancient people buried their dead, but Megan didn't see how anyone could know for sure.

She turned to walk out, but the opening was blocked. Her entire body tightened instinctively when she saw Cedric Forster. She looked for another way out, but unless she wanted to squeeze through the cracks in the structure, Cedric obstructed the only exit.

"Move!" she said harshly.

His slate blue eyes gleamed as he leaned over, his hands resting on the roof slab. " 'Tis the fair widow Dixon I've caught. What shall I do with 'er?"

She stared at him, trying to decide what to do. He wouldn't hurt her. Not only would it be a terrifically stupid thing to do at a Truce Day, but he'd had many opportunities in the past to harm her and had always refrained from it. Just the same, every time she saw him the memory came flooding back of his smiling face while Innes hung dead from a rope.

"Don't be frightened. I'll not 'urt you."

Her back was beginning to ache from stooping, so she knelt. Cedric squatted down, too. He picked up a large stone and held it in one hand as though weighing it.

"Let me out, Cedric."

"You still don't forgive me for your 'usband's death."

"You mean my husband's murder!"

"You won't believe this, but I'll tell you anyway. 'Twas not my wish that your 'usband die."

"You're right, I don't believe you. I was there, remember?"

He shrugged, leaning his head to the side to regard her, looking her entire body up and down. "I heard you've made yourself comfortable with the new warden. Leod would be very jealous. He fought long and 'ard for your prize. He would not like that you give it so freely to another."

"Leod is dead."

His eyes narrowed. "Mayhap he's a ghost. Ghosts have a way of striking back at those who've done them wrong."

"Leod was the wrongdoer! He was a rapist and a murderer! I am the only one who has been wronged!"

She surged forward in her anger, meaning to push him out of the way. He grabbed her wrists.

"Leod told me 'ow sweet you are and I didn't believe it." He pulled her closer, using her wrists. "Your warden cannot protect you forever. Keep the ox. I'll consider it payment for services yet to be rendered."

"What are you talking about?"

He released her and backed away so she could leave the cairn.

"I'm talking about Leod, sweet. He did not think you a whore, but you have proved otherwise of late, eh? I have taken the insult to my friend to heart—as he would."

His strange words confused and unsettled her. "You're insane. Leod is dead. There's no such thing as ghosts."

"That's where you're wrong, but ghosts are of our own making, are they not? You're too bonny to 'arm. I never could do it in the past, thinking you the innocent widow, a victim of the greater forces that move around us all. Since that is not so, mayhap you could give me some of what you spread around so freely."

Her hand shot out and smacked him across the face. The handprint glared white against his darkly tanned cheek, then turned red. It felt good to do it, so she smacked him again. He grabbed her wrist and squeezed until she gasped in pain.

"We'll have no more of that. I like it not."

"If you come near my home, I will kill you."

He was grinning as he walked away. Her wrist throbbed with the memory of his strength. She hurried

down the hill, back into the crowds, tripping and
almost falling on her face. She was trembling when
she finally reached Rory and Johnny. Borderers and
jurors swarmed the table where the wardens sat.

"What is it?" Johnny asked, frowning.

She shook her head, not trusting herself to speak,
looking furtively over her shoulder. She moved
between the two huge guards. Johnny still looked
concerned, but turned his attention back to the table.
What had Cedric been talking about? He wasn't the
brightest man, but neither was he stupid. Maybe he
was planning to raid her and this had been some kind
of warning. She could tell by the way he had been
looking at her, she was no longer safe from him. He
meant to harm her in some way.

And the rubbish about Leod! What was that? He
talks to his ghost? Perhaps Cedric was a bit touched in
the head. That made him even more dangerous.

"Sir Bryan, really, the lad should be executed," Sir
John Forster said, motioning to his men to hang the
thirteen-year-old boy. It was the redheaded messenger
who had been at odds with the Forster boy. Bryan
didn't know whether the boy was truly guilty or not,
but didn't mean to let him hang.

"No! It was just spurs he stole!" Bryan was becoming desperate and finding the cool, cultured Sir John
almost impossible to argue with. It didn't help that the
lad's life he was fighting for was English. Sir Thomas
Kerr was of absolutely no help to him and was, in fact,
pretending to be unaware of the entire conversation,
picking at something on the back of his hand.

The lad was being dragged to a nearby tree. Bryan jumped out of his chair and stood between the boy and the tree. "The spurs were returned. Why kill the lad? No harm's been done. Why not punish him? A few months in gaol? A heavy fine?"

Sir John gave Bryan a condescending smile through his well-groomed white beard. "I have no room in my prison, nor do the other wardens. Who shall pay his fine? He cannot, that is obvious. Come, sit down and forget this nonsense. We're putting him out of his, and our, misery. Left to live, he'd only become a broken man, killing and reiving."

The men advanced to the tree again, dragging the boy behind them.

"I'll pay the fine, whatever it is, and I'll keep him in my gaol."

Sir John sighed. "You cannot save all these young malefactors. He's just a thief. Once you release him from your gaol, he will likely bury a rusted knife in your back and leave you to die."

"Then that will be my fate." Bryan pulled the lad away from Sir John's men. The boy stared up at him with wide blue eyes, but said nothing.

Sir John shrugged. "Do your best, Sir Bryan, for all the good it will do you."

Bryan turned the boy over to his men with orders to keep a strict eye on him. The mysterious Lord Russell hadn't approached him yet, but Lord Russell was son-in-law to Sir John. As long as Bryan stayed around the English warden, it was doubtful Russell would acknowledge him.

He spied Megan standing between Rory and Johnny, looking uncommonly timid. Curious at what could have put such a look on her face, he joined them.

"Is something amiss?" he asked.

She nodded, and he was about to inquire further when a man's face appeared over her shoulder. The man's eyes met Bryan's with an intense, furtive look. Megan saw Bryan staring behind her and started to turn.

"Do not turn around, lass," the man said softly.

She looked up at Bryan quizzically, but obeyed.

"I must be quick. Cedric is following me. I don't understand how—but he knows something."

"You are Lord Russell?" Bryan asked in a low voice, glancing around to ensure no one was taking undue notice of their conversation.

"Aye."

"Your information?" Bryan asked. The crowd around them suddenly seemed to grow and become louder. There was a disagreement nearby, but Bryan ignored it. He wanted this information of Lord Russell's that was so important and dangerous.

"The body you found. It is not Leod Hume."

"What?" Bryan asked in a loud whisper. Megan's eyes widened. Rory remained stoic, but Johnny startled at the news, though he quickly hid it. There was movement behind Lord Russell, and Bryan caught sight of steely blue eyes staring directly into his. He panicked and tried to shove Megan out of the way to reach Lord Russell, but it was too late.

"Aye—" Lord Russell began, but a deafening blast cut him off. The crowd surged forward over Lord Russell and Megan. Bryan grabbed Megan's arm, trying to pull her out of the way, but Lord Russell fell on top of her.

Bryan moved to help them up, but his hand froze when he saw the huge, jagged hole ripped through Russell's back. Blood poured out of it, staining the dirt.

"Christ," Bryan breathed, his head jerking up to search for the culprit. It had to have been Cedric. That was who he saw behind Lord Russell. Cedric was nowhere in sight now. Scotsmen and Englishmen were screaming and fistfighting. A second later there was another gun blast, followed by another.

"Warden!" Johnny cried, pushing Lord Russell off Megan.

Bryan knelt beside her. She was moaning, and her back was covered with blood. Johnny rolled her to her side. Bryan first assumed she was covered with Lord Russell's blood until he saw the hole in her bodice. Terror seized him, and he feared to even touch her or move her. *Anything but losing her*. He could brave anything but that

"It passed straight through Lord Russell and hit her," Johnny was saying.

Bryan touched her face. "Megan, can you talk to me? How bad is it?"

"Not bad, I don't think." Her voice was strong.

"Tell me if I hurt you," he whispered. He lifted her in his arms. It was difficult for her to hold onto him. He had to get her away. The incident was turning into a pitched battle. The Scots broke away and ran for their horses. Sir Thomas was mounted, his armor buckled on, assembling Scots as the English raced for the border. Bryan was relieved. He hoped Sir Thomas planned to impose some calm on the proceedings.

A circle of unyielding metal pressed against his spine. He immediately recognized it as a gun barrel. Megan's head lolled on his shoulder, oblivious to the chaos around them. Bryan knew at such close range, the lead ball would not only rip a hole through his back but Megan would sustain another wound.

"Good day, Cedric," Bryan said quietly.

"Good day to you, Warden. I didn't mean to hurt the lass earlier. If you would kindly set her down, I could kill you without 'arming her again."

Bryan scanned the landscape in front of him. His highly paid guards were nowhere in sight. One of them was retrieving the horses, no doubt, but where the hell was the other? The Scots were lining up in a battle array to pursue the escaping English and paying no heed to what was going on with the warden of the East March.

"If I refuse?" Bryan asked.

Megan lifted her head. Her face was devoid of color and her eyes huge and green. Her pupils seemed a bit too large.

"I'll shoot you anyway."

"Why do you want me dead? What care you about me?"

"Not I, Warden, but someone you threaten wishes your demise."

Bryan dropped his arm that was holding Megan beneath the knees. Her feet landed on the ground, but he continued to support her with his other arm.

"I'm not leaving just so he can shoot you," she said.

"You're hurt. Go find Johnny and have him take you home."

She opened her mouth to reply. Her eyes darted

over his shoulder, looking beyond Cedric. "No!" she said firmly, her eyes on him again.

He mouthed "Rory?"

Her nod was imperceptible.

"This is very sweet," Cedric said, bored. "Well, then move to the side a bit, Meg, so I don't shoot you again."

"Can I not even say farewell?" she asked, stalling. Without waiting for Cedric's answer, she kissed Bryan. Her lips were cold and he could almost taste her fear.

" 'Tis a pattern, I suppose," Cedric was saying behind them, "me killing your men."

Megan glared at him over Bryan's shoulder.

"Don't look at me like that," Cedric said, amused. "Mayhap you and I—"

Megan yanked Bryan to the ground as the gun discharged. He was lying on top of her and quickly rolled off. Rory stood behind Cedric with a rope wrapped around his neck, choking him. The gun was on the ground and no one was hurt. It was obvious Rory had every intention of killing Cedric.

"Rory, no!" Bryan yelled.

Rory looked as though he might disobey. Cedric's face was crimson as he clawed at the rope. His mouth was open, but he made no sound. Rory released the rope, and Cedric fell forward. He made a horrible wheezing sound, but didn't try to escape.

Bryan knelt beside Megan. She was lying too still for Bryan's comfort. He heard a yell and looked up in time to see Sir Thomas Kerr leading the Scots in a screaming charge across the border to pursue the fleeing English. Hell was breaking loose and there was nothing Bryan could do about it. So much for Kerr imposing calm—he was the catalyst.

"Megan, talk to me," Bryan begged.

She turned her head slightly. "I'm fine. Just take me to Cora."

He lifted her in his arms. Johnny rode forward, leading the horses.

"Take Cedric to the garrison and lock him up," Bryan ordered, "then join me."

Johnny and Rory helped Bryan and Megan onto Arthur. Bryan held her close to his chest. He was filled with fear that she might not survive, that he was taking too long to get her to help. He dug his spurs into Arthur's sides.

Bryan paced in the yard, thinking about Lord Russell's last words. Why did Cedric care what Lord Russell was telling Bryan? Cedric had openly admitted he was trying to kill Bryan on someone else's orders. *Someone you threaten wishes your demise.* That someone also didn't want Bryan to have Lord Russell's information. *The body wasn't Leod's . . .* The march widows—Leod's lovers. Their husbands were killed by Forsters. What had Lord Russell been about to reveal when Cedric shot him?

Bryan was having a difficult time concentrating. His eyes kept straying to the house. What was happening in there? Was she dying? As soon as the thought occurred to him he quickly forced it aside. It wasn't possible. He would kill Cedric with his bare hands if she died.

The door opened and wee Innes ran out. "Grand-mum says she needs your help."

Bryan hurried into the house. Megan was still on the table with a sheet draped over her body.

Cora said, "Warden, I need you to carry her to her room."

"I can walk!" Megan's voice was strong.

Bryan lifted the sheet a little. She stiffened until she realized he was only trying to see the wound. Linen was wrapped around her ribs holding a wad of more linen in place. Blood stained it faintly.

"I'm fine. I can walk up the stairs by myself!" She sat up gingerly and swung her legs over the side of the table, clutching the sheet around her.

"If you try you'll tear out my stitches and bleed all over the house. Let the warden carry you and stop being so stubborn."

Megan didn't argue further so Bryan lifted her gently. She wouldn't look at him. He carried her upstairs and laid her on the bed. Innes and Cora followed them in. Innes had the little white puppy and placed it on his mother's belly once she was settled.

"I thought Mary would make you feel better."

Her hand covered the squirming pup, holding it in place. "Thank you, love. I feel better already."

Innes kissed her cheek, and then Cora shooed him out of the room. Bryan felt as if he should leave, too, but he didn't. He stood near the door as Cora busied herself around the room. She pulled a small table to the bedside and set a comb and mirror on it, then left. Megan still didn't look at him, looking instead at the puppy as she stroked its fur.

"Was it bad? Did the shot go deep?"

"Nay, Cora said it should be fine, so long as it doesn't become red and swollen. I think I will be about tomorrow. If Cora allows it, that is."

Cora returned with a bell, a cup, and books. She set the books and the cup on the table. "You ring this if you need me," she said and put the bell on top of the books. "Don't get out of that bed until I say so." She glanced at Bryan. "You make certain she minds me."

" 'Tis really not that bad," Megan said when Core was gone. "She just likes to fuss."

Bryan walked closer. "You should let her fuss. I'll wager you never let anyone fuss on your account." She gave him a small smile, and he was encouraged. He sat on the edge of the bed. "Are you still angry with me?"

"No."

He let out the breath he had been holding. His pleasure at her words was dampened by the fact that she wasn't smiling and was still intent on the puppy. He lifted her chin with his fingers. Her skin seemed so pale. Eyes like watery emeralds gazed back at him. A tear spilled over her lashes and made a trail down her cheek. He wiped it away with his thumb.

"Why do you weep?"

"I have been trying very hard not to think about you and me . . . about when we were together . . . thinking if I forgot it and thought not of you that I could bear it when you were killed. But when Cedric was going to shoot you . . . I just . . ." She shook her head, her lips trembling. "I'm afraid to go through it all again. It was so hard when Innes died . . ."

"No," he whispered, his throat tight, "you're not afraid of anything."

Another tear stained her face. "I am, Bryan. I'm so afraid."

She didn't want to love him. He understood why, but it stung. He slid his hand behind her, feeling only the smooth bare skin of her back. He drew her against him. She rested her cheek on his doublet.

He was a selfish man. He could see that now. He had been determined to force his wants and his will on her, without a thought to what she needed. She was right. She didn't need the kind of worry being the wife of a warden would bring her. Her son deserved a father who would be around. His chest hurt, but he knew what he had to do. There was nothing more important to him than her happiness. He was the barrier to it right now. He had to stop hurting her. But he wanted to stay with her and hold her just a little while longer.

"I have Cedric," he said, hoping to reassure her.

"I know."

He paused, wondering if he should share his suspicions with her. "I don't think Cedric is to blame for what happened today."

She didn't look surprised. "Who is to blame?"

"Leod."

She drew away from him, her throat working as she tried to swallow. Her head moved back and forth, denying his words. "Leod is dead."

Bryan took her hands in his, hating to see her so frightened. She feared nothing. The look of horror on her face was so unfamiliar he became alarmed. "Leod is alive, Megan." He spoke slowly, holding her hands tightly. "I will do everything in my power to find him and make him pay for all he has done."

Her eyes shut tight. "I thought it was over. . . ."

"Listen to me." He took her face in his hands, wanting to drive his words into her head, make her understand he would never let anyone harm her. "I *will* find him."

When she opened her eyes they were hopeful.

"Ah, Megan, do you trust me?" he breathed as he stroked her jaw with his thumb, wanting to memorize her face.

She nodded hesitantly.

Too late, he thought miserably. But he had made his decision to let her be. She deserved better. He knew he should walk away from her now, but he couldn't. She didn't want him to; he could see it in her eyes, feel it in the way her cheek pressed into his hand. Her face turned so that her lips brushed his thumb.

Her hand closed over his, holding it against her face. She pressed a kiss into the palm of his hand. *Oh God*. He couldn't walk away yet. He leaned toward her, meaning only to kiss her one last time. Her skin was cool and tasted of salt from her tears. Her lips parted, inviting. He plunged in, pulling her close, exploring the warmth of her mouth. She murmured his name, winding her arms around his neck.

He was pushing her backward, his hands on her body, pushing the sheet away to feel the round weight of her breasts, when he encountered the bandage. He broke the kiss, untangling himself from her arms. His breath was coming in gasps, his heart racing. *So much for good intentions*. He couldn't even be near her.

She looked at him in confusion, her cheeks flushed, her lips swollen from his kisses. Her lips parted and still inviting . . .

He stood abruptly. "Go to sleep," he whispered. "You need to rest." He pulled the quilt over her and left.

When Bryan returned to the garrison that evening, Francis was there. He sat at Bryan's desk with his feet propped up, stroking his mustache and beard.

"I heard about the Truce Day." He shook his head. "Why would someone want to kill Lord Russell?"

Bryan sat across from him. Pellinore was beside the earl with his snout resting on his thigh. Francis absently scratched the dog's head while regarding Bryan.

"It seems you were right, Cousin. Leod isn't dead."

Francis's feet hit the ground and he leaned forward, dark eyes gleaming. He smiled thinly. "Not dead. Good, I didn't think so. You must find him. Leod is mine."

Bryan eyed his cousin suspiciously. "I don't know what this is all about, but I still say it smells foul. Leod committed many offenses, and I intend to see him punished."

Francis didn't respond and went back to stroking Pellinore.

Bryan was thoughtful. "If the body isn't Leod . . . then it must be Tavish. . . ." The web only became more tangled.

"Perhaps that's why Leod ran? Because he murdered Tavish?"

Bryan shook his head. "Leod had nothing to fear if he killed Tavish. No one would have suspected him. I think he wanted someone to think he was dead. . . ."

He looked at Francis, and a chill suddenly went down his back.

Francis watched him, his eyes hooded, a small smile curling his lips beneath his well-groomed mustache. "Aye. I was wise to seek you as his successor, Bryan. I am well pleased with your performance." He slapped the desk and rose. "Well, done! Keep it up!" He grabbed his cloak and headed for the door. He paused. "Oh, and I'll be needing a detailed report on the incident at the Truce Day—no doubt our good *Queen* James will want to know all about it!"

Bryan sat for a long time after Francis left, filled with unease.

Fourteen

The morning silence was unearthly. All that could be heard were the thick slicing sound of shovels sinking into soft brown earth and the thudding as the dirt clods were thrown into a growing mound. The sun was beginning to dispel the dark shadows. Mist hung thickly around the men surrounding the grave marked LEOD HUME. Bryan was anxious to have this ugly deed done. He held a kerchief over his nose and mouth as the body he and Rory found in the woods was unearthed. Rory stood beside him holding the boots. Bryan had never thought to see if the boots found in the woods fit the corpse. It had been so scavenged and bloated, it had seemed pointless, but he could have at least made a relative comparison.

A collective moan sounded around the grave, and the diggers stumbled back a step, covering their faces. The body was quite ripe and crawling with insects. It had been wrapped in a shroud, but that hadn't stopped the persistent worms from burrowing their way in. That was all right; Bryan only needed one foot. He didn't even need to put the boot on the body, just compare the size.

One of the men was gingerly removing the rest of the dirt from the corpse with the tip of his shovel. Bryan knelt beside the shallow, rectangular hole. His gloves were already on, and he cleared the dirt from around the ankles. Pulling his dirk from his boot, he slit open the shroud. It released a new stench that almost had him gagging. He resisted the urge to step away for a brief respite. The bare feet were gray and mottled. Rory placed a boot in Bryan's outstretched hand. He slid it between the two feet, measuring the length.

The feet were bigger. Not by much, which accounted for no one noticing previously, but still too big to fit into the boots in Bryan's possession. He called the men around to witness, then stepped back, ordering them to rebury the corpse.

Rory and Johnny hurried after Bryan, who strode swiftly back to the garrison.

"It must be Tavish," Bryan said. "We'll have to change the marker."

Rory nodded.

"Did you have any problems with Cedric?"

"Nay, he came along docile enough and is locked up tight in the cellar."

"Johnny, fetch Willie for me," Bryan said when they entered the gates. Johnny ran into the keep. "Shall we visit with our guest?"

They went around the side of the keep. The garrison's excuse for a dungeon was a filthy dirt hole dug below the keep. Two men-at-arms were guarding the door and opened it for them. The ceiling was so low Bryan had to duck his head. The dirt walls were damp and mossy. Stone steps ended in an earth floor that was muddy from the prisoners' urine. Bryan's boots stuck to the floor, making a sucking noise when he walked. A rush light stood near the wall, partially masking the stench of human waste with its fatty odor.

Bryan had emptied the cellar the day before at the Truce Day and now only Cedric squatted in the corner. Bryan's young spur thief had escaped in the confusion. Cedric's head was bent between his knees. He was sleeping.

"Wake him," Bryan ordered.

Rory kicked Cedric. The prisoner raised his head, but didn't stand. "Warden," he said in a rasping voice. His neck was red and scabbed from being strangled.

"Good morning, Cedric."

"Is it morn? I cannot tell in this hole."

"Would you like to come out in the sunlight? You've been in the gaol a while. Were you not just released from the Middle March?"

"Aye."

"I'll give you a room in the keep, with a hot meal and a warm bed. All you must needs do is answer my questions."

Cedric gazed at him steadily, his face expressionless. "Aye?"

"Where is Leod?"

"I thought you buried 'im."

Bryan made a slow circuit around the little room. "Why did you kill Lord Russell?"

"Who is Lord Russell?"

Bryan raised an eyebrow at Rory, who was glaring at the prisoner. "Why did you try to kill me?"

"Eh?" Cedric queried in mock puzzlement.

Bryan smiled patiently. "The gun you had pressed to my back?"

Cedric blinked in surprise. "That was not a gun!" He pointed his finger at Bryan and pretended to cock it. " 'Twas naught but me finger."

Rory kicked him again. He fell on his side, groaning. Rory grabbed Cedric's filthy doublet and yanked him to his feet. "Answer the question," Rory said and gave him another clout aside the head. The door opened, and Johnny and Willie joined them. Johnny held a club that he slapped casually against his palm as he took his position behind Bryan. Bryan could tell Cedric was trying to mask his unease. Bryan didn't like torture, though it was endorsed wholeheartedly by King James, but he had no aversion to using the threat of it.

"I only have one answer for you," Cedric said, eyeing Bryan's two hulking guards.

"Aye?"

"I only follow orders and my orders do not come from a lowly warden thought to be dead. Look you to your own kin, the Earl of Bothwell. Does he have reason for taking your life?"

Rory cocked his fist. "Why you lying, piece of—"

"Hold!" Bryan yelled.

Cedric's slate blue eyes were narrowed. A slow smile split his face. "Aye, Warden, Lord Bothwell has reason to fear you, does he not? Look you there, for Leod is a dead man."

"Come," Bryan called and started for the stairs. The others look confused but followed him out of the dungeon. Bryan emerged gratefully into the fresh air and headed for his chambers. He didn't want to believe Francis would kill him just because he feared Bryan might press some shaky claim to his earldom. But why would Cedric say such a thing? How could he know?

In his chambers, his men lined up behind him, awaiting orders. Bryan stood still, staring at the far wall. "Willie, come nightfall, I want Cedric to escape."

"What?" Rory burst out. "Don't tell me you believe that rubbish? Why would Lord Bothwell mean to harm you?"

Bryan turned. "These are matters you know nothing about, so hold your tongue. Willie?"

Rory fell silent, but his hazel eyes burned.

"Aye, sir," Willie said, nodding.

"Don't make it too easy or he will suspect something. I want you to follow him. You know the marches. Can you do this without him knowing you're there?"

"Aye, I can."

"Fine. I need to know where he goes. Who he reports to."

Willie left. Rory and Johnny flanked the door. They were both broad-shouldered, muscular lads, with biceps as big as most men's thighs. Johnny still held the club and twisted it in his hand, the muscles in his forearm jumping. It was such a waste of manpower to have them guarding him. They were both intelligent and capable of more. And they were loyal. He felt he could trust them completely. The only reason he kept them close was to please Megan.

"Rory," Bryan said.

"Sir?"

"I want you to accompany Willie tonight. Cedric is a big man, though not as large as yourself. See to Willie's safety and aid him any way he might need." Bryan paused contemplatively. "I am appointing you deputy, so you may act in my name. Johnny, you are Captain of the Guard."

"But, sir! You must be protected!" Rory protested.

"You have both done a fine job of it, but I don't think it's necessary."

They both still stood there, looking at each other uncertainly. "You have my leave!" Bryan said in exasperation. "Don't loiter in my chamber anymore. You have duties now."

They both left hastily. He felt as if walls that had been closing in on him before were suddenly lifted. No more Rory like a mother hen pecking at him to be careful. He sat at the desk and pulled out the logbook. He had hardly written in it since he became warden. He leafed back through the pages. It went back almost ten years. He came to Innes Dixon's bold hand. He shut the book abruptly, the urge to write gone.

It was late afternoon, and Megan was resisting all of Cora's efforts to force her back into bed. The lead ball had not hurt her badly, only embedding itself under the skin, not damaging anything deep inside. She had to walk a little slower, and there was a pulling, stinging pain at the stitches, but that was the extent of it.

She found Innes in the yard, sitting on the stump with old Hob. The little puppy, Mary, was curled in her son's lap. As she neared them, she heard Hob instructing Innes on how to train the pup to be a sleuth dog. Innes listened with wide eyes, nodding raptly. She should have gotten him a dog long ago. Why had she not thought of it? Her heart warmed to Bryan. He would make a good father.

She wondered what to do when he returned. She couldn't send him away, or resist him anymore. She didn't want to. Why throw away what little happiness God granted her because of fear? She had been given her first husband, Innes, if only for a short time, and he had given her a son. She knew Bryan could make her happy, she was just so afraid of losing him after they had built a life together.

She was slowly making her way to Innes and Hob when Bryan and Johnny rode through the gates. She was nervous suddenly, unsure of how to act now that she was reevaluating their relationship. He dismounted and came to her. Megan shaded her eyes from the late afternoon sun, watching his approach. He seemed uncommonly serious.

"I see you're up and about," he said, looking her over with a cool, detached expression.

"Aye, like I said before, it's not a bad wound. The shot just went under my skin."

Innes ran over, the pup bouncing in his arms. "Bryan! Bryan! Look! Mary is going to be a sleuth hound!"

Bryan's face broke into a wide grin, and he squatted down in the dirt so he was level with Innes. "That's fine news. She'll make a bonny hound."

They talked and fussed over the hound until Megan thought she might explode. Why was he treating her so coldly?

"Innes, love? Take Mary inside and feed her."

"But, Mum—"

"I said, go," she reiterated in a tone that brooked no opposition. Innes said good-bye to Bryan and sulked into the house. Bryan stayed squatting, watching the boy until he disappeared, then stood.

His brown eyes were still obscure. "I'm glad you're doing fine."

Why was their conversation suddenly so stilted? "Would you like to come in?"

"Uh . . . nay, I should be going . . ." He looked around the yard aimlessly.

She was confused and feeling the beginnings of hurt. She did not want him to leave. "Have you learned anything from Cedric?"

"I have released him."

"What?" The word burst out of her incredulously.

He turned his narrow, hooded gaze on her. "I said I released him."

"But . . . why?"

"It was necessary."

"I don't understand!" she cried, her voice rising in anger, her fists clenched at her sides. "He's a murderer! And you had him! You could have punished him! And you let him go?"

"Cedric isn't to blame."

How could he be so calm about this? It was infuriating! "Cedric was still the one who did the actual killing!"

"I have my reasons, Megan. Reasons I cannot share at this time."

"They must be very stupid reasons. Once he crosses the border he will take revenge on you for capturing him at all." She shook her head again, unable to believe he could be so ignorant. "I thought you were learning something. I thought you finally understood what being a borderer was all about."

"That's enough." He turned and started back toward his horse.

She hurried after him, grimacing in pain from the pull in her stitches. "How long ago did you release him?"

He didn't turn. "Not long."

"You still have time. Recapture him! You must hurry or it will be too late."

He swung into the saddle and glared down at her. "I have not asked for your help on this."

He tugged the reins sharply and cantered away. She gaped after him, furious. What had gotten into him? Johnny had not emerged from the stable. Maybe he could explain what was going on.

Johnny grinned at her over his shoulder when she joined him in the dim stable. "The warden made Rory deputy and me Captain of the Guard today. I'll be moving Marie and Lance back to our cottage so we're closer to the garrison."

"Did he hire another guard?"

"Nay. He decided he didn't want us following him around anymore. He can take care of himself."

His words were like a blow in the stomach, making her weak. "And you just let him? He could be killed!"

He shook his head. "You don't understand, Meg. He is a great warrior. He doesn't need us to protect him. He never did. He did it only to please you."

"If he wants to please me then why has he dismissed his guards?" she asked in a small voice.

Johnny stopped unsaddling the horse a moment, thoughtful, then heaved the saddle off, setting it on the rail of the horse's stall. "I know not."

She stood silently, watching Johnny tend to his horse. When it was stalled and given grain she asked, "Why did he release Cedric Forster?"

"There is much going on that I cannot tell you. But you must trust that the warden knows what he is doing."

"How can releasing Cedric be anything but insanity? It makes no sense!"

Johnny shook his head, and she wished she hadn't asked. She felt betrayed by everyone. First Bryan, and now Johnny was withholding information. She felt weak in his eyes. A woman with a silly heart. She hardened her expression. She wouldn't let him see how badly it hurt her.

"Come inside," she said, turning as briskly as her wound allowed. "I'll get some ale to cool you."

 Fifteen

Rory squatted in the high grass, inspecting the broken shoots in the moonlight. He heard panting behind him. Willie was finally catching up. The old man annoyed him. He was slowing them down. If he had to keep stopping to wait for Willie, they were going to lose Cedric. Rory could follow his trail until they reached the river, but he wanted to be close enough to see Cedric ford it.

His stomach was cramping with hunger and his eyes were tired and itchy from lack of sleep. But he could put those things off. His mind was still sharp and his body strong enough to keep going for a very long time. Willie, on the other hand . . .

"What have you there, son?" Willie wheezed.

Rory controlled his irritation at being called "son." "I still have his trail, but I must see him cross the Tweed."

"Why? Can you not pick up the trail on the other side?" Willie asked. Rory thought he detected a sneer in the old man's voice.

Rory stood, hulking over Willie. "I can, but it will take far longer than if I know which direction he was headed. But if you think you can do it better, I shall defer to you." Rory stepped back and motioned for Willie to take the lead.

In a move that shocked Rory, Willie drew his sword and smacked him alongside the head with the flat of it. Rory stumbled, grabbing the side of his face and working to contain his cry of rage and pain. He looked at his hand in the moonlight, but there was no blood.

"Hold your tongue, whelp! I'm not so old I can't whip your arse. I was asking a question, and you will answer me in the future with none of that bile you save for everyone but the warden."

Rory's jaw clenched, but he nodded stiffly. Willie sheathed his sword. They followed Cedric's trail and slowed as they neared the Tweed. They both lay flat in the grass and scanned the calm water. It was easily fordable here and at first Rory saw no sign of their quarry. He was about to stand and head for the river when Willie's hand stayed him.

"Look," Willie whispered, pointing to the opposite bank. He saw movement, then someone got to his feet. Cedric had been resting. Rory glanced appreciatively at Willie. The old man had eyes like a hawk. Cedric walked along the bank of the river. He unlaced his breeks and pissed into the water. Willie made a gagging noise and whispered, "That'll make for a fine fording!"

When finished, Cedric headed south at a brisk pace. After he disappeared from sight Rory and Willie followed.

"What shall we do when he arrives at his destination?" Rory asked.

"We go home and report to the warden."

"We just leave him? He tried to kill Sir Bryan!"

"And thanks to you he did not. You were following orders then, as you will now. He gave us no instructions to apprehend him."

Rory said nothing, but was angry at Willie's superior attitude. Sir Bryan didn't expect them to blindly follow orders.

A cool breeze blew, bending the silvery-green grass so it looked like a fine rippling sheet stretched out before them. They had been walking several miles when Cedric's trail led them to a cottage next to a loch. Silently, they crept closer. Near the loch was a stand of trees, which Rory and Willie made for. Once they had the cover of the trees, Rory felt safer. He went to the edge near the water and watched the cottage. The windows were covered in horn paper, but he could see the flickering light of a candle within.

"Do you know who lives here?" Rory asked.

"Nay . . . 'tis been standing empty for several years now. I wasn't aware that anyone had moved into it."

"Mayhap he's just stopping to beg shelter and food."

"Aye, mayhap."

They sat quietly, waiting. When nothing happened, Rory became impatient. "We have to move closer."

Willie shook his head. "Nay, I think we should stay put."

"We were told to find out who he answers to." Rory started out of the trees.

Willie grabbed his arm. "We will continue following him when he leaves the cottage."

Rory easily shrugged off the old man's hold. "You sit here, if you like. But we'll find out naught unless we take action. I'm moving in closer." Rory headed for the cottage. Willie followed. They made it to the wall undetected and moved along it until they were next to the window. The horn paper was tacked down. Rory could hear voices through it, but couldn't understand what they were saying. Willie indicated he was going to find another window.

Rory squatted down beneath the window, straining his ears. He almost yelped in surprise when the window above him was opened to let in the air.

"There, that's better," a woman said. She moved away from the window. "Think you he believed your words?"

"Aye," Cedric said, "he left off immediately. Likely to go chasing his cousin down. He's like his father. I'm sure he'll challenge him to duel and one of them will be dead by morn."

He heard a sharp intake of breath, then the woman said, "What was—"

Cedric hissed, cutting her off. Rory sat up straighter, straining his ears to hear. Cedric was moving quietly across the cottage. Rory drew his dirk from his boot and moved from under the window, closer to the corner of the wall. It must've been Willie, for Rory was certain he hadn't made a sound. The door opened. Rory clutched the dirk, his palm sweating.

Cedric left the cottage, but his footsteps were moving away from Rory, toward Willie. Rory followed. When he rounded the corner, he spied Cedric standing over Willie's body, an ax dripping with blood in his hand. Rory gave a cry of rage and ran at Cedric's back. Cedric whirled and caught Rory's wrist before he could stab him. Rory knocked the ax from Cedric's hand and they grappled with the knife. Rory was hot, almost blind with rage. He yanked one of his hands free and crashed his fist into Cedric's gut. Cedric grunted and his hold loosened on Rory's other hand.

Seconds before he buried the knife in Cedric's chest, something struck Rory across the back of the head. He thought he might be all right for a moment and stumbled forward against Cedric, who caught him in his arms like a lover.

"Hit 'im again," Cedric said hoarsely.

This time when he was struck, everything went black.

 Sixteen

As soon as Francis entered the hall of Crichton, his retainers surrounded him, wanting to know where he had been. This annoyed him and he shoved them away, one man tripping and falling on his ass. Francis laughed loudly. At least they were good for something. He climbed the stairs to his chambers, stroking his beard. He stopped suddenly. An elaborate carved wood staircase was being installed, and here it was, half finished, with sheets draped over the rest.

He turned to the men below. "Where are the workmen?"

They exchanged looks, uneasy. "We dinna know, my lord," one man spoke up.

"Well, then, find them! Send me my steward and tell him if he doesn't get the men working I shall flog him myself."

They all nodded and scattered, except one man,

who continued following him. "My lord, my lord!" he yapped, tugging on Francis's hose.

He lashed out, backhanding the man. "Do not touch my person!"

The man shrank back, cradling his cheek where Francis had hit him. "Of course, my lord, forgive me. But this is very important."

"Pah!" He waved his hand at him and continued up the stairs.

"Sir Bryan Hepburn was here to see you—he seemed most unhappy you weren't here. Also, there is a messenger below. He says it is urgent and he is only to speak with you!"

"Is the messenger from Sir Bryan?"

"No, my lord, but the lad says his message concerns the warden."

Francis stopped and turned back to the cowering man. "Send him up."

In his chambers, he removed his clothes and slipped on a light dressing gown. He combed his beard before the mirror, pleased with the effect, then went to the window. He saw the workmen now. They had been working on the courtyard he was having constructed. The walls enclosing it were a rosy stone cut with diamond shapes. It was the latest thing in France.

There was a short knock on the door. Francis bade his visitor to enter. It was a young lad, his black hair curly and his eyes a slate blue. *A Forster.* Francis's lip curled involuntarily. He didn't want this pile of human trash in his chamber for long.

"What is it?" he snapped.

The lad looked around and came closer, making all the perfunctory obeisance.

Francis cut him off impatiently, "Out with it!"

"I 'ave been sent with intelligence that there will be an attempt on your life."

Francis stared down his nose at the whelp. "Indeed? By whom?"

"Your cousin, Sir Bryan Hepburn. He is claiming his mother and father were handfast and he is the legitimate heir to the earldom."

"Then why does he not petition the king? There's no reason for bloodshed to contest the matter."

The lad's brows drew together in confusion. Francis could see the boy had expected him to jump at this bait and begin raging around the room. People were so narrow-minded, listening to every bit of gossip that circulated.

"Surely Sir Bryan knows the king's feelings about his father, James Hepburn. After all, the warden's father killed the king's father. 'Twould be easier for him if there wasn't another Hepburn, free from the stain of regicide," the lad waved his hand to indicate Francis, "standing in the way."

"Hmm, yes . . . It would." He crossed the room at a leisurely pace, stopping in front of the boy. "Who sent you?"

The lad hesitated. "I came myself. I overheard him at the Day of Truce, and being such a great admirer of your lordship, I wanted to warn you."

"Oh? Rushed to save my skin, eh? Because you admire my person so." Francis continued smiling at the lad. He didn't know what game the child was playing, but he was losing his patience with the farce. "So, my dear cousin, Sir Bryan, was standing about at the Truce Day, telling everyone he planned to assassinate me so he could be earl? I daresay, he's as daft as his father, is he not?" He laughed and the lad laughed, too.

Francis struck the lad hard and he fell, blood dripping from his lip. He scrambled across the floor as Francis came after him, grabbing the boy's tunic, and slamming him against the wall. "Tell me who sent you!"

There was a brief knock, and his steward entered. He stood back quietly, waiting for the messenger's audience to be concluded.

"I told you, my lord!" the lad babbled, frightened now, as Francis had intended. "I 'eard him say it myself!"

Francis threw the lad to floor at his steward's feet. "Lock him below and don't give him food or water until he's ready to speak the truth. Oh, and clean up that mess on the floor." He waved at the drops of spilled blood.

The lad was dragged from the room, and Francis went back to the window, admiring how nicely his courtyard was coming along.

Bryan rode out to fetch Johnny to accompany him across the border. He was becoming destitute of trusted men—Rory and Willie had never returned from following Cedric, and Bryan feared the worst. He had sent out search parties looking for the men, but they came back empty-handed. His deputies had tracked Cedric so well, they hadn't even left a trail.

The Olivers' cottage sat alone in the center of miles of lonely plain. Bryan hoped Megan wasn't visiting with Marie. He knew he should tell Megan that her uncle was missing, but couldn't bring himself to do it. He rationalized that she had probably already heard it from Johnny, but he knew it should have come from him. He kept hoping the deputies would turn up—and not in the woods. He would have to face her eventually. He had vowed to protect her and her son—instead he set a known murderer free, lost her uncle, and still had no idea where Leod was hiding himself. After her angry words the last time he visited her, he feared the tongue-lashing he was due for.

Johnny was unloading a wagon when Bryan arrived. Marie sat on a bench in the sun holding their new son, Lance.

"Monsieur Warden! Good day!" she called and waved.

"Marie," he said, leaning over to admire her son. "He's a fine looking laddie."

"Will you come visit us in our home? We get so few visitors." Her large dark eyes were earnest, pleading.

"Of course. I need to borrow Johnny this afternoon. Will someone be coming to stay with you?"

Her lower lip poked out, but she nodded. Bryan patted her shoulder. He went to the wagon and lifted a basket out of it, bringing it into the cottage. Johnny was busy cleaning out the fireplace.

"Is that not woman's work?"

"Not in this house," Johnny shot back. He straightened and wiped his sooty hands on his breeks. "Marie cooks and makes all these pretties," he waved his hand to indicate the lace and embroidery that decorated their home, "and I am grateful for that." Bryan knew Johnny felt fortunate his wife had agreed to move back to the cottage at all, since she hated the place.

"You could always get her one of those scold's bridles, until she learned her place," Bryan joked. "I spied one of the men leading his wife about Edington by a chain. He claims it's most effective."

Johnny grimaced, probably imagining Marie's reaction to having a metal cage placed on her head that was designed to keep her mouth shut. "Don't let her hear you say that," Johnny said, and they both looked through the doorway anxiously, but Marie was out of earshot.

Bryan became serious. "Rory and Willie still haven't returned."

"Think you they're still alive?"

"I can't imagine Cedric sparing them if he caught them following him. I'm going to the English Middle March today to see Sir John Forster. I'd like you to join me."

"Aye, sir," Johnny nodded and looked around the little cottage with a frown of worry.

"Don't fash," Bryan said hastily, "I'll help you finish here first. I don't want Marie in a chuff at me."

Outside, Marie cried, "Madame! Madame!" at the rumbling approach of another wagon.

"That would be Meg," Johnny said, giving Bryan an odd look on his way out the door.

Bryan's heart was heavy with the strange mixture of longing and unease he felt at the thought of Megan. He was torn between wanting to see her and wanting to leave so he didn't have to explain how he had lost her uncle. He was sure her late husband had never lost deputies at such a rate. At the doorway, he ducked his head and went out, but stayed back, his arms folded over the side of the other wagon.

Megan saw him, but looked away quickly. She was angry with him; he could tell. Her golden hair was in a thick braid that hung down her back. She wore her floppy hat. Her dress covered every inch of body except her hands, but he remembered it all well enough. Seeing her reopened the ache, reminding him he couldn't have her.

Megan was walking toward him laden with a basket full of clothes. He took it from her.

"Thank you, Warden," she said, acknowledging him. He followed her into the one-room cottage. "I've heard about Uncle Willie and Rory. Being a deputy in this march is hazardous. What are you doing to find them?"

"Johnny and I are going to see Sir John Forster today," he said tightly, knowing she wasn't going to like that answer.

She pointed to the floor by the bed and Bryan set the basket down. "And you think if he has them, he will just hand them over?"

"I don't think he has them at all—but he might know where Cedric is."

She shook her head, dismissing his plan. "He won't tell you anything. You should take them."

Checking his temper, Bryan said, "I must know where they are first."

"I know where they are."

He raised a brow in disbelief. "Do you?"

"Well . . . I know where Cedric spends most of his time. If they aren't being kept there, I have some other ideas."

He moved close to her. She straightened, her eyes becoming wary. He tapped her forehead with his finger. "Keep your ideas here and stay home. Let me do my duty."

Her green eyes flared with indignation. "I think you have more to learn. Perhaps it's time for another lesson, Warden. I was a good teacher, was I not?"

"Megan, I know what I'm doing."

"No, you don't," she persisted. "You think you do, but your way doesn't work."

He shook his head, exasperated, and left the cottage. He heard her hurrying after him.

She grabbed his arm, stopping him. "Listen to me!"

He was getting heartily tired of her implying he was so incompetent that she must instruct him constantly. "Megan," he said, a warning in his voice that he was losing his temper.

She ignored it. "You must take them! 'Tis the only way you shall ever see your deputies again, if be they in Cedric's hands! Diplomacy doesn't work on the borders."

"Enough!" he said harshly. Marie and Johnny turned toward them, eyes wide. Lance wailed. Bryan lowered his voice, "Your days of tutoring me are over. Keep your counsel to yourself until I ask for it. Are we clear?"

She winced as though he had slapped her. "You shall be fortunate to get it when you ask for it!" She turned on her heel and stalked into the cottage. He fought the urge to follow her and make amends for his harsh words. He returned to the wagon to finish unloading it.

Megan's hands were still shaking with fury when she heard Bryan and Johnny ride away on their futile mission to talk with the English warden. Sir John Forster was the best reiver and raider on the borders. He would never help Bryan.

Who was she, but a woman? Too given to fits of emotion to heed her counsel. Is that what he thought? Indignation burst anew through her as she violently straightened the bedding on Marie and Johnny's bed. She punched a pillow, hard, and was dismayed to see the dried heather it was stuffed with splay out the side. She looked around furtively. Marie watched her with raised eyebrows.

"Sorry," Megan muttered, and crossed the room to retrieve a needle and thread.

Marie laid Lance in the cradle. "You and the warden really should wed. Such agitation is bad for the body's humors." The French woman scowled. "Then maybe he'd leave my Johnny home on occasion."

"Married!" Megan huffed. "As if I would now. He thinks I'm a meddling hoyden." She looked at the gleaming steel needle. "And I think he's the thick end of a horse!"

"Oh my," Marie said, giggling.

Megan chewed her lip, watching the fire play over the silvery metal as she threaded it. "If he's not going to get my uncle back, perhaps I'd better do it myself."

"Madame, I do not think that's a good idea. The warden is already . . . frustrated with you."

Megan shrugged, a plan forming in her mind.

"Why would I have your deputies?" Sir John Forster asked, giving Bryan a perfectly innocent gaze. They sat in the parlor of his stronghold where his servants came in and served him, bowed to him, and murmured deferentially as if he were a king.

"Since they were apprehending your nephew, whom you're notorious for sheltering no matter how heinous his crimes, I thought you might have some idea as to their whereabouts."

Sir John took a delicate bite of apple cake and dabbed the crumbs off his short white beard. "No, no. I know not where your deputies are. But this cake is delicious. Surely you will have some?"

Bryan stared at the man in annoyance. His cool attitude was a farce. Bryan knew it. Something told him Sir John knew exactly where his deputies were.

"Do you know the whereabouts of Cedric Forster?"

"Cedric? No, I cannot say that I do."

It crossed Bryan's mind to threaten the old man and even get violent, but that was not the way to handle him. In fact, there seemed to be no way to handle Sir John Forster. He was too smooth. Bryan was searching his mind for some way to get this man to tell him something, make him slip, when Sir John said, "You know, Sir Bryan, you look much like your mother."

"How would you know?"

Sir John laughed. "Do not act so surprised! Many men knew your mother; she was no blushing maid!"

Bryan clenched his hands into fists. "You dare talk of my mother in my presence in such a fashion?"

"Peace, Sir Bryan," the older man soothed. "Remember your sister, Anna? She is my daughter. So I knew your mother very well and meant no disrespect in my words."

Bryan stared at him in shock, them stammered,

"Anna . . . is she here? It has been a long while since I've seen her."

"Nay. She only recently found out I am her father. Janet and I were very discreet . . . But your mother revealed many interesting things on her deathbed, and Anna's paternity was one of them. Anna came to stay with me after Janet died, but of late . . . I know not of her doings." He gave Bryan a meaningful look.

Bryan narrowed his eyes at the old man, wondering what he was intimating. It wasn't worth his time to pursue, though, and he said, "Do I have permission to send a party of men into your march to apprehend Cedric?"

Sir John was aghast. "Sir Bryan, I do wish I could be of help to you, but that would be unacceptable, having your men raiding and pillaging my march with my blessing. I will send my men to locate Cedric, and I will turn him over to you when he is captured. Is that acceptable?"

It wasn't, but Bryan saw no purpose in continuing their conversation. He stood, bidding Sir John a good day and went to find Johnny, hoping he made out better in gathering information. He was in the hall, drinking and talking with Sir John's guards. When he saw Bryan, he trotted over and fell into step beside him as they walked to the stables.

"Did you learn anything?" Bryan asked.

"Nay, they know naught—I'm certain of it."

When they were mounted and riding back toward the border and the East March, Johnny cleared his throat. "Sir, I believe the only way we will get our men back, if they are alive, is to raid Cedric."

Bryan's stomach felt sour. It was just as Megan

said. Did no man on the border have honor? "If he has them, would he not ask for a ransom? For I fear with no ransom being asked, they are already dead."

Johnny's brows were drawn and his eyes hard. "If that's the case, then we should punish Cedric. He will receive retribution no other way."

It was the way of things here. Bryan had learned that. And it was not so wrong as he had once imagined. "This must be carefully planned if we are to do it. I won't ride onto his land, screaming like a red-shank and hacking away at everything in my path. If we are to succeed, every circumstance must be antici-pated."

"Aye, sir!" Johnny said, a huge grin splitting his face.

There were ten of them riding south. Megan had sent a message to her brother-in-law, Jamie, and he had come to her, bringing friends. She gathered the men on her land who were willing to risk their life for her if they got something out of it. They hadn't even reached the Tweed when they spotted two riders approaching. It wasn't unusual. They were probably other raiders and would avoid a larger raiding party, unless they decided to join.

As they got closer, Megan recognized them and her heart beat wildly in her chest. The warden sat tall in the saddle of his huge horse. The war-horse seemed to be faring well on the borders. Her own men were rid-ing smaller ponies, bred for the border terrain.

"Who is it?" Jamie asked. They were riding stirrup-to-stirrup.

"The warden and his deputy."

Jamie's mouth thinned. Her heart dipped a little when she saw how much he resembled Innes, minus the red hair. Jamie's was long and brown. This was what Innes would have done. He would have taken his deputies back. The anger she had felt toward Bryan had faded and left rational thought in its place. Now she felt like a hypocrite and, not only that, she was infringing on Bryan's duties, a slap in the face and something he would probably never forgive her for. But it was for Willie and Rory, she kept telling herself.

Besides, Bryan already hated her. He had made that clear enough this afternoon. She had gone too far and she regretted it. But it was done, and she would accept it as she accepted everything else in her life. It was better this way, she tried to tell herself, but her heart ached.

Bryan and Johnny rode into the midst of her riders, making everyone stop and cluster around Bryan at the center. He looked immediately to her. "What is this? Are you going reiving?"

"Nay, Warden, we're going to retrieve your deputies."

His dark gaze became hard and inscrutable. "Well, you can all turn about and go home. There will be no raiding tonight."

"What about Willie?" Jamie asked.

Bryan's eyes cut to Jamie. "Who are you?"

"James Dixon."

"I am working on the release of my deputies, Mr. Dixon. Your efforts on their behalf are recognized, yet unnecessary. If I need you, I shall call on the men here, but there will be no raiding tonight. Go home."

To Megan's surprise, her men began turning their horses back in the direction they came from. She grabbed Jamie's reins. "Where are you going?"

"Megan, the warden has seen us tonight and marked us. We can do naught now. Let's go home."

She started to leave with Jamie when Bryan's voice stopped her. "Megan. I want to speak with you."

Her pony was excited from all the confusion and pranced sideways. She pulled the reins, turning to leave, and said loudly, "You asked me to stay out of your business and that I shall do. But now I am telling you to stay out of mine. Good evening to you."

Jamie was looking at her in amazement as they rode away. "What a tongue, lass!" he exclaimed.

She was about to respond when she heard galloping hoof beats. Before she could turn, her waist was grabbed and she was dragged off her pony. She knew it was Bryan, but he wasn't even giving her a chance to think. He reined Arthur and pulled her to the ground. Taking her by the shoulders, he shook her.

"Christ Jesus! It is my *duty* to be in your business!" He stopped shaking her, but still held her shoulders in an iron grip. "Mayhap I'll lock you in my gaol tonight, just to keep you out of trouble."

"You don't understand!" she yelled in his face. "Cedric will kill them. And you let him go. You can do no more than talk; talk and write letters. You will fail and they will die. At least I'm doing something."

He stared down at her, his jaw hard. "Mr. Dixon," he called, without taking his eyes off her face. Jamie rode closer, leading her pony.

"Aye?"

"I'm taking Lady Dixon with me. Please inform her family she is well and I do it for her own safety."

"Aye, sir."

"Jamie!"

"Megan, just do as the warden says." Jamie sounded tired. He handed the reins of her pony to Johnny and rode away. Bryan's hold on her shoulders loosened.

"Get in the saddle. Johnny, don't release the reins."

She climbed onto the pony, her rage barely held in check. He was actually going to lock her up! After they were both mounted and he held her reins securely, he sent Johnny home and they headed for the garrison. She said nothing to him. There was nothing to say any longer. He only thought evil of her and had no trust in her. It cankered her heart.

When they arrived, he led her straight to his chambers. She wondered what he had in mind. She remembered the last time she was here, how he almost made love to her in his room, and then later, in her bed, when he did. Her body flamed at the memory and she tried to think of other things—like spending the night in the damp, stinking cellar below the keep.

He closed the door.

She looked at him in surprise. "I hope I will be provided with my own room. I'm sure you don't gaol your other prisoners in your chambers."

He approached her, hands on hips. "What do you think you're doing, Megan?"

Irritation surged through her. "Your job! Someone has to do it!"

"Then let me do it! You waste my time when I have to keep you out of mischief."

"You are the one wasting time. If Innes were here he'd have his deputies back by now and Cedric strung up from the gates."

He was in front of her before she could think, gripping her shoulders, giving her another hard shake. "I am tired of being compared to your saintly dead husband. I am not Innes Dixon, nor do I want to be!"

She swallowed convulsively. "That's not what I want."

His eyes burned with anger and hurt. "You lie! You loved him so much you have no room in your heart for anyone else."

She shook her head. "That's not true—"

"Then why?"

"Bryan! I don't want to talk—"

His hands tightened on her shoulders. "Why, damn it?"

"Because I'll die this time!" she cried, wrenching away from him. "I never loved him like this!" The tears were hot on her cheeks. "If I make a life with you I will have nothing when you are taken away!"

His hands were on her again, gently pulling her into the circle of his arms. She leaned into him gratefully. She felt his heart beating fast and strong beneath her cheek.

"Megan," he whispered into her hair. "I'm so sorry."

She didn't want to leave his arms. It had been a mistake to let him embrace her, but she no longer cared. She tilted her head up to him. His lips pressed against her forehead. She whispered his name, aching for him to take her. His mouth covered hers in a hard, possessive kiss that left her breathless.

He took her to his bed. She closed her eyes as he

undressed her, restless with longing. When she was naked, she felt him move over her, his hands delicately tracing the lines of her body. His knee nudged her thighs apart, and she clutched him to her. His mouth was hot on her body, stroking and kissing, making her writhe with desire.

Her scalp tingled as he twisted her hair in his fists. He kissed her eyelids. "Open your eyes." His breath was warm against her ear. He took the tender lobe between his teeth.

She shuddered, shaking her head imperceptibly. "No," she whispered. "This is a dream."

His hands clenched in her hair, hurting her. Her eyes sprang open.

"Nay, love, this is real and you'll not run me off in the morning."

He held her gaze until she said, "Very well."

His mouth turned up at the corners. She smiled back, her hands coming up to frame his face. He kissed her, slowly, exploring her mouth. His hand moved between them, caressing and rubbing until she begged him to end the exquisite torture.

When he thrust into her she gasped, arching into him, trying to take him deeper. Pulling his head down, she kissed him, their tongues probing and sparring. She couldn't get close enough to him. She wrapped herself around him, awash in pleasure.

The bed was so small that afterward they had to lie on their sides, their bodies pressed close. Megan loved the feel of his warm, damp skin against hers.

"Is this how you treat all of your prisoners?" she asked, kissing his throat.

He laughed softly. "Nay. I'm sorry I forced you here tonight, but when we raid the Forsters, we won't do a slop job of it, aye? Tomorrow night I will strike, but after much planning. Planning that you can be of use to me in."

"What?" She looked up at him in surprise. "Why did you not just tell me that?"

"Because I don't trust all your men and I feared you might act on your own anyway, thinking me not competent to carry it off."

She averted her eyes. She saw his point. After the way she had questioned his every move, what else was he to think? She had made such a mess of things between them. She feared it was still too late to make them right. She searched for something to say, not wanting to continue this line of conversation.

"Why did you release Cedric? Can you tell me now?"

"I didn't release him . . . exactly. I let him escape."

She looked up at him. "What?"

He twirled a lock of her hair around his finger. "He indicated that he had been directed by someone other than Leod to kill me and Lord Russell. He suggested that person was Lord Bothwell."

She gasped. "Why would he?"

"I have a half sister, and she claims my mother and father were handfast . . . which would make me the heir to the earldom of Bothwell."

Her eyebrows shot up. Bryan, *the Earl of Bothwell*?

He shook his head. "I don't believe it. My mother never mentioned it to me, and from what she has told me, it wouldn't make sense for him to do such a thing." She gave him a questioning look, and he continued, "When my mother and father . . . had their tryst, he had just come into his land and titles. He was very young . . . She was in her forties—but very beautiful. People said she stayed so fetching because she was a witch. She looked no older than two score when she died and she was at least three . . . so there might be some truth to that, though I doubt it.

"Anyway, she found him pleasing, most did from what I hear, and seduced him. He was never under any illusions that he was in love with her, nor she with him, yet they continued their liaison for several years and I was born from it. Why would he handfast this woman who meant no more than a bed partner to him? Who was more than twice his age? And him, with a lifetime ahead of him as one of Scotland's leading lords. It makes little sense."

Megan nodded in agreement. "Then why is your sister saying these things?"

"She means me, or mayhap Francis, ill. I know not. But I fear Francis might have heeded her words and is trying to get rid of the possibility."

"So you sent Willie and Rory to follow Cedric and see who he reports to."

He sighed, his eyes troubled. "Aye, and it seems I only fed them into the jaws of whatever evil is out there."

"Nay, Bryan, you did what you had to. They know that as well as I."

He gazed down at her, his expression softening. " 'Tis strange to hear such things from your lips."

She flushed and lowered her eyes. "Why do you

persist, Bryan, when I have given you more trouble than you deserve?"

"You are worth my trouble."

She smiled, holding him tightly, falling asleep in his arms, not caring if he was the warden or not.

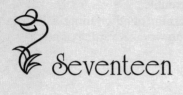 Seventeen

Megan was sleeping, feeling warm and secure, if not a bit cramped in the narrow bed, when screaming and shouting woke her. She sat up immediately. Bryan was already out of bed and dressing. She threw on her clothes and was mostly dressed when the door to his chambers burst open.

"The Forsters are here! Inside the walls!"

Once Bryan was armed, he rushed out of the room, yelling at her to stay put. An explosion rocked the ground beneath her feet. She rushed out the door. The keep was in chaos, the women and children running about screaming, trying to gather up everything they could hold.

Megan darted out into the bailey. The vivid orange and yellow of fire blinded her. Everything was alight. She stepped back, the heat blasting her in the face. Men on horseback tore through the bailey with torches. Bryan's men were attempting to fight, but they were divided between that and trying to put out the fire. The Forster men made full use of their advantage, kicking the soldiers as they rode by.

Megan backed up, horrified by the destruction before her. Her eyes hurt from straining, trying to see Bryan through the smoke, terrified for him. She had been witness to many raids before, but nothing like this. The Forsters were taking things, but they were destroying more. A rider was galloping toward her, and she recognized him even though he was completely black, framed by the fire. He stopped in front of her, his black horse rearing and pawing the air. She shrunk away.

"Where is the girl?" Cedric yelled down at her.

She had no idea what he was talking about and stared up at him uncomprehendingly.

"Lauren. Willie Hume's widow."

Her heart caved in on itself at his words. *Willie Hume's widow.* Willie was dead. Cedric had murdered him. And now he wanted Lauren, too. Megan wasn't going to let him hurt anyone else. She pulled her dirk from her waist and ran at him. He wasn't expecting her to attack him, and she buried it to the hilt in his thigh. He gave a cry of rage and struck her across the face. She fell on the ground, scrambling away from his excited horse. He was pulling the dirk out with both hands as she ran back into the keep. The clop of hooves on stones warned her that Cedric had brought his horse inside to follow her. She looked over her shoulder and fell, rolling through the rushes. She stumbled, trying to regain her feet.

Then she saw Lauren. Coming to her, to help her.

"No! Lauren, run!" she screamed.

Lauren ignored her, taking her arm and helping her stand.

"This way!" Lauren yelled and began pulling her. But Cedric was too close; Lauren's hand was yanked from hers as he lifted the girl onto his horse. Lauren shrieked and fought at him. He shoved her face down across his thighs.

"Cedric, no! She's just a child!" Megan cried, running after him, but the horse was already bounding out of the hall. She heard him yelling, rallying his men to follow. They disappeared through the broken gate. Megan stood in the bailey, tears streaming down her face, gazing at the circle of fire around her, consuming everything. Bryan strode toward her, his clothes torn and blackened. Relief washed through her. He was safe.

His eyes passed over her, hard and glassy. "I told you to stay inside."

"Cedric took Lauren," she said in a gasping breath, her throat raw from smoke and screaming.

His lips thinned and his brow seemed to lower. A shiver of fear passed over her. She had always been acutely aware of his size, of how tall and lithe and graceful he was. But it had never struck her as it did now. She knew his body was solid and packed with muscle, and now she could see it coiling, focusing, directing itself into the anger and hate that surrounded him like a cloud. He was going to kill someone and what shocked her even more was that he was capable of it. She had thought him peaceful, even knowing that he had fought as a mercenary, she thought that was behind him. But she could see now it had only been buried.

He marched past her into the keep. The other men were still frantically throwing bucket after bucket of water onto the flames, beating the fire with wet blankets and with the doublets off their backs. She hurried after Bryan. She found the women closed up in a room, hugging their children to their breasts.

"The raiders are gone, but the garrison is on fire."

The women rushed out to help the men, leaving the older girls to tend the children. Megan went back to Bryan's chambers. He was seated at his desk, four guns laid out on the surface before him. He had a powder horn in his hand and was measuring out gunpowder to load the guns.

"Bryan, what are you going to do?"

He didn't lift his head. "I want you to go home."

"If you're going on a hot trod, you need me."

"You're not coming."

"Willie's dead. Cedric told me. He took Lauren."

He looked up finally, his eyes almost black in the candle's light. He seemed to look straight through her, then he went back to loading the guns. The door opened, and Johnny came in. He was in sorry shape, too, blood drying on his face and his knuckles skinned.

"Where are Marie and Lance?" Megan asked.

"The Foresters passed by the cottage on their way here," Johnny said. "I took them to Cora and came straight there." He turned back to Bryan: "Sir! Are we going after them?"

"Aye. They blew up our gunpowder stores. Are you armed?"

Johnny proffered a musket and patted the pistol in a holster slung over his shoulder. He was also wearing his sword strapped to his belt. It was a two-handed sword, the hilt wrapped with worn leather. She had lived all her life on the border and was used to the killing. Though most of it seemed senseless, there was a sort of purpose to it. To live. Cedric killed because his livelihood was thieving. He removed those who stood in his way. But Bryan and Johnny had gone into battle and hacked men away for money. Their livelihood was killing. She couldn't take her eyes off the battered and well-worn leather of Johnny's sword hilt. How many times had his hands grasped it? Enough times to know he needed that leather when his palms became sweaty from the exertion of cutting men down. She could even see where his fingers gripped it, the indentations a lighter color than the rest.

Bryan stood, shoving a pistol into his waistband. She looked at his sword hilt and saw the leather there, just like Johnny's. He turned to a cabinet and pulled out a leather jack. Her heart seemed to stop. She had never seen him wear any sort of protection before. She felt as if she were watching some ancient war ritual, and she was frightened. She was going to lose him tonight. She felt it to her bones.

When he was armed and armored, he turned to Johnny. "Let's get this fire under control before we go after them."

She grabbed Bryan's arm at the door. "I'm going with you. You can't stop me. If you try, I'll just follow after you leave."

She sensed his mind was elsewhere. He was already fighting and killing Cedric. He nodded and went out the door.

 Eighteen

Rory paced the room he was locked in, trying over and over again, in vain, to find a way to escape. His throat ached from the rope Cedric had twisted around it—payback for the near-strangling Rory had subjected him to at the Truce Day. Cedric had been taunting him, telling him how he planned to raze the garrison to teach Sir Bryan a lesson for meddling in his affairs.

Rory heard boots outside the door, then it swung open. Cedric came in and, to Rory's horror, he was dragging wee Lauren behind him. Sable curls tumbled wildly over her shoulders. Her cheeks were ruddy and wet with tears. When she saw him her enormous brown eyes pleaded with him to help her. Did she know Willie was dead? Had Cedric told her?

Cedric pulled the lass in front of him and held her shoulders. "I am going to release you, Rory Trotter."

Rory raised an eyebrow, looking from Lauren to

Cedric. "W-what? Why?" His voice rasped from his ruined throat, and he swallowed convulsively.

"I am a fair man. You and I are even, I believe."

Rory frowned. "Then what do you want with the lass?"

"I never meant to kill Willie. He was a good deputy to Leod and never caused any trouble. He was not meant to die. I am rectifying the situation to the best of my ability. I shall care for his young widow. Go back and tell your warden that I, too, believe in justice."

Lauren's hands were balled up in fists and pressed to her eyes. Her shoulders shook beneath Cedric's hands. Rory was torn. He could better help the girl if he was released and at liberty. But he couldn't stand to have her think he abandoned her to Cedric. And how did he know what Cedric meant for her? What if he meant to rape her? Rory doubted raping children was beneath Cedric.

"I wish to stay with the lass."

Cedric's eyes widened in astonishment. Lauren's hands dropped from her face and she blinked at him.

"Nay, I cannot 'ave you here. I don't like caring for prisoners. You must go."

Rory clenched his jaw. "She will surely be as much a prisoner as I. I will care for her. Let me take her with me."

Cedric shook his head. "She has nothing—you have nothing . . . She's better off here. I can provide for her. She should wear finery, not rags." He turned Lauren partway toward him and touched her chin gently, so she was looking up at him. Her hair was hanging in her face like it always was, obscuring her features. Cedric brushed it aside with a caressing hand. "She is a stunning child. She will be a beautiful woman. I fancy her." Lauren shrunk away from him and more tears welled in her eyes.

Rory swallowed, sickened by Cedric's words. He owed it to Willie not to allow this. "Then let us fight for her. The winner takes the lass."

Cedric gave a short, incredulous laugh. "You might be an ox, lad, but you 'ave not a chance against me. What is this child to you? Go. She is in good 'ands."

Rory could not let this to happen. He felt enough guilt about the part he played in Willie's death without having Lauren's honor on his conscience as well. "She is my responsibility now," Rory said, frantically grasping for something sufficiently convincing to satisfy Cedric's perverted sense of responsibility to the girl. "Willie made me swear an oath that if anything happened to him I would take Lauren as my wife."

Lauren swooned. Cedric caught her and held her sagging body in his arms, frowning at Rory. Rory didn't like the way he clutched her slight body against his, as though he had already claimed her as his own. Before Cedric had a chance to reply, a man rushed into the room.

"Sir Bryan made it past the ambush! He's here with at least two score men, and I hear he commands Douglas Hume's men as well!"

Cedric's eyes became wild. He thrust Lauren at Rory. "You'll both stay here until I can get rid of the warden."

A black rage drove Bryan on, leaving no room in his heart for reason. He pushed Arthur hard; the horse's sides heaved and its neck was lathered in sweat. He was determined not to let Cedric's trail go cold. No one spoke except when necessary. One of the men held a lighted peat torch; another man carried a bundle ready to be lit. When they arrived at Cedric's stronghold he would burn it to the ground. They weren't far now. He could see the beacon atop Cedric's tower, calling his uncle to help him. Sir John Forster could come, but there was little he could do to obstruct Bryan. According to the law, he was fully expected to cooperate in Bryan's efforts to capture Cedric.

Bryan had sent a messenger to his new deputy, Douglas Hume at Leadwater, and the laird had responded with alacrity that had amazed everyone. Bryan had been studying the border law and intended to follow it to the letter. On a hot trod he had the authority to execute the perpetrator on the spot. He intended to exercise that authority.

Cedric lived in one of the strongholds that protected the English side of the border. It was larger than any of the Scottish border castles, a grim testament to the advantages of being a criminal on the marches. As they drew closer, Bryan observed that Cedric's tower was locked up tight. Archers manned the wall circling the keep, but they didn't fire. Bryan was prepared to lay siege to it if he must, but he wanted to take it quickly. He gathered his two score men around him.

"How long do you think he can last in there?"

"If he's well prepared, he could hold out for months," Megan said.

Bryan looked back at the keep. It was nowhere near the size of some of the towns and strongholds he had taken in the Low Countries. But that wasn't what mattered. It was the spirit of those inside.

"Wait here for Douglas. I'm going to have a look at this wall," Bryan said and rode away to circle the keep.

"We must leave quickly before the guards wake and sound an alarm," Rory said.

He had not expected Lauren to be of much help, and so was surprised when she rose to the occasion. She distracted the guards by screaming rape, and Rory was able to subdue them. They made it to the back of the keep without incident. In the courtyard, they hid in the shadows of the wall so he could survey the area. A strong breeze blew, bending the branches of the trees that lined Cedric's little courtyard. He saw nothing. Not a soul.

He led Lauren through the courtyard to the wrought iron gate. Through the painted leaves and flowers that decorated the iron bars he saw the postern door. Two men stood guard outside it. He could take them easily, except they were twenty feet away. The torch-lit bailey was deserted between the courtyard gate and the postern door. The guards could sound an alarm and end everything before he even reached them.

He was trying to decide what to do when he heard the approach of horses. Two men appeared leading saddled mounts. They stopped at the gate and turned to look directly at Rory and Lauren.

Rory backed up as quickly and quietly as he could, dragging Lauren with him. They hid in some flowery bushes. The door to the keep opened and four people strode out. Two women and two men. One of the men Rory recognized as Cedric.

"Once I have the boy, it will be over," the other man said. "The warden thinks he understands what is happening, and that is enough for now."

Rory knew that voice and parted the bushes to get a glimpse of the speaker.

"What about Bothwell?" Cedric asked.

"Nay, I wouldn't be in my current spot if Bothwell were volunteering such information. He hasn't told Sir Bryan."

Rory got a good look at the speaker's profile, the way he walked. Leod Hume. *Alive*. Rory's hands itched to capture him and bring him before everyone, proving he wasn't dead. The bastard really had killed Tavish. He wished he could determine what they were talking about. What boy? But they were out of earshot.

"Was that . . . Leod?" Lauren asked.

She was huddled by his feet. He squatted beside her, keeping the gate in view in case they returned. "Aye." In the distance they heard the postern gate opened and shut. "Two of them are leaving," he whispered.

"Only two?"

Rory nodded, placing his finger against his lips as Cedric and one of the women returned to the court-yard.

"I can't believe you won't send me to safety," she said, her voice full of hate.

Rory parted the branches again. He couldn't see Cedric's face, but he could tell by his stance that he was angry and ready for violence. "You will be 'ere to witness my death if it comes to that! You told me he was soft; he would not retaliate. You know nothing, woman!" He struck her across the face and she fell. He looked down at her. " 'Tis what I deserve, I suppose, for listening to a woman's counsel."

"I hope he does kill you," she said in a low voice.

He grabbed her hair and dragged her screaming and fighting him into the keep. Rory glanced down at Lauren. Her face was ashen. Rory was glad he hadn't left her to Cedric.

"We must be quick," Rory whispered. "It won't be long before our absence is discovered."

She nodded, sitting up straighter.

"I will approach the men guarding the postern gate as though I am one of them—it should give me the opportunity to surprise them. When that happens, I want you to open the door and run. Don't look back, just find the warden."

"What about you?" she asked. Her eyes were so large they seemed to take up most of her face. She reminded him of his younger sisters, except more fetching.

"I'll be fine," he said, touching her shoulder protectively. "Don't worry about me . Let's get out of here."

Bryan led the small party of riders away from the keep, then circled back so they came out at the rear of the wall. No one was on the wall above or around the postern door for several hundred yards. That probably meant Cedric didn't have a lot of men manning the garrison and they were all concentrated at the front where they were more vulnerable.

Two riders were leaving by the postern door as they approached, and Bryan sent a man after them to find

out who they were. They were probably on their way
to Sir John Forster, seeking succor. Bryan felt some
satisfaction that there was nothing the English warden
could do to help Cedric.

"Perhaps we could send some men back here to
climb the wall?" Megan suggested.

They rode closer, looking at the stones. The wall
wasn't so high they couldn't scale it with grappling
hooks. The nights were short in this part of the country and dawn was already approaching, but a thick
mist was rising from the ground that would limit
visibility.

"Aye," Bryan was saying when the postern door
opened again, expelling a billowing cloud of white
and gray fabric.

"It's a woman," Bryan said. They were being
awfully careless with this door, and Bryan decided not
to let them get away with it. If he was lucky, the door
wasn't heavily guarded. "Let's go." He spurred Arthur
forward.

The woman turned as they approached. It was Lauren! She held her finger to her lips, then pointed inside
the door. Bryan swung off Arthur and reached Rory
just as he was dragging a limp body out.

"Warden! Good to see you," Rory said. Another
man was slumped against the wall and Bryan helped
Rory with him.

"Willie?" Bryan asked.

Rory's mouth flattened into a grim line. "Dead."

Bryan turned to Megan. "Take Lauren to safety and
tell Douglas to stand ready for me to raise the gate."
He paused, then added, "Send more men behind me,
in case I fail."

"Bryan," Megan gasped, frowning. "Don't say that."

"Go," he urged her. "And stay with Lauren. Be safe, I pray you."

She said nothing, smiling slightly before she left, with Lauren in the saddle behind her and flanked by guards. Bryan had a feeling she would be back. "Do you think she'll listen to me?" he asked Rory and Johnny. They were to remain at the postern gate until the others arrived.

They looked at each other for support, then said, "Nay."

"That's what I thought," he muttered. "Stay with her when she returns. I do not want her harmed."

Bryan left them and kept to the shadows beside the wall. He stopped, pressing himself against the cold stones when the sentries passed overhead. He could see the gatehouse in the distance. It would be difficult to reach it without bloodshed. He drew his sword, his fingers itching for a heavy lochaber ax to swing, and crept to the gatehouse.

Cedric limped to the bed and sat down. "Dress my leg again," he ordered.

Anna sighed and rolled her eyes, but obeyed. Blood seeped through the bandage. The pain throbbed, deep inside his thigh. It itched a little, too, telling him it would probably heal fine. He suspected that stupid whore Megan had scraped her dirk against the bone. He planned to exact his revenge if he ever got his hands on her again.

Anna was retying the clean linen over the wound and pulled too tightly. He cried out in rage and pain, and slapped her. He regretted it instantly, as she sat on the floor, glaring at him. It was all too easy to hit her lately, and he could tell she wasn't one to take it for long.

Everything was falling apart and Cedric stood to lose his life, all because he had trusted Leod. And Leod had cleaved himself to Cedric even tighter by wedding his sister. Their destinies were so intertwined now that if one fell, the other must, too. He wondered if Leod had always planned it to be so.

And now Leod had saddled him with Anna. Cedric had heard the stories; she was the spawn of the powerful witch Janet Beaton, and the power survived in her. It seemed so. Though she was five and thirty, she appeared far younger, her skin and figure youthful and glowing. Leod had chosen her for this reason, because he thought she knew the black arts. He had thought he could use her for his own purposes. But instead she had ensnared Cedric. She bewitched him into her bed. Everything was her fault. He wondered if it had been a web of her design all along, weaving it about him like a black widow. And Leod had left him stuck in it, flailing around while he rode to safety.

He shot Anna a look of hatred for all the misinformation she had fed him about the warden. He didn't even desire her anymore. She repulsed him.

"What?" she asked, giving him one of her looks. "Why do you keep looking at me that way?"

He could kill her and be done with her. He suspected if he simply discarded her she would attempt to hurt him in some manner. Leod wouldn't like it, he thought grimly, reining in the urge. He didn't approve of killing women.

She rolled her eyes again and stood. "Are you just going to sit there while the warden's men surround your keep?"

"What do you suggest I do, sweets?"

"I don't know . . . fight him. Don't you have a cannon or something to fire at his men? What about all those archers? Take some of his men out, he'll probably turn tail and run."

He limped over to where she stood, combing her hair in the looking glass. "More of your brilliant advice? What would I do without you?"

He looked at her reflection over her shoulder. He saw the look of disdain on her face before she could mask it. He placed his hands gently on her shoulders and began kneading. Her expression turned tense and wary. She wasn't so stupid as he thought; she knew how inappropriate his tenderness was. She knew how it was with him.

"I don't like women who talk so much, sweets. You are tiresome. I grow weary of your tongue."

"You liked it last night," she said in a nasty voice. He squeezed her shoulders until she cried out, falling limply against him. "Stop it, Cedric! You're hurting me."

"You 'ave touched me with your serpent tongue for the last time. This night will see the end to one of us."

She wrenched out of his hold and put some distance between them.

He thought of the child, Lauren, again. Of her innocence and purity. He grabbed his breeks off the chair and yanked them on.

"Where are you going?" Anna asked, rubbing at her shoulders where he had squeezed her.

"To see the child."

"You dog," she sneered. "Will you violate and beat her, too?"

He grabbed the front of her bodice and punched her. She screamed. Blood dripped from the hands that covered her mouth. He was a little astounded and disturbed he had hit her so hard—he had not meant to—but he shrugged it off. "Do not speak of her so. Her 'eart is pure and innocent, unlike your maggot-ridden soul. She would never give me any cause to 'arm her."

She sat on the floor, crying, holding her face, the blood mingling with her tears. He felt better seeing her like that. She wasn't so powerful. He had smote her with his bare hand. She held no power over him—she was no witch. Looking down on her at this moment, he saw she wasn't beautiful. She was ugly and he hated her. He finished dressing and left. As an afterthought he locked the door behind him. She would surely try to kill him now.

The Trotter lad might actually be of some use, Cedric thought as he hobbled up the stairs. He could threaten Sir Bryan with the lad's life. The guards weren't at the prisoners' door, and a prickle of fear went through him. Inside, both of the guards lay in a heap on the floor. He ran through the keep, into the courtyard, and through the gate. The two men-at-arms were still there, leaning against the wall on either side of the postern door. He heaved a sigh of relief; they were still within the walls somewhere. One of the guards raised a hand in greeting and he waved back.

He cupped his hands over his mouth and called, "The prisoner has escaped with the girl. Keep your eyes open, I want that lass back."

"Aye, sir," one called back and gave him a mock salute. He frowned, wondering if the huge fellow was being sarcastic, and reentered the courtyard.

Megan returned to the postern door with half a dozen Hume men.

"You just missed Cedric," Rory told her, ushering them in. "He asked us to keep an eye out for the escaped prisoners."

Before she could reply Johnny was admonishing her, "You were to stay with Lauren. Why must you disobey the warden constantly?"

Megan glared at him.

"Is Lauren well?" Rory asked.

"Aye, she's with Douglas. I'm here to help."

Johnny shook his head, knowing it was useless to argue with her. Rory sent the Humes around the wall to assist Bryan. Megan headed for the keep. She had a feeling Leod was with Cedric.

"Slow down!" Johnny hissed behind her.

She turned to find both Rory and Johnny jogging after her. Once inside, they found the keep practically deserted. Rory quickly silenced one man they came upon. Megan suggested they spread out, but they wouldn't leave her, which she found annoying. They rounded a corner, and heard a woman beating on a door and screaming to be released.

"Is he holding any other prisoners?" she asked Rory.

"I know not—he didn't discuss it with me."

She noticed for the first time that his face bore the marks of a thorough beating.

"Perhaps we should help her," Megan suggested.

They threw themselves against the door until the door frame splintered and they both fell into the room. Megan stepped over the broken wood in the doorway. Johnny leaned over a woman who was covered in blood.

"Christ, what did he do to you?" Megan asked.

The woman's long brown hair was in disarray, and her face was smeared with blood, as were her hands and her dress. She was shaking and had been crying. "He's going to kill me! You must get me out of here!"

Megan helped the woman stand.

"I've seen this woman," Rory said. "Earlier—with Cedric."

The woman looked wildly at Rory. "When? When did you see me with him?" She clutched at the front of his doublet.

He backed away from her, frowning. "In the courtyard—you were with Leod Hume and another woman—they left through the postern door."

"He's gone?" Megan cried, frustrated and disappointed that Leod continued to elude justice.

"Aye," the woman said. "Leod and his wife escaped—Cedric aided them. I'm Anna, Sir Bryan's sister. That's why Cedric wants me—he wants to hurt my brother." Tears welled in her dark eyes. Looking at her closely, Megan thought she did bear a striking resemblance to Bryan, particularly her height.

"Does she speak the truth, think you?" Megan asked.

Rory nodded. "I think she does. Outside, Cedric struck her and handled her roughly."

Megan bit her lip, not liking the stench of this

whole affair. Bryan had told her some things about his sister—he had said she was trying to hurt him or Lord Bothwell. Anna looked at her pleadingly. But she was Bryan's *sister*. It was the blood covering her that did it, making Megan's decision. It was obvious Cedric had assaulted her—she must be telling the truth. "Very well."

Anna smiled tremulously and wiped her tears. "Where is my dear brother?"

Cedric joined his men on the ramparts. Torches lit the walls surrounding the keep. Most of his men were manning the front of the curtain wall where the warden's men had converged. He was so stupid for listening to that lying whore Anna. He had split with his main body of men, sending some of them to hide the stolen beasts, another small contingent to lay an ambush in case the warden sent a party to pursue them, and the remainder to raid the Kerrs on their way home.

The ambush he set for the warden had apparently failed, and the rest of his men had not returned. Now he had fewer than two score to man the keep. He looked down from the wall. The sun was rising on the horizon, and the stones beneath his fingers were wet from the mist. Hume's men had joined the warden, and there was old deputy frog-eye himself, wearing his rusting armor and carrying a lance. Cedric scanned the men, counting them with his eyes. Over one hundred. Where was that damn warden?

The enemy had gathered around the portcullis, as though the dolts expected Cedric to open it and let them in. He whistled to his archers to stand ready. He would scatter the fools. They looked too relaxed. The laird noticed the archers slipping arrows into their bows and yelled a warning. Cedric raised his arm. The men below frantically untied their targes and shields from their saddles. He dropped his arm, sending a volley of arrows down into the warden's men. Men pitched off their horses, their screams of pain shattering the morning.

Cedric was debating whether to waste more arrows when he heard the groaning creak of his gate being raised. The Humes crowded in close to the portcullis. Panic shot through Cedric. He motioned to the archers to fire at will and took the steps two at a time until he reached the bailey. It was too late; they were crawling under the gate. He ran for the tower to secure the doors. The doors swung open, and he skidded to a stop.

Megan Dixon stared back at him and behind her was Anna, her mouth curved into an evil smile as though she was the master of this design. His heart skipped erratically, wondering if she was. Two huge men flanked them, one of them Rory Trotter. He felt the web closing around him. He swung around. The warden was marching toward him. The bailey was filling with Humes. Cedric's men dropped their weapons, surrendering.

Cedric held his sword in front of him, gripping it with both hands. The warden slowed and unsheathed his. It was slimed with the blood of men he had recently killed. There was no peace in this man. Cedric could feel the rage emanating from him. He had been a fool to listen to Anna.

"Sir John will not be happy if anything happens to me," Cedric said, his eyes blurring from the sweat running into them.

The warden seemed calm. His long body moved with the grace of a cat, circling Cedric. "If Sir John cared what happened to you, would he not be here by now, rescuing you?"

"He's on his way—I'm sure—then you'll have to answer to him."

The warden smiled. "Nay, your uncle can do nothing. I know the border law, and you're mine. You killed my deputy and destroyed my garrison."

"Killing Willie was self-defense," Cedric stammered. "Ask your deputy—Trotter—he was there."

"Rory Trotter saw nothing!" Anna yelled.

Cedric swore. He wished he had hacked that woman up when he had the chance.

Anna stepped forward from behind Trotter, looking every inch the victim, with blood staining her face and bodice. "I was there, Bryan. Cedric murdered Willie. Willie never had a chance to defend himself—and now Cedric plans to violate his widow."

"Lies!" Cedric cried, but he knew no one was going to believe anything he said, so he turned back to the warden, ready to fight with him. But Sir Bryan wasn't looking at Cedric. He was standing straight, his sword dangling at his side, staring at Anna. He took a few steps toward her. Cedric ran at him. Sir Bryan whirled and ducked. Cedric's sword slashed at empty air.

Bryan beat Cedric back with his sword; at first it was pure rage. Cedric *had* killed Willie, and now he wanted to harm Lauren. Anna was covered with blood. Bryan wanted to slaughter him. Cedric was a good fighter and defended himself admirably against Bryan's assault, which gave reason a moment to push its way into his head. What was Anna doing with Cedric? He recalled what Francis had told him— about how she came to him with the handfasting lie. She was still not to be trusted. If Cedric died, the truth might die with him.

The steel blades clashed as Bryan brought his down, again and again, the shocks vibrating up his arms. Cedric was doing nothing more than defending himself, unable to find an opening to attack Bryan. Cedric stumbled against the wall, and Bryan swiped hard. The sound of hissing metal filled the air as Cedric's sword was ripped from his hands and clattered across the stones of the bailey, out of his reach. Cedric's face was greasy with fear. It took all the strength Bryan had not to cut him down. His blade was held aloft, ready to end Cedric's life, his muscles quivering from the effort of stopping himself. Cedric didn't cower or beg, he merely stood there, his eyes locked with Bryan's, waiting to die.

Bryan slowly lowered the sword. He called to his men, "Bind him and bring him into the hall. I'd like to have a word with him."

Nineteen

Leod was relieved to be rid of his wife, if only for a short while. He rode through the Merse, invigorated by the brisk air. It had been so long since he was here. Too long. He was tired of hiding from Lord Bothwell, tired of what his life had become. He was ready to face the earl. But he would have his shield, or else the earl would crush him. He vowed to himself he would not make the same mistakes when he was warden again. This time his actions would appear to be beyond reproach. Besides, he was a bit more respectable now that he was married.

His brows lowered, thinking of his wife. Oh, he had wanted her. Wanted her so bad he couldn't keep his hands off the lass, and now she was carrying his child. Normally, that would not have mattered to Leod, but she was Cedric's little sister. When Leod came to Cedric, seeking shelter from Bothwell, Cedric had

insisted Leod wed Tyna. It ensured Cedric's continued support, so for now, it was a good match. And
Tyna wouldn't give him any grief about his other
activities. The baggage had no spine.

The widow Dixon's tower came into sight. His
pulse sped just thinking about the time he had spent
with Megan. If he had to marry, why couldn't it have
been someone like her, whose fire might keep him
interested? She was so passionate. He longed to spar
with her again.

He reined in his horse, staring at her home. He
imagined himself laird of it, married to Megan Dixon.
The gray stones of her small tower sparkled in the
morning sun, as though it were encrusted with dia-
monds. He wondered if he was in love with her.

Those thoughts were forgotten when he spotted his
quarry, wee Innes running through the grass. Splen-
did! The child was playing outside the protection of
the barmkin. This would be simple. But surely the lad
wasn't out alone. Leod scanned the horizon, looking
for the golden hair of his mother, and was surprised to
see another woman. A vision of loveliness. His horse
seemed to be walking to her against his will until he
realized he was urging it forward with his thighs.

He had never seen this woman before. Her hair was
dark and flowing around her shoulders. Her dress was
simple, yet decorated with pretty lace, and her breasts
looked perfect from where he watched. She tossed a
ball to Innes. The lad's hair reflected the sun like copper. He looked just like his father. Leod's lip curled at
the memory of Megan's late husband. Then he smiled
in satisfaction. He had rid himself of Innes Dixon and
many others. The obstacles before him now were not

insurmountable. He had already achieved much. His current situation was no more than a setback.

The beautiful woman threw the ball too hard, and it went rolling into the trees. She laughed as Innes bounced after it. Leod spurred his horse forward to speak with her. He ran a hand over his hair and mustache, eyeing her body. He could almost feel it beneath his hands.

She heard his approach and turned. She had dark eyes, almost black, and long black lashes. All thoughts of Megan and her son were gone as he stared into her eyes. She was wary, but unafraid, and held her ground. He stopped before her, staring downward. He could see her cleavage from his vantage point, and he was not wrong in thinking she was as close to perfect as a woman could get.

She raised a well-shaped eyebrow at him. "Monsieur?"

She was French! His delight in her was complete. He wanted her badly. *"Enchante! Tu es tres jolie!"* he said, exhausting his supply of French. He wasn't positive what he said, something about her being beautiful, but it earned the intended effect.

She colored pink and clapped her hands, a charming smile curving her lips. "You speak French, Monsieur! I am Marietta, but you, friend, may call me Marie."

He was enamored. The boy was forgotten as he dismounted and took her hand. "I am honored to be called friend by one so fair."

She withdrew her hand. "Might I have your name now, Monsieur?"

"Ah, of course, I can't think straight in your presence. My name is Leod. And I have come recently from a visit to France. I'm here to see Lady Dixon. We're old friends."

"*Bonjour*, Monsieur Leod. Would you come to the house and have some refreshment with me? I miss having people to talk to and would so love to hear news from home. My husband is away fighting the bad men and has no time for me or his new son." She made a little pouty face.

"Then he is a fool," he said suddenly and passionately, taking a step toward her.

She looked slightly alarmed but masked it well and laughed. "You say your name is Leod?" A vertical line of concentration marred her brow. Did she recognize his name? Had Megan talked about him?

"Er . . . Aye, Leod Maxwell, from the West March."

Her brow smoothed and she looked over her shoulder. "I must get Innes," she said.

"Where is the lad's mother?"

"She is also fighting bad men—it is what you borderers do best—fight, murder, and raid." She pursed her lips in displeasure. "Cora is here, though, and she can look after him."

"Verra good," he said. She was dissatisfied with life. Even better!

"Innes!" she called. She lifted her skirts and went into the trees.

He knew the boy would recognize him, so he sheltered himself behind his horse. "I will wait for you, Marie." He rolled her name off his tongue. She looked back at him over her shoulder, uneasy. He would hate to take her by force now, when he was so certain he could make her come to him willingly, but he couldn't risk having that hag, Cora, see him.

He was being foolish. He couldn't take her and the boy. They would both fight him and he had no wish to harm either of them. He could only control one fighting body at a time. He sighed, realizing he would have to stick with his original plan. When he was warden again, he promised himself he would make a widow of her quickly.

"Monsieur! Oh, help me, Monsieur Maxwell!"

He jumped to attention at hearing his lady in distress. She ran toward him from the trees, and he met her halfway. "What is it?"

"I cannot find him! I found the ball, but he is gone!" She clutched the painted wooden ball to her chest.

Leod frowned. They would have seen the boy if he had run to the house, since Leod and Marie stood between the barmkin and the trees. Could Innes have recognized him and gone for help? He hurried into the trees with Marie behind him. He directed her to stay at the edge of the small wood while he went deeper to look. It was impossible to get lost; it was no more than a stand of fifty birch. If he was here, Leod would come across him. And he did. The boy was squatting down at a stream created from the run-off of the recent heavy rains. He poked at a frog with a stick. It was the perfect opportunity to grab him, and Leod started forward. He stopped, peering back into the trees. He couldn't see Marie from here, which meant Innes couldn't, either. Boys tended to become engrossed in their play, forgetting the time.

He backed up. Innes would still be here when he was through. He returned to Marie, who waited, the ball clasped in her hands. He took her by the wrists and drew her further into the trees.

"He is fine, love. He found himself a frog to play with. We can talk here, while he plays."

She pulled her hands away, looking over her shoulder. "I would rather not." He could tell she was beginning to fear him and was trying to gather her courage. His heart ached with love for her. He would hate to hurt her. She tried to walk past him, to where Innes played, but he grabbed her waist and pulled her against him.

"Don't scream, lass, I don't want to hurt you." He could see that didn't concern her and she was prepared to scream anyway. "I will hurt the lad. If you want him safe, do as I say."

"You are the dead warden," she gasped, her face pale.

"Aye, but not so dead."

Her eyes were filled with terror, but also anger and defiance. He kissed her, wanting to show her he would be gentle. Her lips remained firm and unyielding. She twisted her head away. Sometimes it was like this, and Leod accepted that; some women simply liked to be chased. He raised his head and smiled ruefully. "That is fine, there are other things to kiss."

She looked as though she might vomit and tried to escape from his embrace. He forced her to the ground. She was whining and crying, but like a good girl, not making much noise.

"I love you," he whispered to her as he pulled on her bodice until her full breasts were exposed. She was nursing, he could see that now, and he became even more excited. He buried his face in her chest. Something hard slammed down on his head, and he groaned, losing his wits for a moment. She scrambled out from under him and screamed at Innes to run.

Leod stood unsteadily. He had forgotten about the wooden ball. She held the ball in one hand and the other held her shift closed. Innes came running out of the trees.

"Go to the house, Innes, now!"

The lad's eyes widened when he saw Leod. "Marie! Marie! 'Tis the dead warden! He hurt my mum!"

Marie pointed the ball at him as if it were a pistol, her hand shaking. He almost laughed, in spite of the pain splitting his head. Innes tried to dash by him, but he caught the boy.

"We will have to resume our engagement another time, Marie," he said, walking out of the trees, struggling to hang onto the wriggling, crying child. He heard her running behind him, about to hit him again, and stepped aside, tripping her. She fell on her face. He resisted the urge to help her back up. He jogged to his horse and mounted quickly. Innes bucked against him and shrieked for Marie to help him. Marie ran after them, tears streaking her lovely face.

He sighed, disappointed by how the tryst had ended, and rode for the border.

Bryan sat in a large chair positioned by the fireplace at Cedric's keep. His men were scouring Cedric's tower and lands for anything of value they might claim as restitution before they burned it all to the ground.

He felt a presence behind him and turned. It was Anna, clean now, though her nose was swollen and misshapen. Megan had tended her wounds and found her serviceable clothing.

"Lady Dixon is lovely . . . is she yours?" Anna asked, walking around his chair to face him.

He felt somewhat at a disadvantage with her towering over him, but resisted the instinct to stand. "Mine?" He smiled slightly. "If she'll have me, I suppose."

Anna smiled, too, though it dripped of insincerity. She sat on the hearth, lower than him now. "Bryan, it has been too long. Why did you never write?"

"I did."

"You did? I never received any letters." She shrugged wryly. "You know how that goes; tomorrow I'll probably receive one sent a decade ago."

Bryan leaned his elbow on the chair's arm, scratching at his temple. "What are you doing with Cedric?"

"Apparently Sir John told him I was your sister, so he kidnapped me, hoping I would reveal your weaknesses. When I was of no assistance to him, he beat me." Her bottom lip quivered, then she added quickly, "And he violated me."

"He violated you," Bryan mused, staring past her at the fire.

Something about Anna troubled Bryan. It always had. She never seemed quite . . . *right*. She used to play cruel tricks on him when they were children—tricks that were only funny to her. They were usually the normal torments of an older sibling, bees in his bedding, tacks in his shoes, but once, after his beloved hound had died, she had dug it up and situated it on his bed, just as Jasper had always slept. Bryan's reaction to finding his rotting pet in his bed had given Anna weeks of amusement. It had been a rather traumatic moment for a young boy—one he had never quite forgiven her for.

"Aye! He *violated* me," she repeated, snapping her fingers in front of his face, bringing him out of his reverie. "I am your sister—will you not avenge my honor?"

He rested his chin in his palm and gazed at her steadily. "Why did you tell Lord Bothwell our mother and my father were handfast?"

She tossed her thick mane of brown hair over her shoulder. "Because it's true."

"Why didn't you come to me first?"

"Because I knew you wouldn't do anything about it. You're probably content to be warden when you could be a great lord."

"Actually, I didn't even want to be warden—in the beginning, that is."

She smirked and rolled her eyes. "That sounds like the Bryan I remember."

"Tell me, Anna, what you thought Lord Bothwell would do upon hearing there was a threat to his lands and titles? Step down gracefully? Mayhap he *wants* to trade places, aye?"

She stood, glaring down at him, her hands balled in fists on her hips. "You're the same sniveling little brat I remember. That's the last time I do you a favor." She started to walk away.

Bryan stood and caught her arm. "Where do you think you're going?"

"Home."

"I don't think so. I think I'll keep you close a bit longer."

Her eyes flashed with rage, and her hand clamped down on his wrist, her nails digging into his skin like claws. He wrenched her off and turned her over to his guards with orders to lock her up in one of Cedric's rooms.

When he returned to the fire, Lauren sat on the hearth, her arms wrapped around her knees. "Shall you stay on at the garrison, Lauren?" he asked. "There's a place for you, you know that?"

Her head bobbed. "Aye. Since I will be wed to Rory, I will continue on as always."

"What?"

"Rory swore to Willie he would wed me if aught happened to him—just as Willie swore to my da." Tears shimmered in her eyes and she looked down quickly. "I was so frightened. But now I know everything will be fine."

Rory joined them. "Are you ready, Lauren?" he asked. She stood and moved beside him. "Sir, I have your leave?" he asked.

Bryan could only stare at them.

"What is it, sir?"

"Uh . . . wait outside, Lauren. I need to speak with my deputy." Lauren left and Rory looked at Bryan expectantly.

"You are going to wed Lauren?"

Rory shook his head. "Nay. I'm just taking her back to the garrison."

"She told me you swore to Willie you would."

Rory stared at him blankly. His eyes widened suddenly. "Oh, Christ! Did she say that to you? Oh, damn! What did she say?"

"Did you swear an oath or not?" Bryan asked.

"Nay! But I told Cedric that I had, hoping he would believe me." Rory shuddered in disgust. "He wanted her . . . in that way. He is a sick man."

Bryan sighed, his heart heavy. Someone had to tell the poor lass. She would be heartbroken. Bryan was fairly certain Rory was unaware of the affection Lauren had for him.

"I will marry her," Rory said in a brittle voice.

Bryan looked up quickly. "What?"

"This is all my fault. Willie is dead because I wouldn't listen to him."

"What happened?"

Rory swallowed and looked Bryan in the eye. "We followed Cedric to a cottage where he met with a woman. I wanted to eavesdrop on them—but Willie said no. He wanted to wait until Cedric left and continue trailing him. I ignored him. Willie followed me. We split up—one of us on either side of the cottage. Cedric must have heard something outside. I heard a struggle, but by the time I got there, Willie was dead." Rory related the events dispassionately, but Bryan doubted he would be offering to wed Lauren if his guilt wasn't great.

"Do you believe that he didn't mean to kill Willie?"

"I know not."

Bryan laid a comforting hand on Rory's shoulder. "I understand your guilt, but you don't have to wed her."

Rory shook his head firmly. "She has no one because of me, and now I have given her false hope with my lie. I will not let her down again."

"That's not necessary. I'll see to her care."

Rory's face was grim and determined. "Nay. She is of a marriageable age. Will she be pleased with me as a husband, think you?"

Bryan felt the beginnings of laughter tug at him. He

fought for a straight face. "Aye, I think she will be well pleased. This is a fine thing you're doing, lad."

Rory's jaw clenched and he averted his eyes. "It is my duty."

"Should she not observe some period of mourning?"

"I think, sir, it would be best if neither of us has much time to think on it."

The lad had a point. All the thinking Bryan and Megan had done hadn't gotten them very far. Maybe that was the answer—to rush headfirst into your fate. He sent Rory on his way and went in search of Megan. He wanted her counsel on what to do about Cedric. He had promised Cedric his life—in return for Leod's whereabouts. But Cedric wasn't talking. Even when Bryan took the butt end of a musket to him, he still wouldn't speak a word about Leod, though he poured out much bile about Anna, calling her a witch and a whore. Nothing useful. Bryan's rage was gone and all that was left was self-loathing. It had been the old feelings of vengeance that had driven him on the night before, and they were gone now. He had no taste for killing Cedric, nor for beating him earlier. He had done that out of frustration. But how could he set Cedric free after what he did to the garrison? Of course, Bryan's raid to his lands would be difficult for him to recover from; maybe that was punishment enough.

Megan would want Cedric dead, and it was the warden's duty to execute him. And she would be right. The man should be executed. Besides, it was the border way to feud. Bryan's head ached from these thoughts. He was naive to think he was ending anything by showing mercy. He was only prolonging it, for Cedric would surely begin a blood feud with him.

He finally found Megan curled up in a large bed, which Bryan suspected was Cedric's, sleeping soundly. She hadn't even removed her jack or boots. Gunpowder and dirt smudged her cheek and brow. He tried to rub it off with his finger, but she stirred, swatting his hand away.

He was trying to decide whether or not he should crawl in bed with her, when a cabinet with the door ajar caught his attention. Papers were visible within. He went to the cabinet and drew them out. They were letters. He began sifting through them, looking for Leod's handwriting, but didn't find it. Most were just the daily business of running any estate. He returned them to the cabinet and searched the other doors. He found a wooden box filled with sterling. He started to return it when a bit of white caught his eye. It was the corner of a sheet of paper, sticking up from the coins. He dug it out carefully.

It was a list of names written in a chillingly familiar hand—one he had received many letters from while in the Low Countries. Innes Dixon was at the top of the list. There was no date, nor anything explaining what the list meant. But as he read the five names on the list, he realized they were all husbands of the widows of the East March. And the handwriting was his cousin's, the Earl of Bothwell's. He could do nothing more than stare at it for several minutes. What could it mean? Perhaps it meant nothing more than Francis listing men who had died on the March. There was nothing sinister about that.

Why did Cedric have it? That was what twisted Bryan's guts.

Where did Anna fit into all of this—if she did at all? He slid the list into his doublet and returned to the bed. Megan was awake. She lay on her side, watching him, her green eyes troubled. He hoped she wouldn't ask him about the paper.

He stretched out on the bed beside her. "Marry me."

She lowered her eyes, her mouth turning down sadly.

He touched her chin, forcing her to look at him. "What is it?"

"I don't want to be a warden's wife."

He withdrew his hand and clenched it into a fist on the bed. "I see. Then why—"

"I'll marry you, Bryan."

He was confused now. "You aren't happy. Do you want to wed me?"

She lay back on the bed, staring blankly above her. "I want to marry you, not the warden."

Right now, he *was* the warden, and there was nothing he could do about it. Vows to resign before they wed sprang to his lips, but he didn't give voice to them. Until he had Leod—and knew what part Bothwell played in all of this—he would not resign. He had a personal stake in it now. He settled for saying, "What if I will resign when this is over . . . when I understand what Leod was involved in? Would that please you?" It wouldn't please him. The very idea of turning his march over to another corrupt official who would destroy all Bryan had built nearly brought the black cloud of rage back to the surface. But he would do it for Megan.

"There's something else going on here," she said, in a low voice, almost to herself. "Something we can't see. I fear if you dig too deeply, you shall die. Death follows Leod wherever he goes."

He moved over her, placing his hands on either side of her body, so she had to look at him. "I am not going to die."

She smiled slightly. "Innes used to say that, too."

"How many times do I have to say it before you listen?" he growled, leaning closer, so their noses were almost touching. Her hair smelled faintly of wildflowers.

Her eyebrows rose and her smile grew. "Say what?" she asked, her voice breathless, excited. A flush rose in her cheeks.

"I am not Innes." He captured her mouth to prove it.

 Twenty

Riding away from Cedric's tower, back to the East March and home, Megan struggled with the feelings of foreboding and doom that had descended on her since she accepted Bryan's proposal. Johnny was with her, but she hadn't told him of it. She was to be bride to another warden. The fear for Bryan's safety that consumed her was far worse than anything she had ever felt for Innes.

After the past night, she knew if Bryan continued to be warden he would be killed. It was inevitable. She had wanted to protect herself and her son from that kind of sorrow. But she loved Bryan, and her heart mourned him as though he were already dead. Tears blurred her eyes. What was she to do? Just sit and wait for him to be murdered? Regardless of what he promised to her, she could see his heart was in the march now. He was a good warden; he cared. She sniffled and wiped her eyes with her sleeve. How could she make him give it up? How could she take him away from the people of the East March, who needed him? It all seemed so unfair. She loved Bryan to his very bones, but loving him was misery.

A rider was approaching. Megan swiped her tears away and squinted. It was the strangest sight she had ever seen.

Johnny let out an exclamation of surprise. "It's Hob!"

He was perched atop a swayback mule, beating it mercilessly with a stick. The poor mule loped along as fast as it could, its sides heaving. Hob's long wiry hair streamed out behind him.

When he saw them, he waved his arms and shouted. Megan's stomach knotted with unease. Only an emergency would bring Hob this far from home. He had to have ridden for hours on that broken-down mule just to reach her.

She spurred her horse forward. "What is it?" she asked when they reached the old man.

The mule brayed angrily and turned its head to snap at Hob when he dismounted.

"Oh, Meg, 'tis awful! Awful happenings! Wee Innes has been taken!"

"What?" She could barely manage to get the word out of her throat as she slid out of the saddle.

Hob clutched her arm with long, bony fingers. "A man took him. Kidnapped him!"

Megan pried him off, her chest constricting with panic. *Innes*. The copper hair, the freckles, the blue eyes, the intense curiosity, all gone.

"What man?" Johnny asked.

"He attacked Marie and tried to rape her."

Johnny started violently. "Is she well?"

"Aye, aye," Hob said, waving an impatient hand. "He said his name was Leod. Could it be? Leod Hume?"

Megan thought she might vomit. "Did she say what he looked like?"

"Aye, brown hair, mustache, blue eyes, verra comely. And he told Marie he was the 'dead warden.' It must be him!"

Megan's breath caught on a ragged sob. Leod had her son! Why? What did he want with a little boy?

"Surely he knows about you and Sir Bryan," Johnny said, answering her thoughts. "Mayhap he means to trade Innes for Cedric."

Hope filled her. She had to get to Bryan and stop him from executing Cedric. "Go to Marie," she said to Johnny, "and I will tell the warden."

Bryan had returned to his chair by the fire. The scaffold was almost finished and the torches burned hot outside, ready to reduce the keep to ashes. And yet he still hesitated. What part did Cedric play in all this? Why did he protect Leod? The answers to the questions still evaded him. Rory had reported that Cedric had been sheltering Leod. Cedric had the answers, and Bryan was reluctant to kill him.

He stared into the fire, mesmerized by it. The flames were angry, burning like the violence that had consumed him throughout the whole night. But now it was gone and his soul was as cool as the ashes of a burned-out hearth. He thought of the men he had killed. They died because they stood between him and the gatehouse. No other reason. What would their families be told about their senseless deaths? That they were brave? That they died for Cedric? That they failed in their brave fight, because Cedric was hung anyway?

What was this justice? There had to be a better way. He had given in to the border way, and he now regretted it. He wished he could set the wardenship aside, as Megan wanted him to. But if he stepped down someone else would take his place, a borderer probably, who would swat the mystery away. Bryan couldn't bear that—he had to see this through to the end.

And then what? Would another Leod Hume be appointed warden? One who cared nothing for the safety of the march? He didn't think even Megan wanted such a thing to happen.

Someone was walking toward him. He didn't turn.

"Excellent job, Bryan . . . but I hear Cedric still lives."

It was Francis. Bryan didn't look at him. "What are you doing across the border?"

"I go where I want." Francis moved to the hearth so Bryan was forced to look at him. His gaze was probing. "You're growing roots, Bryan. What are you waiting for? Cedric is here, the man who has caused so much tragedy on your march. Kill him and end it."

"There are too many questions unanswered. Cedric has those answers." Their eyes locked. "Leod was here."

The earl's gloved hand curled into a fist and his lips drew into a thin line. "Damn! And he eluded you?"

"I didn't know it was him at the time, but I sent someone to follow him."

Francis smiled. "Good."

"Why do you want Leod?"

Francis leaned his elbow on his knee and stroked his beard, regarding Bryan with hooded eyes. "You've been investigating him. You know what a depraved man he is. I want to rid the world of such scum."

Bryan could feel the folded list inside his doublet, reminding him that his cousin was not being completely honest with him. "But all that is within my duties. Why have you taken such an avid interest in this? Am I doing so poorly you must be at me constantly?"

"You are a most excellent warden. The best I have ever encountered. You please me well." He paused thoughtfully. "Yet, I hesitate to take you into my confidence on things that might bring harm on you simply from the knowing."

Bryan's lip curled. "I knew this smelled foul."

"Aye, but the stench comes not from me, but from Leod and his henchman."

Bryan suspected as much, and try as he might, he didn't believe ill of Francis. No matter how suspicious it all sounded, he believed Francis to be inherently good. They had been friends as children, and when Bryan served in the Low Countries it had been Francis who visited him and brought him letters from his mother. Francis was the one who welcomed him back to Scotland and found him a position of respect.

Yet Bryan refrained from mentioning the list. He would investigate it himself. "I have Anna," he said. "She was with Cedric."

"Indeed!"

"Aye. I don't know what part she plays in this,

either. She insists that my mother and father were handfast and that Cedric held her prisoner and abused her." Bryan stared past Francis into the fire. "I know not what to think. She has definitely been abused." He looked back at his cousin who was eyeing him narrowly. "But I wouldn't be surprised to find she liked to be hit and it was all part of some demented love-play."

"May I speak with Anna?"

"Aye." Bryan led him to the room where Anna was being held and unlocked the door. No candles were lit, and the shutters were closed up tight. He walked forward cautiously. He heard her come out of the dark at him. He crouched low, but was still hit over the head with something hard and blunt.

"Ow!" he yelled. He saw movement and caught her, wrestling her to the ground while Francis lit a candle. She bit him and scratched him and pulled his hair, all the while screaming obscenities.

Francis was laughing as though it was all entertainment for him, and Bryan began to get angry. He was close to striking her, something he had never done before, even when they were children.

"Anna, stop!"

She became still. He was straddling her with her wrists pinned to the floor on either side of her head. Her teeth were bared and she hissed through them like an animal. Her eyes darted to Francis. "What does he want?" Her eyes became so wide he could see the whites of them, and she shrank away, closer to Bryan, the fight draining out of her. "Keep away from me!"

Bryan scowled and stood, pulling her to her feet by

her wrists. "What is the matter with you?" he scolded. "You're acting as if you have no sense."

Francis approached and she clung to Bryan, wrapping her arms around him and screaming. He tried to pry her off, bewildered.

"I think she's gone mad!" he said to Francis.

"Leave me alone with her."

She held Bryan tighter. "No! Don't leave me alone with him! Bryan, I pray you! He will devour me! He is Satan!"

Bryan had to laugh. "Anna! 'Tis Francis. He'll not hurt you. You won't talk to me, mayhap you will talk to him."

He managed to get her arms off, though she was like an octopus and seemed to clutch him with another tentacle each time he pried one off. He pushed her at Francis, who wrapped his arms around her from behind. She was still and straight as a board, her hands balled into fists. She actually seemed terrified of him. Bryan couldn't believe people actually paid heed to the stupid rumors that Francis was a warlock.

Francis murmured softly in her ear and she calmed. He nodded to Bryan.

"Just be careful—she cannot be trusted," Bryan warned. He handed him the key and left. He let out a sigh of relief to be away from his sister. She was a lunatic. He had been foolish to even think anything she said made sense.

Francis was keeping information from him. Bryan meant to get his hands on Leod. He would find out from Leod why he was hiding from Francis. He thought of Megan's words to him before she left. There was something unseen at work. Perhaps she was right.

"Bryan!"

He whirled around. Megan ran across the hall, her hair and eyes wild. She grasped at the front of his doublet. Dirty streaks lined her face from tears. "Innes! Leod took Innes! He's gone! Is Cedric dead?"

"No."

She wrapped her arms around his waist, buried her face in his chest, and began to sob. He held her to him, his mind sorting through this. *Innes. Kidnapped.* He imagined the lad at the mercy of someone as sick as Leod Hume and had to put it from his mind before he did something rash. He must think clearly. No more thoughtless acts of violence, or the lad might get hurt.

The man he sent to follow Leod hadn't returned. He called one of his men over. "Escort Lady Dixon to her home. Stay with her while she packs up her necessities and kin, and escort them to the garrison."

She lifted her head and he saw she was going to protest. He placed a finger against her lips. He changed his mind. "Hold!" he said to the guard, who stopped and looked at him expectantly. "Have you room for us?" he asked Megan. "My garrison is in ruins. I will need a small company of men there anyway after we wed."

"Aye, Innes always kept a score of men in the tower. 'Tis been a while since we've had so many, but we'll manage."

After giving the guard his new instructions, he retrieved a handkerchief and wiped her face. "I need to go back to the garrison first."

She had come to him with this. She hadn't taken matters into her own hands. Perhaps she had finally come to trust him. His arms tightened around her.

She pulled away from him. "I think you should bring Cedric. Leod might want to trade him for Innes."

"I can't just give Cedric up. Look at all the trouble he caused last time I set him at liberty."

Her eyes flashed. "What about my son?"

Bryan sighed. "Go on. I'll bring Cedric along, aye?"

She gave him a long, obscure look before finally walking away. The sky was darkening with a coming storm. A cool breeze swept through the open doors, stirring the rushes. He began readying his men to return to the garrison. Francis came down the steps with Anna docilely by his side. He tucked her hand around his elbow and led her to Bryan.

"Well?" Bryan asked.

"Mistress Beaton is coming with me," Francis said.

Bryan frowned. Anna's eyes were downcast, but she clutched Francis's arm with both hands. Bryan touched her chin, raising her face so she looked at him. She gazed back at him with a small smile.

"Do you want to go with him?"

She nodded earnestly. "Oh, aye."

His frowned deepened. "I thought you said he was Satan!"

"I was wrong," she said softly and looked at Francis adoringly.

Francis shrugged. "I can't control it. Lassies love me."

Bryan was reluctant to set her free, but it was obvious Francis could control her. He stepped aside, shaking his head in confusion.

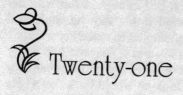 Twenty-one

Francis was glad his wife was away while Crichton was being remodeled. He didn't think she would understand Anna's presence. Of course, there was little the countess understood about him, being more than a decade his senior. But she was a charming woman. Anna's mouth was open and her eyes wide as he led her through the castle. She followed him up the stairs to his chambers. He turned to her when the door was shut. She looked hideous. She would have to be bathed and changed before he touched her.

"Anna? We had a bargain. You are here, with me. I have kept up my end thus far . . . and if you tell me where Leod is, I shall follow through. But unless you give me what I want, I shall strip you, douse you with water, and leave you in my dungeon to freeze."

She gave him a seductive look and advanced on him. No doubt this worked with every other man she encountered, but he only found her amusing. It didn't help that she stank and he didn't want her near him. The ride back had been bad enough. Even with her behind him and the wind in his face he could still smell her. He had been tempted to make her walk.

She laid her hand on his arm. "You won't do that."

He raised an eyebrow. Why did people challenge him? Did they really think he would back down? He grabbed the front of her bodice with both hands and ripped it open. She screamed in surprise and tried to run away. He kept hold of her gown, so her running only succeeded in ripping it further off.

"Henry!" he bellowed. The door sprang open. His steward had obviously been on the other side with his ear to the door. "Dunk her in the horse trough and lock her in the dungeons. Don't give her any clothes or blankets, or I shall take it out of your hide. You'll need a few men to handle her, she's a wildcat."

"What?" she shrieked as Henry caught hold of her. His steward was going to enjoy the task immensely; his hands were already gripping her bare breasts unnecessarily. Francis wondered if he was the only one who could smell her. "You'll learn, Anna, that I mean what I say. I am your master now. We'll discuss it further when you're feeling more . . . agreeable."

He shook his head, irritated at the need to prove his power over her when it should have been obvious to everyone. It often seemed as though he was the only one who could see the whole world, the entire scheme, and his place in it. Everyone else was too caught up in their own stupid problems, their small minds. And in their tiny worlds, they began to think they had some power. Like Leod Hume. Leod was a small man playing small-man games. Blackmail, threats. It didn't work with Francis, and Leod had been slow to realize that. Too slow.

Francis had shown Leod how little he mattered on the grand scale. And how much Francis did. Leod had fled like a terrified rabbit, even faking his own death to escape Francis's grasp. Leod was still underestimating him. He was still using his small mind. Francis had only to shift his vision a tiny bit to snare the rabbit again.

He smiled. After a night with her teeth rattling together, Anna would be his. She had no conscience—she had not even the social graces to pretend one. She would prove very useful.

It had been a productive day! He rubbed his hands together and went to the window to view his courtyard. Everything was going according to his plan. Just like the courtyard. It was coming along splendidly. Even the courtyard was bending to his will.

Megan's home was teeming with soldiers, just as when Innes was alive. Most of them had taken up residence in the tower, though some slept on the floor in her parlor. Half of Bryan's men were here; the other half were repairing the garrison.

Since she had no rooms suitable for housing prisoners, Cedric's ankle was chained to a stake driven into the ground next to the tower door. He had some mobility, but was being treated as an animal. His guard nodded to Megan when she approached. Cedric's eyes were closed. He didn't look so frightening anymore. It appeared Bryan had gotten a little rough with him. His face was cut and bruised and tracked with dried blood.

He opened his eyes. "I am at your mercy now, my lady. What will you 'ave done with me?"

"You're not at my mercy, but the warden's."

He shrugged. "The warden will do anything you ask him to."

She knelt in front of him, but out of his reach should he make a grab for her. "Is that what you think? Is that why Leod took Innes?"

"Aye. It was either you or the boy—and he knows what a difficult quarry you are." He smiled wickedly.

"I could speak to the warden, ask him to treat you lightly, if you tell me where Leod is keeping my son."

"I know not where Leod is," he said with exaggerated innocence.

She sighed. Cedric was useless. She doubted Leod even wanted him. What good was Cedric to him now? Her greatest fear was that Leod would take Innes and leave the country.

"Where is Anna?" he asked.

"Why should I answer your questions when you won't answer mine?" She stood and started to walk away.

"Wait!" he called, his voice sounding strange. She turned back to him and he asked, "How is the lass, Lauren?"

"What care you?"

He licked his lips, then bit them. She moved closer, excitement welling inside her. He was going to talk. "The answers to these questions mean a lot to you?" she asked. "Enough to trade information?"

"I will give you Leod and the boy, if you give me the lass and set me free."

"You know I can't just give people away. Why would Lauren even want to go with you? As for your freedom, well, I would have to discuss that with the warden."

"What's this?" someone asked behind them. She turned to see Rory, hands on hips, frowning down at Cedric. He had wed Lauren the day before when the local parson came to the garrison to bless those who had perished in the raid. The impromptu wedding had been quite a surprise to everyone

"He said," she began hesitantly, "that he would give us Leod and Innes, if we set him free . . . and give him Lauren."

She waited for the expected explosion, but it didn't happen. Rory didn't say anything for a long time. Cedric watched him carefully, then leaned forward. "I see little point in making deals with anyone unless I have some protection. Mistress Dixon would be ideal, but the warden would sooner kill me on the spot than part with her. Lauren will be my insurance against any foul play on your part. You do not love her anyway, do you? You are merely fulfilling a duty by being her husband. Give her to me, Trotter. I will care for her well. Perhaps I will even return her to you when I reach my destination, if you so wish."

Rory contemplated the prisoner for a long time, his face impassive. "I will speak to the warden," he said finally and strode purposefully toward the house.

Megan hurried after him. Inside, Bryan was in a deep discussion with Johnny, but stopped when he saw Rory and Megan. "My man never returned from tailing Leod. I fear the worst."

Rory glanced at Megan, then said, "Cedric has offered to give us Leod and Innes." Bryan's head jerked up in disbelief. "In exchange for his freedom . . . and my wife."

"He expects me to let him go?" He started pacing, scratching his head. "What does he want with Lauren? This is confusing."

"He wants her as a hostage," Rory answered in a tight voice.

"Aye?" Bryan's eyebrows were raised high. "Think you that he would hurt her? It *is* common practice here on the border to use human pledges as an assurance that the parties keep their word, is it not?"

Rory gave a grudging nod. "It is."

"Say we gave her to him and set him free, with the intention of getting her back quickly, as well as Cedric, a deception, mind you . . . think you he would harm her in any fashion, in such a short amount of time?"

"Bryan," Megan said, her voice full of disapproval. "It might be common practice, but generally a man is not asked to offer his bride as a pledge."

Rory shook his head. "He wants her . . . that way, I saw it in his eyes. I won't give her to him, even for an hour."

Bryan sighed. "Then I know not what to do, except wait. I have men searching the march. I sent a man to Kerr, requesting he do the same in his march, but I am certain Leod crossed the border. I can't send men to harry the inhabitants there. I need Cedric to lead me to him."

"Surely Leod will contact us and make use of his leverage with the boy?" Rory offered.

Megan couldn't stand to hear any more. Tears burned her eyes. If Bryan didn't know what to do, what did that mean? She was almost ready to agree with him and urge Rory to give Lauren to Cedric. She went into the kitchen. Marie stood at the wooden table in the center of the room where they prepared the meals. She had a plucked hen in front of her and a cleaver. But rather than cutting the bird up, she stared into space.

"Marie?"

Marie jerked. "Oh, Madame!" She looked unwell. Dark smudges circled her eyes and she looked thin.

"Is something amiss?"

Before Marie could answer, Johnny and Rory entered the kitchen. Johnny went to Marie and reached his hand out to touch her. She set the knife down and left the room without even looking at him.

Johnny slammed his fist on the table after she was gone. Rory and Megan stood awkwardly, looking from each other to Johnny.

"Is there a problem?" Megan asked hesitantly.

Johnny didn't answer immediately and when he did, his voice was tight. "She's leaving me."

Megan gasped and Rory said, "She can do that? She's your wife. She can't just leave you—can she?"

Johnny gave him a withering look. "Shall I tie her up? Beat her? She is like ice toward me. She hates me. She hates Scotland worse. Everything bad that happens is my fault—or so she claims. Once Innes is returned, she is returning to her father. He hates me, too."

Megan's heart ached for Johnny. Maybe she would talk with Marie later. But she couldn't now. Everything in her was focused on Innes. She couldn't spare the energy to think about other matters.

"What will you do?" she heard herself asking.

"I can't stay here and continue on without my wife and son. . . ." His voice became thick. "I'll return to the Low Countries. Prince William's navy, the Seabeggars, still harry the Spanish or so I hear. There's money to be made fighting, and I plan to become rich and win her back . . . or die trying."

They were all silent. It seemed as though life was going sour for everyone. A sharp longing filled her, for something intangible. Something she seemed so close to grasping—and if she was able to, it would help her through this time of miserable waiting. Megan went to the hen and began chopping it up for the stew pot. Rory rifled around in the larder, looking for something to eat.

"Ho, Rory," Johnny said suddenly. "You should join me. Get some real fighting experience for a year or so. When you return, your wife will be a woman, and you'll bring her riches."

"Or make her a widow a second time over ere she's sixteen!" Rory said.

Johnny shrugged.

Rory was thoughtful. "Riches you say?"

"Oh, aye," Johnny said, nodding.

"What about Sir Bryan?" Rory asked. "Willie is dead. We can't just desert him."

"I can't stay here," Johnny protested. "The warden will find other men."

Rory looked doubtful. "But he has told me of his

plans for the watches and beacons. He will set
deputies strategically throughout the march . . ."

They left, talking about Bryan's plans for the future
of the East March. Megan's knife stilled, still clutched
in her hand, but frozen by Rory's words. Bryan told
her he would resign when Leod was brought to justice. Why was he making plans for the future of the
march? Bryan entered the kitchen, and she quickly
focused on the hen again.

He leaned against the table. "I told Rory to round
up some of the outlaws he used to ride with. They'll
be making unofficial forays across the border, looking
for Leod."

Her heart swelled. He was doing everything in his
power. If he couldn't get Innes back, who could? She
fought the burning sensation in her eyes. She couldn't
see for the tears and cut herself. She dropped the
knife, clutching her finger. Blood welled darkly in the
gash. Bryan was beside her. He wrapped her finger in
a clean table linen and pulled her to the basin.

"I'm fine."

He ignored her. He peeled the cloth off and poured
cool water over her finger. He inspected it and
rewrapped it. She tried to pull away, but he held her
wrist firmly with one hand; the other applied gentle
pressure to the wound. His touch burned her and tore
at her heart.

"I can do it," she protested, tugging at her hand.

"You don't need me for anything, do you?"

There was a teasing note in his voice, but his eyes
were intense. She couldn't breathe or tear her gaze
away. She needed him to hold her and tell her everything would be fine. She needed his strength.

She needed him to be there for her. As a man, not a warden. But the man and the warden had become inseparable.

"Rory was talking about all your plans for the march," she said casually. "It sounds quite efficient."

He averted his eyes, nodding, as he ripped a narrow strip of linen from the cloth.

"You have no intention of resigning, do you?

He wrapped the linen around her finger. "I know not." He met her eyes finally. "Does it matter?"

"You know it does."

He took her hands between his and gazed at her beseechingly. "I don't know that at all."

"Leod took my son because he knew it was the only way to get your attention."

He looked away, a muscle jumping in his jaw. "I will find Innes, I swear it. And I will punish Leod for what he has done to you both."

"I know you will," she said, squeezing his hands. "And you will be the best warden the march has ever had."

He brought her hand to his mouth, pressing his lips against her palm. His mouth was warm, and his whiskers scratched her skin. Her pulse quickened.

"And will I be a lonely warden?" he asked, his breath tickling her hand.

She smiled sadly. "Will I be a lonely widow?"

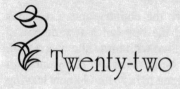

Twenty-two

Leod paced up and down his wife's small house. His mind seethed with indecision. Tyna sat on the floor with Innes, rolling a ball back and forth. Leod had no one now. He had discovered he was being followed after taking Innes. Fortunately, the man was keeping at a distance; in fact, most of the time Leod didn't even see him. He gave the boy to Tyna with no explanation, only an order not to let him escape, and went back to lie in wait for the man. It had been quick. The man had even dismounted for Leod and was taking a piss. Leod slit his throat and took his horse. It reminded him of killing Tavish. His deputy had been relieving himself, too.

But now he didn't know what to do. Tyna had managed to get some information from her uncle, Sir John Forster, that Sir Bryan had taken Cedric's tower and was planning to execute him. The warden also had

Anna. Nothing was going according to plan. Leod was relieved he had thought to take the boy. Innes was all he had left to bargain with.

Tyna wanted to leave the country and take Innes with them. They'd had the boy but a few days and already she'd fallen in love with him. She was a fool. She had a wean in her belly, what did she want with one that didn't even belong to her? Leod knew leaving the country would probably be the best thing to do, but he didn't want to. He was convinced he could make things right with Lord Bothwell, if the earl would only give him the chance. He loved his life on the borders and had no desire to leave. If he left the country, he knew he would never be permitted to return. And his current life as an outlaw did not suit him.

He wanted to be in power again, only this time he would prove to Bothwell that he understood who was master. He had been foolish to tamper with their agreement. He would not mess up and displease the earl again. He shuddered at the memory of Bothwell as he had last seen him in the forest.

It was months ago, though it seemed like years to Leod. He had been hiding in the shadows of Crichton's wall, Tavish Marshall beside him. They had been there for hours. Tavish sat on the damp ground, and was leaning back against the stones and snoring softly.

Leod kicked him. "Wake up, you fool!"

"Huh?" Tavish jerked awake. He gazed into the dark uncomprehendingly, then said, "May'ap 'e wilna be oot tonight, m'lord."

Leod shook his head. "I told you, I have it in good confidence that he will."

They heard something down the wall and both became still, shrinking further into the shadows. The postern door creaked open and a rider trotted out, dressed completely in black. He galloped away without looking back, his dark mantle spread out behind him like the wings of a bat.

"There he goes! Come on!" Leod grabbed Tavish and dragged him back around the side of the castle to where they left their horses.

They rode in the same direction the dark man did. Excitement rose in Leod. He couldn't believe his luck! The widow Dixon had said some very harsh things to him at the fair earlier that day. She had even threatened him! He was amazed at the woman's gall and at the same time enchanted. He sought out a suitable substitute for the lovely widow to sooth his hurt and found a young maid who had been more than willing after a bit of persuasion. She had been a talker, babbling on and on about witches and such as he lay between her thighs.

In truth, he hadn't fully believed her when she told him of the earl's doings in the woods, but if it were so, he would have Lord Bothwell just where he wanted him. His earlier attempt at blackmail, using a third party, had failed. Lord Bothwell didn't bite. And the man Leod had sent to do his dirty work never returned. A summons from the earl had immediately followed. Leod had known he was caught, and so made himself scarce. But now, with this information, he could threaten to tell the king all he heard and saw tonight if Bothwell dared to deny him again.

Leod was almost giddy with happiness. He had always known that someday it would come to this, that he would be granted the power he desired. Being warden and holding the lives of so many men and women weren't enough for him. The Earl of Bothwell could give him more.

The woods weren't far, being situated between the earl's castle of Crichton and Dalkeith, and they soon entered the dark trees.

"I dinna like this, sir," Tavish whispered.

"Shut up, you sniveling coward!"

Tavish fell silent, but Leod could feel his deputy's fear, and it was infecting him. He became angry. He was a man of courage! Tavish was making him frightened with his woman-talk. Leod spied an orange glow winking through the trees. He reined in his horse. He didn't want to mess everything up by the having the earl hear his approach.

"This is it," he whispered. "Leave the horses here."

They dismounted and crept through the trees to the edge of the clearing. Cloaked figures were gathered around a blazing fire. His breath caught as he saw the earl, going to each of the figures. Bothwell stopped before each one in turn and appeared to be blessing them or saying some rite. He then took their heads between his palms and kissed them on the mouth. The figures fell to their knees, prostrating themselves before him. Leod leaned closer to listen, but the earl's voice didn't carry.

There was something about this ceremony or sabbat that excited Leod, made him want to be a part of it. He felt drawn into the circle of worshipers. Tavish's hand on his arm roused him from his reverie.

"What're ye doing?" he whispered hoarsely. "Mean ye to approach him? He will kill you! He is a devil!"

Leod hadn't realized he had been moving forward, and he hunkered back down beside Tavish.

"Haven't we seen enough?" Tavish whined, looking around fearfully. "I keep hearing things, leathery rubbing sounds . . . I dinna like it."

Leod strained his ears and heard it, too. A dry, flapping rasp. The hair on his nape prickled. "Aye, I think I've seen enough."

Tavish made for the horses, and Leod started to back away when he heard the earl's voice say, distinctly, "What are your offerings?" Leod froze, peering through the leaves. One of the figures went to the earl and flung an animal skin, matted with blood, around his shoulders. The creature's long knifelike claws were still attached to the hide.

The shrill scream of a baby crying cut through the night. One of the figures was coming forward with a baby cradled in its arms. Leod was unable to conceal his sharp intake of horrified breath. In his rush to back away and avoid seeing an infant murdered for Satan, he stumbled, crashing into the underbrush. He jumped up and looked back into the clearing. The earl was striding toward him. Leod's heart lodged in his chest. The earl was looking straight at him, and his eyes seemed . . . red.

Leod turned to run, and bats flew at him all around, their leathery wings beating at his face and shoulders, their claws scraping at his neck. He screamed and slapped frantically at them as he tore through the forest.

Someone grabbed him and shook him violently.

"No! No! God save my soul!" he cried.

" 'Tis me!" Tavish said, giving him another hard shake. "Hurry, get on yer horse. I hear them coming!"

Leod vaulted into the saddle, and they galloped through the trees. He could hear the hell bats behind them, their wings beating at his neck. He dug his spurs into his horse's sides, urging it faster. They broke out of the trees and kept going, straight for the garrison. It was over an hour's ride, but they didn't slow down until they saw the wood that flanked the keep. They stopped. Leod looked over his shoulder, scanning the horizon.

Nothing. Empty night. He sighed.

"Good thing he didn't see us," Tavish said in a tired voice.

Leod went cold. But *he had*. Bothwell had looked straight into Leod's eyes. He knew Leod was there, watching. Leod had never really believed the earl was Satan or a devil, he had only looked to blackmail him. But now he knew the truth. The Earl of Bothwell was the Grand Master of the witches. All the rumors were true. His legs were shaking; he was becoming hysterical. The devil would come after him, would send the hell bats, his familiars, to kill him slowly.

He looked at Tavish. The earl hadn't seen Tavish. He probably thought Leod was alone. In fact, Tavish was supposed to be visiting his brother in the north. Leod had delayed his deputy's travels because he needed help on this mission. What if Bothwell thought Leod was dead? He couldn't come after a dead man. And if Bothwell thought he was gone, Leod could come at him from another direction. Destroy him unawares. Tavish could be his decoy. No one would miss a waste of skin like Tavish. He was worthless.

Leod's brow was damp with perspiration from the horrific memories when Innes's shrill cry for his mother jerked him back to the present. Tyna hugged the boy, whispering soothing words.

"Shut him up!" Leod yelled, which only elicited another high-pitched squeal from the boy.

"Leod, stop it! You're scaring him!" Tyna whined.

He would have to make his move soon, but he wanted Sir Bryan present when he spoke with Bothwell. The earl alone was liable to cut him down, boy and all. Sir Bryan held some sway with Bothwell. Leod didn't understand it, for he had thought Lord Bothwell deferred to no one. But the earl had paid scant attention to the handfasting story Anna told him. Leod had hoped to bring about Bothwell's downfall while at the same time ridding the East March of its new warden. But it had done nothing more than bind them closer together. Now Leod would have to grovel.

"Call one of your servants," he ordered his wife. "I need to send a message."

Megan sat on the stump outside the barn. She tried to make herself work, and to her credit, she was getting the necessities done. But try as she might, she couldn't take her mind off Innes. She knew it was useless to sit and lament over it. Bryan was doing everything possible to find her son, going out and scouring the march himself.

Marie came out of the house with Lance in her arms. She started to walk across the yard to join Megan, when Johnny appeared out of nowhere.

"Marie!" he called after her as she ran back into the house. He followed her, and a few minutes later exited with a volley of French curses hurled after him.

He looked miserable. Poor Johnny, Megan thought, sighing.

A young man had entered the gates, eyeing the guards apprehensively.

"Ho!" Megan yelled and waved him over.

"Are you Megan Dixon?"

"I am."

"I 'ave a message for you." The lad glanced around nervously, as though making certain no one was lurking nearby, then leaned close. "I was sent by Leod Hume."

She gasped. "Is it about my son?"

He shushed her. "Aye, it is. But you mustn't tell anyone, or the boy will die."

She covered her mouth to muffle the sob of despair rising. What did Leod want?

The lad looked at her reproachfully. "My lady, someone will see you, and you look as though you've seen a spook. I shall leave now if you cannot control yourself."

She swallowed and nodded, training her face to be bland. "I'm fine. Please, go on."

"Leod wants to meet you at the cairn at Windygyle at noon. Alone. Tell no one where you're going. If you bring the warden, Leod promises you will never see your son again. Understand?"

"Aye, I do."

The lad turned and ran through the gate.

Megan's hands were shaking with excitement and fear. What did it mean? She would do anything to get Innes back, even submit to Leod again. But she suspected that in his present situation he didn't want to

rut with her; he wanted something bigger and more
sinister.

She should tell Bryan. She chewed her lip, wondering how he would react. *He wouldn't let her go*. Since
Innes's kidnapping he had become even more protec-
tive of her. She looked at the sun. It was midmorning
already. Even if she could convince him to let her go,
which she doubted, she would waste time arguing
with him about it.

She could not tell him. She stood and strode casually to the stables. She would have to leave immediately to make it to Windygyle on time.

No one questioned her when she saddled her horse.
Bryan was nowhere in sight. She mounted and headed
for the gates. Her body was strung as fine as a harp as
she watched the gate grow closer, her own progress
unhampered.

Bryan came out of nowhere and grabbed the bridle
of her horse. "Where do you think you're headed,
woman?" He looked larger to her, broader than usual,
now that she was up against him. But he was smiling
slightly, his dimples softening the menace of his size.

"I'm going for a ride," she said coolly, hoping to
discourage him.

"Not alone you're not. I'll come." He tried to lead
her horse back to the stables.

Panicked, she pulled up sharply on the reins. "I
don't want your company!"

He kept a firm hold of the bridle, moving close to
the horse's withers, and glaring up at her with burning
brown eyes. "What the hell is this, aye? Let me protect you!"

"I don't need you to protect me, Warden. You should know that by now."

His face became hard as granite, and her heart wrenched. She swallowed the apologies that rose in her throat. There would be time for explanations later—right now she needed to get away from him.

"That may be so, but I won't let you ride off alone. I'll send Rory with you since I am so incompetent." He turned, looking for Rory. She was desperate to get away from him. She placed her foot on his shoulder and shoved. He was so startled he released the bridle and stumbled backward. She dug her heels into the mare's sides, and it leapt forward. The mare was through the gates and bounding across the countryside.

She knew the march better than Bryan could ever hope to. After skirting around the village she headed for a nearby bog where she was sure to lose him. Then she turned her horse southwest to the Cheviots. In her heart, she feared no amount of explanation would induce Bryan to forgive her for not trusting him with this. But she didn't know what else she could have done. It was her son's life.

When she arrived at Windygyle she could see no one for miles. The grass was beginning to spring up again where it had been trampled during the last Truce Day. She rode to the cairn that sat on the hill and waited. Her stomach churned with anxiety. She would do anything Leod asked to get her son back, but she was terrified of what that might be.

A lone rider galloped across the plain to her. It was Leod. He rode up the hill to the cairn. He stopped when they were facing each other, stirrup-to-stirrup and eye-to-eye. He was smiling, his blue eyes crinkling in the corners.

"Where's my son?"

"He is fine. You don't think I'm fool enough to bring him, do you? What if you had brought Sir Bryan?"

"That would have been stupid since you threatened to kill Innes if I did such a thing."

"I always said you were a clever lass." He looked her over from head to toe. "Ah, Megan, 'tis so good to see you again. I've missed your bonny face. I see it oft in my dreams. I think of naught but you."

"Except mayhap my friend Marie? Whom you attempted to rape. You couldn't have been doing that in my memory."

"Oh, but I could. I was so disappointed you weren't there to . . . entertain me."

He felt no remorse for raping her or trying to rape Marie, and he certainly cared nothing about Innes. Her stomach lurched, but she forced herself not to fall apart.

"What do you want from me, Leod? I want my son, so tell me what I must do."

He smoothed his mustache, watching her with narrowed blue eyes. "I want my life back."

She looked at him incredulously. "If you think I have the power to right all your wrongs, you're insane."

"Not you. The Earl of Bothwell."

She shook her head. "Nay, he wants your head. I can't imagine him letting you be warden again as though naught has happened."

"He will if it means your son's life."

A chill went through her. She had a feeling Lord
Bothwell might consider Innes a reasonable sacrifice
to secure Leod. "Think about this logically! Even if
he agreed to all this, once you were back at your old
life, do you not think he would find a way to dispose
of you quietly?"

He shook his head. "There are things here you
don't understand. All I need is for him to listen to me.
Your son will be that assurance. I want you, Sir
Bryan, and Lord Bothwell to meet me here in two
days time. I will bring your son. Lord Bothwell won't
do anything with Sir Bryan present. I think then he
will hear me."

"Fine," she said, and started to leave, when he
grabbed her wrist.

"If you or the others mean to cozen me in any way,
I swear, I'll slit your boy's throat."

"I will make certain the three of us come alone."

He released her and she rode away, letting the tears
fall at last.

Bryan returned from searching for Megan empty-
handed. He was incensed. What had gotten into her?
Lauren met him outside the stable, Rory trailing
behind her. Her eyes were downcast, her hair escaping
from the coil at the top of her head and completely
obscuring her features.

"Good day, Lauren. How goes things?" Such pleasantries seemed forced after all that had happened, but
she didn't deserve to be ill treated.

"Very well, sir. Prithee I might have a word with
you?"

"Of course." He glanced over her head, giving Rory a curious look. The muscles in the lad's jaw bunched as though he were clenching his teeth hard against something.

"Rory told me what Cedric said."

"Aye," Bryan said cautiously, wondering if this was what had his deputy so wound up.

"I want to help Lady Dixon. I will go with Cedric."

Bryan shook his head. "I've thought on it, too, lass, and I really don't like the idea of sending you off with him."

"I told you," Rory said, nudging her shoulder.

She pushed the sable curls out of her face. Bryan was surprised to see such a firm look on her elflike face. "Sir, he didn't harm me before, he was most gentle, and human pledges are exchanged all the time, it is rare that anyone is harmed, and he promised to release me when he reached his destination which is surely no farther than the Debatable Land, I really think I will be fine." She was running her words together, barely stopping to take a breath.

Bryan raised a brow at Rory. "Is this true?"

Rory shrugged. "Aye."

Bryan placed a hand on Lauren's shoulder. "Are you sure, lass? You don't have to do this."

"You have all been so kind to me, I want to help."

Bryan considered her for a long moment. She lowered her eyes under his scrutiny, staring at the ground, hands clasped in front of her as though ready to receive a chastising.

"When will you be ready?"

She looked up quickly, smiling. "I am ready now."

Bryan pulled his dirk from his boot. "Here. Put it

in your garter; if he tries to harm you, kill him."

Her cheeks flushed and she pulled her skirts up, exposing a rather large dirk already tied to her thigh. "Rory gave me one, sir."

Bryan nodded his approval.

"Go on," Rory said to her.

When she was gone, Bryan said, "You don't have to let her do this, you know. You are her husband now."

Rory gave him a helpless look. "I can't tell her no. I am afraid she will yell at me if I tell her what to do, as Marie does Johnny—as Meg yells at you."

Bryan couldn't stop the laughter that welled up at the lad's words. He doubted Lauren would say a cross word to anyone, let alone Rory.

" 'Tis no jest," Rory said gravely.

Bryan forced a serious expression on his face.

"She greatly admires Lady Dixon, and told me she wishes to be brave like her."

Bryan sighed, humor gone. This *was* something Megan would do. In fact, he was surprised Megan hadn't already volunteered. A sickening thought struck him. What if she was off doing something foolhardy like trying to retrieve her son alone? She thought him so inept that was probably exactly what she was doing. Bryan became even more impatient to get Cedric's information. He feared what a man as desperate as Leod might do to Innes—and to Megan—if she found him.

The afternoon was growing late by the time Megan made it back home. She ran through the house and tower, searching for Bryan. Cedric was gone from his place by the tower door. Where was everyone? Rory was nowhere to be found, either. She finally located Johnny, standing beneath the window of the room he shared with Marie and Lance.

"Where's Bryan? And Cedric?" she asked.

He looked surprised to see her. "You've certainly caused some problems around here. But fash not anymore, your worries will soon be over."

A thread of fear ran through her. "What are you talking about?"

"Lauren agreed to be a pledge and leave with Cedric. The warden returned to the garrison in preparation to go after Leod."

"Oh God," Megan moaned. Leod would kill Innes. Cedric would rape and beat Lauren as he had Bryan's sister. She hurried back to her horse, but Johnny caught her arm.

"Where do you think you're headed?"

"I can't let him do that . . . sacrifice Lauren."

"The lass has consented to it. She wants to help you. I would suggest you start showing some gratitude toward those who do you such favors rather than hindering them." He gave her a hard look. "I would rather you stay away from the warden. I don't know what's the matter with you. He's never been anything but kind to you, and you kick him and ride away when he wants nothing more than to tend to your safety . . ." He shook head in disappoval.

She removed his hand from her arm and shoved it at him. "From a man who can't keep his own wife, I see little value in your counsel. Don't blether on subjects you know nothing of."

His pale blue eyes narrowed, and she walked away.

She was breathing rapidly by the time she was on
horseback again. She couldn't remember the last time
she ate, and she was suddenly so hungry she felt as
though her navel were touching her backbone. Her
hands were shaking, but she had no time to eat, nor
time for ignorant advice from Johnny. Johnny, who
was her friend. Innes's friend. She had alienated him
now, just as she had Bryan and probably Rory and
Lauren, too, since the girl was sacrificing herself on
Megan's behalf.

At the garrison she found many men mounted and
ready to ride out. Bryan wasn't among them, but
Rory's voice rang out across the bailey. "Megan!" He
ran to her and grabbed the bridle of her horse while
she climbed off. "Where have you been?"

"Is Lauren still here?"

"Nay, she's gone with Cedric. Don't fash, I'll be
following soon."

She clutched his sleeve. "Tell me Bryan is still
here!"

"Aye, he's in his chambers, but he's leaving to
retrieve Innes . . . Megan!"

She went straight to his chambers. The door stood
open and he moved about inside, readying himself to
leave. He looked up when she entered, his brows lowering at the sight of her. "Where have you been?"

"You can't go, Bryan."

"I am going to get your son back. If you try to leave
again I *will* lock you up in my cellar!"

He started out the door and she stepped in front of
him. "Please listen to me!" she begged. "I met with
Leod this afternoon."

Bryan grabbed her shoulders and gave her a quick,

angry shake. "You are addled! I cannot believe you've done this!"

"He will kill Innes if you go now. He said he would."

He released her abruptly and began pacing. "Did he hurt you?"

"No, he only wanted to talk."

He faced her, hands on hips. "Well?"

"He wants to meet with you, me, and the Earl of Bothwell the day after tomorrow at Windygyle. If we bring anyone else, he promises to kill Innes." When Bryan just stared at her, she took a step closer. "Do you see why I had to do it?"

"Why couldn't you trust me, Megan?" His voice was heavy with disappointment—as though he was weary of her antics. "Do you realize what I've done?" He sat in a chair, rubbing his temples tiredly.

She had done this to him—pushed him this far. She knelt beside the chair, tears welling in her eyes, and took his hand. "Forgive me—"

He jerked his hand away and stood. She stared at him through the blur of tears as he resumed his preparations to leave. "Bryan," she began hesitantly, terror building in her chest. "You can't still mean to go, after what I just told you."

"No. I am going after Lauren." She was still on her knees, and he stared down at her, his eyes accusing. "She sacrificed herself, wanting to be brave like you. Well, 'tis not bravery, 'tis foolishness."

She looked down at the rushes around her knees, shamed by his words. It *was* her fault. She should have trusted Bryan. She stood, wanting to help. "Let me come."

"No." He didn't even look at her.

She persisted, following him to the door. "You need me."

He swung around, his face dark with anger. "That is where you are wrong. I do not need you. Good Christ, Megan! Let me be the warden." His words went straight to her heart and she backed away. "Stay here and don't cause anymore trouble."

He left and Megan sank down in a chair. She was shaking and her eyes burned. She felt as though she were going mad. She grabbed her hair and pulled, trying to stop the tears from falling, but it was useless. She wanted to scream in her grief. She bit her lip, trying to contain the tortured cries, until she tasted blood.

When the hysterics passed, she began pacing. Bryan was wrong, he did need her. He should have let her accompany him. Cedric was not an easy quarry. He had been fooled once by Bryan and would take care not allow it to happen again. She feared for Lauren. Cedric was a brutal man.

I could find Cedric.

As soon as the thought occurred to her, she tried to put it from her mind. Bryan would be furious. There could be no future for them if she continued to thwart his best efforts. For an outsider, he was an excellent warden.

But he was still an outsider.

She made her decision. No one knew the East March as well as she did, not even Rory, of that she was certain. And this was her fault. Lauren was doing this for her. Regardless of the personal consequences, she had to set things right. A sense of calm followed her decision. She went into Bryan's room and dug through his trunk for suitable clothes to wear in her pursuit of Cedric Forster.

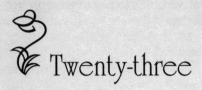 Twenty-three

No fire was lit and the night was cold. Cedric was headed for the Debatable Land. He could trust no one; since he gave away Leod's position, he couldn't go to his sister for succor. Lauren was wrapped in his cloak, lying on the ground while he paced. He was suspicious of the warden. Sir Bryan surely meant to get her back. This was similar to his last ploy, when he *allowed* Cedric to escape. He had anticipated Sir Bryan was playing him false and covered his tracks well this time. He didn't think he would be found, but the warden had proved a more than able adversary and Cedric took nothing for granted. He would use Lauren as a shield if necessary. At the thought, he moved closer to where she slept.

She shivered in the cool breeze. He surveyed the area once more. He heard nothing more than the wind blowing through the grass. An owl circled overhead.

The horse stood a few feet away staring blankly into the night. He sat beside the girl. All he could see was her hair. Dark curls spilling on the ground. He touched it, running his hand over the silken texture. She seemed so innocent, but that could not be so; she was on her second husband.

He plunged his fingers into the cool mass of hair, combing through it. He was becoming aroused by the sensation. He lay beside her on the ground and put his arm around her. She stiffened. She was awake.

"Lauren," he whispered, pushing her hair away from the tiny ear, like a little seashell.

"Sir?" Her voice cracked with fear.

"Do not be frightened. I would never 'urt you. Did your husbands 'urt you?"

"No . . ."

"Not even the first time?"

She was silent for a long time, then queried, "The first time?"

Intrigued by her soft question, he asked, "Didn't you and Willie consummate your wedding vows?"

Her hair moved from side to side in a negative answer.

"And Trotter? Has he had you?"

"No."

How unusual! And exciting. Married twice and still a virgin. He kissed her ear and she shuddered, her small body not moving, but he sensed a straining within her skin to escape his touch. His pulse raced.

"I am very young," she said, her voice was barely audible. Cedric thought it a very practiced reply, probably the explanation her husbands gave for not bedding her.

"Not so young. I have a sister younger than you and she just had a daughter."

She was silent.

"I'm going to give you your first lesson on being a woman, Lauren. Do not be frightened, I won't 'urt you."

He rolled her onto her back. Her eyes were squeezed shut, and her face had a bloodless pallor to it. Her entire body was rigid. He kissed her forehead and her nose. When he tried to kiss her mouth she turned her face away, so he trailed his lips across her cheek. She whispered something that sounded like "courage," and began moving about, messing with her skirts.

Was she bolstering herself for what was to come? Preparing to take it bravely? He was charmed. "What is it?" he breathed in her ear.

"Do I not need to lift my skirts so you can rut on me?"

He laughed softly. "Aye, love." He waited for her to finish, leaning on his elbow and watching her face. After a moment she lay still again. He started to move toward her again, to kiss her. She turned her face to him, her eyes open. Their gazes met, and his heart skipped a beat. Her enormous brown eyes seemed to be staring through him, freezing him to the core with hate. He caught a glint of silver from the corner of his eye as a knife arced toward him.

His reflexes were quick, and he caught her wrist. Anger surged through him. This was how the wench repaid his kindness? He squeezed her tiny wrist. Her hand sprang open, the knife tumbling to the ground. Her lips parted, a soundless gasp escaping her. He heard and felt the bones crack beneath his hand.

"Don't ever do that again or I will kill you," he growled.

Her eyes rolled and her body went limp. He released her wrist, laying it gently beside her. She had fainted. He stared at her broken wrist and felt a pang of regret. Now he would have to splint it or she would be deformed. This was going to cause delays in their journey. He hoped she wasn't a complainer.

He started to rise when he caught movement out of the corner of his eye. Someone was nearby, approaching stealthily. He pretended not to notice.

Megan was on her belly in the grass. She saw Cedric's horse, then Cedric himself. But he lay down in the grass and she saw nothing else, though she heard his voice faintly. She had to hurry. Time was running out for Lauren. She wormed through the tall stalks until she was near the horse. She could see his dark form through the grass, sitting up, looking down at something.

She withdrew the dirk from her waist and crawled on her elbows. She was close enough to see that Lauren's body was limp. She caught her breath on a sob and steeled herself to make no sound. When she was in control again she gripped the hilt of her dirk and rose up from the grass. Cedric's back was to her and she planned to bury the knife right between his shoulders. She ran at him.

Seconds before she plunged the knife into him, he whirled, his arm catching her legs and driving her to the ground on her back. The air left her in a *whoosh*.

Silvery pinpoints clouded her vision as she tried to catch her breath.

"You'll not stab me again, bitch!"

Something crashed against her face. Blackness and pain weighed down on her chest and head. She tried to roll away, but was struck again.

Bryan and Rory had kept a silent vigil on Cedric for hours, waiting for him to either sleep or attempt something on Lauren. Bryan was tense, fearful he would miss something important since their visibility wasn't good.

"He's doing something to her," Rory said in a tight voice as he peered through the grasses.

Bryan squinted. Cedric was leaning over her, but there was no struggling or other movement to suggest he was raping her. Bryan was about to move closer anyway, to get a better look at what was happening, when a dark figure rose out of the grass behind Cedric and ran at him. Bryan's heart seized as he recognized Megan's tall, slim form.

Cedric quickly dispatched his attacker and continued to beat her when she was down. Bryan came to his feet with a roar of blind fury. Cedric jerked around, stumbling over the bodies littering the ground around him. Bryan yanked his sword from the scabbard and slashed at Cedric, cutting him across the chest.

Cedric ran a few paces, retrieving his own sword rather clumsily from his waist, and turned to meet Bryan. "You gave me your word, Warden, I would not be followed."

"And you gave me yours that the lass would not be harmed." He brought his blade down and Cedric blocked the blow. Blood flowed from the wound on Cedric's chest.

"You're as big a liar as any borderer!" Cedric yelled.

Bryan circled him. Megan and Lauren lay motionless nearby. Rory leaned over them. "They're alive!"

"Then your death shall be painless, Cedric. Had you killed her, you would have learned what it is to suffer."

The color left Cedric's face and he turned to run, but Bryan was on him, bringing his sword down across Cedric's neck.

Megan was aware of voices nearby and the cool breeze against her cheek. Her head throbbed, and her stomach was queasy and sour. She opened her eyes to a sky full of stars. She moaned. Bryan's anxious face was suddenly blocking the sky.

"How do you feel?"

"Lauren? Is she . . ."

"She's fine. Her wrist is broken, but that's all. Rory is tending to her."

Megan closed her eyes in relief. "Cedric?" she asked wearily.

"Dead."

She opened her eyes.

His expression was stern. "Did I not tell you to stay at the garrison? Do you ever listen to me?"

"I didn't think you would be able to find him. . . ." she trailed off lamely. He had saved her life. Cedric would have killed her, of that she was certain.

He sat back on his heels, looking past her into the night. Whiskers shadowed his jaw. Thick chestnut hair curled about his neck. "How shall we manage, my lady? If you think me so unfit to protect you and your son's lives that you cannot trust me to do my duties, and I cannot let you out of my sight?"

What was he saying? Had she ruined things so completely between them? "We'll manage . . ." she whispered, her throat tight.

He sighed. "You said once you didn't want to wed a warden. That is what I am."

"I know." She sat up. Sharp pain cut through her head. Her hands went to her forehead and she groaned. He tried to force her back down. "No, I want to sit." She was closer to him now, could look into his eyes.

"Will you never listen to me?" he asked, exasperated, but let her sit. "Will you ever acknowledge that I am not completely daft, and know something of protecting those I love?"

She reached her hand out, tentative, remembering how he rejected her touch before, and lay her palm against his cheek. "I am listening now." She leaned forward slowly and pressed her lips to his. "I do trust you, Bryan. Forgive me for not showing it better."

Her apology didn't seem to appease him, for he still gazed into her eyes, his expression troubled. "What shall we do, Lady Dixon?"

His formal address wrenched at her heart. "You tell me, Warden." She tried to draw back from him, hurt. Did he not love her? Did he no longer want to wed her? But his hand slid around the back of her neck, holding her in place, their lips almost touching, the warm scent of him filling her senses.

"Warden, is it? Not incompetent fool?"

"No. It is most certainly, Warden. A finer warden I have never met."

"Ah, that's what I like to hear." A smile curved his mouth. His eyes searched her face, centering on her lips. "And could you love a warden? Take him as your husband? Bear his children and share his life—how ever short it might be?"

Her heart filled with joy that he had not given up on her. "I would be honored," she said, and sealed her pledge with a kiss.

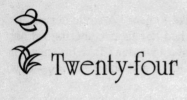 Twenty-four

The Earl of Bothwell listened carefully as Bryan relayed Leod's message. He had brought a pretty blond woman with him, Megan Dixon, and she stood slightly behind him, her hands clasped in front of her. She was thin, with dark circles under her eyes. She was distraught about her son. Francis could feel her despair, though her mind was closed to him, as some people's were. Francis could see he was going to be placed in a difficult position. He turned his attention back to his cousin, who was adamant they should go on this rendezvous with Leod, and follow his terms to the letter, lest anything happen to the boy.

He stroked his beard and mustache, knowing what Leod was up to. It was a clever ploy on his part, Francis gave him that, but not clever enough. Leod would never be clever enough to make Francis stumble. When Bryan was finished, he looked at Francis expectantly. This *would* be difficult. Bryan loved the boy and the woman—Francis could feel it emanating from his cousin. Such powerful emotions Francis had not felt in a long while.

The earl stood and went to the window. His court-yard was almost finished. Soon the gardeners would be called in to landscape the area. It would be magnificent. Grand enough to rival any estate of his cousin, the king.

"Well?" Bryan asked impatiently. "What say you?"

"I say, I want roses along that back wall." Francis turned to the Dixon widow. "What do you think, my lady? Red and large, like blood."

She hesitated then came forward to the window. "Aye, roses would be bonny."

"I care not about the roses. I want to speak of Leod, damn it!" Bryan's voice boomed through the room.

Francis ignored his bad-tempered relative. He took Megan's hand. "Tell me about your son."

Sorrow ran through her like a current at the mention of her son. The lovely green eyes gazed back at him lifelessly. "He . . . he's four. He has red hair like his father. He's very smart."

"Does he have a dog?"

"Who cares if he has a dog?" Bryan roared from across the room where he was pacing impatiently.

"Aye," Megan said, her eyes brightening a bit. "Bryan gave it to me, but it belongs to both of us . . . Innes and I."

Ah, so that was how it was. He had thought he sensed something between them. When she looked at his cousin, she swelled and became stronger. They were lovers. Francis was in a difficult position, indeed. But nothing he couldn't work out.

"Well, then, I don't suppose he will want a hound pup. Mine just gave birth to a litter. A cat then? I have too many running about the place, and the large gray tabby just had yet another dozen. I'm overrun. Would he fancy a kitten?"

She was smiling now, her hand grasping his back warmly. "You'll help me then?" she asked softly.

"Of course. Did you doubt it?" When she just continued to smile at him, he placed his arm around her shoulders. "Come, let us seek out the kittens and choose one."

They stayed the night at Crichton since the three of them would start out early the next morning for Windygyle. Bryan was again feeling that sense of uneasiness about his cousin. He knew it was just Francis's way to regard all situations with amusement, but it still bothered him.

Bryan was a bit jealous to see how his cousin had charmed Megan. She was still subdued and unlike herself, but her mood had lifted since she'd been at Crichton. Francis had also made it obvious that he knew the nature of their relationship by assigning them to the same room. A thin nightshift was spread across the bed when they returned after dinner.

Megan fingered the lawn and lace with wide eyes. It was decorated with emerald green ribbon as though it had been made just for her. Bryan scowled. But when she held it up in front of her, his annoyance eased, seeing how lovely she would look in it. He went to her, running his hands over her shoulders and arms. He wanted to get Innes back badly. He hated to see her in so much misery, and he was very fond of the boy. He kissed her and held her close. She lay her head against his chest.

"Everything will be fine," he whispered into her hair, as though trying to convince himself of it. "Tomorrow we will have Innes back and all will be well."

She looked up at him, giving him a brave smile. She trusted him; he could see it in her eyes. He would get Innes back for her if meant sacrificing his own life.

Later, while she was washing up for bed, Bryan fingered the piece of paper in his doublet thoughtfully. "I'll be back," he said, and left before she had a chance to protest. He caught Francis as he was leaving his chambers. The earl was dressed in all black, a long mantle thrown over one shoulder and secured with a silver brooch.

"My lord? Out so late?"

"Aye, I've much to do before we leave tomorrow." He headed downstairs.

"I need to speak with you on a matter of importance."

They walked through the keep and out into the bailey. "What does your lady think of the gown . . . or should I ask, what think you of the gown?"

" 'Tis bonny; she loves it." Bryan followed him into the stable, becoming increasingly irritated at how his cousin dodged subjects. He pulled out the list of names as Francis woke the stable lad with a swift kick to the posterior and ordered him to saddle his horse. He handed the paper to Francis. "What is this?"

The earl took the list and carried it to a lantern. He studied it for a long time before folding it slowly and turning to Bryan. "Where did you get this?" Bryan could read nothing from Francis's expression, but his voice was uncommonly grave.

"What is it?"

" 'Tis obvious what it is."

Bryan narrowed his eyes. "Aye, it is. But I want to know if the list was written before or after these men died."

Francis's eyes widened and he burst out laughing. "Oh my, Bryan, but you are good for a jest. You're not implying I made a list of men to be raided and killed, are you?"

"I found it at Cedric's keep. Cedric has been working with Leod for years, and Leod is scared witless of you. Why is that, Francis?"

Francis face became cold. "Let me tell you what this is, fool, and you will address me in a manner befitting my rank and yours in the future." He walked toward Bryan, his eyes narrowed and lips thin. "It is a list of the men who served me in some capacity and have been killed in raids. I provide their families with food and other necessities, as they need them. I don't know why Cedric had it or how he got it. It was given to Leod as he was to execute this duty in my name." He folded the paper and stuffed it in his doublet. "But he was taking my money and provisions and using them for his own benefit, leaving the deceased men's families to starve; stupid, greedy, small man that he is. And he will pay for even thinking of cozening me, as any man will who thinks he has it in him to challenge me!"

"Well . . . my lord," Bryan said, scratching the

whiskers on his chin. "Forgive me for questioning your benevolence."

Francis smiled suddenly. "Nay, nay. That's why I made you warden, because I knew what a thorough job you'd do." He winked at Bryan. "I'll wager that lass is up in your room with the chemise on wondering where you're off at. Don't keep her waiting."

"Her son is in a murderer's hands, my lord; a frilly shift will not make things right."

"Of course not. But it cannot hurt."

Francis had no children—at least none that Bryan was aware of—so he could not understand how it was to fret constantly, to never have the fear of losing someone leave his mind. It was a feeling Bryan was becoming accustomed to. Instead of attempting to explain it, he bade his cousin good night and watched him leave from the shadows of the keep. Someone in an enormous hooded cloak emerged from the darkness and mounted behind Francis. They rode through the gates of Crichton and into the night. Bryan went back inside, realizing suddenly that he was no longer in possession of the list.

In the morning Francis had returned, and the three of them set out for Windygyle. Bryan could tell Megan was nervous. Her hands clutched the reins so tightly her knuckles were white. It was a long ride; Crichton was near Edinburgh and they had to travel back to the border. They arrived when the sun was high. Leod was already there, waiting by the cairn on the hill. He wasn't alone. A black-haired woman was with him and she held Innes in front of her on the saddle.

Relief that Innes was safe shuddered through Bryan. Megan met his gaze, and he knew she was feeling the same mixture of joy and fear that he was. As soon as Innes saw his mother, he began crying for her. The woman tried to comfort him, but he squirmed and tried to get down from the horse.

"Innes, be good for Mum. You'll be with me again soon, love," Megan said in a broken voice.

He paid no heed to her words and continued to fight with the woman.

"Well, Leod, it seems you're in quite a spot," Francis said.

Bryan took a good look at Leod, this being the first time he had ever seen the infamous man who caused him so much grief in his short time as warden. He wasn't the impressive man Bryan had been expecting, though he was attractive in a way lasses would find pleasing. He was of average height and build, in his middle years, with sandy brown hair and pale blue eyes framed with lashes so thick they appeared to weigh his eyelids down and lent him a lazy look. He seemed to have a ready smile, and a well-groomed mustache framed a sensual mouth.

" 'Tis the only way I could induce you to listen to me."

"Come now, Leod!" Francis said laughingly. "You felt it necessary to kidnap a child and put this poor woman through hell merely to speak with me?"

Leod nodded solemnly. He appeared scared, but seemed to believe he had the upper hand. He reached toward the woman's horse and took Innes from her. He held the sobbing child tightly. Innes quieted in

Leod's arms, but it was obviously because the boy feared him.

Francis never even looked at the child, keeping his eyes on Leod's face. He folded his gloved hands comfortably over the saddle horn. "Then speak. You've gone to so much trouble to have a word with me, let us not delay any longer."

Leod licked his lips nervously and glanced at Bryan and Megan. "In front of them?"

Francis frowned. "What have you to say that can't be said in front of others?"

Leod's brow was troubled, but he nodded. "You don't have to kill me, my lord. I won't speak of what I saw in the woods. You have my most solemn vow. I pray you, let me resume my duties to you, and prove my devotion. I won't fail you again. I know my place."

"Well, Leod, you've never executed your duties in the manner I wished, and on this other matter . . . of the woods . . ." Francis glanced at Bryan in confusion. "Know you what he speaks of?"

Bryan shook his head.

"My lord, you know well what I speak of!" Leod protested indignantly.

"Nay, I don't. Pray enlighten me."

Leod looked again at Megan and Bryan, his face pale. He clutched Innes so tightly the boy began to whine.

"Leod, please," Megan begged, her voice barely above a whisper. "Don't hurt him."

The hair at Leod's temples was damp with sweat, but he loosened his hold on the boy. "I'm speaking of the . . . sabbat I witnessed in the wood. And the sacrifice . . . or . . . or offering."

"Sabbat? Sacrifice?" Francis said incredulously. "You are clearly delusional."

Leod's eyes became wild. He withdrew the dirk from his waist and held it to Innes's neck. Megan began praying under her breath, tears streaming down her face. The woman with Leod pleaded with him not to hurt the child.

"I will tell everyone you are a warlock!" Leod cried. "I will tell the king of your plan to usurp him through witchcraft. How you mean to be the next king with the help of Satan. I will tell him about your familiars, the bats of hell! You can't stop me this time!"

Leod was obviously insane, and Bryan feared if he wasn't pacified, he would kill Innes. "Leod, listen to me," Bryan said soothingly. "I won't let Lord Bothwell harm you. I'm certain we can come to some compromise." He gave Francis a meaningful look.

Francis sighed, bored. "Aye, let us discuss this."

Leod pulled on the reins of his horse, backing away from them. "Nay," he said, his gaze darting from Francis to Bryan. "I am not insane. . . . I see this was a mistake."

"Leod!" Megan cried and rode forward. "Take me instead of Innes."

Bryan tensed and moved forward to stop her, but knew it would be impossible to dissuade her from this decision. Leod was weighing the advantages of having a woman hostage versus a child. He nodded. Megan rode beside him, and Leod dragged her off her horse and onto his, dumping Innes unceremoniously on the ground. He backed further away. Bryan rode forward, pulling the sobbing boy into the saddle with him.

"If you follow, I will kill her!" Leod spun his horse around and galloped away, the other woman close on his heels. When he disappeared from sight, Bryan started to follow.

Francis caught the horse's bridle. "Hold! Have no fear. I have prepared for this. I know where they're going, and I have men waiting for them. Let's go back to the garrison and wait."

Bryan's stomach was twisted in knots. He was sick with worry about Megan, but he had Innes, and the boy needed tending.

Innes gazed up at him; his blue eyes wide and red rimmed. "Are you not going to get my mum back?"

That made his decision. "Aye, I am. Go with Lord Bothwell. He'll take care of you until I get your mum."

Francis looked as though he might protest, then held out his arms for the child. "Have a care, Bryan. Leod is deranged."

"I will. Take the boy to Lauren Trotter. She'll see to him."

Once Innes was settled in front of Francis, Bryan mussed his hair and smiled with more confidence than he felt. "Fash not, I'll bring your mum home in no time."

Megan's skin was crawling. Leod held her tightly about the waist, the sharp scent of his sweat surrounding her. She was scared, but more than anything, she was relieved her son was out of harm's way. Bryan would take care of him, no matter what happened to her.

The woman beside them was silent until Leod finally slowed, looking behind them fearfully. The landscape was clear, no sign of followers.

"Why did you trade her for the lad?" the woman asked, her voice a shrill whine. Megan looked at her for the first time. She was a Forster, with black hair and blue eyes.

"Shut up!" Leod snapped. She began to cry softly.

"What are you going to do, Leod?" Megan asked. "You can't stay here. Do you really plan to drag a hostage to the continent?"

He grabbed a handful of her hair and yanked her head backward so she could see his face. "Nay, Meg, I have other plans for you." He gave her a nasty smile and spurred the horse forward, releasing her hair. Her scalp tingled and stung. They continued riding until a small tower was in sight. Leod gave the horizon another sweeping look before heading to the tower.

They were almost to the barmkin when men on horseback poured out the gates and headed toward them, swords drawn and screaming. Leod's horse reared, almost throwing them both to the ground. Behind her, Leod fumbled for his knife again, and Megan knew he was going to use her as he had used Innes. She rammed her elbow hard into his ribs and dove off the horse. He gave a cry of rage and grabbed at her, but she hit the ground hard. She couldn't breathe for a paralyzing moment. Hooves were flying near her head, and she forced herself to roll until she was in the safety of the attacking horsemen's shadows.

Leod tried to escape, leaving the Forster woman behind, but the men quickly surrounded him. One of them jerked him off the horse and dragged him down the hill to a large tree stump. Megan stood gingerly, her body aching from the fall, and followed at a distance. Leod was shoved to his knees, his head forced down on the stump. One of the men raised his sword above his head.

The executioner hesitated at the sound of hoof-beats, lowering his sword to his side. They all turned to see Bryan approaching. His eyes lit up when he saw that she was safe. He had come for her. Tears pressed at the back of her eyes as she hurried to him. He swung down from the horse and embraced her tightly.

"Thank God you're safe," he whispered.

She heard movement behind her. Bryan left her abruptly and went to the stump.

"What are you doing to this man?"

"What does it look like we're doing?" the executioner asked as he raised the sword over his head again. Leod's eyes were squeezed shut and his hair soaked, but he had ceased to struggle. A pool of liquid had formed in the dust around his knees.

"Hold!" Bryan's voice rang out, and he grabbed the executioner's forearm. Bryan loomed over the man, taller and broader than he, and the man's eyes widened. "You are Lord Bothwell's men."

"Aye," the executioner said. "And it is under his orders I am killing this man."

"I am warden here. This man will be tried before sentence is passed on him. He deserves a trial, though I believe the outcome will be the same."

The man obviously didn't like the idea of disobeying the Earl of Bothwell and stared at Bryan uncertainly.

Bryan put pressure on the man's arm, forcing him to lower the sword. "Let's take him back to the garrison. Lord Bothwell waits there for my return."

Lauren sat on the hearth with Innes on her lap. The lad was exhausted and had fallen asleep with his head on her shoulder. He was a big child and rather heavy for her, but her heart went out to him, almost being taken away from his family forever.

She felt someone's gaze on her and looked up. The Earl of Bothwell was only a few paces away, staring down at her. She hadn't even heard him approach!

"M-my lord?"

"Why so glum?" he asked, sitting beside her.

He made her extremely uncomfortable, yet there was something exciting about him. He was handsome and dressed in such finery. His long brown hair always looked clean and soft. He had dark green eyes, the color of the deepest forest.

"I'm fine, my lord," she said softly, looking away from his intense stare.

"Did you know Leod very well?"

The question startled her. No one had ever asked her about Leod. "I lived at the garrison, with Willie, when Leod was warden."

His voice lowered and he leaned closer. "Did he ever try to hurt you?"

She understood what he was asking now. Did Leod try to bed her, as he did all women? "Nay, my lord. I don't think he knew I existed."

He frowned slightly then asked, "What think you of the tales that I am a wizard?"

"Why do you ask, my lord?"

He didn't answer, but held her gaze until her cheeks grew hot. The spell was broken when people began pouring into the hall. It was the warden, his arm draped around Lady Dixon's shoulders. They had Leod Hume.

The earl stood and Lauren sighed in relief. Lady Dixon spied her and Innes, and rushed to them, lifting her son from Lauren's arms with a tearful smile of thanks. Innes yawned and blinked tiredly.

"Mum!" he cried, throwing his arms around her neck. After mussing the lad's hair, the warden replaced his arm around Lady Dixon's shoulders, drawing her and Innes close to his side.

"What is the meaning of this?" Lord Bothwell asked his guards. "Did I not tell you to execute him immediately?"

The guard was stuttering, face pale, when Sir Bryan said, "This is my march, and he will not be executed without a trial."

The earl turned slowly to the warden. "*Your* march?"

"Aye. I am the king's appointed warden, am I not?"

"I am lieutenant of the borderlands; that makes you *my* warden."

Sir Bryan's eyebrow twitched, with amusement, it seemed, though Lauren thought he would have to be insane to mock the earl, so surely she must be mistaken.

"That is so, my lord, but as long as I am warden, I will have the last word on executions."

Lauren's eyes widened. He was actually challenging Lord Bothwell! Silence fell over the hall as everyone stared, waiting to see what the unpredictable earl would do.

Lord Bothwell approached him slowly, rubbing his hands together. "So . . . you are not resigning?"

"You may dismiss me if you don't like my ways, but I will not voluntarily desert my post."

Lady Dixon gazed up at Sir Bryan, her eyes shining with pride.

Lord Bothwell clapped him on the shoulder. "Well said, Cousin. Your father would be proud! Lauren, lass," Lauren sprang to her feet when the earl addressed her, "get us some ale. Let us drink to this news! The warden is staying!"

The crowd in the hall, made up of soldiers, widows, and borderers, applauded as the warden leaned down and kissed his lady.

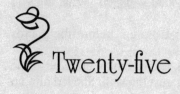 Twenty-five

Leod squatted on the ground in his dank cell at Crichton, shivering from the cold. Since Sir Bryan was busy with repairs to the garrison, Bothwell had generously volunteered his dungeon. *Must escape. Must escape.* But there was no way out. The guards were all huge and surprisingly alert, fearing their master's displeasure, as everyone who had a shred of sense in their head did. Leod had that sense now, but it was late in coming. He should have known no one would believe him. He was a fool to think after taking advantage of the earl's benevolence he could be forgiven.

The door creaked and he stood, fear piercing him. Was it the earl come to kill him secretly? The intruder was shrouded in a hooded cloak and carried a candle. Leod flattened himself against the wall, his bowels becoming watery. The figure threw the hood back and

held the candle close to her face. It was Anna Beaton!
He let out a sigh of relief.

"Anna!" he said in a loud whisper. "What are you
doing here?"

"Rescuing you, fool! Let's go, before the guards
wake up."

She held out her hand, and he took it gratefully. The
guards were slumped against the wall. She led him up
the stairs, then pulled the hood back over her head as
they entered the moonlit courtyard. She blew out the
candle and discarded it in the dirt.

"Come, I have a horse waiting outside the walls."

They ran in the shadows of the wall until they
reached the postern gate. No one was guarding it, and
she had a key. A horse waited outside the door, its
reins dragging the ground as it nibbled grass.

"How—" he started, wondering how she had managed such a perfect escape.

"Quiet! We must hurry! He will kill us both if he
finds out what I've done!"

They mounted and galloped away from Crichton.
He sat behind her on the horse's rump, clinging to her
waist. He leaned forward, pulling the hood from her
head.

"Where are we going?" he whispered into her ear.

"I know a place where you will be safe."

"Where have you been?"

"Lord Bothwell promised me safety in exchange
for certain . . . functions," she was smiling, "but he
didn't come through on his part of the bargain. He
dunked me naked in a trough then left me in the dungeon to freeze to death. When he finally released me,
he expected me to be so grateful I would be his

slave." She laughed loudly, throwing her head back.

Leod had to admit, if anyone was a match for the Earl of Bothwell, it was Anna Beaton. She was full of bile. He eyed the long line of her neck beneath the heavy brown hair and decided tonight would be a good time to finally sample some of what she had to offer.

He asked the question that had occupied his thoughts since his capture, "Anna, did your mother and James Hepburn really handfast?" The story had been her idea and Leod had endorsed it wholeheartedly. But he never considered that it might be true.

"Oh, aye. The earl never would have allowed my mother to give Bryan the Hepburn surname otherwise."

Leod snorted. What a jest! Francis Stewart not the real Earl of Bothwell. Leod wondered if, once he left the country, there was still some way to make use of that information.

They entered the wood, and she slowed the horse. It was dark, the only sound the crunching of the leaves beneath the horse's hooves. Leod's heart began to hammer in his chest. This was where he had witnessed Bothwell and the witches.

"Wait a minute," Leod said, panic filling him. "What are we doing here?"

"Don't be such a coward, Leod. We're almost there." Her voice lowered to a throaty purr. "When we arrive, I have a little surprise for you."

His loins tightened in spite of his mounting terror, and he kept silent. But soon he heard chanting and saw the orange glow of a fire ahead. He reached around her to grab the reins. "No Anna!" he whispered. "We must turn back! You don't understand."

He was trying to turn the horse when the trees around them came alive with figures wearing dark hooded cloaks just like Anna's. They were reaching for him, pulling him down from the horse. "No!" he screamed and clawed at Anna. They pulled him off and dragged him to the clearing where a bonfire was lit.

Lord Bothwell was there, dressed all in black. "Leod! I'm so glad you could join us."

"My lord, I pray you, let me explain," Leod begged, the words falling over each other. The fire played across the earl's face, making his eyes reddish. Anna moved to Bothwell's side, pressing her body against him and gazing at him in adoration. The earl seemed completely unaware of her presence.

Bothwell walked to Leod and pulled a sheet of paper from his cloak. "Look, Leod. I still have the list."

Leod was unable to find any moisture in his mouth.

Bothwell opened the paper and looked at it. "This was never meant to be a harbinger of death. You were to do no more than warn these men to cease calling me a warlock. I never gave you orders to kill anyone on my borders."

"My lord, it wasn't me, but Cedric! I never told Cedric to kill those men."

Bothwell gave him a thin, cool smile. "You didn't waste your time comforting the widows. And attempting to extort money . . ." Bothwell shook his head sadly. "Nay, Leod, many serious blunders lay directly at your feet."

Leod's brain scrabbled for something to say, something to induce the earl to spare his life. "I implore you, my lord," he dropped to his knees and brought his hands together as though praying to him, "I was wrong! Please spare my life and I am your servant." An idea occurred to him and he latched onto it. "I can bring you sacrifices! I have many offerings for you. I have bastards throughout the march and they are all yours!"

Bothwell finally showed some amusement. "I sacrifice no bairns, you fool! My followers *offer* their children to my tutelage at a young age. It is a show of their loyalty and devotion."

Leod's heart sunk. There was nothing left, then.

Bothwell continued to regard Leod with a small grin. "Think you, Leod, that the devil needs servants such as you?"

Leod nodded eagerly. He felt a pang of hope that was quickly quashed by the list Bothwell held in front of his face. His eyes followed the familiar column of names to the bottom and saw "Leod Hume" written in the earl's flowing hand. He was close to sobbing with the intensity of his fear when he met the earl's eyes again.

Lord Bothwell backed away a few paces, his cold smile growing. "As you can see, I have loyal servants aplenty. Ladies?"

The women surrounding him pulled back the hoods of their cloaks. Leod lost control of his bladder. Cathy Armstrong glared down at him. The lass he had forced himself on last year was beside her. He scanned the faces and realized these were all widows whom he had taken advantage of. Many of them he had fathered a child on. And he had just offered their children up for sacrifice. He opened his mouth, and his shriek echoed through the woods.

 Epilogue

Lanterns were strung throughout the courtyard of Bryan's new home. The wine flowed and the food was plentiful, compliments of the Earl of Bothwell. Bryan pushed his way through the crowds of guests, searching for Megan's golden hair, but he was stopped repeatedly by drunken well-wishers. Bryan had been trying to get his bride alone for some time, with little success. He would no sooner get his hands on her than another young man would request a dance.

At the center of it all a wild reel was winding on and on, the dancers twirling 'round so fast he was surprised they didn't become ill, considering all the drink they had consumed. He spotted her, her hair flying out behind her; the daisies that had adorned it earlier were gone, or in tatters, buried in the thick mane. He started toward her and the man she was dancing with, resolute to spend the evening of his wedding with his bride, when Cathy Armstrong appeared in front of him.

"Warden! I've been looking *everywhere* for you!" She grabbed his arm, dragging him to where couples were dancing. Her cheeks were rosy and her hair damp from dancing hard. "Your bride told me you dinna dance! I said, 'We'll see about that!' "

Oh God, no! Bryan strained to escape from Cathy's iron hold, searching frantically for his wife, who had disappeared again amongst the revelers. "No, really, I cannot."

"Nonsense," she said, laughing. She took his hands. "Just do like me!"

He shuffled his feet, giving a halfhearted attempt to please Cathy. Megan skipped by in the arms of his cousin. When she saw him dancing, her green eyes grew wide with laughter.

"How did you manage, Cathy? He refused me!" she called.

"Pardon," he muttered to Cathy and went after Megan. He caught her from behind, his arms around her waist, swinging her away from Francis. "You cannot get away this time!"

Francis had shed his fine doublet. The falling collar of his linen shirt was open. The ribbons that had adorned his love-lock had come undone and trailed down his back.

"You look like a commoner," Bryan said. "Dancing with my common wife."

"Oh, not so common," Francis said wickedly. "She can lead a fine hot trod, or so I hear."

"Aye, she's been leading me on a hot trod since I met her." She twisted in his arms to scowl up at him.

"And it still goes on, aye?" he said, smiling down at her. "I haven't been able to keep up with you all night."

"That's because you won't dance with me," she said, tossing her hair behind her. She looked beautiful and wild. She wore a new blue gown, for constancy, she said.

"I'm saving my strength, as you should be."

Francis hooted with laughter.

"How is my prisoner?" Bryan asked.

"Oh, you!" Megan cried, shoving him. "Don't talk about that now! 'Tis our wedding!"

Francis smoothed his hand over his beard. "Leod? Oh, as well as could be expected, considering."

"Considering what?" Megan was attempting to drag him away, but Bryan resisted. "He *is* still in your dungeon?"

"Oh, aye. I can assure you, he is beneath Crichton at this very moment."

Bryan opened his mouth to ask another question.

"Bryan," Francis cried, laughing. " 'Tis your wedding night; see to your bride!"

"I thank you, my lord," Megan said, giving Bryan's hand another yank.

"A most gracious welcome, dear lady. I think me I'll check on the marriage bed. Cora said something about blessing it."

"You stay away from my mother-in-law!" Megan called over her shoulder. Francis waved her protests away and headed for the house. She looked up at Bryan, wide-eyed. "He wouldn't!"

"Aye, he would." He led her away from the others. "I have something for you."

"What more could I want? I cannot believe Lord Bothwell's gift! Do you know how long I've been trying to purchase the land to the east of us? He would not even talk to me before, and now it's yours!" Her eyes shone with excitement.

"Ours," Bryan corrected her, drawing her into the shadows of a tree.

She smiled shyly. "Ours."

He liked the way it sounded from her lips. He leaned over and kissed her, taking her hand and feeling her finger. Innes's ring was gone. Pleased, he slipped another on her bare finger.

She looked down, her eyes wide. "This . . . this ring bears your father's seal."

"Francis brought it to me. He said he found it among some of my father's things at Crichton. It was in a packet with my name on it."

She blinked at him. "Do you think . . . ?"

"Nay, I do not."

She smiled and slipped her arms around his neck. "Then we shall not speak another word about it, my lord warden."

He held her close. "Ah, so I'm Lord Warden now? I thought I was husband tonight."

"Oh, no." She shook her head with mock seriousness. "There's a great deal to learn about being a husband—on the borders, that is. We do things differently."

"Oh, aye?" he asked, interested. "I'm looking forward to the instruction."

Author's Note

The Earls of Bothwell captured my interest during the research of my first book, *A Time for Dreams*, and they continue to intrigue me. James Hepburn, the fourth Earl of Bothwell, did have an affair in his youth with Janet Beaton, who was known as the Wizard Lady of Braxholm. It has been said that they were handfast, though it is not known for certain.

Having no legitimate heirs, James's successor was his nephew, Francis Hepburn Stewart, the fifth Earl of Bothwell, who was best remembered for his involvement with the North Berwick witches in the early 1590s.

Sir John Forster and Sir Thomas Kerr were both wardens in 1585. Lord Francis Russell was murdered at the Day of Truce in 1585 at Windygyle. Who killed him, and why, is still a mystery. There is a nearby cairn called Lord Russell's Cairn to this day.

I have done my best to portray the border ways and customs as accurately as possible. The wardens had their hands full trying to keep order with no help from the central government. This bred much corruption among the border officials. The lawlessness was so prevalent that the inhabitants did not see it as unusual, merely as their way of life.

All of which set me to musing one day: What would happen if a man with a strong sense of justice were dropped into this mess?